Where I Found You

Amanda Brooke

W F HOWES LTD

This large print edition published in 2014 by
W F Howes Ltd
Unit 4, Rearsby Business Park, Gaddesby Lane,
Rearsby, Leicester LE7 4YH

1 3 5 7 9 10 8 6 4 2

First published in the United Kingdom in 2014
by Harper

A CIP catalogue record for this book is available
from the British Library

ISBN 978 1 47127 227 1

Typeset by Palimpsest Book Production Limited,
Falkirk, Stirlingshire
Printed and bound by
www.printondemand-worldwide.com of Peterborough, England

In memory of Ted and Betty McCulloch

Walking with a friend in the dark is better than walking alone in the light.
                                        Helen Keller

CHAPTER 1

With a history that spanned more than a century, Victoria Park had changed surprisingly little in the intervening years. The original geometric design, which incorporated manicured lawns, intersecting pathways and ornate flowerbeds had been faithfully preserved within its sandstone walls. It couldn't compare to the unrestrained Cheshire countryside that circled the town of Sedgefield, but what the park did offer was a consistent link from one generation to the next.

There had, of course, been some changes over the years. The trees lining the main avenue had matured, dirt paths had been paved, cobbles had been replaced by concrete, and the bowling green, bandstand and children's playground had all undergone various cycles of disrepair and rejuvenation. But for the most part the park's gentle evolution had gone unnoticed.

In one particular corner, on the north side of the ornamental lake, the passage of time had been noticed least of all. It was here you would find a single wrought iron bench nestled between a steep embankment and the water's edge. It was one of the park's originals although it was true to say that visitors were more likely to remember the view they had taken in, the conversations they had shared or the thoughts they had explored rather than the unremarkable seat they had settled back upon.

There was, however, one person who had noticed the bench. She knew each curve of its intricate iron frame and every wooded knot buried beneath the layers of chipped paint. But then Maggie Carter knew Victoria Park better than most. She had grown up in Sedgefield and now lived close enough to hear the creak of the park's gates from her doorstep. It called to her and she rarely resisted, even in the depths of winter when the wind gathered momentum across the playing fields and sucked the air out of her lungs.

The main avenue which sliced the park in half led directly to Sedgefield High Street where Maggie worked, but given a choice she preferred to meander along its circuitous twisting paths. Only occasionally, if the weather was too awful, was she forced to forgo her usual detour to the lake. Thankfully, today was not one of those days.

Harvey sniffed the air as they made their way through a small coppice where, overhead, branches scraped nervously against each other in the breeze. April was being kind and the sun was shining but its fragile warmth was fractured by the shade of the denuded trees. Maggie hunched her shoulders against the sudden cold. Her short dark hair suited her slight frame and gave her face an elfin look but provided no buffer against the chill.

Their pace quickened and the Labrador's paws squelched beneath the slimy mulch, swollen from an early morning drizzle. The dog was powerful enough to lift her off her feet but he matched his mistress's pace perfectly. Rapid footfalls approaching from the opposite direction suggested that they weren't the only ones eager to escape the spindly shadows.

'Hi, Maggie,' Alice called. 'Off to the lake by any chance?'

Maggie and Harvey came to a stop to say hello to one of the regulars at the beauty salon where she worked. 'You can join me for lunch if you like,' Maggie offered, lifting a bag. The air filled with tantalising hints of garlic and sundried tomatoes before the breeze carried them away.

'Thanks, but I'm out for a slap-up meal later so I'd better save myself.'

'Ah yes, how could I forget? Happy birthday!'

'Thanks, Maggie. It's a lot of fuss about nothing but my family do love to celebrate.'

'You can't fool me. I know you're the one who's the party animal.'

'Haven't you heard? Sixty is the new forty,' Alice replied with a gentle laugh that quickly degenerated into a coughing fit. The telltale smell of smoke suggested she hadn't long put out a cigarette.

'I thought you'd given up,' Maggie said, although she wasn't surprised. A forty-year habit was going to be a tough one to break.

'I'm cutting down,' Alice replied guiltily.

'Next time you're having your hair done you should make an appointment to see me too. I might be able to find something to ease your chest.'

An aromatherapist by trade, Maggie ran her own business from a local beauty salon. Sedgefield was a small town and although the High Street was busy, setting up had been quite a gamble. She only worked part-time but in the last eight years she had built up a loyal clientele, which more than justified her efforts, although Alice was yet to be one of them.

'The problem is I have a one-track mind when I walk into that place,' Alice continued. 'There's always some new hair colour I want to try and it'll be even more tempting now I get a pensioners' discount. My granddaughter wants me to have blue highlights next time!'

'The discount applies to my treatments too,' Maggie reminded her. 'And I'll be in all afternoon if you're passing.'

'Thanks, Maggie, I might just do that,' Alice said without conviction.

They said their goodbyes and Maggie hurried towards the warm embrace of the sun. She was a familiar face in the park and there followed a rash of hellos on the way to the lake but no more delays.

Lunchtime was quiet during the working week and although Maggie enjoyed the weekend hustle and bustle she was happy to sit and soak up the peace and quiet which was broken only occasionally by the disgruntled quack of a duck looking for food. Memories flooded her mind, as she knew they would. She and her favourite bench shared a long history. Her mum had brought her to this spot often and one of Maggie's earliest memories was trying to clamber up on to the bench by herself, using its green-painted slats for purchase and pretending not to notice when her mum helped her make that final push.

Harvey, meanwhile, was more interested in the present and pushed his head against her hand. When she began to knead his neck, digging her fingers deep into his vanilla fur, the dog let out a low groan of pleasure followed by a frustrated whine.

'OK, I get the message,' she said and began to unpack their picnic. She filled two feeding bowls for Harvey and he duly ignored the water, opting for the dried food which he devoured eagerly as Maggie set about her own lunch.

Halfway through Maggie's second sandwich, Harvey's tail began to thump against her leg. She could hear little feet galloping along the path towards them, the source of Harvey's growing excitement.

'Harvey! Good boy,' Josh cried as he wrapped himself around the dog, almost knocking Maggie's lunch box off her knee.

The three-year-old's mum arrived huffing and

puffing half a minute later. 'I've told you before, don't go running off like that,' she said before muttering, 'bloody kids,' under her breath.

'I see he's still keeping you on your toes,' Maggie said, trying to keep the mood light. Lorna was another regular to the salon and although they weren't exactly friends Maggie knew the young mum well enough to know that she would launch into a string of complaints about motherhood given half the chance. It was an encounter she could do without right now.

'Can I feed the ducks?' the little boy asked.

Lorna groaned. 'I forgot the bread. We'll feed them tomorrow.'

Maggie sensed all attention being drawn to her half-eaten sandwich and she tore off the crust. 'Here, give them this, Josh.'

'Say thank you,' Lorna told him as he snatched the bread from Maggie's hand.

'Thank you, Maggie.'

The chorus of quacks grew in intensity as the little boy approached the water's edge and Lorna collapsed onto the bench with a loud sigh. 'We're not interrupting you, are we?'

Maggie swallowed up the remnants of her sandwich in one mouthful before replying. 'No, it's OK. I have to head off to work now anyway.'

'That's a shame,' Lorna said. 'I could do with some adult conversation for a change.'

Maggie ignored the subtle hint to stay and began packing up her things. 'Maybe next time.'

'Actually, I'm glad I caught you. There's something I've been meaning to ask.' Lorna spoke urgently but then paused to lower her voice to a conspiratorial whisper. 'You're not pregnant, are you?'

Maggie froze, too stunned to reply. Josh's laughter cut into the silence.

'It's just that I saw you with Mel the other day and . . .'

'Oh.'

'So? Are you?'

To date, only a handful of trusted friends had been told the news but Maggie was having her three-month scan the next day and she had already promised James they would announce the news then so there seemed little point in denying it if Lorna had spotted her with the midwife. 'I'm due in October,' she said.

'Really? I am surprised, I mean, I didn't even think you could.'

'I know, James and I have been married for less than a year but I'm thirty-two and I don't want to leave it much longer.' Maggie was deliberately misunderstanding Lorna's comment.

'No, I didn't mean that,' Lorna said but refused to explain further. Instead, she gave Harvey a heavy pat on the back. He was resting his head on Maggie's lap as if he knew his mistress needed the moral support.

'Oh, you mean because I'm visually impaired?' She wasn't sure how she managed to keep her tone light although Lorna's tactless response was no more than she expected from her less-informed acquaintances. It was the reason she had been more than happy to keep her pregnancy a secret for as long as possible.

'You have to admit that it's going to be difficult. I bet social services will be watching you like a hawk.'

Maggie began stroking Harvey, her fingers following the broad contours of his nose and head. She could feel his eyelashes flutter against her palm. He was watching her. 'Mel is amazingly supportive and yes, there will be challenges – but nothing I can't handle. I simply have to find different solutions to the same problems faced by any new mother,' she said with a confidence she didn't feel. It was only the occasional squeal from Josh as he teased the ducks that kept her spirits buoyed, reminding her that motherhood had its rewards.

Despite having planned to start a family, Maggie had been shell-shocked when she found out she was pregnant. She had been fast approaching thirty before she and James met, by which point the hope of being a wife and mother had dimmed in much the same way as her vision had when she was six years old and had suffered a severe bout of measles, which had left her with only a vague sense of light and shade and no sense of colour. James's appearance had brought a new kind of light into her world and it hadn't taken them long to realise that they wanted to spend the rest of

8

their lives together. They had moved into the house opposite Victoria Park just over a year ago, by which point they were already planning a baby as well as their wedding. But then another guiding light in Maggie's life had been snuffed out. Her mum had died.

When Maggie had lost her sight, Joan had been the one to encourage her daughter to develop her other senses to the point where she found her residual sense of vision almost distracting and often wore sunglasses to filter it out. Together they had found new and innovative ways for Maggie to absorb the beauty of the world around her. Her sense of hearing could pinpoint her position whether from the echo of her voice off a wall, the hum of traffic from the road or a tree shivering in the breeze. Her sense of touch, be it from the tips of her fingers to the tips of her toes, could build up a picture of the world within her grasp and the ground beneath her feet. Taste added texture and depth to the food she ate or the skin she kissed, but it was her sense of smell that had been one of the most exciting voyages of discovery. Joan used an array of spices, fruits and flowers to bring the colour back into Maggie's world, dabbing natural scents onto everyday objects to give her daughter the means to visualise her unseen world. It was almost inevitable that Maggie would one day make her living from her obsession with aromas.

But it wasn't only the practicalities of life that

Joan had helped with; she had instilled a sense of worth in her daughter which gave Maggie the confidence to face any challenges life could throw at her, so much so that she and James hadn't even discussed whether or not they should reconsider their plans to become parents after her mum had died and had let nature take its course.

It was only now, as she sensed the news of her pregnancy being picked up on the breeze and released into the world, that Maggie felt the full force of the loneliness and isolation she had been feeling. She had James, of course, and she had close friends; her closest being Jenny who was her honorary sister and a new mother herself. Only . . . she didn't have the one person who would have been there, not only to tell her that she could do this but to dare anyone to suggest otherwise.

Maggie still had her dad but Stan had moved to Spain to be mollycoddled by his sister. Everyone agreed it was the best thing for him after losing his wife but his daughter would need to choose the right time to tell him the news – as tempting as it was, she didn't want him catching the next flight home. Even his presence wouldn't be enough to fill the gaping hole in his daughter's life, a hole that had allowed self-doubt to creep in.

'I imagine James will have his work cut out,' Lorna said, seemingly determined to erode her confidence further. 'Is he happy about it?'

Maggie was about to answer but a noise caught

her attention. She was turning urgently towards the lake even before she realised it was the sound of feet sloshing about in water. 'Is Josh all right?' she asked but the sound of the little boy's cry for help was answer enough and the splashing grew thunderous.

Lorna launched herself to her feet and Maggie quickly released Harvey from his leash. She could hear his claws scraping against the concrete slipway as he ran to the little boy's aid. Josh's wails intensified as Lorna dragged him out of the water and read him the riot act.

'At least he's safe,' Maggie offered when Lorna returned with a dripping and sobbing Josh in her arms. The smell of stagnant water and bird droppings was strong enough to burn the back of her nostrils and Harvey, who had returned to Maggie's side, summed up his own feelings with a wet sneeze.

Lorna muttered a mixture of apologies and goodbyes as she manhandled her son to his feet and proceeded to drag the snivelling child away. Once tranquillity had returned, Harvey rested his head on Maggie's lap to resume his vigil. He licked her hand, which she had placed protectively over her stomach. No longer in a hurry to get to work, she imagined what might have happened if it had been her child and not Josh wandering into the water. What if she had been on her own and there had been no one to pull him to safety? How would she have coped? What had she been thinking getting pregnant in the first place?

'I'm scared, Mum,' she said as loud as she dared. 'I'm so scared.'

The only response was the gentle lapping at the water's edge. She found herself wondering how deep the lake was and, for a fleeting moment, she imagined plunging into a dark abyss. Her stomach lurched and her hand reached out next to her, hoping for some kind of ethereal resistance but her mum wasn't there. There was no one left who would understand how she felt, but why should they? These feelings of insecurity were new to her, too. Had she become a victim of her own overconfidence?

It was Harvey who eventually led Maggie away from the lake but as she climbed the steep path towards the main avenue she couldn't leave behind the growing sense of dread as easily as she could the lingering smell of Josh's unfortunate dip in the lake. Maggie caught her breath once she reached the top of the slope where she suddenly detected the faintest scent of lilac. It was a synthetic fragrance and stopped her in her tracks. There were no sounds to suggest anyone near but Maggie felt someone watching her.

'Hello? Is anyone there?'

The only response was the gentle waft of Harvey's tail but their greetings went unanswered.

Elsa watched a family of ducks cutting through the glassy stillness of the lake, leaving a sleek trail of ripples to sparkle in the sunshine. Despite their gentle progress, she felt unnerved and began rubbing her forehead as she scanned the water for the more elegant outline of the swans. She was still searching when a young woman appeared like a spectre in front of her but Elsa's attention wouldn't be drawn from the lake and the now-empty bench.

Tucked away in the curved embrace of an embankment, the bench was surrounded by tall rhododendron bushes that looked a little careworn after winter's worst although fresh green buds could be seen peeking through the dark evergreen foliage. In contrast, the flowerbeds had already enjoyed the first blooms of spring and countless purple and yellow crocuses sparkled invitingly.

It was only when Elsa began to make her way down the slope that she realised how exhausted she felt. She spent most days on her feet at the greengrocer's and the hard graft was made harder still by the burden she carried. She tried not to think about the baby. It was bad enough having aching legs – she didn't need to be reminded of her aching heart too.

Her sense of unease increased as she approached the bench. It was a different colour and she expected the dark brown paint to be wet to the touch but it was bone dry and already flaking. Elsa sat down and, closing her eyes, inhaled deeply. Her body melded into the familiar curve of the seat and her growing tension began to dissipate. She pushed out her stomach and stretched her spine.

When she opened her eyes again, Elsa felt calmer and her thoughts cleared. She lifted up her legs to check her feet. They were even more swollen than she had feared and she let them drop back down with a thud. She was only twenty-two but she felt older, her youth eroded by the harsh realities of life. Spreading her fingers she discovered yet more joints that ached – and she felt no emotional connection to the simple gold wedding ring on the third finger of her left hand. But why should she? It wasn't hers. She had borrowed it from Mrs Jackson who had told her she would make better use of it than an old, lonely widow.

Elsa hadn't known a soul when she had arrived in Sedgefield a month earlier but Mrs Jackson had become a good friend and confidant. It had been Elsa's sister Celia who had convinced her that running away to Sedgefield was for the best; she could stay long enough to hide her shame before returning home to Liverpool – alone – to pick up her old life as if nothing had happened. Celia was older by four years and happy enough to be married to a boring civil servant, living in Manchester and popping out children every other year. It wasn't the kind of future Elsa had ever imagined for herself – she had wanted to live life to the full until discovering there was a price to pay for her recklessness. Celia, expecting her fourth child, had taken control when Elsa confessed she might be pregnant too, and it had been her sister's GP who had confirmed their suspicions. Together with the doctor's wife, whose aunt ran a guesthouse in Sedgefield, Celia devised a plan for Elsa's future and that of her baby.

Which was how she had ended up here, claiming to be a distant relative of Mrs Jackson, recently widowed and pregnant. It was all lies but lying was something Elsa had become used to. Her mum thought she was staying with Celia to help her prepare for her next child and would be horrified to discover where she really was and why.

Elsa looked out over the lake. The water appeared darker than it had from the top of the slope, reflecting barren treetops rather than blue sky. 'What in God's name am I doing here all alone?' she asked. Her forlorn words, spoken out loud, were barely audible but trickled towards the water's edge. 'I need you Freddie. I need you to save me.'

As if in answer to her question the future, which had already been laid out for Elsa, flashed before her eyes and she let out a whimper. She wrapped her arms tightly around her body in a vain attempt to hold on to the baby she was destined to lose but it was hopeless. She wasn't strong enough, not on her own. Her chest heaved and the pain of her heart being rent in two was impossible to bear. In slow, deliberate movements, she placed both hands on the bench and pushed against her palms as she prepared to launch herself from her seat and into the lake. Her body shook with an all-consuming need to let the waters drag her body down into the abyss and her misery along with it. But Elsa stayed where she was – she wasn't brave enough.

Not yet.

CHAPTER 2

'**D**o you mind if my daughter strokes him?' a woman asked as Maggie sat waiting to be called in for her scan.

'You'd better ask my wife that question,' James answered. His tone was pleasant enough but there was an edge to it that only Maggie could detect. It wasn't unusual for strangers to direct their questions to a companion rather than Maggie herself and, where she had learnt patience and perseverance, James struggled to curb his frustrations. She had to remind him occasionally that he had been equally ignorant not that long ago and, with few exceptions, such interest was borne of good intent.

'Yes, I'm sure he'd love the attention,' Maggie answered. 'And thank you for asking first. You wouldn't believe the kind of havoc it can cause when someone rushes up and starts distracting him while he's guiding me.'

Maggie introduced Harvey to the little girl who was two years old and in complete awe of him, as was her mum. Maggie pre-empted many of the questions she knew would follow but she didn't mind singing Harvey's praises, he deserved it. She

17

couldn't help smiling to herself as she told the woman how disciplined her guide dog was and how he kept to a strict diet, all the time knowing that Harvey was salivating over the cookie the toddler had offered to share but he had known better than to accept. But then she had been tempted herself to take the little girl up on her offer; she had been too nervous that morning to eat and her stomach was growling.

It wasn't long before the conversation moved on to more maternal matters and for a little while Maggie chatted away like any other expectant mum. She could almost forget her fears, which had been compounded the moment she had entered the hospital. Its corridors of power were part of the system that would judge her fitness to be a mother – or so she imagined.

'Maggie, are you ready?'

'Mel, what are you doing here?'

'I'm on ward duty upstairs and it's unbelievably quiet. Then I thought to myself, I'm sure Maggie's scan is today, so here I am. Hello, James,' she added, leaning in for a peck on the cheek.

'Good to see you, Mel, and what a coincidence that you were free,' James said, a little too brightly.

Maggie heard the lie but chose not to recognise it as such. She was too busy feeling relieved and very grateful to the midwife – and no doubt James – for arranging the additional support that Maggie would never openly ask for. When she stood up, her knees trembled and she held on tightly to

James's hand as she waited for Harvey to extricate himself from the chubby arms of his new friend. The little girl's howls could still be heard long after he had led his mistress into the examination room.

Mel introduced them to the sonographer, who was a young, officious-sounding young man called Joel, while James helped Maggie onto the examination bed. With some discreet adjustment of her top and leggings, she exposed enough of her abdomen for the man to do his job. At fourteen weeks, her stomach was still relatively flat and she could almost convince herself that she wasn't pregnant.

'I'm going to apply some gel first, it might be a bit cold,' Joel said and he was right. Maggie jumped when he squirted it on her stomach.

'It might have been better if you had placed a finger on her stomach first and then said exactly when you were going to apply the gel,' Mel hissed at him.

'Sorry,' he said and there was a nervous cough before he continued to explain what would happen next. With a little more thought this time, he encouraged Maggie to feel the transducer he would be using for the scan. It was about the size of an electric razor and similar in shape. The room fell silent as he began moving it across her abdomen in firm, sweeping strokes. His probing became concentrated on a small area only inches above her groin, directly over her bladder, which was uncomfortably full. She had been drinking water in the waiting room as instructed and would be heading for the ladies as soon as they were finished. 'I'm going to take some measurements now,' Joel said.

'Then I'll be the one to explain what we can see,' Mel whispered, loud enough for the sonographer to pick up her irritation. 'It's a grainy black and white image, lots of indistinguishable blobs really but we can see a steady heart beating. Right now Joel has frozen the image on a particular frame so he can take some measurements. There's a very faint outline of baby's face, a really clear white line which is his spine and I can even make out his arms and legs.'

'He?' asked James.

'I call all my babies he,' explained Mel. 'It's a bit too early to work out baby's sex but if you want our friend here to earn his money, we could have a go.'

'I don't want to know yet,' Maggie said. She was still struggling with the idea that there was a living being growing inside her. 'Do you, James?'

'No, me neither.'

'Did you find out with the boys?' Maggie asked.

The boys were James's two sons from his first marriage. Liam was nine and Sam seven. Fatherhood hadn't been easy first time around for her husband. The divorce had been amicable enough but the strain of his ex-wife moving to Portsmouth after she remarried had pushed him to his limits. The five-hundred-mile round trip to see his children or bring them up north for visits was hard going on all of them but thankfully, it was still worth James's efforts as far Liam and Sam were concerned.

'With Sam we did,' James said. 'But that was only to find out if we could reuse Liam's baby clothes or needed to start saving up for dresses.'

'OK, everything looks fine,' the sonographer announced bringing them back to the present. 'You were given a due date of 24 October and that matches my measurements so everything is going to plan.'

'I suppose there's no going back now,' Maggie said, hoping that no one noticed the serious tone that had crept into what should have been a light quip.

'And now that we know everything is as it should be,' Mel added, 'I've brought my Doppler with me to listen for baby's heartbeat. It might be too early to pick up yet but I can give it a try if you want me to.'

Maggie was obliged to say yes but when Mel placed it on her abdomen and radio static filled the room, she fought the urge to push it away. Hearing the description of an image on screen was one thing but this was something else entirely. Maggie's heartbeat quickened and the Doppler picked up her anxiety for all to hear but then there was another beat. It was only faint, much faster and impossible to ignore. Maggie steeled herself for the crushing wave of panic she expected but instead, indescribable warmth flooded her chest and took her breath away. The trembling smile was on her lips even before she realised that *this* was how motherhood was meant to feel and she prayed for the strength to hold onto that feeling.

As they left the hospital, Maggie and James didn't say a word. Maggie held Harvey's harness in one hand and James's hand in the other. Her ears were straining for the faintest echo of the tiny heartbeat that had swept away weeks of fear and self-doubt. She wanted to laugh. Instead she began to cry.

Her tears slipped silently down her face and it was only as they reached the car that James noticed. 'Are you all right?'

There was no alarm in his voice; in fact Maggie could detect a smile. Harvey was a little more difficult to reassure and whined nervously as he settled into the caged compartment at the back of the car. Maggie rubbed behind his ears. 'It's OK, Harvey. Mummy's . . . happy.'

James cupped his hands around her face and wiped away the tears with his thumbs. 'Are you?'

'Yes,' she replied. 'Of course.'

'It's just what you said in there, about there being "no going back". I got the feeling you weren't so sure. In fact, I've been wondering that for a while. You're not the closed book you like to think you are.'

Maggie took one of his hands and kissed it

gently. The sense of euphoria was still running through her veins and it made her brave enough to confess some if not all of her hidden fears. 'It's more a matter of not feeling ready, that's all. There are so many new things to learn,' she said. 'But when I heard that heartbeat, I felt such a rush of love and it took me by surprise. So yes, honestly, I am happy.'

As James wrapped her in his arms, Maggie buried her head into his broad shoulders. His six-foot frame towered over Maggie's slender figure and even though he was thickset, it was more muscle than flab thanks to an active working life. He was a builder by trade, a gentle giant who would protect her and keep her safe but he had a vulnerable side too and it was this that had attracted her to him more than anything.

Maggie's first impressions of James hadn't come from his appearance but the timbre of his voice and he had sounded lost. His ex-wife had just broken the news about moving down south and he had been suffering from stress-related eczema. It was Kathy, the owner of the beauty salon where Maggie worked and a good friend of James's mum, who had suggested he try aromatherapy. Kathy's poorly disguised matchmaking had cured James's ailments far more effectively than the myrrh and sandalwood Maggie had massaged into his hands.

She raised her head towards her husband. 'And are *you* happy?' It was the first time she had acknowledged that James's reaction to the pregnancy had been as muted as her own.

'Yes.'

'Really?' Maggie asked, not getting the confirmation she needed.

'I love you, Maggie, and marrying you and having this baby is the answer to all my prayers, but if I'm being really honest, the prospect of becoming a dad again is scaring me. I don't want to get it wrong this time.'

'You didn't get it wrong last time. You're a good dad,' Maggie countered.

'And you are going to be a fantastic mother. I know you're missing your mum right now but I'm sure Joan is still around watching over you.'

Maggie recalled the empty seat next to her on the park bench and the sensation of her hand cutting through fresh air. 'Maybe,' she said.

'So now your mum knows, don't you think it's about time we tell the rest of our parents?' James asked as he helped her into the car. It wasn't necessary but she knew he would be just as attentive of his pregnant wife even if she had perfect vision.

'I don't suppose we can put it off forever.'

James didn't answer. He closed the passenger door and walked around to his side of the car giving them both time to collect their thoughts. Maggie had already told him the night before about her encounter with Lorna, although she had been economical with the details, mentioning only that the news was out. James would have phoned his parents there and then if Judith and Ken hadn't been away visiting their grandchildren in Portsmouth. He wanted to be the one to tell Liam and Sam and to reassure them that the baby wasn't going to alter his relationship with them. He hadn't needed to explain why it wasn't a good idea to attempt that while Judith was around to offer her own opinions.

James slipped behind the steering wheel and as he straightened his jacket, she heard the rustle of paper. The baby scan photo was burning a hole in his pocket. 'This is good news we're sharing,' he reminded her.

'I know and I'd like to hold on to that thought for as long as I can but let's be realistic, James. Some people will find it difficult to accept that a blind person could ever be a fit and proper parent.'

'Telling Mum and Dad won't be as bad as you think,' he said, acknowledging who it was they were talking about.

'Do you really believe that?'

The pause that followed confirmed that he accepted that it wouldn't be easy. His parents had struggled from the very beginning to comprehend why their son would take on such a burden as Maggie and despite concerted effort on the part of the newlyweds, she was still a relative stranger to her in-laws.

Maggie and James had been dating for almost a year before he had plucked up the courage to introduce her to his family. Liam and Sam had been staying with James over the summer holidays and he had organised a family barbeque so they could all get to know each other. The boys were curious about Maggie and amazed at her ability to carry out simple day-to-day tasks that they tried to imitate with their eyes closed. Their initial questions were blunt but openly innocent and Maggie had been more amused than offended. Judith's questioning, by comparison, had been more akin to a cross-examination.

'OK, we both know Mum has her own ideas about what's best for her family but maybe when she hears about the baby, she'll finally . . .'

James didn't dare finish the sentence so Maggie finished it for him. 'Accept me?'

'She's a good mum, Maggie. Overprotective of me, yes, but that's only because she doesn't want to see me hurt again. Maybe it would help if we spent more time with them.'

'They seem to be able to find their way to Portsmouth far easier than the fifteen-mile trip from Nantwich. Your mum doesn't like me, James. She doesn't think I'm looking after you properly, she doesn't think I can,' Maggie said. She knew James was about to contradict her so she quickly added, 'Take her reaction to finding out you make a packed lunch every morning. I was trying to explain how it's to stop you pigging out on fast food but she was too busy being horrified that it was you making the lunch and not me.' Maggie shook her head as if to free herself from a web of negative thoughts. 'Even if I had perfect vision, I still wouldn't live up to her expectations. No matter how hard I try, I'm never going to be good enough because I'm not Carolyn.'

'I know, you're nothing like my ex-wife and I thank God for that,' James said with undisguised relief. 'And for the record, I'm more than happy to make my own lunch, thank you very much. You'd only make me eat even more healthily.' He paused hopefully for a smile that wouldn't come. 'Look, they'll be coming home soon. How about we invite them over for dinner on Saturday?'

Maggie let her body sag and as the car engine roared into life it drowned out the sound of the tiny heartbeat that had echoed across her mind. 'With any luck they'll turn you down as usual.'

James chose to ignore her petulance. 'Maggie, it's going to be fine.'

'OK, invite them – but only on the condition that I can invite Jenny along too. She's been looking for an excuse to leave Mark holding the baby for a change and besides, I'll need reinforcements.'

'I don't want you worrying about this. It doesn't matter what other people think. What matters is us, the three of us.'

'And the boys,' she reminded him as if he needed it.

'And our beautiful boys,' he agreed. 'At least I can guarantee you that *they'll* be absolutely thrilled.'

Maggie closed her eyes. She wasn't used to feeling sorry for herself but as she leant back against the headrest she swallowed back the bitter taste of bile. She didn't want to come between James and his mum because she knew how much his family meant to him, but she couldn't imagine how announcing they were having a baby would bring them any closer. As the second wife, Maggie was always going to be second best in Judith's eyes and becoming a mother would only give her mother-in-law a new means of comparison with her predecessor. Maggie suspected that Lorna's reaction would pale into insignificance compared to Judith's – who would refuse to see beyond Maggie's disability and her limitations. And on some matters, Maggie's instincts were never wrong.

CHAPTER 3

Maggie flexed her fingers absent-mindedly. It was Saturday morning and she was taking a moment out of what was going to be a busy day. She had everything she needed for dinner that evening but was trying not to think about it. Her heavy shopping bag lay abandoned at the side of the bench while Maggie filled her mind with the sounds of the park, which was busier than it had been for weeks. The weather was glorious and Maggie lifted her face to the violet sky to soak up the sun's lemon rays and bring subtle light to the grey shadows that played across her vision.

Harvey was steadily lapping up water from his bowl, the soothing sound temporarily drowned out by the chatter of children rushing along the path towards the lake. Next she heard the heavy, rhythmic footsteps of a jogger. The runner took a deep breath before calling out hello to her. He didn't pause for her reply but continued up the slope, his laboured breathing intensifying with the effort.

Harvey stopped drinking and gently nudged her

hand in search of treats. It was a futile attempt and he knew it. To commit to this regime required willpower from both of them but there were occasional lapses and Harvey was hopeful. 'How about some carrot sticks when we get home?' she offered as consolation.

The dog gave a sharp snort of disapproval and then, reading her body language perfectly, settled at her feet. Maggie kept one hand on his leash and let the other trace the familiar contours of the bench and the empty place next to her, which continued to play on her mind.

She braved a smile as she listened to the children's excited calls of encouragement to the ducks and placid quacks were soon replaced by a frenzy of flapping wings and splashing water. To ward off unwelcome thoughts that might drag her down beneath the surface of the lake, Maggie immersed herself in memories of the past. She remembered flinging pieces of bread high into the air as her mum gave a running commentary on the action being played out on the lake, remembered the buzz of excitement listening to the ducks fighting over the remnants of the picnic she and her mum had just shared sitting on their favourite bench.

But the memory was bittersweet, a reminder of all that she had had and all that she had lost. Maggie had always come across as confident and self-assured, but it was her mum who had instilled that sense of self-belief and without her guiding presence Maggie was losing her way. Of all the challenges she had faced in her life, having a baby would be the greatest test of all and one she couldn't get wrong. It wasn't only her life she was responsible for now.

Frightened by the future, Maggie retreated further into the past and disconnected from the world around her. There were so many memories to dip into . . . The park was where her mum had taught her how to explore the world through touch and smell and Maggie recalled the scents from those lost seasons one by one.

The sun dipped behind a cloud and a cool breeze swirled around her, carrying with it the distinctive smell of lilac perfume. It was vaguely familiar but Maggie resisted being pulled back to the present, stretching out her hand across the bench in a desperate attempt to hold on to the tenuous connection to her mum but her fingers touched the heavy material of a woollen coat giving Maggie a start and snapping her out of her reverie.

'Sorry, I didn't mean to frighten you,' the woman next to her said.

Elsa couldn't resist the chance to sit in the sunshine and chase away the chill that had crept into her bones. She wasn't going to be put off by the children's raucous laughter or the woman and her dog, who seemed to be claiming the park bench as their own. It was her bench too.

She had offered a friendly smile as she approached but the woman, whose eyes were hidden behind dark glasses, seemed to be in a world of her own so Elsa sat down next to her without a word. She breathed in the scent of the lilacs that came from the soap at Mrs Jackson's house. Elsa wasn't particularly keen on it but she didn't want to offend Aunt Flo, as she insisted on being called. The old lady had taken her under her wing and seemed to genuinely care for her new charge.

But despite Aunt Flo's fussing, Elsa was feeling more lost and alone than ever and it was as these feelings plagued her that the stranger sitting next to her had reached out her hand. They had both jumped in fright.

'Sorry, I didn't mean to frighten you,' Elsa offered.

The woman, who looked only a little older than Elsa, gave her an apologetic smile. 'No, I'm sorry. I was miles away.'

'It's a lovely spot here, don't you think? A good place to sit back and . . .' she said but then couldn't think how to explain it.

'Let the world go by?'

'Take the weight off your feet,' Elsa added. She was watching the way the woman had placed her hand protectively over her stomach. Elsa groaned as she stretched and let her own bump protrude, hoping the woman might take the hint, but she simply smiled.

'I'm Maggie, by the way. I don't think we've met before, have we?'

'I haven't been in Sedgefield long. My name's

Elsa.' Her voice sounded hoarse so she cleared her throat before adding, 'And who's this cutie?'

Harvey padded towards Elsa's outstretched arm as Maggie said, 'This is my sidekick, Harvey.'

The dog shook himself as his new friend tickled his back. 'I like your fancy jacket, Harvey.'

'Harvey's my guide dog. I'm visually impaired,' Maggie explained.

Elsa gasped in awe. 'You're blind?'

Maggie gave a soft laugh. 'Yes and I'd be lost without him. Literally.'

'I've heard about dogs being trained to help soldiers who've lost their sight but I've never seen one before.'

'Really?'

'Well, I don't think so,' Elsa said suddenly doubting herself. 'I'm from Liverpool so I suppose there must be a few there.'

'Have you moved here for good or are you just passing through?'

Elsa flinched at the idea of returning home, though she knew she would one day. 'I'm not staying forever,' she said and began to rub her stomach in perfect synchronicity with her new friend. 'I'm pregnant too, by the way.'

A look of confusion flashed across the woman's face and her hand stilled.

'You are pregnant, aren't you?' Elsa asked, horrified that she might have got it wrong.

Maggie's reply faltered as she said, 'Yes, yes I am. I suppose now you're wondering how on earth a blind woman can have a baby.' The comment was light-hearted but there was something in her voice that was more of a challenge.

'Why not? You don't need eyes to find your way to a man's heart,' Elsa whispered mischievously.

Maggie laughed. 'No, I don't suppose you do. And I'm sorry if I sounded a bit defensive. I really should stop assuming people will immediately judge me.'

Elsa glanced at the wedding band on her finger. 'I'm the last person to judge anyone,' she said, her words catching in her throat.

'Is something wrong?'

Elsa didn't dare answer.

'It's all a bit frightening, don't you think?' Maggie said to fill the lengthening silence.

Elsa looked out over the glassy surface of the lake. 'Too frightening, sometimes,' she agreed.

'Want to talk about it?'

Elsa shook her head vigorously. The story of how she was recently widowed was a well-rehearsed one but she couldn't bear to tell one more person how the love of her life had been taken from her: it would break her heart. 'I'm supposed to tell you that my husband died and I'm staying with Aunt Flo until I've had the baby.'

'But . . .'

'I can't say.' Elsa put her hand to her mouth to hold back the confession that was ready to tumble over her lips.

'My mum always said there was something

special about this bench,' Maggie said, after another lengthy pause. 'Now you don't have to tell me if you don't want to, but me and this old bench are good listeners and neither of us will tell a soul.'

'I've wanted to tell someone for so long,' Elsa said. 'You promise you won't tell?'

'I promise.'

She let her hand drop to her side and her fingers followed the gentle curve of the wooden slats beneath her as she steadied herself. 'Aunt Flo isn't my aunt, she's not even a distant relative and there is no husband, dead or otherwise. The only grain of truth in the story is that I am pregnant, five months by my reckoning.'

'These things happen, but it's not exactly unheard of. If you don't mind me asking, Elsa, how old are you?'

'Twenty-two.'

A frown creased Maggie's brow. 'That's still very young,' she said hesitantly. 'Don't you have any family to support you?'

'Oh, my parents would kill me if they found out. Dad kept telling me if I didn't curb my wild streak, it'd end in tears, and Mum made it clear that if I got in trouble she would rather see me on the street than bring shame on us all. It would destroy them if they found out. Only my sister Celia knows.'

'So what will you do when the baby's born? Surely your parents will come around once they see their new grandchild.'

35

Elsa would have laughed if the hope that was being dangled in front of her wasn't so impossibly beyond her reach. 'They won't,' she said stoically. 'And there's no way I can manage on my own so I'll go back to Liverpool and the baby will go to a respectable family.'

'Is that what you want?'

Elsa pulled her coat around her tightly as she imagined her newborn baby being wrenched from her arms. 'What I want is Freddie. I want him to ride into Sedgefield on his motorbike and rescue us both,' Elsa said. 'But that's a silly dream, isn't it? Freddie doesn't even know I'm here. Or why.'

'You won't tell him?'

'He's an American serviceman. We met at a dance while he was stationed at the Burtonwood airbase.'

'Burtonwood? I thought that site had closed down years ago?'

'No, I know some people who are still there, just not my Freddie. He broke my heart.'

'You fell in love,' Maggie said simply.

'A man in a uniform, how could I resist? When I found out he was being posted to Germany, it felt like someone had ripped out my heart. But we made the most of those last few weeks together – and that's how I ended up like this. If I'd known then what kind of trouble I was in, I wouldn't have been so eager to break things off when he left. I thought I was being all grown up about it. I didn't want to wait around for the rest of my life while he would eventually go back to America and forget about me.'

As Elsa spoke, she continued to stroke Harvey. He had stayed close and whined once or twice, offering his own note of sympathy as Elsa revealed her heartbreak.

'So why don't you contact him now and let him know?'

'Because I wanted him to come back for me and not because he found out I was pregnant. And in my heart that's what I thought he would do, even on that last night together when we said our good-byes.' Elsa took a breath and held it. She could feel the tears stinging her eyes but she refused to let them fall. She kept her gaze on the lake. 'I'm a silly, romantic fool.'

'There's nothing wrong with a bit of romance.'

'Oh, but there is! This is my punishment. I should have listened to my mum. I don't deserve Freddie and I certainly don't deserve to keep this baby.'

'I may not know you very well, Elsa, but I don't believe you deserve to have your baby taken from you, not if it's something you don't want to happen and I get the feeling you don't.'

'Some days I just want to jump in that bloody lake and let it swallow me up and then no one will ever take my baby from me. But what kind of mother would even think such a thing?'

'A desperate one,' Maggie said, her voice choked with emotion.

★   ★   ★

The young woman sitting on the bench next to Maggie had fallen deathly silent, in fact Maggie wasn't even sure she was still there. Perhaps she had vanished into the ether, leaving as silently as she had arrived. Maggie's blood ran cold at the thought and she strained her ears for the slightest sound that would reassure her of the woman's earthly presence but she could hear nothing above the hammering of her own heart.

Maggie depended on her instincts and they were telling her something was wrong. Elsa's appearance had been accompanied by so many conflicting messages. There was something about her voice that didn't quite ring true and the dated perfume belonged to a different era, as did some of the things she had said. And yet despite all of this Maggie felt an immediate connection to Elsa, perhaps because they were both terrified of becoming mothers, albeit for very different reasons. Nothing added up and yet everything made sense because Elsa needed a friend and Maggie needed to help someone. More than anything, Maggie wanted to prove she wasn't as hopeless as she would have herself believe.

'I don't want to let her go. I can't.'

The voice came from nowhere and gave Maggie a start. 'Elsa? Are you OK?'

'I don't think I'll be able to live with the pain of losing my baby,' she replied, her voice wet with tears. 'I won't survive it.'

As Elsa shifted uneasily, Maggie placed her palm

flat against the wooden slats of the bench and was grateful for the gentle vibration that confirmed Elsa's presence had substance. But then Maggie felt that sense of connection again, a connection that travelled through the painted layers of the bench, peeling back time itself . . . Realising how irrational she was being, Maggie put these thoughts to one side and let her heart reach out to Elsa. 'Then fight for your baby. Swallow your pride and tell Freddie. At least then you'll know that you've done all you can. Can you still contact him? Could you phone or send him an email?'

'A what?'

'Could you write to him?' she asked, refusing to acknowledge why Elsa might not know what an email was.

'I could ask someone at Burtonwood to pass on a letter for me, I suppose,' Elsa said. There was a spark of hope in her voice now, although she was quick to dampen it. 'But even if he did turn up, I don't think I'd fit on his bike any more. And I can't help thinking he's vanished out of my life just like the swans have disappeared from the lake.'

Maggie turned her head towards the lake as if to scan the waters she couldn't see. 'What swans? I don't think there have ever been swans in Victoria Park.'

'But I've seen them,' Elsa insisted, and the spell that had been cast over the two expectant mothers began to splinter. 'I'd better go,' Elsa added sharply. 'I'm going to be late for work.'

'Don't rush off. Please, Elsa, let me help you,' Maggie said, reaching towards her but she wasn't quick enough and her hand passed through thin air. Elsa was up and away, leaving only a lingering scent of lilacs and a little of her soul which the bench was intent on keeping for itself.

CHAPTER 4

Experience had taught Maggie not to let anyone help when she was in charge of preparing a meal. Cooking wasn't an impossible task; far from it, it was something she enjoyed doing, but there were challenges and it required her full concentration. All she had to do was keep track of what she had put where and as long as well-meaning helpers didn't come in and move things around, she could turn out a pretty mean curry. Maggie especially loved working with spices that would release delicious aromas when crushed, ground, toasted or simply left to simmer in the pot.

Tonight, Maggie was more than happy to enforce her rules, which afforded her a little respite from more onerous duties. Judith and Ken had arrived and James had been left to play host to his parents with only Harvey as reinforcement. Jenny was predictably late but at least she had phoned to say she would be on her way very soon. Maggie had warned her that if she didn't hurry up then she'd be around personally to drag her out of the house. Jenny lived in a large 1930s semi-detached house, similar in size and style to Maggie's and only two streets away, so she knew the threat wasn't an idle one.

Stirring the lamb curry, a cloud of steam billowed upwards and Maggie breathed in the spiced air. The mix was the perfect balance of earth and fire and it made her mouth water. She used a wooden spoon to scrape across the bottom of the pan and judged that the curry needed a little longer for the sauce to thicken and the vegetables to soften. A quick taste confirmed that she had the balance of flavours and seasoning just right. Everything else was ready and there was nothing left to keep her from her guests – the quick hello on their arrival wasn't good enough and she knew it.

Maggie opened the kitchen door and stepped out of her haven. The hallway was long and wide with a solid timber floor and ceilings that reached the full height of the house above the staircase. She could hear the distant thud of heavy raindrops hitting the skylight above.

Her pensive footsteps made only the barest whisper but as she slipped past the living room door on her right, a floorboard creaked. Maggie stopped immediately and explored the floor tentatively with her socked foot. This part of the house had seen the most change since moving in and the flooring had only been laid six months ago so the boards were still settling into place. She stepped gingerly to the left until her outstretched hand brushed against another door on the opposite side which was nestled beneath the stairs and had once led to a large garage that was now divided into two separate workspaces. This door gave access to her office while the remaining space, accessible from the front of the house, was James's workshop.

Maggie's nerves were getting the better of her and she tried to regulate her breathing as she approached the dining room door. Her leg hit something and it clattered to the floor. Cursing herself, she scrambled around to find what had fallen over. At the same time, a series of measured creaks marked the approach of someone on the other side of the door. When it opened, she detected the scent of her husband's aftershave.

'I knocked an umbrella over, that's all,' she whispered.

'Time for a stiff drink?'

'If only I could,' Maggie mumbled as she entered the room.

The dining room had been recently redecorated and as Maggie walked in she was thankful for the sense of security it gave her. This was her territory. The newly plastered walls had been painted a soft shade of green that was almost blue, complementing a feature wall which had been papered in a raised art deco pattern of silvers and greys, and the soft furnishing and accessories picked up the reflective tones of the wallpaper. Before the cloud of curry spices had a chance to overwhelm the room, Maggie could detect the scent of the rosemary- and peppermint-scented oils she had left warming to welcome her guests.

'Ready for some help yet?' Judith asked.

'No, everything's under control,' replied Maggie, her false cheerfulness a perfect match for that of her mother-in-law.

'Here you go, love, you've earned this,' Ken said.

Maggie could hear the glug of a wine glass being filled. The bouquet of dark plum mixed with notes of oak cut through the already heavily scented air. Whether it was nerves or delayed signs of morning sickness, her stomach flipped as she took a seat at the dining table.

'Not for me, thanks, Ken. I'll keep to sparkling water for now.' The pause she left was the perfect opening for the announcement but the only sound from James was the clink of glass as he poured her water. She had no choice but to continue and said, 'I need to keep a clear head while I'm in charge of dinner.'

'Mum was saying how Liam's been pestering Carolyn for a dog.'

'I wonder where *that* idea came from,' Maggie said, patting her hand against her thigh and within seconds Harvey was by her side, nuzzling her hand with his wet nose as he deciphered the scent of the meal she had been preparing. A soft sneeze confirmed that he wasn't impressed with her choice of menu.

'So is she going to give in do you think?' James asked his mum.

'I hope so. A dog would be good company for her. She gets so lonely with Tony working away so much. I'm a bit worried about her if I'm being honest.'

'They were debating different breeds when we left,' Ken said when everyone else fell silent. Neither James nor Maggie was prepared to launch into a debate about the state of Carolyn's marriage. 'It was a good job we came home when we did. Given half a chance, your mum would have marched them all off to the nearest kennels to put down a deposit on the first puppy they saw.'

'I hope they don't get a Labrador,' James said. 'The boys might be less inclined to come up here otherwise.'

'You know there's more for them here than just Harvey,' Maggie said, picking up immediately on the insecurity in James's voice that he was trying hard to disguise. 'They might love him to bits but they love you more.'

'And let's not forget their wicked stepmother,' James reminded her.

Maggie's gentle laughter helped her relax a little. Her first taste of motherhood had felt daunting at the time but in hindsight it had been nothing compared to the prospect of caring for a newborn. There had been a gradual introduction into the boys' lives and, with her mum by her side, Maggie had embraced her new role and the challenges that came with it. 'The one who can see through walls, you mean?'

Liam and Sam had learnt very quickly that they couldn't get away with quite as much as they had first expected with Maggie. Her hearing could see around corners and through closed doors and occasionally she had even been able to detect the sound of wet tongues being poked at her. But that had been in the early days. Their reluctance to accept a rival for their father's affections had been overpowered by Maggie's winning charm, one that had four legs and a wagging tail.

'How's Kathy doing?' Judith asked her, clearly not willing to dwell on her daughter-in-law's virtues. 'Still working at the salon until all hours? It's high time that woman slowed down.'

'She never will and I can't imagine the place without her,' Maggie said of the person who had been pivotal in getting her business up and running eight years ago. Aromatherapy had been little more than a hobby before then, and the offer to rent out an old storeroom in Kathy's salon had been too good to turn down.

'We all thought she was mad moving away from Nantwich and setting up in Sedgefield, of all places. Her mum was absolutely against it but Kathy was as stubborn then as she is now,' Judith said.

'*She's* stubborn?' asked Ken before turning to Maggie and saying, 'I have to take cover when those two are in the same room. How they've remained friends for the best part of fifty years is beyond me.'

'I'm glad they did,' James added. 'It's thanks to Kathy that I found Maggie.'

Judith had taken a breath to berate her husband but James's comment knocked the wind out of her sails. She exhaled with a sigh.

'You've done a lovely job in this room,' Ken said to break the silence that Maggie was waiting for James to fill. 'In fact, the whole house is really coming along.'

'Yes, it's been a hard slog stripping everything back. This room must have had about six layers of wallpaper underneath,' James explained. 'But the end result is all down to Maggie.'

'Oh, James, you always did hate taking credit for anything. He was exactly the same when he was little,' Judith said.

When Maggie spoke, her tone was that of a frustrated schoolmistress who was tired of repeating herself yet still managed to keep up a façade of good humour. 'I chose rosemary and peppermint for the theme because they both have properties that help with digestion, perfect for a dining room, and of course the blue-green of the peppermint complements the silvery rosemary leaves. I may not be able to see colours any more, but I can still visualise them with my sense of smell. My mum taught me the basics and training for my accreditation as an aromatherapist brought even more depth to that visualisation,' Maggie said,

47

using the opportunity to remind Judith that she was a skilled professional. 'Every room has been carefully thought through and my next project will be the third bedroom.'

Maggie turned towards James in grim expectation.

'It's a fair-size room,' Ken said, 'not one of those boxy third bedrooms by anyone's standards, but the boys will still fight over who keeps the bigger one.'

James didn't answer immediately and the sense of anticipation was tortuous. Maggie had to bite her tongue to stop herself from jumping in. As he cleared his throat, his discomfort was obvious and contradicted all his previous assurances that his parents would take the news well.

'Actually,' James paused, 'it's going to be a nursery. We're going to have a baby. Maggie is due at the end of October.'

Maggie couldn't see Judith's jaw drop but she imagined it had just hit the table. She looked in her direction and dared her to speak her mind.

'Son, that's fantast—' Ken began but the first spark of delight was brutally snuffed out by his wife, whose reaction was true to form.

'Oh, James, what were you *thinking*?'

'What do you mean?' James's question had an edge to it.

'Have you really thought this through? What about your plans for the future?'

'This *is* my future, Mum.'

Judith was only momentarily silenced. 'I know you're coping now but wouldn't a baby be taking on too much? I was worried about how you would manage to keep your business going once you and Maggie moved in together but credit to you, in fact credit to you both, you've proved me wrong but, son . . . seriously? How are you going to manage looking after a baby too?'

Maggie remained silent as Judith blustered on.

'I'm going to help, of course I will,' James said. 'But Maggie is perfectly capable of caring for the baby, just like she's perfectly capable of caring for herself and her husband.' He reached over to take Maggie's hand and, as the tips of her fingers brushed against his wrist, she could feel his pulse racing.

Despite wrestling with her own doubts, Maggie refused to let it show. 'There will be changes and there will be challenges,' she said. 'But we'll overcome them and we'll be the best parents we possibly can.'

'But—' The single word came out like a torpedo, a warning shot for the tirade that would follow but in a rare display of assertiveness, Ken disarmed his wife.

'We're both surprised by the news, that's all. Congratulations, both of you. You can count on us for our support.'

'I'm glad you said that, Dad,' James jumped in. 'Maggie wants to carry on working, don't you?'

Maggie was stunned and could only nod as she

realised where the conversation was leading. When they had first talked about starting a family, the plan had been for Joan to help with childcare so Maggie could return to work and she had wanted to return quickly. There was no one qualified to cover her absence at the salon and she risked losing clients if she stayed away too long. She only worked two or three hours a day and her mum had been more than willing to help but those plans had been made an impossibly long time ago. Everything had changed since then and she had assumed James would have realised that. He continued:

'So how do you feel about being a little more hands-on with your next grandchild?'

There was a sharp intake of breath from Judith and deservedly so. Judith was fifty-eight and, unlike Kathy, was already planning her retirement. She had cut back her hours as a volunteer at a charity shop and intended to give up work entirely when Ken retired from his job as an architect the following year. Taking care of a baby wasn't part of her plan and Maggie could sympathise: the idea horrified her too. Thankfully, Judith was rescued from the need to answer by a knock at the door. Jenny had arrived.

Inviting Jenny had been a stroke of genius. Not only was she a much-needed ally but she could talk to anyone about anything and she kept the conversation flowing over the awkward pauses during dinner.

Maggie had met her when they were both fifteen. Jenny's family had been new to Sedgefield and the arrival of a quiet, surly teenager at school had been a blessing in disguise. Maggie had been managing reasonably well in a mainstream school but once surging hormones had entered the mix, her peers had begun to develop at a faster pace and slowly but surely Maggie had become marginalised. The two girls formed an alliance that gave each of them the courage to face the world and eventually Jenny's true personality had emerged and she hadn't shut up since.

'So, Maggie,' she said. 'When are you going to tell us all about this ghost of yours?'

'We have a ghost?' James asked.

'No, we do *not* have a ghost,' Maggie said through gritted teeth, regretting having said anything to Jenny about her encounter by the lake earlier that day, when she was still trying to make sense of it herself. But despite her denial, Maggie couldn't easily dismiss the idea that Elsa belonged to the past more than the present. It was, after all, where Maggie often retreated and would it be so terrible to believe that her favourite park bench held the power to resurrect the people who had once rested upon it?

Jenny had homed in on the supernatural aspects of Maggie's story and even though Maggie had told her very little about Elsa, and nothing at all about the secrets she had sworn to keep, her friend's curiosity had been piqued. But Maggie wasn't going to be drawn into the conversation at the dinner table. 'I met another mum-to-be in the park and she was a little eccentric, that's all. So how's the job going, Jenny?'

Realising her mistake, Jenny didn't object to the swift change of subject. 'I thought I would hate going back to work but it's so nice having conversations that don't revolve around a baby's sleeping, eating and toilet habits.'

'And if there's one thing you can count on when you visit Jenny at the bank, it's conversation,' offered James.

'I like to spend time getting to know my customers, that's all. And I'll have you know, that kind of personal service is a dying art.'

'I wouldn't be surprised if they made it bank policy,' Maggie added with a mischievous smile. 'I think all staff should be able to update customers on which celeb is sleeping with who, what's going on in all the TV soaps, not to mention advice on the latest high street fashions.'

'I keep you on trend, don't I?'

'Yes, you do,' Maggie conceded. Jenny was her official stylist while Kathy could be relied on to keep her beauty regime up to date. When she had first met James, it was thanks to their help that she had looked more like the young woman she was and not the old spinster she thought she was destined to become.

'And I'll have you know that I provide a community service, advising on the opening times at the health centre or where to buy the best bargains. I'm like a living, breathing bulletin board and people choose me to serve them. And before you two come out with any more smart remarks, my manager has finally recognised my talents and has told me to apply for the assistant manager's job that's coming up later this year.'

James paid no heed to Jenny's warning. 'If anyone can talk themselves into a promotion, it's you.'

Judith and Ken were in danger of being completely sidelined as the banter continued. Maggie had one ear to the conversation and the other to the uncomfortable silence that wrapped around her in-laws as they drank their post-dinner coffee in awkward gulps. 'Would you like another one?' she asked when she heard Judith replace an empty cup onto its saucer.

'Not for me, thanks.'

'Care for something a bit stronger, Dad?'

'I wouldn't say no, son.'

'Can I get you ladies anything?' James asked and was met with a flurry of polite refusals. 'It's just you and me then, Dad.'

'I suppose that means I'm driving,' Judith commented.

'Thanks, love.'

'But don't blame me if I crash into that gate. It came off its hinges again the other day, like it does every time your dad tries to fix it.'

'Do you want me to take a look?' James asked.

'Oh, we'll manage. I might even have a go at mending it myself.' The refusal was half-hearted and when James insisted on coming over to fix it, Judith had her way, as she knew she would.

Chairs scraped against the floor as James and Ken made their excuses and scurried off to the kitchen, followed soon after by Harvey who didn't need an invitation to go into his favourite room in the house.

'So,' Jenny announced, 'let's talk babies.'

Jenny had realised within moments of her arrival that the announcement had been made and the news received as badly as Maggie had feared. But that hadn't stopped her best friend from bringing babies into the conversation at every possible opportunity. There was a distinct possibility that Jenny wouldn't let Judith leave the house until she was gushing with enthusiasm.

'Lily is such a pretty thing,' Judith said, referring to the myriad of photos of Jenny's six-month-old daughter that had been thrust under her nose throughout the evening.

'I'll try to remember that when she's bawling at three o'clock in the morning.'

'I don't think anyone appreciates how much a baby can turn your life upside down until you have one. But you're lucky you can leave her with Mark. Ken never was one for babysitting.'

'Babysitting?' Jenny demanded. 'He's her dad and we're equal partners. He might need reminding of that now and again but that's the deal. Wouldn't you say so, Maggie?'

'We'll see.'

'I'm so excited that Maggie and I are going to be mums together, Judith. It wasn't that long ago when I thought it would never happen and I think Maggie probably thought the same. I couldn't get pregnant and she thought she'd never find Mr Right but now look at us!'

'Yes, James was a very good catch,' Judith said.

Jenny kept her tone light as she responded to the cutting remark that sliced through the air. 'And Maggie's a bit of a catch too. Just look at those high cheekbones and that gorgeous body,' she said, turning to her friend whose high cheekbones were starting to glow with embarrassment. 'I'd give anything for a figure like yours, even now you're three months gone. You don't look pregnant at all.'

'I certainly never would have guessed,' Judith added, her reply measured and meaningful.

Jenny wouldn't be put off. 'I'm hoping she has a girl so she inherits Maggie's looks. What about you, Judith? Wouldn't it be nice to have a granddaughter for a change?'

'I don't know. I hadn't thought about it.'

'I expect it's still a bit of a shock,' Jenny said, a sting of accusation in her observation.

Judith sighed as if the weight of the world had been placed on her shoulders. 'I still don't know what they were thinking, Jenny.'

Maggie's jaw clenched as she reeled in her emotions. There was frustrated disbelief that her mother-in-law was talking as if she wasn't even in the room; there was anger that Judith wasn't willing to give her a chance to prove herself as a parent; and then there was the ever-present fear for a future Maggie felt she no longer had control over.

'Maybe they were thinking it would be nice to start a family?'

For a moment, all that Maggie could hear was the hammering of her heart then, without warning, music started blaring from beneath the table. Jenny muttered under her breath as she dug out her mobile from her bag. 'It'll be Mark. I can't have one night off without some emergency or other. Sorry, Maggie, I'd better take this.'

Jenny slipped out into the hall and left the two women alone. Judith's chair creaked softly as she was forced to turn and acknowledge her daughter-in-law's presence again. 'Have you seriously thought this through, Maggie?' she asked. 'How are you going to manage? We *could* help but we're not getting any younger.'

Maggie would have been amused at the forced frailty in Judith's voice if she hadn't been quietly fuming. 'I agree. I don't know what James was thinking by asking you. I do want to go back to work but I can use the same nursery as Jenny. You really don't have to worry on that count.'

'But I do worry. How will you be able to afford

it, especially if James is forced to cut back his hours too? It's bound to affect his ability to provide for his family – and by that I mean the boys. I know it sounds harsh but I don't see how this is going to work. I just don't see it.'

'And I thought I was the blind one,' Maggie said. 'My mum brought me up to believe that there's nothing I can't do if I put my mind to it. OK, so maybe I can't drive a car and never will but I can still get myself from A to B.'

'I agree. There are things you do that genuinely amaze me. The meal you made, the way you explained how you helped James decorate this room—' Judith began.

'Then give me a chance. These aren't tricks I'm performing; this is the way I live my life.'

High heels tapped across wood as Jenny made her return. 'Lily's teething and Mark can't settle her. Not surprising really given that he's not home enough these days for her to recognise him. I'm so, so sorry, Maggie, but I have to go. I'll say goodbye to the boys and send them back in to you,' she said.

There were anxious hugs and a promise from Maggie to make up some teething gel once she was back in the salon on Monday and then Jenny was gone.

Judith sighed and, hearing James and Ken coming back down the hallway, couldn't resist one parting shot. 'If Jenny finds it hard going, how will you cope?'

It was the first statement from her mother-in-law that Maggie couldn't argue against and in a desperate attempt to hold on to her crumbling confidence, she tried to recall the steady rhythm of her baby's heartbeat. But it was the sound of waves slapping against the edge of the lake that filled her mind and she felt herself drowning in self-doubt.

CHAPTER 5

On Monday morning, between her steady stream of clients, Maggie caught up with other chores. Occasionally she picked up the telephone but didn't dial. She wanted to phone her dad and at least capture some of the joy being denied her, but now was not the time to tell him she was pregnant. Stan had struggled through the first year without his wife but by all accounts he was slowly adapting to his new way of life in Spain. If Maggie was ever going to convince him that she could manage without him then she would have to at least sound stronger than she felt right now.

Maggie inhaled the scent of clove bud as she prepared a gentle ointment to ease Lily's teething pain. The essential oil's stimulating properties weren't enough to give her the courage she needed to step out of her treatment room but she left anyway.

'You've had a busy morning,' Kathy remarked. 'I was starting to think you were avoiding me.'

Kathy had a perceptive eye that was an equal match for Maggie's ability to read a person's face by the tone of their voice. They each had their own ways of recognising a lie when they heard it so Maggie didn't try. 'I know she's your friend, Kath, but—'

'It's all right, I know. I've spoken to Judith and she's worked herself up into a right state. And I'm afraid I haven't helped.' Kathy sighed. 'I let slip that I'd known for a while about the baby.'

'Surely she can't be surprised that I didn't want to tell her? Her reaction was always going to be awful.'

'And was it?'

This was exactly the line of questioning Maggie had wanted to avoid. So far she'd kept Judith's most cutting remarks to herself, not wanting to put James in an awkward position, and it was the same with Kathy. 'Why are you two such good friends again?' she asked now.

'Having an old grouch around makes me feel younger.'

Maggie returned the smile she had heard in Kathy's voice. 'And I always thought it was owning a beauty parlour that guaranteed you eternal youth,' she said, although Kathy had a point. The two might be the same age but that was where the similarities ended. Whereas Judith was already changing down a gear, Kathy had no intention of growing old gracefully. Her hair was cut in a modern style, short and spiky to accentuate her fine bone structure and she described the colour as platinum blonde although it felt coarse enough to be completely grey without the helping hand of peroxide. As a regular to Maggie's massage table, Maggie knew that Kathy hadn't completely avoided the signs of aging, but although there were the odd wrinkles here and there, her skin was smooth and retained enough elasticity to keep her looks as youthful as her outlook.

'Please don't go losing sleep over Judith. She's only panicking because she wants what's best for James. And you,' Kathy added but not quickly enough.

Maggie shrugged. 'You were right first time. Sorry, Kath, but I have to go. I promised to meet Jenny at the bank,' she said and made her escape before her resolve to keep quiet weakened even further.

Slipping on her sunglasses to block out the muted sunshine trickling across her vision, Maggie and Harvey headed in the direction of the bank, but no sooner had they set off than they came to a sudden halt.

'Hi, I'm here,' Jenny announced. She sounded out of breath as if she had been running. 'The nursery phoned and they're desperate for this miracle cure you promised me.'

'How is Lily?' Maggie asked as she handed it over. They turned together and continued along the route to the nursery, which was the same direction as the park where Maggie was heading next.

'Red-faced and grumpy.'

'And you?'

'The same,' Jenny quipped.

'I've been worried,' Maggie confessed. 'I know you were annoyed with Mark for dragging you away last night but it sounded like there was more to it than that. What's going on?'

'Oh, something and nothing.'

They had reached the entrance to the park and came to a stop. 'And the truth?' Maggie said not willing to accept the prevarication.

Jenny sucked air through clenched teeth as she tried to hold back her feelings. It didn't work. 'Mark's been working all the hours God sends and I know it's tough for estate agents right now but he doesn't seem to recognise how hard it is for me too. I've only been back at work a few weeks but I seem to be the one who's expected to juggle everything: the baby, the job, and the house. Look at me now, rushing over to the nursery to look after our daughter on my so-called lunch break. It's bloody hard, Maggie.'

Jenny's breath caught in her throat but it was Maggie who gasped back the sob. The seed of doubt planted by Judith had burst through to the surface and was tearing up the foundations of the life Maggie's mum had spent decades building for her daughter.

'Maggie? What's wrong?' Jenny grasped both of Maggie's hands in her own.

'If you can't cope then what hope do I have, Jen?' she said in the barest whisper.

Jenny squeezed Maggie's hands. 'Don't pay any

attention to me, all I need is a bit of "me" time. What's happened, Maggie? It's bloody Judith, isn't it?'

'Yes . . . no . . . I don't know. She thinks I'm deliberately setting out to destroy James's life and I'm starting to think that's exactly what I'll end up doing. So much is going to change and it scares me. I want to have it all, Jenny. The baby, the job, the house,' she said, making a feeble joke of Jenny's earlier complaint, 'but how can I? It's not just about finding the time for everything; even the finances don't stack up. If I went back to work then I'd have to put the baby in a nursery but I doubt I'd earn enough to cover the fees. That's why James wanted Judith to help look after the baby. Thank God she doesn't want to. Am I being selfish?'

'You're feeling overwhelmed, that's all, but why make it harder than it needs to be? If I had the choice, I'd give up work like a shot and it might give you the time you need to settle into motherhood.'

Maggie's heart sank. It wasn't the answer she had wanted to hear. She wasn't ready to give up the business she had worked so hard for.

'But,' Jenny continued, 'if you're insisting on being superwoman, so what if you can't cover the nursery fees? Make James work twice as hard to make up the difference. It's the least he can do for letting Judith upset you.'

Maggie wanted to smile but despite Jenny's faith,

her superhuman powers failed her. 'James is blissfully unaware. All he remembers of Saturday night is demolishing a bottle of single malt in the kitchen with his dad to wet the baby's head.'

'He knows. Maybe he didn't hear everything Judith said about the baby but he couldn't ignore the constant references she made to Carolyn.'

'Comparisons, you mean. I think she's still waiting for the day when Carolyn realises she's made a terrible mistake and begs James to take her back. But in answer to your question, yes he can ignore that too. Given the choice, James is more than happy to stick his head in the sand,' Maggie said but then regretted her harsh assessment of her husband. 'But that's only because he's such a gentle soul and that's why I love him so much.'

'Gentle soul or not, he won't appreciate his wife pretending everything's fine when it's not. Talk to him.'

'I don't want to be the cause of a family rift, not after everything James has been through already.'

'*You* wouldn't be the cause of a rift, Judith would. Tell him.'

'OK,' Maggie said with no intention of doing so. 'But only on the condition that you talk to Mark about how you're feeling overwhelmed too.'

'OK,' Jenny said, sounding even less convincing than Maggie. 'And we'll make some time for us too. How about we hit the town and go clubbing?'

Maggie couldn't help laughing even though she

suspected Jenny wasn't joking. 'Or how about a yoga class?' she countered, recalling the nights out with Jenny in Chester where she had spent most of her time apologising for standing on people's toes on the dance floor.

Jenny relaxed now there was a smile on Maggie's face and said, 'Yes, I suppose we are meant to be sensible, married women these days. Now, I really am sorry, Maggie, but I have to get this to the nursery. Are you going to be all right?'

Maggie assured Jenny that she was and could almost believe it herself. As she and Harvey switched to autopilot and stepped into the park, she reminded herself of all the people in her life, willing her to succeed. Did it really matter that Judith wasn't going to be one of them? She had good friends and a loving husband, not to mention an amazing midwife who was already putting together a support network that would give her all the necessary skills to take on motherhood.

It was only when she paused at the top of the slope leading down to the lake that Maggie's fragile confidence began to disintegrate again. She turned her face towards the park bench as if she could see its wrought iron frame and achingly empty seats. Her mum was meant to be there, to share her daughter's joy at fulfilling her lifelong ambition to be a mother and to help her prepare for her baby's arrival. She was meant to be there to silence her doubters. But her mum wasn't there and Maggie felt her absence more keenly than ever before.

Her legs had turned to lead as she made her way down towards the bench but each juddering step felt like a body blow. Her heart thudded against her chest, which had an invisible weight pressing against it. Gulping air desperately into her lungs, Maggie began to feel light-headed. Tears stung her eyes but couldn't blur the image of the empty park bench she held in her mind. Why had she ever thought she could do this? She couldn't stand up to Judith and, more importantly, she couldn't look after a baby. Not on her own. She couldn't do it.

Overwhelmed by a growing sense of panic, Maggie ignored the uplifting scents of spring flowers around her and she was too engrossed in the rhythmic sound of water slapping against the slipway to pick up the scent of lilac perfume. Her pace raced alongside her pulse as she drew closer to the lake. She was ready to give herself up to the dark and silent abyss and would have done so if Harvey hadn't been so determined to guide her towards the safety of the bench. Maggie wasn't sure if it was the realisation of what she had been about to do or the sound of a woman's voice that brought her to her senses.

'Are you all right?' Elsa asked.

Elsa couldn't for the life of her remember how she came to be sitting on the park bench. The twisted branches of the giant rhododendron bushes growing up the embankment made her feel like she had been caught up in a huge spider's web but it was her mind that was full of tangles.

Smoothing over the creases of her dress and resting her hand on her stomach, Elsa watched a woman stumbling down the sloping path with her dog. For a moment, she thought she would march straight into the lake and Elsa's heart jumped into her mouth.

'Are you all right?' she called.

The woman's breathing was ragged as she approached the bench. 'Elsa?'

'Have we met before?' Elsa asked when the dog greeted her like an old friend.

'Yes, the other day.' The woman took a seat next to her and put her hand on her chest in an effort to steady her breathing. It took a moment or two before she could speak again and even then her voice trembled. 'I'm Maggie and this is Harvey. Remember?'

Elsa placed the palm of a hand on the surface of the bench and a memory seeped out from its painted surface and into her mind. This was where she had shared her secret. 'You're pregnant too, aren't you? Is that why you're so upset?'

Maggie tried to give her a winning smile but it crumpled with the effort. 'I'm upset because I miss my mum. We used to sit here together.'

The vision of a child being separated from its mother struck a chord in Elsa's heart. 'Do you think my little one will cry for me?' she asked.

67

'Are you still thinking of giving the baby up?'

'I think of nothing else.'

Maggie took a deep breath and, as she focused her attention on Elsa, she brought her tremors under control. 'I have to admit, I've been thinking a lot about you since you disappeared last time. I've been worried about you.'

'I'll survive,' Elsa said as if that wasn't a good thing but she was comforted by the idea that Maggie had been concerned about her. She could do with a friendly ear. She had done something reckless, even by her standards, and if her hopes held out then she was going to upset a lot of people.

'You sound tired,' her friend said.

Elsa looked at her hands; they had been completely destroyed by hard graft. 'I'm on my feet all day at Flo's Fruit and Veg. I think every bone in my body aches.'

'Flo's Fruit and Veg? I've never heard of it.'

'It's on the High Street. Don't tell me you go to Mr Flanagan's? Aunt Flo's fruit is much fresher. Cheaper too.'

'Aunt Flo,' Maggie repeated as if she was struggling to follow what Elsa was telling her. 'She's the woman you're staying with, isn't she?'

'Yes, and she's a bit of a hard taskmaster but why have a dog and bark yourself, isn't that right, Harvey?' Elsa rubbed the dog's neck until he groaned with pleasure.

'I hope she's not pushing you too hard. You need to take care of yourself.'

'She's not that bad really. I was a complete stranger when she took me in but now she treats me like family. She has a will of iron sometimes but soft as a brush the next. She's going to hit the roof when she finds out I've written to Freddie.'

'You've written to him?'

Elsa had her sister to thank for that. Celia had given birth to a bonnie little girl and Elsa had rushed over to Manchester to see them and, more importantly, to be there when her mum arrived to inspect her latest grandchild. Elsa was five and half months pregnant and had to bind herself up so the bulge didn't show but her weight gain had been the first thing her mum had noticed.

'You'll never get a husband if you let yourself go,' she had warned.

Celia had leapt to her defence, fearful that Elsa might break down and confess all. 'I'll make sure she does. We both need to get in shape.'

Her mum continued to scrutinise her younger daughter. 'Still, you've got those lovely eyes and such beautiful hair. Don't go cutting it short like your sister here. I don't understand why girls want to look so much like boys these days.'

'I won't, Mum,' Elsa said as she tried to staunch her tears. 'I would never let you down, you know that.'

'Being around Celia and the children has clearly been a good influence. I don't see that wild streak of yours any more,' her mum said with a note of approval. Her face softened. 'You're a good girl,

Elsa, I know that.' It was then that her mum had put a loving hand on Elsa's cheek and it was a wonder she hadn't noticed her daughter's body trembling with the effort to keep her emotions in check. If anything was going to push her over the edge then it was that simple touch of her mum's hand.

But it wasn't her mum's touch that had made Elsa go against the plans that had been laid for her but the defenceless newborn she had held in her arms. 'How can I hand something so precious over to someone else?' she had asked Celia. 'How can you make me?'

'You can barely look after yourself, Elsa. You've still got a lot of growing up to do,' Celia had said, repeating old arguments.

'I'm old enough to feel a mother's love – and I swear I'm going to love this baby growing inside me until my dying day.' She was holding on desperately to her sister's baby now and refused to let Celia take her from her. There was a look of horror on Celia's face as she was forced to imagine it was Elsa's baby being wrenched from its mother's arms. 'Please, Celia,' Elsa had whimpered. 'Please, I'm begging you.'

What else could Celia do but promise to help?

'I've written the letter and left it with my sister Celia,' Elsa explained to Maggie. 'She's contacting the friends I know at the base and by hook or by crook, that letter will find its way to Freddie.'

'What did you tell him?'

'Everything. I've told him everything,' Elsa said, the rasp in her voice laced with emotion. 'And if he doesn't reply now then I'll know there's nothing left for me to live for.'

'Please don't say that. I know how daunting it must seem but don't give up. Believe me, I know how easy it is to convince yourself you can't do it because that's what everyone's telling you, but you have to believe in yourself, Elsa. We *both* do.'

'I have to face facts. I can't work and look after a baby at the same time. I can't provide for both of us.' As Elsa spoke, a cold breeze bit into the nape of her neck. She raised a hand to the back of her head for protection and her fingers touched cropped locks. She was such a disappointment to her parents.

'I really hope your hero comes back on that motorbike of his.'

'And if he doesn't? The thought of handing my baby over to someone else . . . It's breaking my heart already.' Elsa cast her gaze over the lake. The day was bright but the spring sun was not yet warm enough to chase away a lingering mist that covered it like a shroud. She imagined the water would be deathly cold. 'I can't see the swans.'

Maggie turned her head as if to follow Elsa's gaze. 'No, there are no swans,' she said hesitantly.

'Would it be so bad if the lake swallowed me up and I spent the rest of eternity with my baby?'

'That isn't the answer,' Maggie said, turning

71

away from the lake. 'Listen to me, Elsa. You can't think like that. You've got to stay strong. I just wish there was more I could do for you.'

Rummaging in her bag, Maggie pulled out a small card and handed it over to Elsa. It had pretty swirls of colour printed on it and a delicate script.

'What is it?'

'My business card, but don't get me wrong, I'm not touting for work,' Maggie added quickly.

Elsa squinted at the print. Reading was never her strong point and she couldn't quite work out the letters. 'Aroma . . .'

'Aromatherapy. That's what I do. I could give you a complementary treatment if you like, something to ease your aching joints. But call in anyway, even if it's just for a chat. I'm not always there but the opening times are printed on the back and it has my mobile number too. If ever you feel like there's nowhere else to turn, turn to me. Please, Elsa.'

The numbers and symbols on the card were indecipherable but Elsa understood the sentiment perfectly. 'Thank you. You really are so very kind.'

'I'm not being completely selfless in all of this. If I can persuade you to believe in yourself, then maybe I'll start believing in myself again, too.'

Maggie's words of kindness were too much for Elsa and it didn't help that Harvey was staring at her so intently. The look of sadness in his eyes took the last remnants of her self-control and Elsa reached out to grasp Maggie's hand. For a fleeting moment, they held on to each other but then Maggie recoiled from her touch. The look of horror on her face was unmistakeable.

'I'm a monster, I know I am!' Elsa cried. 'If I'm the kind of person who can give up her baby without a fight then I don't deserve Freddie and I don't deserve to be happy.' Her whole body began to shake as the weight of her guilt pushed the air out of her lungs. 'I can't stand this any more.'

Elsa stood up so quickly that she frightened a family of nearby ducks. The world around her erupted into chaos and above the angry quacks, the flapping of wings, and the furious splashing of water, Elsa barely heard Maggie's desperate pleas as she stepped closer to the water's edge.

CHAPTER 6

The splashing was thunderous but didn't quite drown out the more frightening sound of Elsa's wracked sobs. Maggie rushed towards the noise, not hesitating at the water's edge or stopping when the cold water rose up over her ankles and then her knees. Once she was waist deep, she used her arms to propel herself forward, all the while calling out to Elsa. For a moment, Maggie grabbed hold of what she thought was Elsa's hand but it was deathly cold and the skin papery thin. She cried out, imagining it was the hand of a long-forgotten corpse trying to pull two young women towards a watery grave. Maggie staggered backwards but lost her footing on the slimy floor. She managed to call out to Elsa one last time before the lake swallowed her up as surely as it had her friend. All was lost and the silence coiled itself around her body and pulled her down towards the abyss. Maggie didn't fight it, not until she heard the urgent heartbeat of her unborn child.

'No!' she screamed, and her arms began to flail in a bid to escape the water that had taken the form of a cotton sheet.

Muscular arms wrapped tightly around her. 'Shush, shush, it's all right, Maggie,' James whispered into her ear and his gentle rocking eased her slowly from the nightmare.

When Maggie was able to speak, all she said was, 'Sorry.' She didn't need to explain further. She'd had the dream half a dozen times already. Her night terrors were forcing her to relive that heart-stopping moment in the park when she had thought Elsa was going to throw herself in the lake. She hadn't, but her latest encounter with Elsa had left Maggie even more unsettled than the first. Her instincts told her that all was not as it seemed. Elsa had been talking about shops that didn't exist, not in modern-day Sedgefield at least, but while Maggie's mind focused on the contradictions, her heart clung to the similarities. They were kindred spirits.

James kissed Maggie softly. 'Don't be sorry,' he said. 'I'm always going to be here to save you.'

Maggie squeezed her eyes shut to hold back the tears. She felt blessed to have James in her life but she also felt guilty. Who would save Elsa?

'I'm going to have to insist you have a smile on your face before you come into this salon, Maggie Carter,' scolded Kathy. 'You'll frighten away the customers with that scowl.' As Maggie drew closer to the reception desk she added, 'And I should also insist that you're dry. Have you been wandering through that park in the teeming rain?'

Maggie's visits to the park had become more of a daily pilgrimage in the last three weeks but once again her hopes of crossing paths with Elsa had been dashed. She forced a smile. 'Morning, Kathy.'

'That smile reminds me of the one I had fixed on my face all weekend.'

'That doesn't sound good.' The smile on Maggie's face, false or otherwise, faltered as her mind raced ahead to the possible cause. 'You were going home, weren't you?'

Kathy had moved to Sedgefield in the late seventies but Nantwich would always be her home town. 'To see my mum, yes, and before you ask, no, I didn't see Judith. I'm keeping a safe distance until she comes to her senses otherwise I may not be responsible for my actions. She has a habit of speaking before she thinks and I have a habit of acting before I think. *Not* a good combination.'

'I don't want you two falling out over me,' Maggie warned, 'but we have to accept that she's not likely to come to her senses any time soon. The news about the baby might have come out of the blue but she reached the conclusion that James was throwing his life away by marrying me a long time ago.'

'Which I take as a personal insult since I was the one who brought you two together. Maybe I should have a word.'

Maggie shook her head. 'James was over there the other day and he says they're slowly getting used to the idea. I doubt that's true but it's what

76

he wants to believe and I'd rather leave it at that for now. But enough about me, tell me about your troubles.'

'Oh, it's nothing I can't handle. Mum has me running round in circles, that's all,' Kathy said with an uncharacteristic sigh of resignation. 'She's not getting any younger and whether she likes it or not, she needs more support. But my mum can be quite single-minded when she wants to be.'

'I wondered where you got it from,' Maggie said. 'You'll have to bring her over to the salon some time, I'd love to meet her.'

'Getting her to Sedgefield is part of the problem. I've suggested she move in with me and Joe but she's refusing point blank to leave her friends,' Kathy complained before adding, quickly, 'We haven't all been blessed with mums that were as easy-going as Joan. But we'll find a compromise somehow. If Mum won't move here then I'll simply have to convince Joe that it's time for us to downsize. We could always look for somewhere with a granny flat nearer Nantwich.'

'I know how much you love that house of yours but maybe it's for the best,' Maggie offered, recognising that moving house wasn't going to be as easy as Kathy made it sound. She lived on the outskirts of Sedgefield in the kind of house that was big enough to be split into apartments and had been a nurses' home before Kathy took over the place. It was half-empty now that the kids had grown up and moved away but despite being careworn and high maintenance, was much loved and it would be a wrench for Kathy and her husband to leave it.

Maggie and Kathy's soul-searching was drawn to a swift conclusion by the tinkle of the bell above the salon door as someone came in. Harvey, who had been sitting patiently next to Maggie, stood up and sniffed. He took in a lungful of hairspray-tainted air and quickly snorted it out before sitting back down. Maggie surmised that the person wasn't someone he, and therefore she, knew particularly well. She stepped to one side as the stranger approached.

'Afternoon, ladies,' the man said. 'Could you sign here for me please?'

A package had been placed on the counter and Kathy signed for the delivery. In a moment, the courier had disappeared but he had been enough of an interruption to remind the two women that they had work to do.

'I suppose I'd better start setting up for my afternoon appointments. I've got two new clients today and the first is due any minute now,' Maggie said. She had flipped up the cover on her tactile wristwatch and was horrified to discover how short of time she was. It wasn't only meandering through the park that had made her late; she had lingered too long at home too. She and James had spent the weekend clearing out the spare room and that morning had been her first opportunity to get a feel for the place so she could start planning the theme for the nursery. Preparing for the future was still frightening, but she could either sink or swim and thanks to her recurring nightmare she had already chosen which.

'Make sure you dry off first and I'll let you know when Mrs Smith arrives.'

There was an inflection in Kathy's tone and Maggie latched onto it. 'Did you take the booking? Do you know anything about Mrs Smith? Is she pregnant by any chance?'

'What is it about this Elsa woman that has you so obsessed?'

'I'm not obsessed, I'm just concerned.'

Before Kathy could interrogate her further, the door jangled again. Harvey stood up and began to wag his tail furiously but it was the aroma of chamomile and cloves that gave away the identity of the salon's latest arrival.

'I didn't expect to see you here on your day off. Is it a social call or have you chipped a fingernail?' asked Maggie.

'Neither,' Jenny replied.

Maggie waited for her to explain further but Jenny was being reticent for a change. 'Don't tell me Mark's getting his hair done,' Maggie asked as she turned her attention to the person she heard soothing a grumbling Lily.

'There's no way I'm handing over my gorgeous husband to one of these vixens. No offence, Kathy.'

'None taken,' Kathy replied. 'In fact, I think my girls would take it as a compliment.'

Mark cleared his throat to get their attention. 'Actually, I'm on babysitting duties this afternoon.'

The growled response from Jenny was no doubt as he intended. 'It's not called babysitting when it's your own daughter.'

'You should be grateful he's willing to help you out at all,' interjected Kathy.

'This joke is wearing very thin,' Jenny warned.

'Who was joking?'

'Will you two stop teasing her,' Maggie said before Jenny started hyperventilating. 'Now is someone going to tell me what's going on? If you're here to see me then I'm afraid I can't hang around. I need to get ready for Mrs Smith . . .' Her voice trailed off as she finally recognised the deceit. '*You're* Mrs Smith?'

'I'm being treated to a day of pampering by my darling husband and that includes a relaxing massage.'

Maggie folded her arms and gave them a stern look. 'So why go to the trouble of booking an appointment under a false name – and a pretty unimaginative one at that.'

'I picked that,' Kathy added curtly.

'Did *you* know?' Maggie asked, redirecting her glare at Kathy.

'Jenny wanted you to treat her like any other client – or should I say, charge her like any other client. If it was left to you to manage your own business affairs, you'd have gone bankrupt in the first month.'

'I'm not so busy or desperate that I can't help out a friend now and again.'

'Except half of your clients would end up being treated like friends if you had your way,' Kathy insisted.

Maggie raised a hand in submission. In her own mind, she offered a therapeutic service to people in need which often made it difficult to see them simply as clients and it was undoubtedly Kathy's business acumen that kept Maggie's accounts in the black. What had started out as a simple agreement to provide space and reception services for Maggie's business had quickly developed into Kathy becoming a not-so-silent partner. 'I don't suppose there's any point in arguing?'

'None,' Jenny and Kathy said in unison. 'Besides, it's Mark's treat.'

'And it's my pleasure. I don't know how she manages to take care of us all but even with her boundless energy, she needs to recharge her batteries now and again.'

'You work hard too,' Jenny reminded him.

'Ah, but I couldn't do what you do. I'm only a man, not good at multitasking like you ladies.'

Maggie sensed Kathy preparing to stick her fingers down her throat so she jumped in to divert the conversation. 'Mark, do you ever remember seeing any swans in Victoria Park?' she asked. He was the only one of the group who had lived in Sedgefield all of his life.

'No, I can't say I have.'

Undeterred, Maggie tried another tack. 'Ever heard of a shop in Sedgefield called Flo's Fruit and Veg?' She heard Kathy sigh; she had heard these questions before.

'No.'

'Not ever?'

'Ah, has it got something to do with this ghost of yours?' he asked.

Jenny nudged Mark so hard that he let out a short gasp. 'You're not allowed to use the "G" word.'

'And that would be because I don't think she *is* a ghost,' interjected Maggie. 'A restless soul, perhaps, but not a ghost.'

'Really?' Jenny asked. 'So your next question isn't going to be whether or not Mark has heard of anyone drowning in the lake?'

'I'm only asking in case Elsa did do something silly. I'm worried about her and I wanted to know if the lake was deep enough, that's all,' Maggie said, hoping only she could hear the lie.

She couldn't blame her friends' gentle mockery. Away from the lake and the connection she had felt with Elsa, Maggie was finding it impossible to justify or explain why this relative stranger should occupy her mind so much or why she feared for her future.

'It wouldn't take much water if someone was determined enough to drown themselves,' Mark offered helpfully.

'Thanks, Mark,' Maggie said. She had no desire to revisit the countless theories that had kept her mind turning and her stomach churning for the past few weeks, so she made a point of checking her watch again. 'Now I'll be late for my second appointment if we don't get a move on.'

'Then if you've finished with me, I'll be on my way,' Mark said and turned to leave.

Maggie may have begun to doubt her senses but in some respects, she was as sharp as ever. 'Don't you think you're forgetting something, Mark?' She had heard the footsteps that marked his retreat but not the telltale squeak of pram wheels.

'Nice try,' muttered Jenny.

'And don't forget to come back and pick your wife up,' Maggie added. 'Now, Mrs Smith, would you like to come this way?'

The treatment room had been designed to make the most of the limited space available. There was a massage table in the centre, a small table and chairs for consultations in one corner and shelving lined up along all the available wall space. Jenny was currently reclining in the treatment chair, which took up the last of the available space.

Maggie had begun with a head massage and there had been gratifying groans from her mystery client as she dug her fingers deep into her neck and scalp in wide, curving arcs. Together they had selected a relaxing mixture of bergamot, chamomile and neroli, taking account of Jenny's preferences and needs.

The aromas had already worked their magic on Harvey who was snoring peacefully in his bed tucked away in a corner. Jenny was another challenge entirely: between groans her chatter had been incessant. She had been telling Maggie how the property market wasn't picking up fast enough and that Mark's boss was considering further redundancies. Rather than relaxing, Jenny was becoming more agitated, so when Maggie moved her to the table for a full body massage, she refused to start until her friend had taken a vow of silence. She called it tough love.

By the time all the knots in Jenny's shoulders had been kneaded away, her groans had reduced to whimpers. 'I'll massage your feet next,' Maggie whispered, 'and then that's it.'

'It won't tickle will it?'

'Shush,' Maggie instructed.

'But you started talking first.'

'Shush.'

Maggie had learnt different therapies over the years and reflexology had proven to be an effective technique for mind as well as body. It often evoked an intense and emotional reaction so when the first sob came, Maggie wasn't as surprised as Jenny, who had been warned of the side effects but had been convinced she wouldn't succumb.

'It's OK, Jen, don't fight it. Let yourself go. I'm here to catch you.'

Jenny's reply was unintelligible, little more than a mumbled snivel. Maggie guessed her friend was still trying to fight against the tide of her emotions but the next sob came nevertheless.

When the treatment was over, Maggie didn't say a word as she poured a glass of water for her client who was weeping in loud, ragged gasps.

'I . . . I . . . I'm just so scared. What if Mark loses his job? What if it's me working all the hours God sends? What if I'm the one missing out on Lily growing up?' Jenny stammered as she finished dressing and took the glass. 'I don't know if I could cope with that.'

'Those "what ifs" haven't happened yet but if they do you *will* cope. You have Mark and Lily and you have me too. You're not on your own,' Maggie said. She handed Jenny a tissue.

'I feel like a gibbering wreck,' her friend said with a hiccup.

Maggie gave her an enigmatic smile. 'You look ready to face the world to me.'

Jenny laughed. 'Thanks, Maggie.'

'The boys are with us next week for half-term so I won't be in the salon but I can still do home visits, armed with a bottle of massage oil or a bottle of wine; your choice.'

'Wine sounds good,' Jenny said. She was doing her best to sound upbeat but her voice trembled very slightly. She blew her nose. 'I think I'm ready.'

'You haven't seen the bill yet,' Maggie said, although she had already decided that if she was being forced to accept payment from a family whose financial future was in doubt, then it would be heavily discounted no matter how much Kathy protested.

Lily's cries could be heard from outside the salon as soon as Maggie opened the door of the treatment room. More sobs erupted behind her. Mother and daughter were howling in stereo and the crescendo of wails was enough to wake up Harvey who hurried past them.

Maggie did her best to usher Jenny towards the exit without disturbing the other customers but it was an impossible task. Harvey didn't have his harness on and she hadn't thought to pick up her cane. Jenny's floundering was getting them nowhere until Kathy came to the rescue.

'You know, Maggie, we might need to invest in a rear entrance,' Kathy said once they had handed Jenny over to a bemused Mark and promptly closed the door on them. 'If your scowls earlier weren't enough to frighten away our customers then that little performance certainly will.'

'I think she means me,' came a voice that was immediately recognisable.

'Elsa?'

Jenny's treatment oils had overpowered the scent of lilacs when Maggie had walked past the waiting area earlier but she could smell the perfume now.

The woman gave a throaty laugh. 'People haven't called me that for sixty years. Even the doctors know better than to use my proper name. I don't care what's written on your forms, you can call me either Mrs Milton or Elsie. I prefer Elsie.'

Maggie tried to swallow but her mouth was bone dry.

86

'Are you all right, love?' the old lady said. 'You look like you've just seen a ghost.'

'You don't remember me, do you?' Maggie managed.

'I'm afraid my memory isn't what it used to be. Should I?'

Maggie didn't know what to say or think. Her mind had stalled and a shiver crawled down her spine. She wanted more than anything to tell this woman, who was undoubtedly in her twilight years, that they had met when Elsa was twenty-two-years old, alone and pregnant – not because Maggie believed it to be true but because she wanted it to be true. She had an irrational need for Elsa to remain within reach of her help.

'Would you like me to wait while you get yourself ready?' Elsie asked when Maggie still hadn't responded.

'You do look a bit pale,' Kathy added.

Maggie insisted that she was fine but there was no fooling Kathy.

'How about I make you some hot, sweet tea?' Kathy asked. 'Would you like one, Mrs Milton?'

'That would be lovely. I'll let my husband know what I'm up to first. I won't be a minute.'

Mrs Milton headed for the small waiting area and Kathy lowered her voice to ask the burning question: 'Mrs Milton is Elsa? *The* Elsa?'

'Yes.' There was no hesitation in Maggie's reply but there was a note of puzzlement.

'You do realise she's in her eighties? I'm pretty

87

sure that rules out the possibility of her being pregnant.'

'I know,' Maggie said as she tried to think back to when they had first met. The dated perfume and the gravelly voice were the clues Maggie should have used to build up the picture of an elderly woman despite the youthful lilt that had obviously been forced. Had Maggie been so eager to believe that Elsa was some kind of lost soul that she had ignored her instincts? How could she have been so foolish?

'At least the search can be called off,' Kathy added kindly when she realised Maggie was finding it difficult to reconcile the two opposing images she now had of her new friend.

'What have I done, Kathy? She doesn't remember a thing about me. That poor woman was stumbling around the park thinking she was in her twenties and I did nothing to help her.'

'Hello, ladies,' Alice announced as the bell above the door gently tinkled. She tried to muffle her cough as Maggie turned towards her. 'I know what you're going to say and I *will* make an appointment for one of your massage thingies but my roots are showing and that's my priority for today.'

'OK, Alice, I'll be with you in a minute,' Kathy said. She sounded disappointed that her conversation with Maggie had been cut short.

'Is that Mrs Milton over there?' Alice asked. 'It's such a shame.'

'What is?' Kathy asked before Maggie had a chance.

Alice whispered, 'I found her in the park the other day. She was a bit confused, poor love. It took me a while to get her to tell me who she was and where she came from but we eventually tracked down her husband. It's an awful thing, dementia. I saw my dad go through it and I wouldn't wish it on anyone.'

'At least you helped her,' Maggie said, comparing Alice's abilities to her own. She felt humiliated; there was no other way to describe it.

'Hello, Elsie love,' Alice said as she directed her attention to the woman whose heels scraped across the tiled floor towards them. 'Are you feeling better today?'

'Erm, yes thank you . . .'

'I'm Alice.'

'Of course, how could I forget?' she said, clearly uncomfortable, then turned to Maggie. 'I've told my husband we could be a while and to go home but he's having none of it. How long do you think it will take?'

Maggie painted on a smile. 'That really depends on you. What is it I can help you with?'

'I'm not sure to be honest. I came across your card and I thought I'd give it a try. Something to ease my aching feet would be good.'

'I'll see what I can do for you,' Maggie said. The old lady was either unaware or unwilling to acknowledge the episodes in the park where she had been transported back to another time in her life so Maggie was going to have to earn Elsa – no, *Elsie's* trust all over again. 'I don't have any more clients today so we can take as long as you need.'

'Then we'll take our time and make the daft old sod wait,' Elsie whispered, loud enough to be heard ten feet away.

'Don't worry, I'll look after him,' Alice promised.

As Maggie took her latest client into the treatment room, she couldn't help but wonder about the man waiting patiently in reception. Had Freddie returned to save Elsa and refused to leave her side ever since?

The rigid plastic chairs in the treatment room squeaked as Maggie went through a formal assessment with her new client: taking some personal details; a brief medical history; checking for known allergies; and forming an idea of what fragrances Elsie preferred while she did her best to silence the internal voice that wanted to ask more probing questions.

She used a digital recorder for her notes and from experience knew that when she played the recording back, the squeak of the chairs would be as irritating then as it was now. Today the recorder would also pick up the chink of china as Elsie sipped her tea.

'I'm sorry, these seats aren't very comfortable, are they?'

'With my joints, there aren't many chairs that are.'

'If I can convince you to try out some of my therapies, then the treatment chair over there will be much better.'

At this point, Maggie was meant to go through some options to help ease Elsie's aches and pains but she still hadn't told her how they had met before. The deceit played on her mind and she was about to confess all but the seemingly frail and vulnerable woman in front of her was already one step ahead.

'I'm afraid I have a confession to make,' Elsie said and if the squeak of the chair wasn't enough to give away her agitation then the nerves constricting her throat certainly were. 'Do you mind if we turn that thing off?'

Maggie switched off the recorder without a word.

'This is a lovely room, so clean and colourful. It's not what I was expecting at all,' Elsie said as she scanned the shelves which held an intriguing mix of jars and bottles with bright labels that brought a splash of colour to counter the clinical white of the walls and the chrome fittings.

'I'm a bit obsessive about adding lots of colour to the packaging of my products to match the colourful scents inside but as for clean, the dog hairs can be a problem,' Maggie said, tapping the side of her leg to call Harvey over.

'Hello, boy,' Elsie said. 'You are a cutie, aren't you?' The dog shook himself as she tickled his back. 'One of our neighbours in Liverpool had a guide dog. They were quite a team. Mr . . .' Her voice trailed off.

'It doesn't matter,' Maggie offered.

'Remembering names is a bit hit and miss I'm afraid.' There was a frustrated pause but Elsie wasn't giving up. 'Woodhouse, that was it. Mr Woodhouse. Anyway,' she said, turning her attention back to the dog, 'he had a German Shepherd and he wasn't a patch on you, Harvey.'

'You remember his name?'

Elsie laughed but it was hollow. 'Like I said, hit and miss.'

'That wasn't what I meant.'

Elsie stopped stroking Harvey. 'I don't remember meeting you before but I'm not denying that we may have.'

'We've met twice before in Victoria Park. We sat together on the bench by the lake,' Maggie said gently.

'That bench has certainly seen a lot of comings and goings in its time.'

A flush rose in Maggie's cheeks as she imagined Elsie trying to work out how much she had told her. Maggie wanted to explain but something held her back. Bizarre as it seemed, it was Elsa who had trusted Maggie with her innermost secrets and she was loath to break that trust, even with Elsa's older self. 'It's a beautiful spot.'

'And one that has played on my mind for a very long time.'

'Do you remember anything of our meetings?' There was the soft swish of hair brushing against her collar as Elsie shook her head. Struggling to find a diplomatic way to bridge Elsie's present with her past, Maggie asked, 'How long have you been having problems with your memory, Elsie?'

'You mean how long have I had Alzheimer's? That's the medical term the doctors in Liverpool labelled me with. Now, when was that?' she asked herself. 'We moved to Sedgefield a couple of months ago . . . I think . . . So, oh, I don't know, six months ago, a year maybe? It was when the police got involved.'

'The police?' Maggie asked, unable to hide her shock.

'I kept trying to find my way back to Sedgefield and the local bobbies got used to picking me up and taking me home so I eventually agreed to see the doctor. Of course it started long before then, lots of silly things that we could joke about at first, like when I put my shoes in the oven and claimed I was making Dover sole,' Elsie said. 'But there are some things I can't laugh off.'

'Like your trips to the park?'

When she replied, Elsie's words were choked. 'I come out of the fug feeling so lost and confused and it terrifies me. I keep trying to convince myself that it'll take time to settle in a new place but I'm not getting better, only worse.'

'There's a reason this town is special to you, isn't there?'

There was a telling pause. 'You know I've lived in Sedgefield before, don't you?'

'When we met, you introduced yourself as Elsa and told me you were twenty-two, which would be back in 1953 by my reckoning,' Maggie said, having worked it out from the date of birth Elsie had given. But that was only one small piece of the puzzle. 'I think you trusted me, maybe because I'm pregnant too.'

'I did wonder how I came to have your card in my pocket. Can I still trust you?'

'Yes,' Maggie replied, eager to hear Elsa's fate.

'Then forget everything I may have told you.'

When Maggie reached out to take Elsie's hand, the chair squeaked as the old lady pulled away.

'But you came back to Sedgefield for a reason, surely? Perhaps I can help,' Maggie offered although for the life of her she didn't know how.

'You can help by taking absolutely no notice of my ramblings.'

But the image of Elsa that Maggie had conjured in her mind persisted. She couldn't shake the feeling that the young woman she had befriended was still there, hiding in the corners of Mrs Milton's mind, still frightened of the future, still needing her help. 'And if you find yourself at the lakeside again?'

When Elsie spoke, it was in the barest whisper and had echoes of Elsa. 'Don't try to save me.'

Maggie's skin crawled. She reached over and this time took hold of Elsie's hand firmly in her own.

Elsie's fingers were icy cold, the flesh slightly sagging and her arthritic joints swollen and gnarled. Little wonder Maggie had recoiled when she had taken hold of Elsa's hand in the park, expecting the taut, delicate skin of youth. 'I can't promise you that.'

'Do you have any idea what it's like to wake up next to the man you've been married to for fifty-odd years and think an intruder has found his way into your bed? Can you imagine how terrifying that is for me and for him too?'

'No, I can't. But if you jump into that lake then I promise you, here and now, that I'm going to dive straight in and drag you out.'

There was a moment's pause as the two women squared up to each other then Elsie sighed. 'You don't have to worry – my husband won't let me out of his sight these days.'

'Is it Freddie waiting for you outside?' Maggie ventured.

'There *is* no Freddie,' came the rather stoic reply.

Forced to consider that the American had been a figment of her fractured mind just like the swans, Maggie asked, 'He didn't exist?'

'Freddie is a ghost from the past that my illness seems intent on bringing back to life. I have to keep reminding myself of who I am and where I am. My name is Elsie; I've been married to . . . Ted . . . for God knows how many years. I have . . . I have two daughters,' she said, faltering as her mind failed to keep up with the sense of conviction she had wanted to convey.

'I still want to help if you'll let me,' persisted Maggie. 'There's empirical evidence that aroma-therapy can help with some of the symptoms you're experiencing. Are you having any treatment?'

'Why do you think I ran away from Liverpool? I couldn't be doing with all that. And this could just be a storm in a teacup. My trip to the park was probably a one-off while I get my bearings in a new town.'

'I met you there twice,' Maggie reminded her. 'And Alice found you there too.'

'All right, I'm not daft and before that frown of yours gives you premature wrinkles, I'm not in complete denial either. I've promised . . . I've promised . . .'

'Ted?' Maggie offered and immediately regretted her haste.

'I know my husband's name. Now, you've made me forget what I was saying,' Elsie said with more than a hint of irritation. 'I've promised Ted I'll go back to the doctor's so I don't need your inter-ference. My Ted will look after me.'

'I'm your friend, remember?'

When Elsie exhaled, the anger left her body. 'I wish I'd had someone like you around sixty years ago.'

The silence that followed, rather than creating an awkward pause, brought a connection that spanned the decades. Maggie still hadn't asked the burning question but it would take time for Elsie to trust her enough to reveal what had happened to the baby. However, that didn't stop her from skirting around the edges.

'Do you have any family in Sedgefield?'

'No. My eldest daughter, Nancy, lives in America and Yvonne lives up in Scotland. As for the rest of my family, I only have a brother left now and he's in his seventies. I do have plenty of nieces and nephews though, some close enough to be called upon if needs be.'

'And you have me, not sixty years ago but now. Please do go to see the doctor but that doesn't mean you can't come here too for some complementary therapy. In fact, you might want to try this cream,' Maggie said, jumping up so fast it made Harvey start. She quickly found the jar she was after and checked the label, which was written in Braille as well as print. 'You can apply it to your arms, neck and chest before bedtime to help improve your sleep patterns or you could use it during the day to keep your thoughts clear. It contains lavender and lemon balm,' she explained, undoing the lid.

'I prefer lilacs,' Elsie said without taking the proffered jar.

'I've noticed but I'm afraid lilac isn't widely used as an essential oil. It's very expensive and even the lilac perfume you wear will be made from a synthetic scent rather than a natural oil.'

Maggie heard a surreptitious sniff; Elsie was checking the remnants of her perfume on her wrist. 'It was my Aunt Flo who introduced me to lilacs. I stayed with her when I was last in Sedgefield and I can remember back to that time as if it was yesterday. She could walk into this room right now and I wouldn't bat an eyelid.' Elsie's voice trailed off as her mind wandered for a moment but then she sighed. 'Now, where was I? Ah yes, Flo Jackson. She had lilac trees in her garden and made all kinds of concoctions from the flowers, including soap. I didn't like it at first but I'd be lost without my perfume now, even if it's not quite the same as the one the old lady used.' Elsie laughed to herself. 'Listen to me talking about an old lady. I sometimes forget I'm one myself.'

Maggie's smile didn't reach her eyes. 'Well, I can't claim to be another Flo Jackson but if this one doesn't help then there are other recipes to try or I could always acquire some lilac oil if you really wanted it.'

Elsie didn't respond immediately and Maggie felt herself being scrutinised. 'My instincts still work no matter what state my mind's in and they tell me you're a good person, Maggie.'

'I try to be.'

'And you'll make a good mother. Don't let anyone tell you otherwise.'

'You remember me telling you how scared I am about becoming a mum?'

'No, I'm afraid not,' Elsie said although there was something in her voice that made Maggie think she did, even if her mind failed to register the fact. 'It was your friend outside.'

'Kathy?'

'She went to great lengths to tell me how capable you are and how anyone who dares to suggest that you wouldn't make a wonderful mother would have her to answer to. She talked quite a lot, probably to drown out the noise of you torturing that poor girl who was in here. Is she all right, by the way?'

'Jenny? Yes, she'll be fine. It's good to have that emotional release now and again, especially in a safe environment with someone you trust,' Maggie explained. 'She's actually my closest friend and despite appearances, she'd say the same about me.'

'Once she stops sobbing,' added Elsie.

Maggie could feel herself relaxing and would have been happy to chat some more but she heard the plastic chair squeak one last time as Elsie hauled herself up. 'I'd better get going before Ted starts fretting.'

'Will you come and visit me again? We could make another appointment for you now if you'd like?'

Elsie didn't answer immediately and Maggie willed the old lady to reach out to her, but without the park bench to unite them, Elsie's determination to keep her distance was too strong. 'Let's see how I get on with this cream first,' she said with a groan as she straightened her back. 'Who knows? It might be a miracle cure.'

Maggie took the jar and, tightening the lid, popped it into a paper bag. 'I hope so, Elsie.'

'So how much do you charge for miracles?' Elsie

asked, putting her handbag on the table so she could find her purse.

'This one's on the house. No arguments.'

Elsie thanked her and when she took the paper bag, Maggie heard her flip it over to twist and seal the corners, reminiscent of a fruit and veg seller in the town market.

'When's the baby due?' Elsie then asked.

'October.'

'You'll be just fine.'

Many people had said the very same thing but it was the first time that Maggie had come close to believing it. There was something in Elsie's tone that dared to be challenged, a tone that Maggie hadn't heard since her mum had died.

CHAPTER 7

Maggie stirred her tea as she sat perched at the breakfast bar. It was Saturday afternoon and the house was quiet, unlike her thoughts. After Mrs Milton's visit earlier that week, she had been left shell-shocked and not a little ashamed. She should have known immediately that Elsa wasn't the young woman she claimed to be. Even without the benefit of sight, her perceptions were better than that but whereas Alice had coaxed Elsie out of her fug when they had met, Maggie had only reinforced the old lady's illusory world, leaving her even more confused.

To make matters worse, Maggie felt completely impotent. Mrs Milton would not be returning to the salon despite her assurances to the contrary. She had said her piece and now she wanted to draw a line under the past while that choice remained in her control. There was nothing else Maggie could do except ponder Elsa's fate and grieve the loss of a friendship that, for the briefest time, had made her feel less alone.

There was one good thing to come from the whole mess: failing Mrs Milton had made her all the more determined not to fail anyone else, not least the baby growing inside her. She could still hear the raw pain in Elsa's voice as she contemplated giving up her child and behind it that fierce love that only a parent could know. It was that inner strength that prompted her to make one particular call that was well overdue.

'Hello? Are you there?'

The only reply was the combined sound of shuffling and heavy breathing.

'Dad? It's Maggie,' she said.

She could hear shuffling footfalls as the person on the other end of the phone, no doubt her father, went in search of assistance. Stan had moved to Spain not long after Maggie's wedding and she had given him a mobile phone so that they could keep in touch. Her dad was hard of hearing and technology wasn't his strong point so he always seemed mildly annoyed when the phone started to vibrate and disturb his peace. 'This thing isn't working again,' he growled.

'Come here, Stan.' It was the matronly voice of Maggie's aunt. Dot was ten years Stan's junior, which put her in her late sixties, a spring chicken compared to Stan in body and in mind. The sound of metal scraping against the handset suggested that Dot's ring-embellished hand had pulled it from Stan's grasp.

'Hello?'

'Hi Dot, it's Maggie. I take it he hasn't switched on his hearing aids.'

'It's your daughter,' Dot said loudly before turning her attention to the caller. 'I swear I don't know why he even bothers to wear them. How are you, love? Any news?'

'I just wanted to speak to Dad,' Maggie said as casually as she could, her pulse racing.

There was a curt exchange between brother and sister and a short pause as everyone waited for Stan's hearing aids to be switched on. After an interminable wait, the phone was handed back to her dad.

'I wear them as earplugs to drown out your chatter,' Stan told Dot gruffly then said to Maggie, 'Hello, sweetheart.'

'Hello, Dad. I haven't interrupted anything, have I?'

'No, of course not. I was just sitting outside on the porch playing solitaire.'

'It's not a porch, it's a veranda!' Dot called.

Stan tutted. 'Sorry about the interference on the line, love. Bear with me; I'll take the phone out on to the porch.'

Maggie held her smile as she listened to her dad's laboured shuffling, more confirmation that it was better for him to be too far away to insist on being more hands-on in his daughter's life. Her parents had both been in their forties when Maggie came along and their maturity and patience had been a crucial factor in her development, but time had marched on and Stan's hearing wasn't the only thing to have deteriorated in recent years.

They had each been set adrift when Joan died and had needed to find new anchors. Maggie already had James so it had been a godsend when Dot offered to take Stan under her wing.

'That's better,' he said. 'So, how are things with you? What's the weather like over there?'

'It's teeming down at the moment,' Maggie told him knowing how pleased he would be by the news. It dampened his homesickness and she had been known to occasionally embellish the bleakness of the British weather for his benefit.

'Never mind, it's warming up nicely here. Warm enough for a bit of sunbathing if Dot didn't insist on slapping on two layers of sun block every time I step out of the shade. That stuff stinks to high heaven.'

'She's only looking after you.'

'No wonder Jim spends half his time on the golf course.'

'You're still not tempted to take it up yourself then?'

'Someone's got to keep the old girl company,' he said. It was the closest Stan would ever come to admitting a reluctant affection for his sister.

'The golf widow and the widower, a perfect team,' Maggie said. She was playing for time, trying to decide when and how to break the news but the words came out before she could hold them back. 'Dad, I'm going to have a baby.'

At first it was only the shuddering gasp that gave Maggie any clue to her dad's reaction but it was enough. It was a mixture of joy and sadness at receiving the long-awaited announcement, the release of years of frustrations and fears that his daughter might never achieve the kind of completeness she had longed for since she was a little girl. 'Oh, sweetheart,' he said at last, a sniff exposing the tears that would be welling in his eyes.

'I'm only four months pregnant so there's a bit of a wait yet,' Maggie said as her own tears slipped down her cheeks.

'Oh, sweetheart,' he repeated but this time there was a note of regret in his voice.

For a moment, Maggie considered the possibility that he was about to reproach her in the same way that Judith had. 'Dad? You *are* happy about it, aren't you?'

'Happy? Of course I am, Maggie. I couldn't be happier,' Stan said and his smile beamed across the miles. He started laughing. 'I can't believe it. Really, I just can't believe it. I'm going to be a granddad!'

There was a squeal of delight somewhere in the background and then Dot was there, gushing with excitement as she wrestled the phone from Stan. Maggie was laughing and crying as the two began talking at once, asking questions and barely listening to the answers as their opponent interjected with the next question. Even her Uncle Jim's voice was added to the mêlée and it took almost half an hour before the tidal wave of excitement settled into a satisfied lull.

'I wish your mum was here to enjoy the moment too,' Stan said when he had his daughter to himself. His voice was the barest of whispers as if it was a confession he didn't want to reveal.

'Me too, Dad. I could do with her guiding arm right now.'

'I should come home. I'll check the flights.'

Yes, please come home, she wanted to say and was thankful she had waited until she felt strong enough to hold back the urge. 'No, Dad, I'm fine. Mum spent her life preparing me for this by showing me first-hand how to be a good mum. I'll try not to let her down.'

'You are your mother's daughter.'

'That's some compliment. But you can expect loads more calls from me in the next few months because I might need you to keep reminding me of that,' she said.

'Anytime, day or night.'

'As long as you've got your hearing aid switched on,' she reminded him.

'Yes, you're definitely your mother's daughter!'

Maggie wasn't only smiling now; she was practically glowing. 'Thanks, Dad.' She was about to end the call but found herself returning to an obsession she hadn't quite relinquished. 'Before I go, could I pick your brain?'

'You can try.'

'Do you remember a greengrocer's in Sedgefield called Flo's Fruit and Veg? It would have been around in the fifties.'

Stan muttered to himself as he put his memory to the test. 'Your mum would remember stuff like that, not me.'

Maggie wasn't ready to give in. 'Apparently it was owned by someone called Mrs Jackson.'

'Ah yes, of course! You mean Flo Jackson. Her shop was somewhere on the High Street, I think.'

'Really? You remember her?' Maggie asked. She was surprised at how relieved she felt from the confirmation that the shop and Mrs Jackson had existed at all. Even in her most lucid state, Mrs Milton had been reluctant to give Maggie any indication that Elsa's story was fact or fiction.

'Vaguely. Her husband died and she ran the shop on her own for a while. She was quite lonely, as I recall. I don't think she had any kids.'

'Do you remember any other relatives? Or maybe a young woman staying with her in the early fifties?' There was a flutter of excitement as Maggie considered the possibility that her dad had once met Elsa.

Stan thought a little while longer. 'Now you're asking. There might have been some kind of falling out with family . . . Could it have been a niece? No, I'm sorry, love. I probably didn't pay enough attention at the time, let alone remember it now.'

The sound of the front door opening brought Maggie back to the present. James was home from what would be his last day at work for a whole week and he would be curious to know why his wife had started digging into Elsa's past when she had already told him how Mrs Milton's appearance had exorcised that particular ghost. And she didn't have a convincing argument, not even to herself. Her only answer was that you had to be there, sitting with Elsa sixty years ago by the lake, so she preferred to avoid the debate. 'Never mind, it doesn't matter,' she said.

'Why on earth are you asking anyway?'

'Oh, just some research,' Maggie said. Heavy footfalls grew closer and then James was there. 'Thanks, Dad. I'll get James to email the scan photo to Aunt Dot so you can have the first glimpse of the baby.'

'All right, love, and tell James I said congratulations.'

'Yes, I'll tell him you said congratulations and then I'll thank him for not taking off his work boots and making a mess of my nice, clean floor.'

'Hello, Stan!' James called as he backed carefully out of the kitchen.

When Maggie put down the phone, she sent James upstairs to take a bath while she set to work mopping up. Fortunately for her husband, she was too distracted by the fading path that led to the past than the trail of mud down the hallway.

What sounded like a herd of elephants charged through the front door and down the hallway. With a well-developed sense of smell, they picked up a scent too delicious to resist and raced towards the kitchen.

'We're here!' they screamed.

Maggie dropped the wooden spoon in her hand and it landed in the bowl of chocolate butter icing with a choreographed thud. The startled look was melodramatic as was the gasp. 'You scared me!'

The boys laughed as they hugged her. 'Hello, wicked stepmother,' Liam chirped.

'Sam, take your fingers out of that bowl,' growled Maggie.

There was a sucking sound as the youngest of James's sons sampled the butter icing. 'Dee-licious!' exclaimed the seven-year-old.

'Can I lick the bowl when you've finished?' Liam asked.

'No, I want to.'

'Since you've already had your lunch of . . .' Maggie said with an analytical sniff, 'burger and fries with way too much tomato sauce if I'm not mistaken, then you can have the bowl and two spoons to share. The cake is for later.'

'But not until you've unpacked,' James added. He had been watching from the kitchen door. 'Now.'

'We haven't said hello to Harvey yet,' Sam cried.

'Where is he?' Liam added.

'I think he's behind you,' Maggie told them.

Harvey had watched from the sidelines but at the sound of his name, he rushed over to the boys. His years of self-discipline and training were quickly forgotten as he jumped up and began to lick them ferociously. Sam's chocolate-flavoured fingers were particularly irresistible.

'Come on, let Maggie finish her baking,' James said. 'You can take Harvey upstairs with you – but do not feed him.'

Sam and Liam muttered but didn't object. No sooner had they left the kitchen than the troop of elephants resumed their charge and headed up the stairs, closely followed by the lighter but no-less-excited footfalls of Harvey.

'How was the drive?' Maggie asked when the noise had died down.

James had driven only as far as a service station near Birmingham where his sons were waiting to be handed over by Carolyn and her new husband.

'Far easier than travelling all the way to Portsmouth and back,' he said. 'All I need to do now is convince Carolyn to do this every time.'

James and his ex-wife had found an uneasy friendship, which occasionally allowed for compromise, although Carolyn would always have the upper hand because James would travel to the ends of the earth to see his sons and she knew it.

'Have the boys mentioned the baby at all?' Maggie asked.

'Briefly. They wanted to know if you were fat yet.'

Maggie laughed. 'I hope you told them I'm not.'

James stepped towards her and slid his hand over her bump. 'It is starting to show a little.'

She placed her hand over his and a smile reached her lips before the frown could crease her brow. Her baby was further ahead with its own preparations than she was. 'So what else did they say?'

'Not much really,' James said, trying to disguise the anxiety in his voice. Liam and Sam had been excited when first told the news but that had been a month ago and the novelty had quickly worn off.

'That's not necessarily a bad thing. It means they don't feel threatened.'

'I hope so, Maggie. They spent most of the journey talking about their new puppy.'

'I should have known they'd opt for a Labrador in the end. So when will they get it?'

'The pups haven't even been born yet but the plan is to pick up Hartley sometime in the summer,' James said.

'Hartley?'

'So they say. Very imaginative, don't you think?'

Maggie's aim was perfect as she smacked James's hand, which was poised over the mixing bowl. 'You're as bad as the boys,' she scolded. 'Why don't you go and help them unpack. I need to finish this cake while I've still got enough butter icing to cover it.'

'You're the boss.'

James was retreating out of the kitchen when the phone rang. The house phone had been programmed for specific callers and this ringtone had a persistent chirp that would not be ignored.

'Judith must have a sixth sense when it comes to locating her grandsons,' Maggie said wryly.

'I'll get it,' James said as if there had been any dispute.

Maggie began scraping her spatula against the

bottom of the bowl as she sought out the last pockets of cocoa powder that hadn't been incorporated into the mix. A quick taste test confirmed that the icing tasted as good as it smelled and she could almost forgive Sam for giving into temptation. But these thoughts barely registered and her stirring slowed as Maggie listened to one half of a conversation between mother and son.

'Yes, the traffic wasn't bad for a bank holiday weekend,' James was telling her.

Maggie used the spatula to push the mixture towards one side of the bowl as she heard James answer more questions about his early morning journey. It took a couple of minutes for Judith to get around to the real reason she had phoned.

'I'll have to check with Maggie first. We wanted to spend as much time with the boys as we can.'

Maggie didn't need to hear the other side of the conversation to know that her mother-in-law was trying to engineer some time of her own with the boys. Judith would be persistent; she liked to get her own way and with James she usually did. It was this apparent hold on him that terrified Maggie. Fixing gates and trips out with the grandchildren were one thing but Judith had views on James's future too and Maggie suspected she wasn't a part of that vision.

'I know, Mum, but you were down there not so long ago,' James continued. 'We've got a lot of catching up to do.'

James's sigh suggested he still wasn't getting

through to her. 'Wait a minute.' There was the click of a button. 'It's on mute, Maggie,' he said. 'She wants to have the boys over for a night next week.'

'Which means two days out of our week with them.'

'I said I'd check with you . . .'

Maggie's patience was wearing so thin that it showed in the flush rising to her cheeks. She was often the fall guy when James couldn't get through to his mum. Little wonder Judith hated her. 'Tell her we've got the week all planned but if they want to come over for tea or maybe join us when we go to the zoo then they're welcome.'

James returned to his conversation with Judith and promptly invited her over for tea. It wasn't only the spatula that had stopped moving. Maggie held her breath as she hoped for a refusal.

'Oh, OK then,' he said. 'How about a trip to the zoo? We don't know what day yet. We were going to see what the weather's like first.'

There was another pause, another sigh from James.

'Look, Mum, it's an important week for us. I want to make sure that the kids are happy with the idea that I'm going to be a dad again.' There was a tone in James's voice that was almost alien, especially in a conversation with his mum. He was losing patience too. 'It would be good for the boys to see us all pulling together, don't you think?'

The spatula resumed its slow, steady movement

and by the time James finished the call, Maggie had already started to smooth the icing over the top of the cake.

'That looks good enough to eat.'

'But not until teatime,' Maggie warned. 'And there's no point looking at the empty bowl. The boys would never forgive you. So?'

'It took a while but she's relented. Dad's working but Mum will try to meet us at the zoo as long as she can work around her shifts at the charity shop,' James explained.

'It can't be that difficult considering she was hoping to have the boys over anyway,' Maggie said sceptically.

There was a thud upstairs and an argument began to rage.

'I'd better see what they're up to.'

James kissed the top of his wife's head before leaving Maggie to her baking and her thoughts. She had been looking forward to the week ahead but now all she could see was another day of judgement looming. The call from his mum had poured cold water over Maggie's enthusiasm and it rose up over her head. She was back in her dream again, fighting to escape the murky depths of the lake only this time Judith was there, pushing her back down.

CHAPTER 8

Typical of a bank holiday weekend, the weather had been foul and the forecast for the rest of the week didn't look promising. So when James looked out of the window on Tuesday morning and saw blue sky, the house erupted into a frenzy of activity as they put their plans to visit the zoo into action.

'Go upstairs and put those toys back in your room,' James ordered.

'They're only for in the car,' whined Sam. Some of his toys were left permanently at his dad's house so when he was reunited with his Transformers it was like Christmas all over again. To mark his displeasure, Sam pressed a button on one of his killer robots. A burst of gunfire was followed by an earth-shattering explosion that set Maggie's teeth on edge.

'No, Sam!'

'But why?'

James had to shout over the sounds of warfare. 'That's why!'

'Can I take my game?' Liam asked next while Sam stomped upstairs.

'As long as you use your earphones and you leave it in the car when we get there. Today is about doing things together and having good old-fashioned fun without the aid of electronics.'

'The overhead train runs off electric,' Liam pointed out.

'Less lip or I might change my mind.' As the words left James's mouth, his mobile phone began to ring.

'I hope you're leaving that in the car too,' Maggie said, much to Liam's amusement.

She enjoyed playing the good cop if only to exaggerate James's often lacklustre bad cop impression. He struggled to remain firm with his sons when all he really wanted to do was spoil them rotten so today he would need a will of iron. Nana Judith was meeting them at the zoo and would make sure her grandsons had everything they wanted and more.

Answering the call, James said, 'Hi, Gerry, hang on a second,' then turned to his wife. 'Sorry, Maggie, I won't be long. Could you get everyone loaded into the car and I'll bring the picnic from the kitchen?'

When James eventually emerged from the house ten minutes later, Liam was in the front passenger seat while Maggie was in the back with Sam playing a game of 'I spy'. Maggie was allowed to pick anything that came to mind and it usually involved weird or otherworldly objects that Sam found hilarious. Harvey, meanwhile, was trying to

116

lick the back of Sam's head through the mesh that separated the boot space from the rest of the car.

Rather than taking the driving seat, James opened the rear door where Maggie was sitting.

'You're going to hate me for this,' he said.

It took far longer to empty the car of sulking children than it had to fill it with their growing excitement. Fortunately for James, he was in too much of a rush to set off for an emergency job to take in the full measure of his sons' displeasure or that of his wife. He had been working on a house extension the week before and had thought his timing perfect by taking a week off to let the concrete set. But he hadn't factored in the rain or been aware that the roof wasn't as watertight as he would have hoped.

'I'm really sorry, Maggie,' he said as he pulled on his work clothes in their bedroom. Her silence had finally registered in his psyche. 'I know I should leave it to Gerry to sort out but he's on another job and this one is my responsibility. I should have checked the roof before I left.'

Maggie knew there was little point in arguing. She loved James for many reasons and his character flaws were often his strengths. He was too easy-going, too generous and too conscientious. That was why he wouldn't shirk his responsibilities and leave his business partner to fix what he considered to be his mistake, even though she knew the roofing work had been subcontracted.

She picked up his discarded clothes and began

to fold them neatly. 'As long as it's only today that you're needed.'

'I'll do my best but I can't make promises. It's an important contract and if I mess this one up then it could go against us for future work.'

'Surely once you've checked it over you can leave it to Gerry to supervise?' Maggie persisted.

'I need to do everything I can to keep the clients we've got, Maggie, but I promise that, whatever happens, we'll get the boys to the zoo before they go back.'

'And that's supposed to make up for us not having a whole week together?'

'Maggie, please. I'm doing my best.'

Her body sagged but then she grasped at the silver lining. She didn't have to face Judith. 'What about your mum? She'll be on her way.'

James came over to put his arms around her, thankful the argument was over. 'All sorted. I phoned her as soon as I finished speaking to Gerry. She was almost out the door but I managed to catch her in time.'

'Did she give you a hard time too?'

'No,' James said.

Maggie detected the lie as soon as it had left his lips. 'James?'

'She was happy to put it off for another day,' he insisted.

'But?'

'Well, Mum did suggest coming over to help you look after the boys while I was out.'

The pressure that rose from her chest and set her cheeks on fire was fuelled more from irritation than alarm.

'Don't blow a fuse,' James said, trying to laugh it off. 'I told her you're more than capable of keeping the two horrors in check.'

He still had his arms around her and Maggie's neck was starting to ache but she kept her face lifted towards him and narrowed her eyes in determination. 'I might take them to the park,' she said as if there remained a point to prove. 'We can still have our picnic and the kids can play with their remote control boat on the lake. In fact, we'll make a little adventure of it.'

James leant down to kiss her forehead. 'I am sorry,' he said and was about to release her but stopped. 'Actually, I'm not. It's good to see that spark again.'

'What spark?'

'The one that makes you light up a room and dare anyone not to be in awe of you. The one that made me fall in love with you,' he said with a soft slow smile in his voice. 'It's been lost in the shadows since your mum died but it's there now. I can see it.'

'Yes,' Maggie said carefully as she recognised in herself what James could see. 'The phone call to Dad helped. I'm feeling almost ready to face the future again.'

'Almost?'

'Give me time. Now off with you,' she added

as she pushed him away. 'You've got work to do.'

When James left, Maggie was smiling. She wasn't convinced the spark was anything more than a flicker – but given a chance it would blaze a light towards the future. Assuming, that was, no one came along to snuff it out.

Elsa turned her nose up in disgust as she tried to wipe away the pervading scent on her hands. She recognised the lavender but there was something else too, something lemony and she didn't like it. Rummaging through her bag, she found a bottle of perfume and tested it on her wrists.

'That's better,' she told herself before spraying it liberally on her neck and body.

The lilac fragrance was strong enough to disguise the other scents but the sense of familiarity did little to ease her mind. She was looking down towards the lake. A gust of wind swept across the water and the bright reflection of the sun shivered on its surface. The nearby shrubs and trees whispered to each other in the breeze and Elsa was reminded of the hushed conversations between Aunt Flo and Anne as they conspired against her.

She felt exposed on the top of the embankment and her eyes searched out the safety of her bench, secreted beneath the shadow of giant rhododendrons in full bloom, their bulbous purple flowers reflecting softer pinks in the sunshine. There was someone already sitting there and close by, two small boys playing with a model boat at the water's edge. A frown creased Elsa's brow as she watched the woman shouting over to the boys. She thought she recognised her but couldn't understand how she could have children.

Turning her attention back to her handbag, Elsa began to sift through its contents. When she couldn't find what she was looking for she became more and more agitated and began pulling things out. There was a purse and a handkerchief along with other items that completely baffled her. She paid them no heed.

'It's got to be here somewhere,' she whimpered but then froze as soon as she heard the rustle of paper beneath her fingertips.

Elsa almost tore the envelope in her eagerness to pull it from her bag but her heart sank when she realised it wasn't the airmail letter she was searching for. She groaned in frustration and dropped the accumulated clutter back into her bag, some of which fell to the ground. But Elsa was more aware of her growing panic than the detritus scattered around her.

Looking back towards the lake, she watched as one of the boys went to sit next to the woman on the bench. She wrapped a motherly arm around him, yet Elsa was sure this woman had told her she didn't have children. She had lied. Was there no one left who she could trust? Her first instinct was to turn and run but she still hadn't found

Freddie's letter. A sob escaped her as she stumbled down the hill.

'Can you feel the baby inside your tummy?' Sam asked.

'I keep waiting,' Maggie said with a smile, 'and there have been a few times when I thought I could feel it moving but it turned out to be my stomach gurgling. It won't be long though and one day you'll be able to feel him or her kicking too.'

'I want it to be a girl,' he said in a whisper so his brother wouldn't overhear, but he needn't have worried: Liam was too busy chasing the ducks with his boat.

'I always wanted a sister,' Maggie told him. Her parents had spent many painful years trying to have a baby and at forty-one her mum had all but given up hope of ever having children when Maggie, their miracle baby, arrived. 'But to be honest, a brother would have been better than nothing.'

'I wouldn't say so,' muttered Sam. 'Liam's a pain.'

Maggie put her arm around him. 'At least you'll get to play big brother to the new baby. It'll be your turn to boss them around.'

'But I won't be a proper brother.'

'What do you mean, Sam?' she asked, completely dismayed.

'Nana Judith said the baby will only be my half-brother or -sister. That means we'll only love each other half as much, doesn't it?'

'Nana-bloody-Judith!' she said with a hiss loud enough to disguise her words. Taking a breath she explained, 'No, Sam. It means that you share only one parent: in your case you have the same dad but not the same mum. That's all. I think you're going to love this baby as much as you possibly could, even if it is a boy.'

'OK,' Sam replied.

Maggie felt as if she ought to say more but the sound of heels scraping along the path caught her attention.

'Did you take it?' Elsa demanded.

As Elsa approached the woman on the bench, her golden-haired dog stood up to greet her. His ears were pricked and his tail wagged furiously but his body froze as she spat out her accusation.

There was a look of shock on the woman's face. 'Elsie? What's wrong?'

'My name is Elsa, as well you know! Did you take Freddie's letter?'

The woman had the nerve to turn towards her son. 'Sam, why don't you go and play with Liam so Elsa can sit down?' The boy looked warily towards Elsa but didn't move other than to take hold of his mother's hand. 'I'll be OK,' the woman reassured him.

'Is everything all right?' It was the other boy this time. He had abandoned his boat and was creeping closer to them.

'Don't worry, Liam. Elsa is a friend. We'll be

fine. Why don't you take your brother and carry on playing with your boat?'

The boys skulked away but didn't return to their play, reluctant to leave Maggie's side. The fearful look on their faces wrenched at Elsa's heart. She didn't want to frighten the children but she was scared too. She didn't know who she could trust any more and her mind was becoming so muddled. Through it all, one single thought stayed in focus.

'Well? Did you?' she demanded.

'Please, Elsa, sit down.'

Elsa shook her head. 'And you're not coming near my handbag.'

'I didn't take Freddie's letter, Elsa. I didn't even know he'd sent one. Please, sit down and tell me what's happened.'

Elsa refused to move closer. 'You said you didn't have any children but here you are with them!'

'They're not my children; they're my husband's from a previous marriage. I don't have any of my own, not yet.'

'So you stole them and now I bet you want to steal my baby too! Well, I'm telling you now: no one is taking my baby away. I won't let you and Freddie won't either.'

The dog was looking at her with his deep brown, imploring eyes. His friendly face was irresistible and he wagged his tail when he sensed her resolve weakening. Maggie let go of the lead and the dog stepped confidently towards her. She patted his head.

'I want you to keep the baby, Elsa. Really, I do. I'm pregnant too, remember? I'm Maggie and this is Harvey. Tell me about the letter from Freddie. Please, Elsa,' Maggie said.

Harvey led Elsa towards the bench but she sat as far away from Maggie as she could. Her breathing was still ragged but as she settled into her seat and took in the view she knew so well, her thoughts began to calm. She could picture Freddie perfectly, as if he was standing there in front of her. 'You have no idea how lucky I am,' she said. 'Freddie's so dashing and out of all the girls at the dance, he chose me.'

Elsa didn't flinch when Maggie moved closer. Amongst the memories she was able to grasp, she recalled that Maggie was indeed a friend.

'I'll never forget the first time he took me for a ride on his motorbike. I was all dressed up for the dance in a red polka-dot dress, which was hardly appropriate for riding pillion. I had to hold on to Freddie for dear life and couldn't stop my skirt from blowing up but Freddie said my legs were too good not to show off.' Elsa giggled at the memory and her anger was all but forgotten. 'That was the night he told me he loved me.'

Elsa's smile was enough to put the two boys' minds at ease and they sauntered off towards the lake. Within seconds they were consumed in their own arguments over who was in charge of the remote control.

'I don't know how I ever thought he would go

off to Germany and forget me,' she continued. 'I should have had more faith in him. He told me in his letter that he only agreed to the break-up because he thought someone would snap me up as soon as his back was turned and it would have broken his heart.'

'Does he know you're pregnant?'

'Yes, and he wants to marry me! So I'm not going to spend the rest of my life grieving – I'm going to be happy. Freddie's letter proves it,' Elsa said, but the joy in her voice left her body in a sob. She looked in her bag for her handkerchief but it had disappeared along with the proof that her one true love really would come back for her. 'I suppose I should be grateful I got it in the first place. He used Celia's address rather than Mrs Jackson's, because as good as Aunt Flo is, she'll do whatever Anne says and that niece of hers wants me to forget all about Freddie. Anne says not to get my hopes up and now she's stolen the letter just like she's going to steal my baby.'

'Anne's going to adopt the baby?'

'Not now, she isn't. I explained everything to Freddie and he's said no one else, not even a posh doctor and his wife, could be better parents than us. Of course Anne doesn't agree and nothing I could say or do would convince her otherwise.'

Elsa's voice cracked with emotion as she explained, 'I was so foolish, so trusting. When I first met Anne and she offered to help, we didn't even discuss how the baby would be adopted. All I knew was that she would be better off with a family who could give her the kind of things I couldn't. When Aunt Flo just happened to mention how her beloved niece couldn't have children of her own, I was the one who actually suggested that Anne and her doctor husband should take her. But I can't help but wonder . . . Do you think they planned it from the start? Have they trapped me?' When Maggie didn't answer, Elsa became more desperate. 'He will come back for me, won't he?' she asked, looking to her friend for reassurance but it was already too late and the ghosts of memories came back to haunt her.

Elsa's restrained sobs transformed into a heart-rending wail and amidst the returning confusion she was left with one indisputable fact. Freddie wouldn't be coming to save her.

When Elsa had arrived, Maggie had been acutely aware this time that she was in the company of a very confused old lady. She was still trying to work out how she could have got it so wrong before. Everything about the way Mrs Milton moved suggested old bones and aching joints but once she sat down on the bench, those subtle distinctions were lost. The old lady's perfume was dated but as the breeze curled around them it was diluted with the natural scents of the park. And then there was the voice. Tight with emotion, tempered by forced youthfulness, and dulled by the acoustics of their little alcove, the aged rasp was all but obscured.

As she sat back and listened to Mrs Milton reliving her fears, Maggie's spine followed the curve of the bench that had absorbed the lives of the park's former visitors. The seat was as hard and unyielding as the past and yet Maggie found herself melding into the world Elsie was creating around them. It took the old lady's tormented sobs to jolt her completely back to her senses and she wrapped her friend in her arms. Maggie's slight frame was strong and taut in comparison to Elsa's fragile soul captured inside the crumpled body of an old lady.

'I want it to be over. I don't want to feel like this any more!'

Mrs Milton had lifted her head and looked towards the lake as she cried out. Maggie's stomach churned as snatches of her nightmare came back to haunt her again. She had to find a way of helping Elsie while taking care of the boys at the same time. They were ominously quiet.

'Harvey, go find the boys,' she urged.

The dog had become wedged between the two women but followed his mistress's command and went to offer his comfort elsewhere. Maggie's next challenge wasn't going to be so easy. The past was too painful for Elsie to bear and she needed to be drawn back carefully into the safety of the present, but Maggie had two children in her charge and they were her first priority, so she waited as long as she could for the sobs to ease.

'The last time I saw you, you visited me at the salon. Do you remember?'

The only response from the elderly woman, holding herself as if heavy with child, was to bury her head into Maggie's shoulder.

'I'm an aromatherapist,' Maggie said, speaking slowly but firmly. 'Do you remember coming to see me?'

There was an imperceptible nod of the head.

'I gave you some cream.'

Elsie sniffed back her tears with a hiccup. 'That smelly stuff? I don't like it.'

'What does Ted think? Does he like it?'

'He thought it was OK,' she said hesitantly.

'Maybe we could try something else next time.'

'Maybe.'

Maggie held her breath. She had detected a change of tone in her voice. The forced youthful-ness had disappeared. Elsie lifted her head tenta-tively. 'I've made a fool of myself again, haven't I?' she said. The only remnants of her sobs now were the persistent hiccups.

'You were looking for a letter. The one from Freddie.'

'Oh,' Elsie said, pausing to hold back a hiccup as well as her emotions. She didn't quite succeed with either and her next words trembled over quivering lips. 'Why do I keep putting myself through this?'

'I suspect there are some things you can't forget, no matter how much you try. You went through such a lot here in Sedgefield, didn't you?' Maggie asked.

'I sat here many times and wondered what would become of me,' Elsie admitted. 'Holding on to hope only to have it ripped from my arms.' The confession was painful but there were no tears to accompany the suppressed sob. They had been spent, not only in the last few minutes, but perhaps over decades.

'He never came back for you, did he?' Maggie asked, and as she did she was acutely aware of the hard wooden surface of the bench keeping her connection with Elsa open.

'No.'

Maggie was about to summon up the courage to ask about the baby but then she heard Elsie rummaging through her bag again. 'What are you looking for?'

'My handkerchief; I know I'm losing my marbles but I'd never leave the house without a clean handkerchief.'

'You're not losing your marbles,' Maggie assured her.

'Oh, but I am. I hate what this illness is doing to me and there's nothing I can do to stop it,' she said. 'After everything I've been through in my life, you would think I could have some peace in my old age.' Elsie had every right to be angry but there wasn't a trace of it in her voice, only an

130

overwhelming sense of resignation. The fight had gone out of her. 'Maybe it's what I deserve.'

'I can't believe anyone deserves to go through this, least of all you.'

'I'm scared, Maggie,' Elsie whispered.

That simple statement tore at Maggie's heart and she groped around for a glimmer of hope. 'Things are bound to be more confusing right now. You said yourself that you've had a lot on your mind with the move.'

'Thank you for being so kind,' Elsie said, 'but there's little point in ignoring the facts. I've lost my mind *and* my handkerchief.'

The sound of footsteps and the accompanying rattle of Harvey's harness drew Maggie's attention. Sam and Liam were running up the path and away from the lake. 'Liam, I don't want you and your brother going far,' she shouted.

The two boys didn't answer and a moment later Maggie could hear them talking to someone at the top of the slope. Before she had time to panic, she heard the boys returning and, judging by the number of footfalls, they weren't alone.

Sam arrived first. 'Here's your tissue,' he told Elsie in the barest whisper as if he was afraid that the old lady would shatter if he spoke too loud.

'And you dropped some other stuff too,' Liam added. 'But look who we found, Maggie.'

'It's Judith,' Maggie's mother-in-law said. She spoke slowly and clearly as if Maggie was hard of hearing and it was true to say that Maggie was finding it difficult to believe her ears.

'Nana Judith says she's come to the rescue,' Sam piped up.

'I thought you might need some help,' Judith explained, the forced cheer a challenge to Maggie's brusqueness. 'And from what Liam's told me, it sounds like you've had your hands full.'

Maggie clenched her teeth but she had no idea if the smile she painted on her face deceived Judith or not. 'This is my friend Elsie. Elsie, this is my mother-in-law, Judith.'

'It's lovely to meet you,' Judith said, surprisingly kindly.

'And you too. Your grandsons have been real gentlemen, putting up with a silly old lady like me,' she said. 'And Maggie here is a godsend. You're lucky to have such a lovely family.'

'Thank you,' replied Judith, less convinced than Elsie.

'I'm new to the area and managed to get myself lost,' Elsie said by way of an explanation. 'Have you lived in Sedgefield long, Judith?'

'Oh, I don't live here,' Judith said. 'My son moved here a couple of years ago and a friend of mine has been here for over thirty years so I should know Sedgefield fairly well – but I'd probably get lost too given half the chance.'

'Judith's friend is Kathy. You met her the other day at the salon, do you remember?' Maggie said then regretted putting Elsie's failing memory to the test. She waited for Mrs Milton's response, which was only the vaguest acknowledgement before turning back to Judith. 'You really didn't have to come over.'

'It's no bother.' Her tone suggested there wasn't a choice. 'What did you have planned for the rest of the day?'

Maggie was about to reply that they were going to have a picnic but Liam interrupted. 'I want to go back to your house, Nan.'

'No, Liam,' Maggie said quickly. 'I think your dad wanted you to stay with us.'

'But he's not here, is he?'

There was a harshness to Liam's voice that unsettled Maggie. 'But Liam . . .'

'Nana Judith said there's a bird's nest in her garden. I want to see the baby chicks,' Sam added.

'Oh, why not let them? Ken can bring them back later and I know he's desperate to see them too.'

'Yes!' shouted the boys in unison as if it had already been decided.

Elsie blew her nose and returned her belongings to her bag as she too prepared to leave. Maggie didn't want to let her wander off on her own. She could hear the gentle lapping of water, a reminder of how close to the lake they were. She tried to weigh up her options, which were narrowing by the second. She should stand firm and say no to Judith, but instead she sat where she was, paralysed by indecision.

'I'll leave you to it. Ted will be looking for me,'

Elsie said, hoisting herself to her feet and shocking Maggie into action.

'Harvey, come,' she said and stood up too. The decision she was being forced to make broke her heart but she made sure she salvaged at least some self-respect. 'OK boys, you can go as long as you promise to behave yourselves or you'll have me to answer to.'

'We will,' they chorused.

'That's decided then,' Judith said, barely able to disguise her sense of victory.

Even as she made the arrangements for returning her grandsons later, Judith was gathering them up and all too soon Liam and Sam's goodbyes were receding into the distance. Harvey whined after them but remained steadfastly by Maggie's side. Rather than pick up his harness immediately, she reached for Elsie's arm. 'We'll help you home.'

'I don't suppose there's any point in arguing,' Elsie said but no sooner had they prepared to leave than another problem presented itself. 'Doesn't that toy boat belong to you?'

Maggie sighed. 'I pride myself on doing most things but steering a remote control boat to shore isn't one of them.'

Elsie took a step towards the lake but Maggie pulled her back instinctively. 'It doesn't matter. Leave it.'

The old lady patted Maggie's hand, which was tightly gripping her arm. 'Don't worry, I won't lead you straight into the water,' she said but the laughter caught in her throat as she realised that Maggie knew her of old. 'I was inconsolable back then. Would it be so bad if I had the courage of my convictions sixty years on? Wouldn't that bring an end to all of this suffering?' She sighed in resignation. 'Oh, don't look at me like that and don't worry! The lake isn't that deep anyway.'

Maggie was about to ask how she knew but Elsie was determined to move forwards, not return to the past. 'Come on, let's have a go at getting this boat back.'

The toy boat was a pleasant distraction and the two women were soon laughing as they struggled to retrieve it. Maggie did her best to show Elsie how to use the remote control but she had to confess that she was a complete novice too. The boat seemed to head further away the more they tried to turn it around.

'Would you like me to help?'

The voice was deep and although it wasn't familiar to Maggie, the distinctive Liverpool accent meant an introduction wasn't exactly necessary.

'This is my husband . . . Teddie,' Elsie said.

'Ted,' he corrected and then set about piloting the boat to shore. When he handed it to Maggie he was unable to hide his disbelief. 'Is it yours?'

Maggie realised how it must look and the same thought crossed Elsie's mind too. They collapsed into a fit of girlish giggles again. 'It belongs to my stepsons but they've rushed off and left it behind,' Maggie explained once she could draw breath.

Ted hadn't shared the joke. 'Kids are far too spoilt these days,' he said flatly.

'I was about to walk Elsie home but now you're here, would you like to share a picnic with me? It'll go to waste otherwise.'

'Elsie spends too much time here as it is. Thank you, but we have our own lunch waiting at home which is where we'd be now if she hadn't done another disappearing act.'

Maggie found herself wondering how this man measured up to the hero Elsa had been waiting for. 'That's a shame, maybe another time,' she said.

'Not in the park,' he said quickly. 'If it was up to me, I'd have the gates chained up. We were out shopping on the High Street. I turned my back for two seconds and she was gone. You shouldn't come in here, Elsie,' Ted said, turning to his wife.

Maggie knew he was right. Elsie's illness had resurrected painful times and the old lady had already let slip how she would lay Elsa's ghost to rest but Maggie now believed there was another way. She had a growing conviction that if they could spend enough time sitting together on the bench and unravelling the secrets of 1953 then Elsie might be able to let go of the past before her illness took everything else. 'Your wife has an affinity to this spot by the lake,' she said.

'We came to Sedgefield because I thought she

would settle,' Ted answered. 'She hasn't. Now come on, Elsie, the sooner I get you back home the better.'

Elsie ignored him. 'Why don't you come over to ours for lunch one day, Maggie? It's the least I can do to thank you for all your help. Maybe by that time my husband will remember his manners and stop being such an old grouch.'

Maggie smiled. There had been genuine affection in Elsie's voice despite her harsh words to her husband. 'Only if Harvey can come too,' she said.

'Oh, he would be our honoured guest. Wouldn't he, Ted? What about Monday?' she suggested.

'You have an appointment on Monday,' Ted reminded her.

'Ah, so I do,' Elsie said. 'Typical. I make an appointment to see the doctor about my memory and then I go and forget it. Can we make it Tuesday?'

'I'm at the salon in the morning so I could call around straight afterwards, say about one o'clock?'

Maggie used her phone to store the Miltons' address and phone number, its automated voice repeating the buttons as she pressed them.

'I could do with one of those for myself,' Ted marvelled. 'I can't see past my nose some days.'

With the arrangements made, and in the knowledge that Elsie was in safe hands, Maggie began to relax as she set off for home with Harvey but her sense of achievement didn't last. She had helped Elsie but at what cost? She had no idea how the events at the park had affected the boys or how she was going to justify to James why she had handed them over to Judith. The only thing she was sure of was that the day was going to end as badly as it had begun.

CHAPTER 9

Maggie was standing in the hallway facing the front door as she listened to the sound of James's car pulling into the drive. Her restless fingers explored the smooth contours of the wooden balustrade at the foot of the stairs as she waited. She hadn't phoned to forewarn James. News that his mum had taken the boys with Maggie's apparent blessing would have been a distraction, she had told herself. He needed to be left in peace to finish what he was doing if they were to stand any chance of salvaging the rest of the week.

It was only when James was stepping over the threshold that Maggie blurted out her confession. 'Your mum turned up today and she's taken the boys back home with her.'

'What? You just let her take them?'

The accusation stung but it was deserved. 'We were in the park. I'd taken them to play with the boat and then . . . and then . . .' Maggie's words caught in her throat.

'Hey, it's OK,' James added quickly. 'I'm surprised, that's all.'

She allowed him to wrap her in his arms even though she knew she didn't deserve his sympathy. He didn't know the full story yet. The smell of dust and sweat tickled her nostrils as she inhaled one last breath to steel herself. 'We met Elsa by the lake,' she began.

James pulled away slightly. 'I thought she didn't exist?'

'Yes, of course – I mean *Elsie*,' she said. 'But she was confused again and worse than before. She was really upset.'

'And the kids? They were still with you at that point?'

Maggie bit her lip. She felt like a child herself and fought the impulse to run away. 'Yes.'

'Why do I get the feeling you're going to tell me that's when Mum turned up? Was that why she took the boys away?'

For the first time in a long time, Maggie couldn't read James's voice. It was devoid of emotion as if he hadn't quite decided how he should be feeling.

'Elsie was sobbing, James. She was on her own and I couldn't leave her.'

'You weren't on your own, though. You were in charge of a seven- and nine-year-old.'

'I was watching over them too. They were playing with the boat and they were lovely; they even helped Elsie collect up some of the things she'd dropped,' Maggie said. 'I'm not saying they weren't scared but I think they were more worried about me than anything.'

'And I bet Mum loved coming to the rescue.'

'If I could have split myself into two I would have done. I know the boys needed me but Judith was there by then,' Maggie said as she tried to defend the indefensible.

'And doesn't this Elsie have family of her own? Where were they? Why should you be expected to come to the rescue all the time?'

'Her husband did turn up eventually,' she said. 'But I'm not sure about him, James. I can't help wondering why she would rather jump in the lake than face the prospect of her husband caring for her.'

James wasn't listening. 'I don't want to seem heartless, but we've got enough going on in our own lives as it is. This could have been your chance to prove to Mum exactly how capable you are at looking after the boys.'

'It's not like I haven't looked after them before,' Maggie said but then a spark of anger caught her off-guard. 'And why do I have to prove myself anyway? What gives her the right to make me feel like I'm auditioning for a role in her family every time I see her?'

'I'm not even getting into that argument now. The point is we were meant to spend as much time as we could together as a family this week.'

'Really? So where have you been all day?' Maggie reminded him.

'OK, I know. I let them down too,' James said, ready as always to back down from an argument but the gentleness in his voice was forced. 'So now all I have to do is prise the kids back from their nan's clutches. I'll give her a ring.'

'Sorry,' Maggie said, although she wasn't sure what she was apologising for any more. She wasn't the only one at fault and she hoped James wouldn't lose sight of that when he spoke to his mother.

'I know you want to help this old lady of yours, but you should have put the kids first,' he said as he moved towards the living room. His footsteps sounded heavy but Maggie thought better than to remind him to take off his boots.

Maggie sat down on the stairs and buried her head in her hands as she listened to James's conversation with his mum. With each response, his voice grew more and more distant.

'I suppose,' he was saying. 'If that's what they want.' A pause, then a sigh. 'OK, Mum. Tell them to behave. I'll pick them up first thing tomorrow.'

When James returned to the hall, he was in his stocking feet. He didn't so much drop his boots onto the shoe rack as he did launch them at it and a waterfall of shoes tumbled to the floor. 'They're shattered and ready for bed so I said I'd pick them up tomorrow. And, surprise, surprise, they've just got back from the zoo.'

Maggie's body tensed as she held back her annoyance. 'We'll find something else to do with them, something extra special,' she promised but James wasn't listening. He swept past her and up

142

the stairs, closing the bathroom door before she had finished the sentence.

Alone, Maggie was forced to accept that she was no match for her mother-in-law and she could almost admire her. Not only had Judith got her own way with the boys but she had demonstrated quite succinctly how Maggie wasn't up to the job of wife and mother. She certainly had Maggie convinced.

The sense of unease that had settled over the Carter household had been impossible to dispel and Maggie felt no less alone while James was in the house than she did when he left to collect his sons the next morning. She was standing in the hallway, listening to his car speeding off, when another sound caught her attention. It was the creak of iron gates as Victoria Park welcomed in another visitor.

Five minutes later, the gates creaked again when Maggie opened them. Her jacket was thin but warm enough for a spring morning. The rain was a fine mist that didn't so much fall as float around her, sneaking under her hood and soaking her face and neck. If Harvey was objecting to the damp weather then he was hiding it well and didn't complain when she stopped at the side of the lake.

The bench was soaking wet but Maggie was too absorbed in what was going on inside her head to react to the cold shock of wet jeans pressing against the back of her legs as she sat down.

'I give up,' she said above the hiss of raindrops hitting the surface of the lake. 'I'm not going to sink but how do I swim?'

She waited patiently for an answer and when it didn't come, her hand searched out the tiniest shred of comfort from the flaking paint on the empty seat next to her. 'I want you here, Mum,' she whispered, digging her fingers into one of the bench's open wounds. 'I can't do this on my own.'

James had been right. She should have put Liam and Sam first. She had failed again and her sense of defeat had crushed the little self-confidence she thought she had regained. She didn't want to face a future where she would be put to the test time and time again. And with people like Judith around, she would always be tested.

Her desperate search for a long-lost connection was rewarded with sharp pain as a splinter bit into her fingertip. She sucked her wound and tasted blood. The pain was fleeting but enough to shock her out of her self-indulgent misery. She returned her hand to the empty space next to her only this time she placed the palm of her hand flat against its surface. She would have to dip into her own memories rather than the splintered wood to find the comfort she had sought.

She tried to recall a time in her life when giving up wouldn't have been an option and clung to the first memory that sprang to mind. Joan had borrowed a bike from a friend of Maggie's one summer and had taught her how to ride it. She had listened to her mum's instructions behind her and concentrated on the vibration of the wheels as she rode along the park's main avenue, adjusting course whenever she ventured on to grass. She had fallen off a few times but had picked herself up again and again. It was never going to be a regular form of transport but Maggie had proved to everyone, most importantly to herself, that she could do it, and the sense of exhilaration had been worth the scraped knees.

What would her mum be telling her now? she asked herself.

By the time James arrived home with Liam and Sam, she had found her answer. It was time to stop agonising over how to be a good wife and mother. She simply had to pick herself up and try again. Returning home, once she and Harvey had dried off, Maggie headed straight for the kitchen. Her empty home was in need of some aroma-therapy but not necessarily the kind that could be found in a bottle. The warm and welcoming aroma of gingerbread men baking in the oven would go some way to making her home feel safe and secure again.

Sam was the first to rush in to see her. 'Can I have one now?'

'How about some vanilla milkshake to go with it?' Maggie asked, turning towards the fridge. 'It's homemade.'

James came in. 'They smell nice,' he said, kissing the back of her neck. It was the first time he had kissed her since their argument last night and the sensation of his lips on her bare skin sent a tingle down her spine. 'I'm sorry,' he whispered.

Maggie didn't reply immediately but poured Sam his milkshake and sent him off to the living room to watch TV. Only then did she turn to face her husband. 'And I'm sorry about how things turned out yesterday, but I won't apologise for coming to the rescue of a distressed old lady who needed my help.'

'I don't want you to apologise.' He had said each word quietly but forcefully. 'How can I blame my wife for wanting to help people? The boys are home now, let's put yesterday behind us and enjoy the rest of the week together.'

Maggie ignored him and continued with the argument she had prepared. 'And I'm going to stop trying to prove myself to your mum. If she can't accept me for who I am, if she can't appreciate that, yes, I have my faults but actually being blind isn't one of them, then that's *her* problem. I won't make it mine. I can manage without her help.'

James cupped Maggie's face in his hands. 'I know.'

'Good.'

'But,' he added, 'it would be so much easier with more people to help.'

Maggie's fiery defiance wouldn't be smothered with gentle words. 'You really must give up on this idea that Judith will help out when the baby's

146

born. I don't care how much the nursery fees are – we'll manage. In fact, I wouldn't accept if she did decide to help out! I won't be beholden to her, James.'

She could feel James tensing but the touch of his palms on her cheeks remained as tender as ever. 'For the record, Mum was impressed with how you dealt with Elsie in the park.'

'Really?' scoffed Maggie, doing her best to ignore the sincerity in his voice.

'That's what she said, but far be it from me to convince you that she has a heart. She thought it was so sad that Elsie keeps returning to the same park bench she'd sat on all those years earlier.'

'Please don't say you told her I thought she was a young woman when we first met,' Maggie said, thankful that she hadn't told him enough to reveal all of Elsa's secrets.

'No, I wouldn't do that.' James sounded frustrated, but for the time being at least he seemed ready to accept that any conversation about his mum would ruffle Maggie's feathers. 'Now, are we ready to start our holiday again? Please.'

'OK,' Maggie conceded and allowed herself a cautious smile, which would have remained fixed on her face if James hadn't kissed it into submission. She snuggled into his chest and let him rock her until their bodies were back in sync.

'I was thinking we could always go to the aquarium today since the weather's so miserable,' she said, unwrapping herself and turning her attention to the second milkshake she had poured. 'Where's Liam?'

'He's sulking upstairs.'

'Why? What happened?'

'He didn't want to come home.'

Maggie put together a peace offering consisting of the milkshake and two gingerbread men. 'I'll take these up to him,' she said.

The front bedroom was the boys' domain and had been designed to their own specification. James had built the bunk beds himself. Both boys had wanted the top bunk and the only way to settle the argument had been to create two bunks at right angles to each other with enough space below for a communal computer and games area.

It was the expanse of floor between the beds and the door that was Maggie's immediate concern. She slid one foot tentatively in front of the other as she tried to navigate the obstacle course her stepsons had constructed with their discarded toys.

As she drew nearer, she could hear Liam's soft breaths, slightly muffled by the duvet cover. 'Liam? I've made you some gingerbread men. I was hoping you'd help decorate them but you'll just have to eat them naked.'

'Don't want any.'

Maggie was at eye level. 'Liam,' she said. 'Could you pull back the cover, please?'

'Why? You can't see me anyway.'

Maggie put down the glass and plate on a nearby table, her actions slow and deliberate to make sure she was placing them on a level surface. Her laboured actions also gave her time to collect her thoughts and take the sting out of Liam's comment. Without warning, she flipped back the duvet from his face and to her surprise Liam didn't try to pull it back over his head.

'Move over,' she commanded and proceeded to climb up the ladder. She squeezed in next to him, lying on top of the covers. Liam was next to the wall and because his arms were still beneath his duvet, he was effectively pinned down. Maggie had no intention of releasing him until the problem she had created had been fixed.

'I'm sorry about yesterday,' she said. 'I know it must have been a bit scary seeing Mrs Milton upset like that.'

She felt Liam shrug. 'Didn't bother me.'

'Sometimes people can become confused, especially when they're older like Mrs Milton. They can recall things perfectly from years and years ago and yet not be able to remember what happened the day before. I think Mrs Milton remembers things so clearly about her earlier life that she actually believes she's back there and that's when she gets scared and upset. She's expecting things to be like they used to be and they're not.'

'I know. Nana Judith explained it to me.'

'So what's upsetting you?'

Liam shrugged again and then turned his face to the wall.

'Why are you mad at me, Liam?'

She heard him take a gulp of air and knew she had hit a nerve. She waited patiently for an answer.

'Why did you tell Mrs Milton that you didn't have any children?' he asked.

'Because I . . .' she began, then stopped herself when the penny dropped. She turned on her side towards him and tentatively put a hand on his shoulder. 'When the baby comes, your dad will say he has three kids, I can promise you that. But I'm only your stepmum, Liam, and even though that means a lot to me, I don't think I have the right to say you're mine. I didn't think you'd like it.'

'When we're here you act like our mum.'

Maggie suppressed a smile. 'I know, and that's nice, but I'm only borrowing you off your real mum, aren't I? You don't call me Mum and I don't think your mum would be too happy if you did.'

'Maybe,' he said, 'but sometimes we call Tony Dad.'

'Oh,' Maggie said. She knew that was one of James's fears. 'I imagine it gets pretty complicated for you, having two homes, two sets of parents.'

'You can say that again,' Liam said. To Maggie's relief, he had stopped muttering his replies and a little of his mischievousness was re-emerging.

'What you have to remember is that it's not

about the labels we give each other, it's about how much we love each other and how we treat each other. I've been your stepmum for less than a year but I can tell you now that I love you and Sam just as much as I'm going to love the new baby. If it seems sometimes like I'm not putting myself out there as your mum then that's because I'm trying to tread carefully. I'm scared sometimes that I'll do or say the wrong thing and you won't want to come here any more. I guess I messed up, didn't I?'

Her gentle cajoling worked and Liam turned to face her. 'Sorry about what I said.'

Maggie's face was a picture of innocence. 'What do you mean?'

'About you not being able to see me.'

'Hmm, that wasn't very nice, was it? But you've said sorry now which helps make it better, because we're family.'

'Thanks mmm . . .' Liam was taking his time to form the word so that Maggie was left guessing. 'Maggie,' he said at last.

'You're welcome, son,' she said and then kissed the tip of his nose.

'Good shot.'

'Actually, I was aiming for your forehead.'

When they had stopped giggling, Maggie twisted around so she could get up and fetch him his snack but then froze mid-action. She lay back down carefully and remained perfectly still.

'What's wrong?' Liam asked. He was still trapped

beneath the duvet and couldn't get up. 'Is it the baby?'

'Sort of,' Maggie said. Unlike Liam, there wasn't a trace of fear in her voice. She had placed a hand firmly over her abdomen. The tiny flutters had felt like a butterfly trying to escape. 'I think I just felt the baby move.'

'Can I feel?' Liam wriggled beneath the covers but couldn't release himself.

Maggie reached over and tugged at the duvet, pulling it away from the wall and releasing one of her children from their cocoon. She placed his hand where she had felt movement and they both held their breath and waited. She was about to admit defeat when the baby moved again and Liam pulled his hand away in fright.

'Wow, did you feel that?' he cried.

Maggie nodded, not trusting herself to speak.

'Can we go tell the others?'

'Can I have a hug first?' she asked.

Liam rationed his hugs, finding other ways to express his emotions as he had proven today, but he complied with his stepmother's request without hesitation. 'Love you,' he mumbled and Maggie could feel the heat from his glowing cheeks.

'And I love you, Liam. Don't you ever doubt it.'

CHAPTER 10

The Miltons' bungalow was in a small cul-de-sac to the west of Sedgefield and within walking distance from the High Street. The route was a new one for Maggie and Harvey but she knew the way to her old primary school, which was close by, and with a little help from a passer-by they arrived only ten minutes after leaving the salon.

Maggie was feeling nervous, unsure what to expect or what it would take to put her mind at rest. She supposed she needed reassurance that Elsie had the care she needed, but she also wanted to know that Elsa's story had a happy ending even if Freddie hadn't been a part of it.

'I should warn you that Harvey's moulting at the moment,' Maggie apologised when Ted and Elsie opened the door to her. 'I've brushed off the worst of it but you wouldn't believe how much hair he loses once the weather starts warming up.'

'Will you stop fretting and get yourselves inside? It might be warming up but that rain is still wet,' Elsie insisted.

'I've got a cloth with me to clean his feet,'

Maggie continued as she wiped her own feet on the coarse mat she had stepped onto.

Elsie touched her arm. 'You and Harvey are guests. Let me worry about cleaning up muddy paw prints after you've gone. It's a small price to pay for good company. Come in and make yourself at home.'

'These are for you,' Maggie said handing Elsie a posy of flowers.

'Now you shouldn't have – but thank you. They smell beautiful.'

Ted took Maggie's coat and let his wife escort their guest into the living room.

'Here, we saved the best seat in the house for you,' Elsie said, ushering Maggie to what felt like a deeply padded but well-worn armchair.

Maggie sat down and took off Harvey's harness before she allowed herself to relax. Above the smell of damp fur she detected the scent of more fresh flowers. Far more intense than the delicate sweetness of the freesias she had brought with her, these blooms were a sophisticated mix of lilies and roses. 'I take it you like flowers then?' she asked.

'Oh, they're amazing, aren't they? They're all the way from Australia.'

'America,' Ted corrected. He was hovering at the door as Elsie took a seat opposite Maggie. 'And they're from the florist on the High Street.'

'But the thought came from Aust . . . America.'

'Are they from your daughter?' Maggie asked.

'Yes, it was my birthday at the weekend and Nancy always spoils me.'

'You have two daughters,' grumbled Ted.

'Yes, Yvonne fusses over me too. She was here not that long ago to help us settle in.'

'She didn't stop complaining, though. She thinks it was a mistake moving to Sedgefield,' Ted explained Maggie.

'So do you,' Elsie said.

'We would have been better off moving up to Scotland to be closer to Yvonne but you can't argue with Elsie once she's set her mind on something. Now, I'll leave you ladies to have a chat while I make the tea.'

'There's a pot already brewing,' Elsie told him, 'and here, put Maggie's flowers in a vase for me.' Cellophane rustled as the flowers changed hands.

'I'll make a fresh one just in case,' Ted muttered under his breath as he left.

'And put that pie in the oven while you're at it,' Elsie barked before turning her attention back to her guest. 'It's meat and potato. You're not one of those vegetarians, are you, Maggie?'

'No, not me.'

'Would your little chap like some water?' Ted shouted from the kitchen. The bungalow was relatively small so he was still nearby. 'Or perhaps something stronger?'

Elsie tutted. 'Ignore him, Maggie; he's as daft as a brush.'

Maggie insisted that water would be absolutely

fine and Ted whistled as he set about his chores. Harvey kept his ears pricked as he listened to the noises coming from the kitchen but stayed at Maggie's side.

'I'm sorry I missed your birthday, Elsie. I should have realised when I took your details at the salon.' In truth, she had been more interested in working out the exact year a twenty-two-year-old Elsa would have first visited Sedgefield. Presuming Elsie had reached an age where she would be proud of her years, she added, 'By my calculation I'd say you've just turned eighty-three, am I right?'

'Am I?' she asked as if Maggie had imparted a secret. 'I wondered how these hands had got so wrinkly. So I don't work at the school canteen any more then?'

Maggie blushed as she faced the latest incarnation of Elsie's illness. 'You're enjoying a well-earned retirement.'

'Tea's up,' Ted announced with the rattle of teacups on a tray. Moments later he guided Maggie's hand to a china teacup. 'Sugar?'

'No, thanks.'

'She's sweet enough,' Elsie said. 'Did you put the thing in the oven?'

'Yes, of course I put the pie in the oven.'

'I'm only checking. What about the water for the dog?'

Ted had only just sat down and there was a painful groan as he stood up again. 'I'd forget my head if it wasn't screwed on.'

'Lunch should be ready in twenty minutes,' Elsie told Maggie. 'You're not a vegetarian are you?'

'No, I'm not a vegetarian,' Maggie answered patiently. 'I'll eat anything you put in front of me. Harvey would too, given the chance, but he's already had his lunch.'

'That's a pity,' Ted said as he re-entered the room. He walked with slow, deliberate steps so as not to spill the water. The dog stood up and wagged his tail with polite gratitude. 'I was going to save you my crusts, boy.'

Harvey replied with a low whine as if he knew what he was missing out on.

'I was telling Elsie that I'm sorry I missed her birthday. Although I have brought along some massage oil that I was going to leave with you,' she said turning back to the birthday girl. 'I could always give you a massage here after lunch if you like. Call it a belated birthday present.'

'Oh, I don't know if I'd feel comfortable having a massage.'

'It could just be a head and shoulder massage if you like. The oil has a different mixture of essential oils this time,' she added, trying to engineer some time alone with Elsie in the hope that she would reveal more of her past. And if Elsie weren't willing, then perhaps Elsa would resurface to tell her tale. 'It's not lilac but I think you'll like it. Will you give it a try?'

Maggie wouldn't take no for an answer so as soon as lunch had settled, they left Ted and

Harvey snoozing and retired to Elsie's bedroom. Elsie sat awkwardly on a cushioned stool, her blouse unbuttoned to expose bare shoulders.

'You do realise a massage is supposed to make you more relaxed, not terrify you?' Maggie asked when she placed her hands on Elsie's tensed shoulders. 'And I'm afraid I might make a mess of your hair but it's good for your scalp.'

'It's been a while since I was worried about my looks,' Elsie replied, making a concerted effort to sound more at ease than she was.

Maggie warmed some oil in her hands and released exotic scents into the air. 'Do you like this fragrance better?'

'Yes, it's quite nice. Is that rosemary I can smell?'

'With a little basil in there too.'

'Are you sure you're not trying to baste me?'

They both laughed harder than necessary but it helped ease the tension. Maggie's fingers would do the rest as she began kneading Elsie's neck and shoulders. This was where Maggie encouraged her clients to relax into their own thoughts, but she held her tongue and willed Elsie to fill the silence. Their conversation over lunch had been animated but it hadn't touched upon the problems of the distant past or the present. Nor had anyone mentioned that Elsie's homemade pie had a distinctly sweet taste, almost as if someone had used sugar instead of salt . . .

'I suppose you're wondering how I got on yesterday?'

'Yesterday?'

'Don't go acting daft, Maggie. I'm the one with the memory problems. I'm sure you remember I had a doctor's appointment.'

Maggie paused, resting her hands on Elsie's shoulders. Rather than massage, she gave her a comforting squeeze. 'So how did it go?'

'He didn't tell me anything I couldn't have worked out for myself. I'm getting worse. I have a new prescription and he's sending me for more tests for all the good it'll do. It's Ted who worries me more than anything.' Elsie put her hand over Maggie's and it trembled.

Maggie's pulse raced. Her first impression of Elsie's husband hadn't been great but she had wanted to believe that beneath the rough exterior was a heart of gold. Was Elsie about to confirm her worst fears? 'Why, Elsie? What does he do?'

'Everything,' she said. 'I know you're worried about me but if you really want to help then promise me you'll look out for my Ted. He won't ask for help for himself, but he'll need it.'

Thankful that Elsie hadn't been able to read her mind, Maggie's heart swelled as she heard the confirmation she had hoped for; Mrs Milton was loved as much as her younger self deserved. She was also flattered that Elsie had so much faith in her. 'I promise I'll be there for both of you,' she said with a smile that was pulled down by thoughts of the future.

'You're a good girl and if you don't mind me saying so, you're blooming very nicely.'

'Thank you. I've spent the last week chasing after my two stepsons and rather than tire me out, I feel more energised than ever. They've stayed before but I felt more like a mum this time. The house felt so empty after they left and I can't believe how much I'm missing them.' After such an inauspicious start, the week had gone amazingly well. Letting Judith get her own way early on had worked out well and other than a brief phone call on Sunday to say goodbye, she had left them in peace.

'They looked like a bit of a handful.'

Maggie was relieved that Elsie could recall at least part of their encounter in the park. 'Not as much as their grandmother.'

'I met her too, didn't I?'

'Yes. I've known Judith for two years but she doesn't have a fraction of the trust you have in me,' Maggie said as she continued with the massage. She was surprised how, rather than engineer Mrs Milton's confessions, the old lady was extracting one from her without even trying. 'She's still not convinced I can look after myself and, unlike you, wouldn't dream of entrusting me to watch over someone else. That's why she turned up at the park; to rescue her grandchildren.'

'So she hasn't known you very long?'

'Two years,' Maggie said, aware she was repeating herself. 'James and I moved into the house eighteen months ago but I think you could count on one hand the number of times she's visited.'

Maggie could feel Elsie finally relaxing into the massage. Her breathing had slowed and her response was punctuated with soft groans. 'Maybe if she got to know you better she might start seeing things differently.'

'That's what James keeps saying. We were all meant to have spent the day together last week but James got called into work. That's why I ended up taking the boys to the park – where all I succeeded in doing was proving to Judith how hopeless I am.'

'You're not hopeless and what's more, you know you're not. Try again.'

Maggie imagined being back in the park with her mum, nursing a grazed knee after falling off the bike. The memory wasn't quite sharp enough this time to weaken her stubborn streak. 'I'm not sure I want to. I know she's James's mum but I can't help thinking we'd be better off if she stayed away completely.'

It was almost imperceptible, but Maggie felt Elsie's body tense up a fraction. 'It's wrong to separate a mother from her child, even a grown-up one.'

'I lost my mum a year ago so I know how important this is to James,' Maggie answered by way of a defence.

'But?'

'But becoming a mum isn't going to be easy

161

for me. There's so much I have to learn, and without my mum it's going to be harder still. I know I'm my own worst enemy. I'm determined to go back to work once I've had the baby. Running my own business has helped me retain some kind of independence over the years and I don't want to give that up. But that means I'm going to face some tough challenges and the last thing I need is someone like Judith waiting for me to fail.'

'You're young and you're allowed to make mistakes. But isn't that when you'll need your family most of all? I'm sure someone like you can make Judith see the error of her ways and, who knows, maybe she'll be the guiding hand you've been missing?'

'*You're* the one who's sounding more like my mum.'

'That's probably the biggest compliment anyone could ever pay me but I'm not exactly a good example to follow.' Her harsh assessment of herself was tinged with regret and it didn't go unnoticed.

They both fell silent as Maggie began to massage Elsie's scalp. The sensation of coarse grey hair was at odds with the image of the young woman who was never far from Maggie's thoughts, or Elsie's for that matter.

'I had all my hair chopped off after I got married and had my girls but once upon a time it was so long I could sit on it.'

'Back when you called yourself Elsa?'

'Hmm,' Elsie said with a soft sigh. 'It was the colour of golden sand, probably only a shade or two lighter than Harvey's. Oh, I'm sorry, I keep forgetting. I don't suppose colour means a lot to you.'

Maggie smiled as she tried to picture Elsa with her long vanilla hair. 'More than you would imagine.'

'My hair was my crowning glory, my mum said, and I loved wearing it down. I can remember that feeling of the wind blowing through my hair as if it was yesterday.' Elsie allowed herself a short chuckle. 'Better than yesterday, I should say.'

Elsie went quiet for a moment and as Maggie kneaded her scalp, decades-old connections were remade.

'If I tell you how my hair got in such a mess, you won't tell anyone will you, Celia?'

Elsa's sister didn't answer immediately. She was standing behind her trying to undo the tats in her hair. 'How did it happen?' she asked hesitantly.

The smile on Elsa's face broadened. 'Freddie took me for a ride on his bike. I was holding on to him for dear life, my head buried in the back of his neck, and he just laughed when I started screaming. But then I was laughing too. He makes me so happy.'

There was no need to turn around to see the look of disdain on her sister's face. Celia had never approved of Elsa's boyfriends; there had been quite a few, but none like Freddie. 'He calls me his little firecracker,' Elsa said with a giggle, knowing she was about to shock her sister. 'And he certainly knows how to set me off.'

'He really loved you, didn't he?'

'Loved?' The use of the past tense was like a slap across the face. Elsa's eyes darted across the room as panic bloomed in her chest. It wasn't her bedroom. Something was wrong. She could almost feel the gaping hole in her heart as it beat a little faster. Something awful had happened. Her hand reached up to her hair.

'It's all right,' Maggie soothed as Mrs Milton let out a low mewl.

Elsa's appearance had been fleeting. She had called out for Freddie as she pulled at her hair but then the youthful tone in her voice had washed away with tears.

Maggie gave up on the massage and came around to sit on the edge of the bed in front of her. She took hold of Elsie's hands to still them.

'Freddie's gone,' Elsie sobbed.

'You think about him a lot, don't you?'

'You never forget your first love, no matter how much it hurts to remember.'

'Do you think you could tell me about him?' Maggie asked. 'Please.'

The story that Elsie revealed was carefully edited. Unlike the scenes that had already been played out in front of Maggie, this version made no reference to an unplanned pregnancy but it did include one vital fact that the young woman who called herself Elsa had been unable or unwilling to share with Maggie.

'I can barely bring myself to think about that awful, awful day when Celia turned up at Mrs Jackson's shop but I'll never forget that look on her face. At first, I thought something had happened to Mum or Dad but then I saw the airmail letter in her hand. It was sent from Freddie's commanding officer and Celia, being Celia, had already read it.'

Maggie had often wondered what would have kept Freddie from fulfilling his promises to Elsa. She had wanted him to be the hero to the end but for that to happen there would have to be a very good reason for him to stay away. She dreaded what Elsie might say next but asked, 'Why didn't Freddie come back to you?'

Elsie had barely regained her composure and her next words caught in her throat. 'Celia put her arms around me so that I wouldn't drop to the ground when she told me.'

'Told you what, Elsie?'

'Freddie was dead.'

The shock Maggie felt was as real sixty years on as it would have been if she had been there with Elsa in 1953. 'How?' she managed to ask.

Elsie shrugged as if she had insulated herself from the past, and perhaps she had. It was only her dementia that found her weak spots. 'A motor-bike accident.'

Maggie couldn't stop herself from imagining a lonely and pregnant young woman sitting on a park bench waiting in vain for her hero to appear. 'I'm so, so sorry.'

Elsie sniffed back unshed tears. 'It broke my heart, but I suppose I should be thankful I found out at all. I would have gone on waiting for him forever otherwise. Still, it was my Ted who came along eventually. Our marriage may not have had the same fiery passion – but it was built to last.'

'Why come back here, back to Sedgefield, after all of this time, Elsie?' Maggie asked, stepping a little closer to the question that still remained unanswered.

'We came here when the girls were little to visit Aunt Flo and I do like the place.'

The response wasn't as sincere as Elsie would have had Maggie believe. 'But it's the more painful memories you're revisiting now.'

'Maybe it's my way of punishing myself.'

Elsie had so far chosen not to talk about the baby but Maggie sensed she was getting nearer the truth. 'Or you want to retrace your steps? It would be perfectly natural to want to come back to trace—'

'Trace my fingers across an empty bench,' Elsie said before Maggie could finish. 'I can't change the past. What's done is done. Now,' she said, patting Maggie's hand, 'if memory serves me right you're supposed to be giving me a massage.'

Reluctantly, Maggie did as she was bidden. She couldn't bring herself to push Elsie further. Losing Freddie would have been painful enough but she imagined there had been worse to come.

'Tell me all the latest gossip at that salon of yours,' Elsie asked. 'Have you made anyone else cry lately?'

'It's Kathy's salon and no, there haven't been any more cases of hysteria.'

They chatted a little longer but Maggie's massage worked to better effect than either had expected and Elsie was soon in danger of nodding off. 'I think we're just about done. So how was that?'

'It was a pleasure and I hope I remember your kindness. You will forgive me if I don't, won't you?'

Maggie cleared her throat as if to swallow back the useless words of comfort that she had quickly learned would only insult Elsie's intelligence. A last squeeze of the shoulder was all she could trust herself to offer.

'Try not to wash off the oil immediately,' she said, her bump protruding as she straightened her back. 'And I'll leave you the bottle so you can apply it yourself. The oil will moisturise your skin but it's the smell that will give you the most benefit.'

Maggie was rubbing her stomach as Elsie eased herself up, her stiffened joints making the process slow and painful. She couldn't resist laying a hand over Maggie's. 'You know, it's not so much the things I forget as the things I remember that scare me most. You need to start believing in yourself, Maggie. Take my word for it, you don't want to fail this little mite before it's even been born.'

Elsie's words echoed in Maggie's mind as she returned to the living room, sending shivers down her spine.

'Where's Elsie?' Ted asked when he realised she hadn't reappeared with Maggie.

'I'm afraid I made a bit of a mess of her hair so she's trying to make herself presentable. Has Harvey behaved himself?'

'We've had a great time watching the snooker,' Ted said. 'It's still pouring down outside. Do you want me to phone for a taxi?'

'Erm, yes, that would be kind of you,' Maggie replied, a little disappointed to be ushered out so soon. If Maggie was ever going to fulfil her promise to Elsie and help her husband, first she needed to know him. She was starting to realise she would have her work cut out trying to chip away at his rough exterior.

'How is she doing? Really?' Maggie asked once the taxi was ordered.

The question was probing, but thanks to Elsie's pep talk, Maggie was feeling assertive enough to challenge his obstinacy. Ted didn't answer straight

168

away and the only sound in the room came from the rhythmic ticking of a clock on the wall.

'The doctor's given her some tablets,' he said at last.

'For Alzheimer's?'

'Alzheimer's, dementia,' Ted said dismissively. 'It's all the same thing in the end. We've seen it before with my dad and Elsie's mum. The tablets will stop her forgetting so much.'

'Or remembering things,' Maggie added. 'Has she had many episodes like the ones in the park?'

'She always comes back to me.'

'I know it can't be easy for you, Ted, so I'm telling you what I've told Elsie. I want to help as much as I can.'

'That's very kind of you but you're not really in a position to help, are you?'

'I might be blind but I'm not completely useless,' Maggie said, her tone a warning that she was a force to be reckoned with.

Ted coughed nervously. 'I meant because you're pregnant. You'll have your hands full soon enough.'

Maggie's cheeks flushed. 'Sorry.'

Ted laughed. 'Don't apologise, I like your spark. I can see why you and Elsie get along so well.'

'You have my number; call me if I can help. Your wife seems to be able to talk to me when she's confused. She's told me quite a bit about herself.'

'Complaining about her aching feet after a hard day's work at Flo's Fruit and Veg?' he ventured.

'Or waiting for someone to return,' Maggie offered.

'So you know about Freddie, then?'

'Yes. Did you know much about him?'

'I didn't when we first met but she told me eventually,' he said and then laughed. 'We must have been married at least five years before she got around to it though. Apparently, she thought I'd be jealous.'

'And were you?'

'I wasn't then,' he said.

Having hit a nerve, Maggie took a more gentle approach to her next question. 'I'm beginning to understand why she dwells on her time here so much. It was quite traumatic, I think.'

'You shouldn't go reading too much into what my wife tells you,' he warned. 'Not everything she says really happened. She's not well, remember.'

This time Maggie didn't pause long enough for self-restraint. She was too busy overstepping the boundaries of politeness. 'Did Elsie have any children before she met you? I was wondering if Nancy . . .'

'Is my daughter?' Ted asked, unfazed by Maggie's directness.

'I know I have no right to ask, but maybe knowing more about her life in Sedgefield will help me give her some kind of comfort when she needs it.'

'I don't think there's much comfort anyone could give her. Freddie's death affected her more

170

than I ever imagined but as far as I'm aware there was no baby back then. Maybe she pretended to be pregnant just to get him back. I wouldn't put it past my Elsie, she was a little minx in her day,' he said with deep affection. 'Nancy was born in 1957, two years after we were married. My daughter is selfish and thoughtless, so she most definitely takes after me. I hope that answers your question.'

'What if . . .'

'Maggie, my wife has kept her feelings locked away for sixty years. If she wanted me to know about everything that happened before I met her then she would have told me. Whatever she says when she's not herself, real or imagined, is of no consequence. If she has secrets to keep then far be it for me – or you, for that matter – to take any notice of her ramblings.'

They both heard the taxi beep its horn but only Maggie felt the disappointment. Elsie came in as Ted was helping her with her coat.

'Leaving so soon?'

'The taxi's here,' Maggie said.

'I hope you didn't go pushing our guest out of the door,' Elsie said to her husband. 'He's terrible, you know. As soon as Yvonne arrived the other week, the first thing he asked was when she was going home.'

'Someone has to be organised and I was only trying to help,' Ted protested.

'Don't be so hard on him. I can tell he has a

good heart, however hard he tries to hide it,' Maggie said, more in hope than belief. 'And I really do have to be going but I'd like to do this again soon. You can come over to my house next time, I insist.'

'You live by the park, don't you?' Ted asked.

Maggie could feel a polite refusal forming on his lips. 'Yes, but I can always ask the park warden to lock the gate if you want,' she joked. Despite Ted's compelling arguments earlier, Maggie still wanted the chance to sit and listen to Elsa talk of her time in Sedgefield, whether her view of the world was flawed or otherwise.

'You're beginning to sound as bad as he is,' Elsie said. At that moment, a car horn sounded again and she immediately became flustered. 'That must be the oven. The pie will be burnt to a crisp!'

Neither Maggie nor Ted could stop her from rushing off to the kitchen.

The reminder of Elsie's frailties was a reality check for Maggie. 'If it's easier, then I can come over to you,' she conceded.

'Yes, it would be easier,' he said. 'Now, if you have everything then I'd better see what she's up to.'

Maggie heard Ted releasing a deadbolt before opening the front door for her. 'You lock her in?' she asked.

'It's easier that way.'

Maggie shook her head, dismayed by this glimpse

of their life together. 'I don't imagine it's easy at all,' she said.

Maggie and James snuggled up together on the sofa. Both were shattered but for Maggie it was more mental than physical exhaustion. Soft music filled the warm air, which was laced with the scents of juniper berry and sweet marjoram, a perfect reflection of the purples and greens in the living room's colour scheme. But despite all the ingredients for a relaxing evening, Maggie's pulse raced.

She had expected lunch with the Miltons to go some way to allaying her fears but it had had the opposite effect. Whether she called herself Elsie or Elsa, her newest friend had sneaked into Maggie's heart and she worried what the future held for both. Her own problems were insignificant by comparison and it had been Elsie who had given Maggie the courage to confront them head on. It was a poignant gift considering how little control the old lady had over her own fate.

'Have you spoken to your mum today?' Maggie asked.

The arm that James had around his wife was strong enough to demolish brick walls but when he gave her a gentle squeeze, his touch was as delicate as his response. 'Only a quick hello, this morning.'

'She doesn't work on Fridays, does she?'

'No,' James answered and would have followed through with a question but Maggie was already pulling away from him.

173

Her tired body objected as she stood up and it took the adrenalin rush pumping through her veins to get her to the house phone. She was dialling before James had time to ask what she was doing.

'Hi Judith, it's Maggie,' she said, relieved that the tremors making her hands shake had not transferred to her voice.

'Oh. Hello, Maggie.'

Judith had been taken by surprise so Maggie still had the upper hand. 'I hope I haven't disturbed you?'

'No, of course not. It's lovely to hear from you,' she said, more confidently this time.

Maggie bit down hard on her lip, the pain giving her the final push to carry out her plan. She wished she could see James's face. She had heard him sitting up and leaning forward to listen in on the conversation. 'The thing is, Judith, I'm after a favour.'

'Really?'

'I've got an antenatal appointment on Friday afternoon and James was supposed to go with me but he's just been asked to quote for a job. He says he can cancel but it sounds important and I don't want him to miss out on any opportunity for more work.'

'Yes, I understand,' Judith said. She didn't.

'So . . .' Maggie paused to take a deep breath '. . . I was wondering if you wouldn't mind coming with me? I could go on my own but I'd rather have some company, if you're not too busy.'

There was a pause and then, 'Oh.'

Maggie's nerves jangled and it took all of her self-control to stop herself from immediately retracting the offer. Of course she could manage on her own, and she was well-aware that admitting a weakness, albeit a fabricated one, could work against her but she needed some kind of bait to get her mother-in-law to visit.

'What time?' Judith asked hesitantly.

'Two thirty at the health centre in Sedgefield.'

With a sigh of relief, Maggie made all the necessary arrangements for them to meet at the salon later that week. They would go to the health centre from there.

'Do you want to tell me what that was all about?' James asked when Maggie ended the call.

She waited until she was back on the sofa, wrapped in her husband's arms once more before she said, 'I want your mum to accept me, that's all. I want an opportunity for the two of us to be on our own so that I can get to know her a little better and she can get to know me. I know we've tried before but I was told today that I need to start believing in myself. And I do. I can do this, James.'

'For what it's worth, I already believe in you.'

Maggie's emotions bubbled to the surface and she only just managed to say, 'I know.'

'So do we have your Mrs Milton to thank for this change in attitude?'

'It's not fair that my mum isn't here to see her grandchild come into the world. She would have moved heaven and earth for me and it took Elsie to remind me that the same could be said of many mothers, even yours. I'm taking a leap of faith that Judith is going to be worth the effort.'

'I promise you she will be,' he said with iron in his voice that wavered when he added, 'She has to be or she isn't the mum I thought she was.'

Maggie was even less convinced but there was hope. 'My plan is to concentrate on your mum's positives. I'm going to remind her how good a mother and grandmother she is, how strong and protective she is. And then all I have to do is convince her that I'm part of that family too.'

'And how exactly are you going to do all of that?'

Maggie let out a soft but nervous laugh. 'I wish I knew.'

'Maybe you should ask Elsie what to do next.'

Although it was intended as a joke, Maggie considered James's suggestion in all seriousness, if only for the briefest moment, before shaking her head. 'I'd rather be the one helping her,' she said and wished, not for the first time, that she could sit next to Elsie on their park bench and help her confront the ghosts of the past once and for all. 'Do you think it's possible that someone could find their happy ending even if it is sixty years too late?' she asked, already knowing that no one, not even Elsie herself, could answer that question with any certainty.

CHAPTER 11

Maggie had been busy in the salon all morning and only allowed herself a quick lunch break in the park with Harvey before returning to prepare for Judith's visit. She systematically checked every inch of the treatment room, eliminating any possibility of fumbling or tripping over a forgotten obstacle in full view of her harshest critic. She was in the process of checking the bottles on one particular shelf for the second time when Kathy knocked at the door.

'A royal visitor for you,' she said mischievously. 'I've got the china cups ready and waiting if you fancy a cup of tea, your majesty?'

Maggie heard the clip of stiletto heels halt at the door. Judith wasn't ready to step over the threshold just yet. 'Haven't you got customers to scalp?' she asked Kathy.

With so little contact, Maggie rarely witnessed the two together. This lively exchange served to remind her that Judith was different things to different people. Her friendship with Kathy was surely a testament to the virtues her mother-in-law had yet to reveal to Maggie.

'Yes, probably,' Kathy said. 'And I can easily add you to the body count if you don't behave.'

It was a veiled threat that didn't go unnoticed, by Maggie at least. Kathy was proud to have brought James and Maggie together and she saw Judith's obstinate rejection as a reflection on her.

'Don't worry, I'm not hanging around,' Judith said. 'I wouldn't want to upset your customers by showing them what a proper haircut looks like.'

'Your roots could do with a touch up,' Kathy said with a sniff.

'Actually,' Maggie interrupted, 'a cup of tea might be a good idea.' She smiled in Judith's direction as the next part of her plan took the form of a lie on her lips. 'I'm afraid the clinic has phoned and asked if we can put the appointment back by half an hour so we don't have to leave straight away.'

'Oh, right. Well then . . . Maybe I could do a bit of shopping and come back later.'

'I was hoping I could persuade you to have a quick treatment here. Maybe a hand massage.' Maggie could hear the refusal forming in Judith's mind as clearly as the air being drawn into her lungs. 'I insist,' she added quickly. 'It's my way of thanking you for helping me out today.'

'Oh go on, Judith,' Kathy encouraged. 'I can't believe you have an aromatherapist in the family and have never taken advantage of it.'

Kathy disappeared to fetch the tea while Judith reluctantly settled into the treatment chair. Maggie did most if not all of the talking as she introduced Judith to her world of colourful aromas. As she talked, she went from one side of the room to the other, selecting the items she needed with rehearsed precision. Harvey remained in his bed. He had decided long ago that Judith was not one of his favoured visitors and had not deigned to greet her.

Sitting down on a stool at Judith's side, Maggie took her hand. The intimate contact made an already anxious Judith tense even more but Maggie was far from relaxed either. 'Do you moisturise your hands regularly?' Maggie asked as she detected a few rough patches of skin.

'Only when I remember.'

Maggie poured a little of the oil she had prepared into the palm of her hand, a mixture of chamomile and rose to relax patient and therapist alike. She rubbed her hands together to release the aromas before taking hold of Judith's hand again.

'You should take better care of them. Dry skin obviously runs in the family. I can see you work as hard as your son.'

'I keep promising myself I'll slow down, that's why I went part-time at the shop, but I still manage to find new things to fill my days.'

It was the opening Maggie needed and she took it. 'I've told James it was unfair of him to ask you to help look after the baby and that I won't entertain the idea,' Maggie said. It was at least a half-truth. 'So please don't worry, we'll manage. I'll need to shelve the business for a while but when I'm ready and I can convince James we can afford it, we'll use the same nursery as Jenny. Lily seems happy enough there.'

'I don't suppose a business like this could be left for too long without losing custom, but nurseries can be so expensive. I should imagine you'll be working just to cover childcare costs.'

'Maybe not even that,' added Maggie.

'And I'm not saying we wouldn't be able to help out occasionally . . .'

Maggie's head was bowed so Judith couldn't see the look of confusion on her face but she would have felt Maggie's grip tighten on her hand. It had never occurred to her that Judith's position would relax. She had been relying on them both finding the whole idea implausible.

'But it would have to be on your terms. I understand that,' Maggie said, giving them both an easy way to sidestep the issue. She poured more oil and concentrated on Judith's other hand. 'It's not the only reason you're unhappy about the baby though, is it?'

'I'm not *unhappy* about it. James is my only son. I love my grandchildren and I will love this one too,' Judith began before adding the 'but' that would contradict her previous statement. 'But babies are hard work under the best of circumstances and you've accepted yourself that keeping your business up and running will only add to that pressure. These things are bound to add stress to any relationship.'

180

'It's not the only thing that adds stress to a relationship.'

'Exactly,' Judith said as if they were in perfect agreement but as Kathy tapped on the door and entered with a tray of clinking china, she and Maggie were still worlds apart.

'Ready for some tea, ladies?' Kathy asked.

They both mumbled their thanks and the awkwardness that hung in the air was as tangible as the scent of chamomile and rose. Kathy, wisely, chose to leave as quickly as she had arrived.

'I think I'm about done,' Maggie said, her words flowing uncomfortably over the lump of anxiety lodged in her throat. 'I'll give you a pair of cotton gloves to wear while you drink your tea.'

'Thanks, Maggie.'

Silence fell as Judith sipped her tea and Maggie filled the time by clearing away her equipment and washing her hands. Each practised move was completed to perfection despite her mind being elsewhere. She had pushed the conversation but, in her own inimitable way, Judith had used Maggie's openness to contrive more fault lines in her daughter-in-law's life. She checked her watch. They would have to leave in ten minutes but perhaps there was still time.

Maggie sat back down on her stool, a flush rising to her cheeks as the questions lined up in her mind. Why are you adamant that James has made a big mistake in marrying me? Why, now that I'm pregnant, are you still willing the

181

marriage to fail? What do I have to do to get your approval? Her mind raced as fast as her heart but as she steeled herself, Judith jumped in with her own questions.

'How's that lady doing? The one with you in the park the other day?'

'Mrs Milton?' Maggie asked, her thoughts stumbling as the conversation steered away from its intended course. 'She's doing OK, I suppose.'

'Has she been suffering from dementia long?'

'Yes, quite a while I think.'

Judith's curiosity had been piqued by what James had already told her but Maggie wasn't about to fill the gaps. Ted had been right, Elsie was entitled to keep her secrets even if the old lady's mind insisted on making them public. As Maggie concentrated on her replies, the adrenalin that had quickened her heart slowly washed away. Crockery clinked as Judith placed her empty cup on the saucer and dropped a pair of cotton gloves onto the table. The opportunity for confrontation had slipped through Maggie's fingers and her growing confidence cut back down to size.

'It was good that you could help her like that, amazing really. And I hope you didn't mind me interfering but no one could expect you to look after the children and be a Good Samaritan at the same time. I would have hated to see you getting into trouble over it and you never know who's watching.'

'In trouble with who?'

There was a long pause while Judith fumbled with her bag as she prepared to leave. 'Oh, I'm guessing James, for one,' she said at last. 'I hope you didn't fall out too badly over it. Those boys have seen too many arguments and they know how quickly things can turn ugly.'

Maggie listened in stunned silence. Judith's voice was soothing and sympathetic, too intent on imagining the collapse of James's second marriage to consider that he might have been angry with his mother, too. Her daughter-in-law's mouth was agog but by the time she had the presence of mind to close it, Judith had moved the conversation on again. 'I should come here more often – my hands feel amazing. You've still got a little tea left in your cup if you want to drink up. We'd better leave soon.'

Judith was rising to her feet when Maggie took a deep breath, hoping that the remnants of the essential oils in the air would be enough to steady her for one last attempt to speak openly and honestly.

'Judith,' she said. 'I wish you would come over more often. I wish we could know each other better.' It was hardly the no-holds-barred discussion she had imagined; it was a plea and a desperate one at that. Maggie could feel her heart thudding against her chest as she waited for Judith's answer.

'Shall I get your coat?' Judith said.

The hurt cut deeply into Maggie as Judith deftly

ignored the proffered olive branch. She was about to respond, all sense of tact and diplomacy abandoned but luckily Judith spoke first.

'How about I make another appointment with you so I don't go undoing all your good work?'

'I was stunned, completely stunned,' Maggie confessed in a hushed whisper. 'I still am.' She was in the kitchen with Jenny, out of earshot of their husbands who were engrossed in their own discussions in the dining room about the dire state of the economy.

'I know how frustrated you are with Judith but you can't rush these things.'

'In case it's escaped your notice, I've been married to her son for precisely one year,' Maggie said. She and James had invited their friends over for a quiet dinner to mark their first wedding anniversary. It was Sunday evening and Lily was sleeping soundly in the living room allowing her parents some much-needed time off to share a meal and a celebratory glass of champagne. 'And we were living together for six months before that. She's had plenty of time.'

'You mark my words, one minute you'll think you're getting nowhere and the next she'll be interfering in your life as much as she has with James's for the last thirty-five years.'

'I know you're trying to put me off but right now that would be the lesser of two evils! Keeping her at a distance was quite tempting, but the more

I glimpse how her mind works, the more I've realised I need to be around to correct all the outrageous assumptions she jumps to.'

'So how did she wind you up so much that you're in danger of curdling the soup?'

Maggie was standing over a large saucepan, the contents of which were still swirling around long after she had the presence of mind to stop stirring. 'I don't think you'd believe me if I told you. Let's just say that she asked the midwife some pretty damning questions.'

'Like?'

So far Maggie had kept the events of her ante-natal appointment to herself. She hadn't even told James; she didn't want to shatter the illusion that she and his mother were making progress. 'It doesn't matter. It was just lucky that Mel was there to deal with her. Well, I say lucky but actually I'd forewarned her and she made sure she was at the clinic to see us.'

'You're nothing if not prepared,' Jenny said. She was on the far side of the kitchen rummaging in the fridge. 'Ooh, that looks nice.' A freshly made cheesecake was taking pride of place on the top shelf.

'And I'll know if you try putting your finger in it,' Maggie warned, trying to keep the mood light when her insides were tied up in knots. 'You'll find the butter on the second shelf from the top.'

'You always did have eyes in the back of your head.'

185

'And I'm going to need them with Judith around,' Maggie said under her breath. She could hear the roiling soup that was a perfect match for her emotions. She tipped her head back so that the tears brimming in her eyes wouldn't fall. 'I really thought it was going to work, Jen.'

'Hey, don't get upset,' Jenny said turning towards her. 'If I know you, you'll win her over eventually. Give it time.'

It wasn't so much the words as the sympathy in Jenny's voice that knocked some sense into Maggie. She sniffed back her tears and straightened up. 'I'm sorry, Jen. I should be the one consoling you. How's Mark dealing with the news? How are *you* dealing with it?'

Jenny had picked up a bread knife and was cutting a granary loaf into wedges, her efforts slow and deliberate as she tried to make sense of how her life was about to change. After living under the shadow of redundancy, Mark had been served notice that week. It was official. He would be unemployed come September.

'It's awful – for me and for him. Just awful.'

Maggie looked over in Jenny's direction, shocked by how all the colour had been drained from her voice. 'I can't believe you've let me rant while you're there putting on a brave face.'

'Take my word for it,' Jenny said. 'This is not a brave face.'

Maggie left the soup simmering and stepped towards her friend. She placed a palm gently against her cheek. Thankfully there were no tears but her jaw was set firm, pulling her mouth in a downward direction. Her bottom lip trembled.

'So this is where you take up the strain?' Maggie asked.

Jenny tried to nod but she didn't seem to have the energy. 'I'm going to apply for the assistant manager's job even though I don't know if it's what I really want. I have no choice, we need the money, but with so much pressure on me now I'm bound to mess it up. Mark isn't particularly sympathetic and why should he be? I'm panicking about the possibility of getting promoted, for goodness' sake. It's already driving a wedge between us and it's bound to get worse.'

'Not necessarily and who's to say there isn't a new job for Mark right around the corner?'

'Actually, he's been talking about retraining once he's worked his notice.'

The question was begging to be asked. 'Retrain as what?'

'A joiner,' Jenny said deliberately. 'He started an apprenticeship when he left school but then took the job at the estate agents. He was pretty good by all accounts and if he can persuade someone to take him on, I don't think it would take long for him to become qualified.'

'Someone like James?'

'Do you think it's possible?'

The soup began to bubble ferociously and Maggie had a short reprieve before giving an answer. She returned to the stove and turned off the heat. 'I don't know, Jenny. I don't think James is taking anyone on at the moment. Things are tight.'

'There are probably grants that he could claim for apprenticeships and if not, Mark wouldn't ask to be paid. We could live off the redundancy money for a while. It would be a way of investing in our future.'

Jenny wasn't going to take no for an answer but Maggie knew it wasn't in her gift to offer Mark a job, even an unpaid one. 'I'll mention it to James,' she promised.

'I know you'll convince him,' Jenny said, suddenly reanimated. She joined Maggie at the stove and gave her arm a quick squeeze. 'Now, let's sample the chef's work.' She slurped a spoonful of scalding hot mushroom soup. 'I'd say it needs a little more pepper.'

'It's perfect as it is,' Maggie said. A quick check of the oven confirmed there was still another half hour until the roast was ready. 'Time to serve.'

Buoyed by the lifeline Maggie had handed her, Jenny's effervescence still wasn't enough to lift the mood around the dining table. Mark was distinctly subdued and James not much better.

It wasn't until after the second course, when Jenny disappeared to check on Lily and Mark sloped outside for a quick cigarette that Maggie had a chance to ask James about the apprenticeship.

'Please don't say you've promised her anything.'

'I said I'd talk to you, that's all,' Maggie answered.

'I'm sorry, Maggie, but there's no chance. I could tell Mark was angling for an offer when he mentioned it before but I deliberately ignored the hints.'

'Couldn't you find some way of helping? They're our friends, James.'

'Maggie, estate agents aren't the only ones losing their jobs, builders are laying people off too.' Their conversation was in hushed tones, which made the exasperation in James's voice all the more pronounced.

'Is it that bad?'

James took her hand and gave it a squeeze. 'We're supposed to be celebrating tonight. Let's not talk about it.'

'Not interrupting anything, am I?' Jenny asked.

Maggie forced a half smile. 'How's Lily?'

'Sleeping like a baby.'

The conversation stalled, Jenny not willing for once to fill the silence. She was waiting for someone to put her out of her misery.

'Did I tell you about my lunch at Elsie's the other day?' Maggie asked, knowing full well that she had.

'Yes. It's such a shame isn't it? She and her husband have been in the bank a few times and I don't know what to say to them.'

'That's not like you,' chipped in James.

'It would help if Maggie filled in some more of the gaps,' Jenny said. 'We know she came here

189

when she was pregnant and no one believes this story that she'd lost her husband. So what became of the baby? Was it adopted?'

Even though Maggie had refused to break Elsa's confidence, Mrs Milton's frequent dips into the past had meant she was already the subject of local gossip. 'If there ever was a baby. She gets a bit confused and imagines all kinds of things which probably never even happened,' she said. It was the explanation Ted would have her believe and Maggie hoped she sounded more convincing than he had. 'But on her better days, she's quite a character.'

'Maggie was saying her husband doesn't want her going back into the park,' James said.

'Does he think she might throw herself in the lake?' Jenny asked. 'You thought that yourself once, didn't you?'

'She had nightmares about it,' James agreed.

It was a memory that Maggie occasionally wrestled with, but the spot by the lake still held more comfort than fear. It had been a place of quiet reflection for both of them and the bench had bound them together. Maggie couldn't bear the thought of Elsie never visiting there again. 'If she's reliving her past life then obviously she didn't come to any harm. I think she's safe on that count.'

'I thought you just said she was making it all up?' Jenny asked.

It was guilt rather than embarrassment that brought a flush to Maggie's cheeks. She didn't enjoy lying and obviously couldn't do it very well. 'I don't know what happened to Elsa, Jen, honestly I don't. She did a lot of soul searching while she sat on that bench and maybe that's where she thinks she'll find herself again.'

'It's easy to see how she could slip back into another time so easily,' James said. 'I doubt the park's changed that much in the last sixty years, especially down by the lake where it's so enclosed.'

'She notices the changes and that's what upsets her most,' added Maggie.

'Is this the crazy lady who was looking for the swans?' Mark had returned to the dining room as they were talking. The smell of stale smoke drifted in too and Maggie heard Jenny sniffing the air in disgust.

'She's not crazy,' Maggie corrected.

'And you would understand that if you hadn't been outside burning money,' Jenny sniped.

'I think you'll find it was a cigarette – and while I'm still earning, I can do what I like with my money.'

'Who's ready for some cheesecake?' Maggie offered quickly.

'I'll get it,' James said, jumping up as if his seat was on fire. He hated arguments and one between friends would be particularly tortuous. Maggie heard Harvey scramble to his feet too and he squeezed between a forest of legs, table and human, to follow James's retreat.

'Did you ask him?' Jenny asked as soon as James was out of earshot.

Maggie wished she had insisted on helping James with dessert. 'I'm sorry, Jenny, but I don't think it's possible at the moment. I knew James was struggling but I'm beginning to think he hasn't been telling me everything.'

Mark let out a long sigh of exasperation. 'You asked Maggie? Jenny, I told you not to get involved,' he said to his wife. 'I'm sorry, Maggie, she shouldn't have put you in that position. I was talking to James before and it's clear he's barely managing to stay afloat himself.'

'But you have to put yourself out there, Mark. It's not like someone is going to come knocking at your door,' Jenny said angrily.

'I *will* put myself out there. Me. Not my interfering wife.'

'Would James be able to have a word with some of his contacts?' Jenny asked, her desperation making it impossible to heed Mark's warnings. 'Maybe there's someone he knows who could take him on.'

Maggie was starting to feel drained and just a little nauseous. 'Jenny, please,' she begged as she heard James returning from the kitchen.

No more was said on the matter and little else was said for the remainder of the evening. There were the compulsory compliments on the chef's coup de grâce, polite interest in the recipe for the cheesecake but an uncomfortable silence fell as they concentrated a little too much on savouring their dessert. No one argued when Jenny suggested making it an early night and it was only after their guests had wrapped up a softly snoring Lily and headed out into the bleak night that James realised that they had forgotten to open the champagne.

'Shall we?' he asked. They were in the kitchen, clearing away the dishes.

'Not unless you're planning on demolishing it by yourself. I was only going to have a sip anyway and to be honest I'm not even in the mood for that any more.'

James sighed. 'Me neither.'

'I hate to see them at such odds with each other.'

'They'll be fine,' James answered, but there was little hope of convincing Maggie when he sounded so unsure himself.

The nausea she had been fighting hit her like a wave. 'And what about us? Are we *fine*?' she asked.

James actually laughed. 'Where did that come from? I know I was a bit short with you before but that's hardly grounds for divorce.'

Maggie wouldn't be cajoled. Mark's words were still ringing in her ears. In one conversation he had worked out that James's business was in dire straits, something that had barely registered on Maggie's radar. 'I didn't know you were struggling to find work. How much are we not telling each other, James? What's happening to us?'

'Nothing's happening to us and nothing is going to happen. Look, business is tough at the moment and maybe I should have told you more but I didn't want to worry you unnecessarily. We're managing, just not enough to consider taking on someone else, that's all. If there was ever a real problem then I promise you'll be the first to know.'

Maggie had been rinsing crockery while James loaded the dishwasher. She scrubbed away at one particular plate until James had to abandon what he was doing to take it from her before she wore away the pattern. 'Maggie?'

'Your mum asked Mel if there was a risk that the baby could be born blind,' she blurted out.

The pause James left was too long and Maggie had to fill it. It was either that or burst into tears. 'Even though she knows I lost my sight after contracting measles, she thought I might still be able to pass the virus on to the baby. I could almost forgive her that one, but it gets better. She thinks our baby could end up with learning difficulties, James,' she said, her voice croaking as she forced out the painful confession. 'Not that she came right out and said as much, but there were enough questions about how the baby could possibly develop normally with me as its role model.'

James's mouth sounded dry as he swallowed and simply said, 'Oh.'

'Oh?' Maggie asked in disbelief having expected her husband to feel at least some of the anger that had been twisting at her insides.

'I'm sorry, Maggie, and please don't hate me but she asked me the same things.'

194

'And you're OK with your mum harbouring those kind of prejudices about me?'

'Of course not. I put her straight and I hoped that would be the end of it. And I didn't tell you for exactly the same reasons you didn't want to tell me.' James took a deep breath and let it out with a long sigh. 'We've fallen into the habit of only telling each other what we think the other wants to hear, haven't we?'

The hairs on the back of Maggie's neck stood on end, her senses telling her there was more to hear. 'What else haven't you told me?'

James didn't immediately answer. Instead he turned to put the last plate in the dishwasher and made a good impression of being occupied selecting the right settings. He switched the machine on and the sound of churning water matched the churning of Maggie's stomach.

'I've done the maths, Maggie. If you're determined to go back to work after the baby's born then you'd have to increase your turnover to justify the cost of a nursery. Realistically, that isn't going to happen.'

Maggie tried to remain calm. It was good that they were talking openly and honestly at last but it didn't make what James had to say more palatable. 'I know, but going to work isn't only about making money, you know that.'

'But it's not a sustainable option. Your business will become a luxury we can't afford.'

'Would you give up your business so easily?' she

demanded. The argument wasn't a rational one but Maggie refused to give in.

James chose to ignore her question and, from the tension in his voice, her stubbornness was testing his patience. 'Of course I know how important your work is to you and that's why I was trying to get Mum to help. I know she wouldn't be your first choice but what if she was the only choice?'

The dishwasher rumbled on, its pumps washing away the debris from their disastrous dinner. 'She isn't a choice at all though, is she? I've tried my best, James and I don't like admitting defeat but your mother has defeated me. Do you have any idea how humiliating it was to listen to her talking to Mel? Talking to her, I should add, as if I wasn't in the room; and having my ability to be a mother challenged and questioned? I can't face that again,' she continued, her voice rising as she felt herself being hemmed into a corner. 'And while we're at it, why is it me that has to make things right? I didn't make them wrong in the first place, your mum did. *Your* mum! *Your* responsibility.'

Maggie's chest was heaving as she waited for James to react. He didn't say a word. He wasn't going to fight and his inertia turned the waves of nausea into a surge of panic. She could imagine Judith rubbing her hands in glee. Her dire prediction about the longevity of James's second marriage was becoming a self-fulfilling prophecy. They were ending their first year of marriage with an argument that had exposed the cracks in their relationship. Maggie gave into the need to run and pushed past her husband.

James grabbed her, taking both of her hands in his. The gentle giant wasn't so gentle as he put her hands behind her back and pulled her towards him. He waited for her ragged breaths that verged on sobs to quieten before he spoke. His voice trembled and his words were as tender as his soul. 'OK, I get it,' he said. 'I've been here before, I know the signs and right now I'm terrified.'

Maggie wanted to contradict him but she couldn't. 'I'm scared too.'

'Well, I've got news for you, Maggie Carter. I'm not going to give up without a fight. If I keep my head stuck in the sand then one day I'll look up and you won't be there. So, I get it.' James inhaled deeply as if he could hold back the tears she imagined welling in his eyes. 'A year ago today I promised to honour you but already I've let other people dishonour you. I get it, Maggie. I know how difficult Mum can be. I've had a lifetime of trying to get around her and failing miserably but I promise you this much. If I can't get Mum to accept you and there's ever a choice to be made then I choose you. I hope it never comes to that but I need you to know. I choose you.'

Letting go of her hands, James waited for Maggie to make a choice of her own. She still wanted to run, the problems were still there and they still defeated her but as she wrapped her arms tightly around James her emotions rose in waves through her body, a mixture of pride, relief and pure love.

'I think I would like some champagne,' she said when she could finally speak. 'We do have something to celebrate. We have each other and I don't ever want to take that for granted.'

CHAPTER 12

Maggie's mood seemed to follow the seasons and, as the weather began to brighten and bloom, so did she. There was no escaping it: at five months pregnant she had grown out of most of her old clothes and had no choice but to start wearing maternity wear.

There was also no escaping the fact that she would have to give up work. It was difficult to accept, but not as difficult as accepting help from Judith. Fortunately that remained unlikely. James was doing his best, but in a battle of wills with his mum he was always going to come in second. There was nothing for it: she was going to have to tell Kathy that when she went on maternity leave at the end of the summer, she wouldn't be coming back.

Although she had her regrets, Maggie refused to feel sorry for herself. There were too many other people to worry about. She had spoken to Jenny almost daily since the ill-fated anniversary dinner and talking seemed to ease the pressure her friend imagined piling up on her. It was hardly a solution but James had made it clear that there was nothing else they could do.

She had been to see the Miltons again and here, too, there was very little practical help she could offer. While Ted pottered about the house or in the garden, Maggie sat and listened to Elsie talking about her life in Liverpool – although occasionally she was called upon to fill the silences that fell when Elsie faltered. There were brief snatches of Elsa, too, but an easy chair couldn't summon up the desperate hours she had spent sitting on the bench by the lake. It would seem that Ted's determination to keep Elsie away from the park might be enough to put Elsa's ghost to rest and Maggie had to keep reminding herself that wasn't necessarily a bad thing.

On one particular Monday morning in late June there had been a steady flow of customers in the salon but Maggie hadn't been so busy that she couldn't find a space in her diary to come to the aid of another friend.

'I'd all but given up on you,' Maggie said when she had Alice exactly where she wanted her, lying prone on the treatment table.

At a time of year when the days were at their longest and warmest, Alice still hadn't shaken the winter blues. A chest infection had left her weak and a rattling cough persisted, day and night.

'I'm desperate for a good night's sleep and if I'm being honest, Maggie, it's starting to get me down.'

'So you had to wait until you were desperate before you came to see me?'

'Oh, you know what I mean. But I'm warning you now, if you can stop this cough long enough, I'll be asleep in no time.'

'It's allowed,' Maggie assured her as she began warming some almond oil in her hands. It was laced with eucalyptus oil and would have set Harvey into a sneezing fit if he hadn't already been sent out to keep Kathy company.

'The last time I was in this room all I could smell was shoe leather.'

'I think you need to explain that one,' Maggie said with a laugh.

'Don't worry; sleep deprivation hasn't made me lose my senses. I worked here when this place was a shoe shop. Once upon a time this was a store-room piled high with boxes of shoes. It was quite a nice smell as I recall.' The memory made her chuckle, which immediately turned into a coughing fit.

'You really should go back to see your doctor again, Alice.'

'I will,' she gasped between suppressed coughs.

Maggie raised an eyebrow. 'There's a phone in reception. I'll help you dial the number.'

Alice was about to answer when Kathy ran into the room. 'Jenny needs you over at the bank, now, Maggie.'

Sick with dread, Maggie asked, 'Why? What's wrong?'

'It's Mrs Milton. She's outside the bank and in quite a state by the sounds of it. They can't find

Ted and Jenny's asked if you could try to calm her down.'

Maggie was already reaching for a cloth to wipe her hands. 'I'm so sorry Alice, do you mind?'

'No, not at all! I know what they're going through. Is there anything I can do to help?'

'Thanks, but I should be able to manage,' she said as she helped Alice manoeuvre herself up and off the treatment table. She held on to Alice's hand but it was unclear who was steadying whom.

'Your hands are shaking,' Alice said.

'I'll be fine once I know Elsie's OK,' she said, turning her attention to Kathy. Her frown deepened along with her anxiety. 'Where's Harvey?' She didn't like the pause Kathy left before answering.

'Sorry, one of the girls has taken him for a walk.'

'But I need to get to the bank.'

'I'll take you,' Alice and Kathy said in unison.

'You need to get dressed first,' Kathy reminded Alice.

'Then I'll follow you over,' Alice promised, still intent on offering her services.

Grateful for Kathy's calming presence as much as her guiding arm, Maggie hurried out of the salon. It was a hot summer's day and the air was thick with car fumes. The bank was on the opposite side of the High Street and the seemingly endless stream of traffic frustrated their progress. Maggie was ready to take a chance and dart across but Kathy insisted they use a pedestrian crossing. Waiting for the lights to change was excruciating.

When they arrived outside the bank, there were plenty of passers-by but no suggestion of the commotion Jenny had described to Kathy.

Maggie tried to catch her breath but the fumes were acrid and her lungs strained for fresh air. 'They must be inside,' she said. 'Can you see any sign of Ted? He's bound to be looking for her.'

'Maybe he's already here. Let's go in.'

Despite being heavily pregnant and tired, Elsa wouldn't go back to Aunt Flo's where she would have nothing to do but watch the hours drag towards the conclusion of another day. Mrs Jackson meant well by telling her not to build up her hopes, but the constant suggestion that Freddie might not fulfil his promises had started to grate on her nerves. Aunt Flo didn't know Freddie and she hadn't seen his letters, which were full of love and plans for their future as a family. Elsa wanted to believe that Mrs Jackson's heart was in the right place, but blood was thicker than water.

Thankfully, Anne was keeping away but only because Elsa had warned her that if she didn't stop needling her, then even if she was forced to give up her baby, she wouldn't let Anne have it just to spite her. It was a hollow threat because there was no doubt in Elsa's mind that Freddie would turn up. Eventually.

But now, as she walked up and down the High Street, she was starting to fear that it could be Anne's wishes coming true and not her own. She wrapped her arms tightly around her as if Anne's hands were already reaching out to snatch her baby. It was still her child and always would be. Only the other day she had been lying in bed, marvelling at the unfathomable rise and fall of her exposed stomach, probing the intriguing lumps and bumps, when all of a sudden a tiny foot had pushed upward. It was a tantalising glimpse of the baby growing inside her and made her more determined than ever to hold onto her dreams.

But where was Freddie? she asked herself. He had told her he would go straight to Aunt Flo's when he arrived in Sedgefield and she had been afraid to step over the doorstep for two whole days. On the third day she had started to suspect something had happened, imagining all kinds of dirty tricks that Anne might be up to with Aunt Flo's help. She couldn't wait any longer and thought there might be a chance that Freddie would track her down to the greengrocer's but as she looked up and down the High Street, she couldn't make head nor tail of the myriad of gaudy signs and walls of glass that lined the busy road. Flo's Fruit and Veg was nowhere in sight and she was starting to think she had somehow managed to wander into another town when she had seen the unmistakeable red sandstone façade of the bank on the corner.

★   ★   ★

The bank wasn't air-conditioned but with its high ceilings and shuttered windows, it was insulated from the outside world and the cool contrast made Maggie's skin prickle with goose bumps. She didn't need to ask Kathy what was happening because she could hear Elsa's plaintive demands for someone to give her directions to the greengrocer's. Her voice rasped with age but it was the familiar youthful lilt that echoed off the walls.

Jenny hurried over to meet them. 'She's been rushing up and down the High Street looking for Flo's Fruit and Veg,' she explained. 'She kept coming back to the bank to try to get her bearings, sobbing her heart out, and we eventually persuaded her to come in here but I don't think she'll stay put for long.'

'I have their home phone number in my mobile,' Maggie said reaching into a pocket in the tunic she wore at the salon. 'Damn, I haven't got it with me.'

'No matter, we already had their number,' Jenny said. 'There's no answer.'

'Why don't I wait outside and keep looking out for Ted while you try to speak to Mrs Milton?' Kathy offered.

Maggie agreed and was already moving towards the sound of the familiar voice before Jenny had a chance to guide her. Mrs Milton was sitting in a small waiting area at the far side of the bank. A young cashier had been doing her best to comfort her and was more than happy to give up her seat for Maggie.

'Who are you?' Elsa demanded as Maggie sat down. She had reached out a hand but Elsa pushed it away. 'I don't know you.'

'It's Maggie. Maybe you don't recognise me because I'm usually with my guide dog,' she explained. 'You remember Harvey, don't you?'

'Why does everyone keep asking me what I remember? Yes, of course I do,' Elsa snapped. 'We met in the park.'

'That's right and I'm here to help.'

'Then tell these people to stop fussing around me.'

Maggie heard tentative shuffles as the crowd of onlookers, staff and customers alike, gave them more space. Somewhere amongst them she recognised Alice's voice. 'Come on now, less of the gawping. Give the poor lady some dignity.'

Elsa sighed and the air hissing across her lips sounded pained and desperate.

'What's wrong, Elsa?' Maggie asked. She tried again to reach out and this time Elsa took her outstretched hand and squeezed it tightly.

'Freddie should be here by now,' she whispered. 'Anne will have something to do with it, mark my words. She'd do anything to keep the baby.'

Maggie felt her chest tighten as she imagined the raw grief Elsa would have gone through when her sister arrived with news of the accident, an unimaginable pain that her fractured mind was intent on putting her through again unless Maggie could guide her back to the safety of the present. 'Maybe we should just sit here and rest awhile.'

There was another frantic squeeze of her hand. 'What if he's already on his way back to West Germany?'

'I'm sure Freddie wouldn't give you up without a fight. He'd be here if he could,' Maggie told her. 'I know all of this is very frightening for you, Elsa. Your mind is probably racing and it's making you confused. I promise you'll start feeling better soon and I'm going to sit here with you for as long as it takes.'

Maggie was talking slowly and her voice was gentle. In contrast, Mrs Milton's grip on her hand was fierce and Maggie was getting pins and needles. As she tried to replace one hand with another, Mrs Milton slipped from her grasp.

'I'm not giving up without a fight. I'm stronger than anyone realises,' the old lady said with a forced youthfulness that recaptured the past. 'I'm going to find him!'

Elsa wrenched her hand away and stood up. The woman she had been sitting next to tried to catch hold of her again but Elsa was too fast. She ignored her aching bones and pushed through the crowd. It was as if she was in a nightmare and she recoiled from the countless hands reaching out towards her.

Her heels clicked and scraped across the marble floor but she raised her gaze upwards, seeking out the familiarity of the bank's vaulted ceiling. She knew where she was. Now all she needed to do was find the greengrocer's and if she failed this time she would go to the park and if he wasn't there then she would keep looking. She wouldn't give up.

'Elsa, please come back!' the woman called after her but Elsa ignored the plea. She was already stepping out from the dimly lit bank into the bright light of day.

The glare from the sun was blinding and Elsa raised a hand to shield her eyes. She could see only the silhouette of a woman standing in front of her, blocking her way.

'Leave me alone,' Elsa cried. She was trying to look past the woman but the flashes of sun glinting off speeding cars stung her already red and swollen eyes.

'I'm sorry, I can't let you go,' the woman said.

Elsa tried to make out the features of her latest adversary. The woman was tall with short blonde, almost white hair. Through blurred vision she looked into the woman's eyes and wondered why she hadn't recognised her immediately.

'Celia?'

'Come back into the bank with me, please,' her sister said.

Despite the cloying heat, a cold shiver ran down Elsa's spine as she caught a glimpse of the future and her mind recoiled. 'No, no, you have to help me find Freddie. If I lose him now then I lose the baby too. Do you really want that? You said yourself you couldn't have given up one of your own babies. Why make me give up mine, Celia? It's not fair! You have so many and I only want one, one little baby. Don't do this to me, Celia. Please, don't do this. Help me!'

Celia was lifting her arm and at first Elsa thought she was trying to stop her from passing but then she knew. Elsa's eyes opened in horror. Celia was about to give her the letter that would rip out her heart and one day tear the baby from her arms.

'No!' she cried in a desperate mewl. 'He can't be dead! No, please God, no.'

'It's going to be all right,' Celia pleaded. 'Please, take my hand.'

'No, it's not going to be all right. You know what's going to happen and I can't face it. I might as well be dead too. I can't do this, I can't go on.' Elsa practically shoved her sister out of the way and stumbled towards the road. *Am I really that strong?* Elsa asked herself. *Am I brave enough to end it all now?*

With Jenny's help, Maggie had followed Mrs Milton out of the bank and although she didn't see what happened next, she heard enough of the exchange between the old lady and Kathy to follow the heartbreaking drama as it unfolded. It was the fear in Kathy's voice and the shocked gasps around her that warned Maggie that Mrs Milton might be about to do something drastic.

'Elsa,' Maggie called, her voice deceptively calm

and her tone authoritative. 'Come back inside the bank. Please think about the baby.'

There was a heart-stopping pause and even though Maggie couldn't see that Mrs Milton was about to step off the pavement she heard the choked cry from the old lady as she lost her footing and stumbled into the road.

Maggie could only listen on helplessly to the screech of brakes and the ensuing chaos. Her only comfort, if it could be called that, was that the thud she heard before the car juddered to a stop had been Mrs Milton hitting the ground and not the thump of flesh hitting metal.

Maggie's breathing was no longer coming out in shuddering gasps but her body was still shaking as she accompanied Mrs Milton on the fraught ambulance ride to the hospital. In the mêlée that had followed the accident, Kathy had had the presence of mind to go back to the salon and fetch a few of Maggie's essentials, the most important being Harvey who had returned from his roving. He hadn't left Maggie's side since and as she sat on a small seat at the back of the ambulance the dog leant against her leg, the shivers coursing through his body barely distinguishable from her own.

The ambulance had arrived quickly enough but it had seemed like an age as Maggie comforted Elsie as best she could at the side of the road. Jenny was a trained first aider and assured her that there were no obvious signs of trauma and that Mrs Milton had a strong pulse but she couldn't explain why the old lady remained completely unresponsive.

A friendly paramedic had introduced himself as Ronnie and he too confirmed that Mrs Milton's vital signs were strong. But until Mrs Milton was conscious and aware of her surroundings and, perhaps more importantly, aware of who she was, only then would Maggie allow herself to relax.

'Mrs Milton, can you squeeze my hand for me?' Ronnie was saying as the ambulance swayed from side to side.

'Still no response,' he told Maggie. 'There's no sign of concussion but she'll be thoroughly checked out at the hospital.'

The ambulance rocked as they turned a corner a little too fast. Ronnie cursed under his breath as he stumbled but it was the sound of metal scraping metal that caught Maggie's attention. It was a wedding ring clinking against the handrail of the gurney as someone clamped her hand around it.

Ronnie had noticed too. 'I think you can hear me after all, can't you, Mrs Milton?'

'Elsie? It's Maggie. Are you OK?'

They both waited patiently, unwilling to let their questions be ignored any longer.

'Freddie,' she said with a sigh.

Maggie sighed too but hers was one of relief not regret. The voice had been frail and weak but it was Elsie's voice, not Elsa. Maggie made a move to stand up to be closer to her friend. The vehicle was still rocking but rather than insist she sit back down, Ronnie let Maggie take the seat closest to her friend. He stepped away to let the two women talk.

'It must have been awful for you, to lose him when you needed him most,' Maggie said.

'The worst,' Elsie agreed. 'I've made a bit of a fool of myself again, haven't I?'

'You've made me more in awe of you than ever,' Maggie assured her. 'I can't imagine what it must have been like to be an unmarried mother in the fifties, but from the glimpses you've given me, you were a formidable character.'

'But I wasn't an unmarried mother, was I? I never got the chance to be a mum to my Tess.'

Maggie's smile was tinged with sadness as another layer of Elsa's past was revealed. At last Maggie had the confirmation she had been longing to hear: the baby was as real as Freddie had been. 'You had a little girl and you called her Tess,' she said, more as a statement than a question. 'And you were and always will be her mother.'

'I failed her.'

'You've come back for Tess, haven't you?'

'I might be daft but I know I can't change the past however much I try. I'm a lost cause, Maggie.'

'You are not, you're an inspiration.'

'Now I know you're lying,' chided Elsie. 'All I really wanted was to return to that bench in the park, to remember all that I'd lost and to find some peace. Not a day's gone by without me thinking about that place and everything that happened.'

It was a simple wish and one that Maggie understood better than most. She knew exactly what it was like to sit at the side of the lake and reconnect with the past but for Elsie, her visits to Victoria Park had been far from peaceful. 'Even though it's so very painful?'

'Yes. If I had a friend sitting next to me I'm sure I'd be safe. We just need to convince that husband of mine. Where is he?' Elsie groaned as she tried to pull herself up into a sitting position but Ronnie was quick to step in.

'Oh, no you don't, young lady. You lie still until the doctors have said it's OK for you to get up.'

'Another charmer,' Elsie said. 'I should warn you I have a thing for men in uniform.'

He was grinning as he said, 'I always knew these bright green overalls would be irresistible to women. It's what drew me to the job.'

The banter was brought to an abrupt end as the ambulance pulled up outside the Accident and Emergency Department. Maggie was beginning to feel calmer but as she stepped out into the fresh air her legs trembled, a reminder of the shock her own body had been through. She was ushered into a waiting area while Elsie was taken through to be examined. Maggie needed to phone Jenny and let her know what was happening in case Ted had been found but first she needed to sit down and let her mind settle.

She rested a hand on Harvey's head as he sat patiently and watched, her mind turning. Elsie was going to be fine, physically at least, and with that initial fear laid to rest, Maggie let her thoughts wander a little further into the past. She could still hear the pain etched in Elsa's voice as she relived the moment she had discovered how Freddie had been taken from her, knowing that one day her baby would be taken too.

Elsie had said she hoped to find peace but Maggie recalled an earlier conversation where she had suggested she was also punishing herself. Maggie couldn't help wondering if what Elsie really wanted was the one thing she felt she didn't deserve and so hadn't been able to voice. Could a child given up for adoption in 1953 be traced? Could Tess be found quickly enough for Mrs Milton to have the presence of mind to find some kind of resolution and, more importantly, could Maggie be the one to give Elsa her happy ending?

The afternoon began to fade into evening but Maggie had no thoughts of going home. She had been sitting in the waiting room for so long that her back had seized up and her only break from the monotony had been to take Harvey outside to relieve himself and find him a drink of water. The fresh air had been a welcome contrast to the sterile environment that drained the hospital of any colour. But it was only a brief respite and she had quickly resumed her vigil.

Ted had eventually been tracked down and Maggie had spoken to him only briefly. He had been busy in the garden that morning, only realising that Elsie had vanished when he came in for a break. His first instinct had been to go to Victoria Park and it was only when he couldn't find her there that he had started to panic. On his way back to the High Street he had bumped into Alice Bowden. She had not only told him what was happening but had been good enough to enlist the help of one of her sons to take Ted directly to the hospital; he had been in no fit state to drive himself.

'Come on, Maggie, I'm taking you home.'

James had appeared from nowhere and the sound of his voice made Maggie start. She had already phoned to warn him that she intended to stay as long as she was needed, but if she had been under the illusion that he had arrived to keep her company, she was quickly corrected. James hooked his hand under her elbow and gently coaxed her to her feet. It wasn't an easy task. Maggie's stubborn mind and her stiffened body protested, but James wasn't taking no for an answer.

'I can't leave without seeing Ted first, if only to let him know that I'm going,' she said. 'He might need me to fetch some of Elsie's things.'

'I thought you said Alice was already doing that?'

Her delaying tactics had been exposed but Maggie was undeterred. 'Ted's here on his own, he might need something.'

'I don't think either Mr or Mrs Milton will expect you to wait here all night. Please, Maggie, if not for yourself then what about Harvey? He must be starving.'

Harvey heard his name and when he whined in agreement, Maggie knew she had been beaten. 'For Harvey's sake then.'

Her first steps were tentative as her body adjusted to an upright position but no sooner had their pace quickened than James stopped them all in their tracks.

'I think someone's trying to catch your attention,' he said. 'It's an elderly gent, so I presume it's your Mr Milton.'

Maggie heard Ted walk slowly and heavily towards them. 'Hello, Maggie,' he said, sounding not only tired but utterly despondent. Maggie imagined a frail old man standing in front of her rather than the surly husband who was Elsie's rock.

'How's she doing? Will they need to keep her in?'

'Yes, but only for observation, thank God. The doctor doesn't think she's done herself any real harm,' Ted said.

'Can I see her?'

'She's being moved up to a ward at the moment.'

'We can wait, can't we, James?'

Maggie wasn't asking her husband's permission

but he answered as if she had. 'I really think you need to go home and rest, Maggie. You need to take care of yourself too. I'm Maggie's husband, James, by the way,' he added, having given up waiting for Maggie to make formal introductions. 'I've heard a lot about you and your wife and I'm only sorry we have to meet under these circumstances.'

'Pleased to meet you,' Ted replied as the two of them shook hands.

'We could come back in later then,' Maggie insisted. 'If there's anything you want me to fetch from home, we could pick it up on the way.'

Ted cleared his throat. 'I'd rather you didn't.'

'I'll come in first thing tomorrow then,' she said, almost stumbling over her words in her eagerness to help. 'Will they let me visit so early do you think?'

'No,' he said. Ted's shoes squeaked against the linoleum tiles as he shifted uncomfortably.

'Of course not; it's afternoon visiting, isn't it? I'll phone in the morning then and if she's being discharged, I could always call around when you're home and check if you need anything.'

'I'm sorry, Maggie, but I think it's best if you don't,' Ted said.

Maggie's innate ability to read people by the tone of their voice hadn't failed her; she had registered Mr Milton's unease, she knew what he was trying to tell her, she simply refused to acknowledge it. 'You're right, I should leave her to rest for a couple of days,' she said.

Ted had no alternative but to make his point bluntly. 'No, Maggie; I'm sorry but I'd rather you didn't see her at all. I know you mean well, and I know you and Elsie have been developing a bond that, in other circumstances, she would really enjoy. But for some reason, when you're together, it only strengthens that connection she has with the past, opens up old wounds when they should be left to heal.'

'Those wounds have been open for sixty years, Ted. I know it must be hard for you to hear her talk about Freddie but you must realise that her pregnancy isn't a figment of her imagination. She wants me to take her to the park. She wants to go back to a time when she was closest to her baby.'

'Tess, you mean?'

Maggie felt awash with relief. After stubbornly refusing to acknowledge the baby's existence, Ted was even willing to say her name – she was winning the argument. 'Yes and I've been thinking about that. What if Elsie didn't have to rely on memories, what if we could find her daughter? It might help.'

'It won't mend her,' Ted answered. His voice was leaden.

'But—' Maggie started.

'No, Maggie! After everything that's happened today, I'm more convinced than ever that the only way to help Elsie is to bury the past, not rake up old ghosts. I'm sorry but my mind's made up.' His voice finally cracked with emotion when he

218

saw the tears welling in Maggie's eyes and his hardened shell showed signs of weakening, but he wasn't about to break his resolve. 'Elsie's getting worse with each passing day. The drugs the doctors have given her are too little, too late. There's nothing I can do other than protect her from herself the best way I can. I hope you'll understand why I'm doing this.'

Maggie couldn't agree to that. She wanted to be there for Elsie, and she wanted to be there for Elsa too. It took all of her strength to nod her agreement.

'Is there *anything* we can do to help?' James asked.

Maggie took comfort from the strength in her husband's voice and the arm that had slipped around her waist. 'Even from a distance,' she added.

'I appreciate the offer, really I do, but right now I have to prove to everyone that I can manage. Yvonne's on her way down from Scotland and I've promised that we'll sit down and talk through the options. I already know what she'll say but I'll grow eyes in the back of my head if I have to. I won't have her going into some care home.'

'Whatever you decide to do, I'm sure you'll make the decisions that are best for your wife, as difficult as they may be,' James said.

'I know I'm being greedy but fifty-eight years with my Elsie isn't nearly long enough. It's a cruel thing, to see the woman you've loved for all that time disappearing right in front of you, layer by layer.'

'She's still there,' Maggie said, putting aside her own feelings so she could concentrate on easing the pain of the man who had devoted his life to his wife. 'It may be hard to find her sometimes . . .'

'Literally,' Ted said with a brave attempt at a smile if not a laugh.

'But she's still there and she's still the woman you married. I'll agree to stay away, Ted, but only on the condition that you don't stay away from me. I promised Elsie I'd look after you too. I'm here whenever you need me. We both are, aren't we, James?'

James agreed and he meant it. He was seeing first hand why Maggie had been so determined to help these relative strangers. Amongst the maelstrom of emotions building inside her, Maggie recognised a thin shred of relief that she no longer had to fear Elsa's fate alone.

As they left the hospital, the little light that Maggie's vision allowed pushed away her darker thoughts. Her head was held high and her shoulders pulled back as she let the warm air ease her tensed muscles and the knot in her stomach. She didn't dare think about Mrs Milton's future, even less so her past. Her friend was safe for the moment and that would have to be enough; she could do no more.

'Are you OK?' James asked, as Maggie stood motionless while he put Harvey into the back of the car.

'I'll survive. If nothing else it's reminded me how fortunate I am despite all my complaining. Are you OK?' she questioned, having detected a reflection of her pain in her husband's voice.

James didn't respond but finished what he was doing and then came to Maggie's side. He raised his hands to her face and wiped away the ghostly trail of her tears. 'I will be. All I want now is to go home and hold my wife and thank my lucky stars that I can.'

CHAPTER 13

'You don't have to say anything, I know what you're thinking,' Maggie said. She didn't need to be told not to wallow in self-pity and she really was trying to fight against it but it was getting so hard to ignore the invisible weight pressing down on her chest.

She leaned back to make herself more comfortable but the hard surface of the bench didn't meet the curve of her spine as well as it should. Her back was still aching from spending so much time at the hospital the day before and now her feet ached too after a morning in the salon. In fact, everything ached, her heart included.

Harvey stood up in the vain hope that her fidgeting was a precursor to getting up but Maggie didn't have anywhere else to go. When it didn't happen, he sat back down with a disgruntled snort. She consoled him with a pat on the head. 'Sorry, boy, we could be here a while.'

Maggie started to say something else but a sigh escaped before her words had formed. She tried again. 'I thought I was strong, an independent woman who could be a good wife and daughter and a reliable friend, but lately I've been failing on all counts. I can't help Jenny, I've shipped Dad off to another country, I let Liam and Sam down, and I've been giving James such a hard time about his mum. What if he falls out with her because of me?'

When Maggie stopped berating herself it wasn't because she had run out of failings to list, but because there was still one left that hurt most of all.

'What if Ted was right and I have made matters worse for Elsie? And God forbid, what if Judith's right too? What if I can't care for my baby properly? Have I been fooling myself? Is it time to accept that I can't be everything I want to be or achieve everything I want to achieve?' She raised her hand to ward off the response. 'Don't answer that! Of course you'd say I can still do anything I set my mind to but not everyone believes in me the way you do, me included. I've tried, but I have to face facts. The only reason I managed to be so strong and independent was because you were there helping me, which is kind of a contradiction in terms, don't you think? And there lies my problem. You're not there any more, are you, Mum?'

Maggie's body sagged and she had to put her hands out to support herself, only to recoil from the cold touch of smooth, varnished wood. There were no memories to be drawn from the surface of this bench. Her mum had never sat next to her here. She was lying six feet under the ground in front of her.

Covering her face with her hands, Maggie pushed her fingers against her eyes, forcing back the tears. She wouldn't cry. That would be letting her mum down completely. She strained her ears, still waiting for an answer to her questions from beyond the grave but the only sound came from a more earthly source. The approaching footsteps belonged to someone with a long and powerful stride. A man, she guessed. Harvey jumped up and his tail began to wag ferociously. *Her* man, she corrected.

'Playing truant?' she asked.

'I decided to give myself the afternoon off,' James said. He swept his hand under her chin and, lifting her face towards him, kissed her gently on the lips.

'That's not like you.'

James sat down next to her and she heard the rustle of a paper bag being set to one side. 'I missed my wife. Nothing unusual in that,' he said, wrapping his arm around her and pulling her close.

She rested her head on his shoulder. 'So how did you find me?'

'Kathy told me you were avoiding the park so this was my next best guess.'

Maggie had walked around rather than through the park that morning to reach the High Street. It wasn't that she was afraid of bumping into Elsie and breaking her promise to Ted – Elsie would still be in hospital. It was for reasons she barely knew how to express. She felt something akin to betrayal by, of all things, the park itself. It had been the place where she not only felt safe and secure but connected to the people who meant the most to her, even though they weren't there any more. Elsie had made similar if not stronger connections but rather than bring her comfort, their beloved bench had been complicit in her self-inflicted torment. Ted was right, it might be what Elsie wanted but it was never going to help her. Was it possible to feel anger against an inanimate object? She knew she had no rational justification for her feelings and yet still she responded to them. Her surrogate bench was a poor substitute but with James's arrival, she would find comfort in the present rather than the past.

'So what's in the bag?' Maggie asked.

'First I have a confession. I wasn't in work this morning either.'

Maggie raised an eyebrow. The tone of his voice was soothing, the steady rhythm of his breath calm. His confession held the promise of some-thing good. 'So why did you act like you were? What have you been up to, Mr Carter?' It was only now that she noticed that the usual smells of acrid dust and sweat from heavy labour were absent. The aromas she could detect, however, were familiar, just not on James. She sniffed the air to let him know that he had been caught out. 'What have you been up to?' she said again.

'I've been letting you down lately and I know I've got to take more responsibility for resolving things with Mum,' he started.

Maggie's breath caught in her throat. 'What have you done?'

James laughed. 'Nothing yet, not about Mum at least; this has nothing to do with her. I suppose it has more to do with your Mrs Milton.'

'Yesterday really got to you, didn't it?'

James pulled away from her to retrieve the bag he had set to one side and then handed it over. 'This is my way of telling you I'm sorry. I know I'm too soft for my own good and this probably only goes to prove the point but I don't care and . . . well, please stop me talking, Maggie, and open the present.'

Maggie prolonged James's agony a little longer by exploring the shape of the gift bag rather than delving straight in. It was roughly the size of a carrier bag and had an embossed picture of a teddy bear on one side. There were curls of ribbon attached to the handle.

She wanted to savour the moment. A rift had been growing between them and they had already started to bridge that gap with words and promises but so far there had been a distinct lack of action. This felt different. It was a ground shift and the chasm didn't feel so deep or so wide.

Slowly, Maggie slipped her hand inside the bag and removed three separately wrapped gifts. She couldn't decide which to open first. 'What are they?' she asked. They were similar in size, flat and oblong. From their weight and softness, she guessed they had something to do with the baby.

'You'll have to open them to find out.'

Peeling back the paper of her first parcel, Maggie discovered a plastic Ziploc bag and pulled it open. The scent of roses filled the air and seeped into her senses, painting them pink. She lifted out a Babygro. It was impossibly small and had a scalloped neck with embroidered flowers. 'It's a girl,' she laughed.

'Or . . .' James prompted.

With growing excitement and urgency, Maggie unwrapped the second parcel to find another secret contained within a plastic bag and this time released a clamour of bluebells. 'Or it's a boy,' she said, her words now choked with emotion. 'So what on earth is the third option?'

She didn't wait for an answer but ripped the paper and opened the final gift. Lemon scents were now fighting against those of rosebuds and bluebells so she lifted it to her face. The delicate material felt baby-soft against her skin and, unlike the other two gifts, she knew without doubt that one day her baby would wear the yellow Babygro grasped in her trembling hand.

'I thought I'd cover all angles,' James said.

'And raid my office while you were at it?'

'Guilty as charged.'

Maggie's office was for her use and hers alone, no clients visited there and even James rarely ventured inside. She remembered the first time Judith had seen it. She had been dumbfounded that Maggie used a computer, a skill she had never acquired herself. But Maggie's office wasn't only the place where she kept client records; it was where she experimented with her bottled rainbows. James had shown no more than a passing interest in what went on in there and although she had slowly introduced him to her alternative understanding of colour, this was the first time he had painted her world without supervision and she was stunned.

'You don't want to give up work completely, do you?' he asked when Maggie fell silent.

She thought about it for a while, recalling all the long hours she had put into developing her craft. 'I always thought of my business as my baby. I thought it might be the only one I would ever have,' she said at last. A smile trembled on her lips as she felt the now-familiar flutter of a real baby inside her. 'But now that I'm about to be a mum, I'm beginning to realise that the business was just that, a business. It's not such a big sacrifice; in fact, it's nothing at all.'

'Maybe we could manage. It would be a stretch on the finances but not impossible.'

'Let's assume not, for now at least. And maybe if I do need to find something to make me feel like I'm earning my keep, I could work from home.'

'You don't have to earn your keep, Maggie. I

made a promise to your mum,' he said. They both turned their heads to the grave in front of them as if someone was listening in. 'I told her I'd look after you and that's what I intend to do. If you'll let me.'

The offer hung in the air and as Maggie returned the baby clothes to their respective bags, the colours began to fade. She couldn't be sure if her desire to retain her sense of independence was being driven by determination or desperation. It had come as a shock to her to realise how much of a safety net her mum had been in her life and it hadn't helped that she had vanished from her daughter's life without warning.

Joan had woken up one morning feeling unwell and by the time Stan had returned upstairs with a breakfast tray, a massive heart attack had taken her from them. Maggie dreaded to think what life would be like if James hadn't been in her life, then – but she had yet to accept that he could be a safety net too. She had asked him to take care of the problems with his mum but she hadn't asked him to take care of her. She could feel him tensing as he waited for her to let him in.

'Yes, I'll try,' she said with a smile.

They sat quietly for the longest time, holding on to each other and letting go of the past. It was Harvey who broke the spell. He pushed his nose into the space between them – which was no distance at all.

'How about we take Harvey for a bit of a run?' she suggested.

'The park?'

'Why not?' she asked, and this time she couldn't think of a single reason to stay away.

CHAPTER 14

'The gate's broken again,' James said as he joined Maggie in the garden.

She was making the most of the sun during one of its rare appearances so far that summer, tending to the small herb garden that James had built for her soon after they had moved in. There were slim pickings. The lavender had plenty of buds but the flowers weren't quite ready and the thyme had yet to recover from the harsh winter, its straggling stems too delicate and precious to harvest; but at least the rosemary had grown in abundance and offered some reward. Its velvety green aroma could ease the mind and improve the memory, but for Maggie, the memories it enticed to the surface were far from settling.

Rosemary had been one of the oils she had used on Mrs Milton in her feeble attempts to counter the effects of her Alzheimer's. She wished she could do more but she had been true to her word and had kept away in recent weeks. Elsie had been discharged quickly from hospital but that was as much as she knew. There had been no sightings in the park, not even the faintest scent of lilac.

'And I suppose you're going over there to fix it,' Maggie said. She already knew whose gate he was referring to; the shrill ringtone a few minutes earlier had been unmistakeable. 'I can't believe that with an architect *and* a builder in the family, it hasn't been mended yet.'

'Do you want to come with me?'

'Did your mum invite me?'

James knew how easily she would detect a lie and so tried a half-truth. 'You don't need an invitation. You're my wife.'

Maggie pursed her lips. It was Sunday morning and she had been looking forward to some quality time with her husband. She hadn't seen her in-laws for some time and this could be the perfect opportunity for another attempt to break down Judith's prejudices. On the other hand, James could step up to the plate and have a long talk with his mum. He might decide now was the time to tell her that while she couldn't drive a wedge between husband and wife she might very well strain relations between mother and son. 'I think I'll leave you to it,' she said.

'I won't be long,' he said before bending down to kiss the top of her head.

Left on her own, Maggie refused to let thoughts of Judith pull her down and it didn't take long before she was absorbed in her favourite obsession. And it wasn't only Elsie she was thinking of now, but Tess also. Was it possible that she could be traced? Would Ted ever give his permission to even begin the search? And even if he agreed, if they did find her, would Elsie be well enough by then to recognise her as her baby? And what of the baby herself? Would it be fair to reunite Tess with her birth mother only to lose her all over again?

The debate raged inside Maggie's head until rudely interrupted by a phone ringing from inside the house. In her urgency to answer the call, Maggie stubbed her toe and, gritting her teeth to suppress a cry of pain, she said, 'Hello?'

'Hi, Maggie, it's Carolyn.'

Maggie could feel her hand tingling but the electric current running down the phone line was all in her mind. There had been some lingering animosity between James and his ex-wife when Maggie had started to date him, mostly caused by Carolyn's move to Portsmouth, but that had eventually dissipated. James had even considered inviting her to the wedding but Maggie had said no, citing her mum's recent death as reason enough to keep the day as intimate as possible, but there had been another reason too. As Judith often pointed out, it had been Carolyn's decision to leave James and even though Maggie didn't believe for a minute that James was still Carolyn's for the taking, she was wary of letting her get too close. There was a rivalry between the two, even if Carolyn wasn't aware of it.

'Oh, hi,' Maggie replied as pleasantly as she could. 'James is out at the moment but he shouldn't be long.'

'Never mind. I was only going to check the arrangements for the summer holidays.'

The rash of goose bumps that pricked Maggie's arms had nothing to do with stepping into the cool shade of the kitchen. She had heard the tell-tale signs of someone sidestepping the truth. 'So have you settled on a holiday yet?' she asked, not so eager to end the call any more. Had Carolyn been phoning James as a shoulder to cry on about the state of her marriage? Another, more rational voice reminded her that the only evidence that Carolyn's marriage was in trouble had come from Judith.

'We might be giving it a miss this year,' Carolyn said.

There was an almost imperceptible inflection in her voice that set Maggie's nerves on edge. 'I suppose it's going to be difficult with a new addition to the family,' she said with a forced laugh.

There was a sharp intake of breath. 'Oh, the puppy? Yes, we're picking him up in a couple of weeks, perfect timing for the start of the school holidays.' Carolyn laughed nervously before rambling on. 'I want to enrol him in obedience classes but I think the kids are going to be disappointed when our pup doesn't turn out quite as well-behaved as Harvey.'

When Carolyn finally took a breath, Maggie threw caution to the wind. 'What new addition did you think I meant?'

She could hear Carolyn slow her breathing as

she summoned up the courage to answer honestly. 'It's early days,' she warned. 'And we've not even told the boys yet but I'm pregnant too.'

The knot of suspicion that had been growing in the pit of Maggie's stomach dissolved. The news not only washed away the irrational doubts that had plagued her moments earlier but some of her more deep-seated anxieties. 'Does Judith know?'

'Good grief, no,' Carolyn said. 'Actually, that was why I wanted to speak to James. I wanted to forewarn him.' As difficult as it was to believe now, Carolyn had fallen out of favour quite dramatically with her mother-in-law after she walked out on James. Judith put the blame for their failed marriage squarely on Carolyn's shoulders and relations didn't improve when she remarried and announced she was moving down to Portsmouth. It was only when Maggie appeared on the scene that Judith miraculously mended her bridges with Carolyn; given a choice of daughters-in-law, Carolyn was clearly the lesser of two evils; but Carolyn hadn't forgotten how difficult Judith could be.

'You don't think she'll take it very well, do you?'

'About as well as your news I should think,' Carolyn agreed. In recognising a common foe, the two women formed a tenuous bond. 'On the bright side, she might actually begin to accept that James and I are both happy and settled in our new lives.'

'We can hope,' agreed Maggie, 'although I think

hell will have to freeze over before she accepts that I could make James happy.'

'She is *impossible*. And I know you don't need to hear it from me but you *do* make James happy, far more than I ever could. Why Judith can't see that, I don't know. She's never going to give up on this idea that you trapped him.'

'Trapped him?'

There was silence at the other end of the phone, not even the sound of Carolyn's breathing until she said, 'I'm sorry, I shouldn't have said that. It's just the way Judith is; she has to make the story fit to justify her rigid view of the world. Honestly, when you've had the baby, she'll have no choice but to welcome you with open arms. If I'm honest, she was a bit aloof with me before the kids came along. Anyway, I'd better go, the boys have gone too quiet and that's never a good sign.'

'OK, I'll get James to phone you later then.'

Maggie put the phone down on the kitchen counter and stood still for a moment. There was no sense of shock. Carolyn hadn't exposed Judith: she had simply confirmed Maggie's suspicions about how her mother-in-law's mind worked. Surprisingly there was no surge of anger either, only a wry smile as she imagined what Judith's reaction to the latest baby news would be. Surely now she would have to accept that both James and Carolyn had moved on with their lives.

As Maggie's mood lifted she felt as if she could

overcome any obstacle: and that meant considering doing something she had all but convinced
herself not to do. Rather than return to the garden,
she headed for her office. It was time for some
preliminary research on the adoption process and
how a birth mother might go about tracing a long-
lost child.

CHAPTER 15

'How's the diary looking?' Maggie asked after saying goodbye to her latest client. She leaned against the reception counter as Kathy leafed through her appointments book.

'Busy, busy, busy,' Kathy recited as she turned the pages. 'Right up to the end of August and then . . .' She let the remaining pages in her hand flutter and drop. 'Nothing.'

They were barely halfway through July but Maggie had already started to count off her last days at the salon. She stared down despondently at the pages she couldn't see.

'Don't look so miserable. Most people would be looking forward to taking it easy,' Kathy added when she didn't get the response she wanted.

'Maybe I'm finishing too soon. We have a two-week break with the boys but then there's still six weeks left before the baby's due.'

'No,' Kathy said. 'We discussed this. You want that time to prepare and besides, you could have the baby early and you don't want to be paying rent on a place that you can't use.'

'And it's not like I have to worry about keeping the business going any more,' Maggie added bleakly. She had already surrendered her lease agreement and told Kathy to find a better use for her beloved treatment room. 'Have you found someone else?'

'Not yet,' Kathy said. 'Let's see what tomorrow brings.'

'Tomorrow isn't the problem. Fifteen weeks away, that's the part that worries me.'

'Maggie, I don't doubt for a minute that you'll surprise some people by how good a mum you're going to be but I never thought you'd be one of them. Stop feeling so damned sorry for yourself!'

Maggie should have been shocked by Kathy's tough love but she expected no less from her friend and she was grateful for it. She pulled herself up and let Kathy see a mischievous glint in her eye. 'Maybe I could phone Carolyn and ask for some tips on motherhood.'

'You mean now that she's expecting too?'

Rather than Kathy, Maggie was the one who was shocked. 'Who told you?' she demanded.

'James.'

'When? He didn't say. He hasn't even told his mum yet,' Maggie spluttered. She had told James about her conversation with Carolyn as soon as he had returned home but he was less concerned about the baby news than he was about the idea that his mum thought Maggie had trapped him.

Typical of James, he fumed silently and had avoided speaking to his mum, about anything.

Before Kathy could explain further, the bell above the door jangled and the latest visitor to the salon introduced herself in her own inimitable way.

'I'd know that cough anywhere,' Maggie said as the footsteps drew closer.

'Yes, and I know what you're going to say next,' Alice said. There was another surreptitious cough as she stroked Harvey.

'So have you seen the doctor yet?'

'No.' For a sixty-year-old, Alice made a good impression of a toddler as she ground her foot into the tiled floor.

'Are you busy now?' Maggie asked, picking up the reception phone.

Alice tried not to laugh. 'I came here to make an appointment for a haircut, not a checkup.'

'You can do both,' insisted Maggie. She knew the number from memory and dialled it.

The phone was handed over to Alice who was too stunned to object and the appointment with her GP was made without any further prevarication.

'I'd better go before you railroad me into something else,' Alice muttered and turned to leave.

'Hold on, you haven't seen the Miltons lately, have you?' Maggie said, trying to hide the desperation in her voice for news.

'I've been calling in now and again and things are much the same. Elsie has her moments but nothing like that day at the bank. Whatever happened to her in the past must have been heartbreaking. If it happened at all,' she added quickly.

'I'm sorry,' Kathy said in exasperation. 'I know you want to protect her, but it's too late for Elsie to keep her secrets, they're already out there.'

'But that doesn't mean we can't pretend that they're not, for Elsie's sake,' Alice said sternly, daring Kathy to contradict her. They were old friends who weren't afraid to argue. 'On the positive side, if you can call it that, she's raking up all kinds of other memories. We've worked out that I must have bumped into her a couple of times. After she married Ted, they used to visit her Aunt Flo quite regularly. Yvonne and Nancy would have been a bit younger than me but I can remember playing in the park with two little girls from Liverpool and I'm sure it was them.'

'Wow, really? Do you remember Flo Jackson then? Would you know what happened to her family?' Maggie asked, now wondering if Alice could help with the search for Tess. She had discovered that the search through the adoption agency could be a lengthy process and couldn't even begin until the Miltons agreed. If Maggie could track down Mrs Jackson's niece in the meantime, they would at least be one step ahead and time was of the essence.

'Sorry,' Alice said. 'I knew of her, but she became a bit of a recluse and died sometime in the sixties. Believe it or not, I would have been

241

quite young back then. Like I said, I can only vaguely remember playing with the girls and Yvonne doesn't remember being here at all.'

'You've met her daughter? What's she like?' Kathy asked, jolting them back to the present.

'Very friendly but a bit bossy. Reminded me of you,' Alice added under her breath. 'She only stayed a week but she didn't waste any time. There were all kinds of meetings with doctors, specialists and social workers – the lot. She even took her mum and dad to look at care homes.'

It wasn't the news Maggie wanted to hear. 'Ted thought Yvonne might do that. How did they get on?'

'To be honest, Elsie is more open to the idea than he is because she doesn't want to be a burden. Yvonne suggested they could try it for a few days' respite when things get too much for Ted but he still said no, not while he's got breath in his body. He says he can manage and, with a bit of help, he will.'

'He's lucky to have you.'

'Oh, I live close by so it's no trouble. I only hope that one day someone will do the same for me. In fact, I'm insisting on it. I've got two strapping lads and my daughters-in-law are a blessing. I've already told them that I have every intention of being a burden to them,' she said with a raspy laugh. 'Jack said he could always convert his canal boat into my very own granny flat.'

As Maggie waited for another coughing fit to

ease, a thought occurred to her. 'I'd forgotten Jack had a barge. They're supposed to be a great way to relax, aren't they?'

'They go at a snail's pace so it takes forever getting anywhere but that's the point, it forces you to slow down. I'm sure Jack wouldn't mind if you and James wanted to use it. He loans it out to his friends all the time.'

'James loves boats,' Maggie mused. 'But I'm hoping to take advantage of another friend's generosity for our summer holiday. She has a place in France and has been trying to convince me to go there but the time has never been right.'

'Until now?' Kathy asked, completely taken aback. The place in question was a farmhouse that had belonged to her father as part of his property business. James had been there with Carolyn and that had been reason enough to turn down the offers in the last couple of years but Maggie was beginning to realise that time moves on. And at least if they were abroad James couldn't be called away for emergencies at work.

'We were thinking about it, if you didn't mind and it's available?'

'Of course I don't mind! It's yours.'

'Well, it looks like I've been outbid,' Alice agreed. 'But the offer still stands if ever you need a short break.'

Maggie couldn't hide a mischievous smile; her meddling wasn't over yet. 'Do you think you could extend that offer to someone else? It's Jenny who could really do with a break right now. I don't mind paying Jack, it could be my early birthday present to her.'

'You will not pay! I'll let Jack know to expect a call and the two of you can sort out the details.'

Eventually Maggie released Alice from her clutches but it would be hours later before anyone realised that she had left without making the hair appointment she had come in for. Maggie for one was too distracted making plans for Jenny and Mark. Assuming Jack agreed, she would have the time and place, which only left the small matter of persuading the troubled couple to go away together, not to mention explaining to James that they would be babysitting Lily for a whole weekend. But other than that, it was all planned.

'That's what I like to see,' Kathy said.

'And what would that be?'

'The old you.'

Maggie knew exactly what Kathy meant and she had James to thank more than anyone. By giving him permission to take care of her, she now felt secure enough to take care of other people, including someone else's baby.

'And since you're in the mood for accepting invitations, I'd like to invite you to a bit of a do I'm having next week. It's my birthday,' Kathy said.

Kathy's voice had given nothing away but Maggie's instinct told her there was something afoot. 'I thought you didn't celebrate birthdays? Are you planning something special?'

'Yes.'

'So why am I starting to suspect I won't like it?'

'I can't imagine,' sniffed Kathy. 'I was wondering if you could be persuaded to forego your usual lunch in the park and come over to my place for a bit of a girlie afternoon.'

'Just the two of us or were you planning on inviting more girlies?' Maggie barely suppressed a smile as her mind made huge leaps and bounds. Kathy knew how desperate she was to catch up with Elsie, perhaps . . .

'You, me and Judith.'

Somewhere in the salon, a tray clattered to the floor but it could easily have been the sound of Maggie's jaw hitting the counter.

CHAPTER 16

As Maggie knocked on the heavy wooden door, she breathed in the scent of lilacs. As always it evoked thoughts of Elsa but on this occasion the fragrance was completely natural and had floated across from the garden. She had forgotten Kathy had lilac trees and as she waited for the door to be answered, she wondered if it was too late in the season to extract some oils from the flowers in the same way Mrs Jackson once had to make her soap.

Kathy swung the door open wide. 'I hope you're hungry,' she said.

Harvey sniffed the air in anticipation. 'She didn't mean you,' Maggie warned as they were ushered into the house. She was hoping to be the first to arrive to give her a little extra time to get her bearings. She knew the house well enough but even a subtle change in the layout of furniture could lead to jarred limbs and stubbed toes and she would rather make those painful mistakes without Judith's pitying gaze.

Carefully wiping her feet on the thick bristles of the welcome mat, Maggie stepped into the cavernous entrance hall. Then her heels clicked against porcelain tiles and echoed through the house. Her first visit had been eight years earlier and while her initial impression had been that of a substantial home, it would be James's later descriptions that had given it the grandeur it deserved. It was a large Georgian villa, three storeys high, four if you included the basement. Many of the features were original, including the black-and-white tiled floor she was now standing on. James was called upon now and again to keep the place from falling into disrepair and it was as much a labour of love for him as it was for Kathy and Joe. It had been the couple's family home for the last thirty years or so, but now their children had families of their own, it had become what Kathy lovingly termed 'a money pit'.

'I can't believe you're finally giving it up,' Maggie said as she breathed in her surroundings. Beneath the pungent aroma of garlic and herbs wafting through from the kitchen there was a distinctive old house smell. She picked up the scent of dried-out wallpaper sealing in decades of history.

'There are some rooms I don't go in from one month to the next,' Kathy explained, 'and when I do it's only to air them or check that the ceiling hasn't caved in. It was an easy enough decision to take, in the end, and we've already had a few enquiries about renting it out.'

'Another addition to the family portfolio?' Maggie remarked without a hint of envy. She had no idea how many properties Kathy's dad had acquired over the years but she'd gathered that it had given his wife quite a headache when she had been forced to take over the business when he died. At close to ninety, Kathy's mum was a wily business-woman, by all accounts, but had finally accepted that she couldn't go on forever. It was her daughter who would be picking up the slack now and although it was clear who Kathy had inherited her work ethic from, she was going to need more hours in the day to cope with it all.

'This house always was part of Dad's portfolio, as was the salon, but if I had my way the only other property I'd keep is the farmhouse in France. You'll know why when you go over there,' Kathy said as she led Maggie and Harvey into the living room.

The smell of an astringent perfume stung the back of Maggie's sinuses and gave her the advance warning she needed to paint on a smile as Judith spoke.

'James said you were going to France. The boys will be so excited. They've had some lovely summers there – Ken and I went along with them one year.'

While Judith was reminiscing about the good old days, Maggie worked her way around to the far side of the living room. By the time she took a seat opposite her mother-in-law, her smile had become more of a grimace.

'As I recall, you complained that the house was

a bit too rough-and-ready for your high standards,' Kathy said. 'It's worse than ever now. Just in case you were dropping hints about going too.'

The tightness of the false smile on Judith's face made her reply sound all the more clipped. 'I wasn't thinking any such thing,' she said but then clasped her hands as a thought struck her. 'Why don't you invite Carolyn and her husband along, Maggie? I know it sounds a bit unconventional but stranger things happen these days. She could help out with some of the practicalities and the children would love it, I'm sure.'

Maggie's mouth opened and closed like a stranded fish as she struggled to find an appropriate response that didn't involve expletives.

'I'm toasting up some paninis for lunch, nothing special,' Kathy interrupted. 'And I know it's early but how about a glass of wine, Judith? Imagine you're a teenager again, sagging school and drinking in the middle of the day.'

Judith's reluctant refusal was left hanging in the air but Kathy wouldn't be deterred. 'I've got some pretend wine for you too, Maggie. I'll be two minutes.'

Silence filled the space that Kathy left behind her. Maggie still didn't trust herself to speak.

'So what do you think?' Judith asked, oblivious to the tension building around them. 'Shall I ask her or would it be better coming from James?'

Maggie wasn't known for her patience and the little she possessed had been stretched to its limits.

She could almost hear it snap. 'I don't think *anyone* should be suggesting it, Judith,' she said firmly. 'Carolyn has her life and we have ours. The boys are used to the arrangements and I don't think going on holiday together would be at all helpful, especially when there are going to be so many changes for them. I'd rather we took Liam and Sam on our own so we can reinforce their security, not threaten it.' A flush rose to Maggie's cheeks. She had only just stopped herself from telling Judith about Carolyn's pregnancy because she knew it wasn't her place to say anything.

'It was only a suggestion. I thought it might help, given how we've ended up where we are.'

'And where exactly is that?'

Judith bristled at the sharp tone of Maggie's voice. 'Truthfully? I can't help thinking that bringing a new baby into the family right now will do more harm than good. I know James tries to please everyone but he should have talked you out of it, for the sake of the boys.'

'I'm not denying that it will take time for them to adjust but I think with enough support and reassurance they'll come to love their new siblings.'

'Plural? Oh, don't tell me you're planning more?'

'Not me,' Maggie said, now that she had been backed into a corner – or at least that was how she would explain it to James later.

'Sorry?'

'I'm not the only one fulfilling my maternal needs. You do know Carolyn's pregnant too, don't you?' Maggie didn't wait for the answer. 'We're all moving on with our lives, Judith, and maybe it's time you did too.'

'I can't believe it! What on earth is she thinking of?'

'As I recall, you asked the same thing of me and James,' Maggie replied. 'And I'd say Carolyn thinks the same as I do, that having a child with the man you love couldn't be more natural.'

'But things have been so strained between them.'

'Clearly not any more,' Maggie said, only just stopping herself from suggesting that any strain that Judith had observed in Carolyn's relationship with her husband might have had something to do with the proximity of her ex-mother-in-law.

'Having a baby doesn't mend a marriage, it adds to the pressure,' Judith countered.

'It can also cement relationships that are strong enough to take that extra pressure.'

'And you think you have that kind of relationship?' It was framed as a question but Judith was challenging what she saw as Maggie's misplaced confidence in her marriage.

'Why don't you tell me what kind of relationship James and I have,' she answered, deftly avoiding the trap of extolling the virtues of her marriage only to have Judith dismiss them one by one.

With her heart hammering against her chest, Maggie realised the time had come for an uncensored exchange of views. She was absolutely terrified but also felt such a sense of exhilaration that it stopped her from holding back or worrying about the consequences: she only wished she'd had the courage to do it sooner.

'Maggie, you're a strong-minded woman and I don't blame you for wanting the security of a marriage—'

'You mean you don't blame me for trapping James?' interjected Maggie.

'I'm only thinking of my own family!' Judith said, by way of an explanation. 'My grandchildren have been through enough and all I want is for them to be happy and secure.'

'And you think the only way that can happen is for James and Carolyn to get back together, don't you? You're willing both marriages to fail so that they can be one big happy family again.'

'I should never have stopped James from moving down to Portsmouth. He loved Carolyn and he didn't want to let her go. I tried to convince him to move on with his life but when he turned to you on the rebound I realised what a mistake I'd made. I'm genuinely sorry that you've been dragged into this, Maggie. Really I am.'

'I don't want your pity, Judith. All I want is for you to give me a chance.'

Judith didn't even acknowledge Maggie's heartfelt plea. 'It's my fault entirely – I know that. I'm just trying to put things right.'

'If this is your way of putting things right, Judith, then God help us all.' Kathy was standing at the door where she had been listening for some time.

Maggie had heard her return and was wondering when she would re-join the conversation. Although her tone was forthright, her voice crackled with emotion. 'Apart from Liam and Sam, Maggie is the best thing that ever happened to James. He was never this happy or content with Carolyn and it amazes me that you can't see that. What you're trying to do now is unforgiveable and I won't keep quiet any more. Maggie's carrying your grandchild and he or she has as much right to your protection as the boys! Do you want another grandchild dragged into the middle of a divorce? Shouldn't you be doing your damnedest to make sure this marriage works instead of trying to sabotage it? I thought you were better than that.'

Judith sniffed the air. 'Is this why you invited me here? To gang up on me?'

'Get over yourself, Judith. I brought you here because you are my oldest friend and I brought Maggie here because she's one of my dearest friends. I respect you both immensely but I'm officially too old now to put up with any more nonsense. Judith,' Kathy said, her tone assuming that of a lawyer about to present the case for the prosecution, 'Maggie is the first to accept that there are things that she can't do but she *more* than makes up for it with the things that she can do because she does them better than most. *You* on the other hand have only been willing to see her limitations and how they might limit your son's life. It's time to give up on this stupid idea that James is toying with Maggie's affections while he waits for Carolyn to come back to him. That idea is so flawed, it's laughable – and as much as I love laughing at you, Judith, this is breaking my heart.' As if to make the point, Kathy's voice broke at the last.

Judith sounded as if she was about to respond but Kathy hadn't finished. Harvey whined and tried to squeeze himself into the gap between the chair and Maggie's legs, as if he knew the battle was far from over.

'Maggie,' Kathy said, beginning her case for the defence, 'as hard as it is to believe right now, your mother-in-law is actually a very nice person when you get to know her. She can be manipulative but it's usually to someone else's advantage, or at least that's how she justifies it to herself. But you can be manipulative too – you had Alice eating out of the palm of your hand the other day, remember?' She didn't wait for a response. 'Judith is also tenacious, especially when she thinks she's protecting her family, but once she's willing to consider the possibility that you and James are meant to be together, when she realises that you're her family too, then I promise you she is going to be one serious ally in your life. I had hoped that once you told her you were pregnant she would have worked it all out for herself but don't give up. When she sets eyes on her newest grandchild, her heart will melt. If it hasn't already withered and died, that is.'

Judith snorted and Maggie prepared herself for another derisive comment but when Judith spoke,

Maggie caught a glimpse of the woman that Kathy clearly admired. 'I still have a heart,' she said. It wasn't a challenge, but rather a promise.

Maggie felt Judith's gaze on her and had to fight the urge to run. She didn't want to be judged and she certainly didn't want to face rejection again. Was it too much to hope that her mother-in-law was looking at her with new eyes, seeing past her prejudices? Maggie sensed her acceptance was within touching distance. She was surprised by how much she wanted it and her pulse raced as she said, 'I know I'm not the wife you had in mind for James and it's clear you don't like me but I swear I didn't trap him. I fell in love with your son and he fell in love with me. And our marriage is going to work because I love him too much to see him go through another break-up. It would destroy him – and that would destroy me too.' Maggie ran out of breath and gasped for air, determined to carry on as if her life depended on it. 'If I'm being brutally honest, then the biggest strain on our marriage so far hasn't been my disability but your inability to accept me. You called me strong-minded but that isn't how I've felt recently, far from it,' she confessed and her next words were laced with the kind of emotion she hadn't been prepared to reveal to anyone, least of all her mother-in-law. 'Your opinion matters to me, Judith, because it matters to James, and your rejection of me, my baby, and everything my marriage stands for has pushed me to the brink of despair. So much so that I would have gladly jumped into the lake in Victoria Park and let it swallow me up whole!' When Maggie spoke again it was in the barest of whispers. 'That's how worthless I felt. That's how you made me feel.'

There was the sound of tears being swallowed back as emotions got the better of everyone in the room.

'I never meant to . . .'

Maggie pulled her shoulders back; she wasn't going to be a willing victim any more.

'I'm not expecting things to change overnight but I would like to try. Yes, Kathy's right, I can be manipulative but I promise you my affection for your son is genuine. And I should warn you that you don't have a monopoly on being tenacious. I came close to giving up but I won't do that again. I'll fight for my marriage and my family.'

Maggie's pulse thumping against her eardrums was deafening and she almost didn't hear Judith's reply when it came.

'For the record, I don't dislike you, Maggie. If anything, I'm a little scared of you.'

'Scared?'

'You can be quite . . . intimidating,' Judith said, but then corrected herself. 'No, perhaps I mean forthright. When I first met you, I didn't know how to react and I could see your mum watching and judging me. Now she *was* intimidating.'

Maggie could recall that first meeting. James had arranged a family gathering with both sets of parents and the boys. Joan and Stan had the upper hand because they had already met James and had welcomed him with open arms. Joan expected Judith to welcome Maggie with equal enthusiasm and when it wasn't immediately forthcoming, she had been furious.

'And that's where the battle lines were drawn,' Maggie concluded. 'Do you think there's a chance we could start again?'

'I'd like to try.' Judith spoke hesitantly, as if somewhere in her mind new beginnings were forming. 'It would be nice to have a little girl in the family, don't you think?'

A shiver travelled down Maggie's spine. 'I can't promise you a girl,' she said, talking over the sound of Kathy blowing her nose, 'but I can promise you a grandchild who will need a nana. You're the only one he or she has.'

'James is an amazing dad.'

'And he's a devoted son,' Maggie said. 'And I don't want our relationship to give him anything to worry about.' She had chosen her words carefully, not wanting to apportion blame and reopen the argument. 'If we can get this right then maybe we'd all be a lot happier.'

There was a moment's pause as both women reflected on what had passed between them. The ground had shifted beneath their feet and they both needed time to steady themselves. Kathy, on the other hand, had no such problems adjusting. 'There, that's settled then,' she said.

'You always were an interfering so-and-so,' Judith accused her.

'Me?'

'You!'

'Definitely a case of the pot calling the kettle black,' Kathy said.

Maggie bit her lip but she couldn't hold back her smile any longer, even as her heart still raced. 'Is this what you two were like at school?'

'Yes,' they said in unison.

'I think I can smell burning,' Maggie said, detecting the first signs that the paninis were officially warmed up.

'Damn,' Kathy said. 'Quick, here's that wine you didn't want, Judith.'

There was the sound of sloshing as a glass was quickly handed over. Maggie could hear Judith taking a generous gulp as Kathy gave Maggie her own drink. 'I think we've finally worn her into submission,' she whispered loudly before scuttling off towards the kitchen.

'Maybe you *could* come with us to France,' Maggie suggested bravely.

Judith laughed softly. 'Kathy's right. It is a bit too rough-and-ready for me. But thank you for asking, I do appreciate it.'

The smell of melted cheese and garlic filled the room. 'And would it be too rough-and-ready to eat off your knees?' Kathy asked as she placed a large tray on the coffee table in the centre of the room. 'We haven't used the dining room in months and it's a bit musty in there.'

Without asking, Kathy had placed some food on

a plate and handed it to Maggie, avoiding the need for her to ask for assistance. Between them, they were breaking down Judith's prejudices, but eliminating them altogether was going to take more than a firm talking-to.

'You should get James to look at it if you think there's rising damp,' Maggie said.

'I suppose he does owe me a favour now I've sorted out the two of you,' Kathy said, sounding more than willing to call it in.

'How are you getting on with finding a new place, then?' Judith asked.

'We're almost ready to make an offer on a house we've seen. It has a lovely little granny flat and it's not too far from Nantwich. Mum will still be able to see her friends which means there's absolutely no reason for her to object.'

'I think you're really brave taking her on. If you think we're bossy, Maggie, you should have seen Kathy's mum in her heyday.'

Maggie smiled. It was the first time she had noticed Judith making a reference to her 'seeing' something without getting all flustered.

'That's why I have every intention of carrying on working at the salon,' Kathy said. 'It's going to be a tall order with all the extra property management stuff but I'm planning on getting extra help and besides, I don't mind keeping busy. Unlike you, you part-timer.'

'I'm still at the charity shop three days a week,' Judith reminded her, 'but I make no apologies for slowing down a gear and at least *I'm* not afraid of getting old. I can't wait until I get my free bus pass. Eighteen months and counting,' she joked.

'Which you can use to take your newest grandchild out on little trips when the time comes,' Kathy added, less afraid than Maggie of reopening old wounds.

'We've already agreed that James and I won't impose on Judith and Ken's well-deserved retirement.'

'Oh, we'll see,' replied Judith with a smile. 'It has to be better than making my chores stretch across the whole day. Although on the bright side, at least none of my rooms get musty.'

'I thought it was too good to last. Being polite just isn't in her nature,' Kathy explained to Maggie.

With all the excitement, Maggie had almost forgotten why they had been invited, or at least the reason Kathy had used for bringing them together. 'Now I know you didn't want any fuss,' she said when the food had been cleared away and wine glasses topped up. 'But I can't let the occasion pass without some kind of offering. Here, it's nothing much but I hope you like it. Happy birthday, Kathy.'

Maggie passed over a gift bag and there were mutterings of disapproval but a gasp of delight when Kathy unwrapped a handmade plaque. It was a solid piece of oak that had been cut to form the shape of four letters. 'The wood is from the old back gate James replaced for you the other month,' Maggie said. 'He cut out the shape for me and I just sanded it down and added some finishing touches.'

Kathy breathed in the smell of the aged oak, which had been polished with linseed oil and a hint of ylang-ylang for good measure. 'Home,' she said, reading the plaque. There was a tremor in her voice.

'I thought it might be nice to take with you when you move.'

'This is Braille, isn't it?' Kathy asked. 'Hold on, this bit says Kathy, am I right?'

Maggie had carefully applied tiny metal studs along the outer edges of the plaque and although Kathy couldn't read Braille, she had learnt enough from Maggie to recognise the letters of her own name. 'It's your name, along with Joe's and the kids'. The people you shared this house with.'

'It's beautiful,' Judith added. 'And so thoughtful of you, Maggie.'

'That's Maggie all over,' Kathy said, gushing with pride.

'I'm beginning to see that.' Judith cleared her throat and put down her drink. 'Now if you'll excuse me, I need to use the powder room.'

'I can't believe I just invited Judith to France with us,' Maggie gasped when her mother-in-law had disappeared upstairs. 'What on earth was I thinking?'

'You were thinking of building bridges, two at a time.'

'Am I trying too hard?'

'You're doing fine, Maggie,' Kathy assured her. 'I'm sorry I never realised how bad it was getting for you.'

Maggie's smile, which had been so broad it made her cheeks ache, didn't falter. 'It's all in the past now,' she said. She was looking forward to the future and getting to know Judith better. It wasn't going to be easy, Maggie wasn't going to be as compliant as James, but she suspected Judith already knew that. 'I'm not really manipulative, am I?'

'I only said that to make Judith feel better,' Kathy promised.

Maggie gave a dramatic gasp to let Kathy know she had recognised the lie. 'It's amazing really how you've managed to remain so innocent while surrounded by such bad influences,' Maggie said and she didn't even try to sound convincing.

'The same could be said of your husband.'

'James?'

Kathy laughed. 'You can thank him for this little get-together. He told me all about Carolyn's faux pas when she phoned you. He was ready to confront his mum but we talked it through and decided I probably stood a better chance of getting through to her. Which of course he was very relieved about.'

'If not hoping for,' Maggie added. 'So didn't

you know Judith had convinced herself that I'd trapped James?'

'It might have been better if I had. We would have had this showdown long before now,' Kathy whispered. They could both hear the creak of floorboards as Judith crossed the landing above their heads.

As she came downstairs, Judith's footsteps faltered and rather than returning directly to the living room, she walked down the hallway towards the front door. For a heart-stopping moment, Maggie thought she might be having second thoughts and was trying to escape but then Judith was rushing back in to them.

'I don't want to worry you, Kathy, but I've just seen someone peering through the glass in your front door. She wandered off but I think she's still in the garden.'

Kathy jumped up and went towards the large bay window. Maggie stood up, not sure how she could help but not wanting to stay on the sidelines. She had taken off Harvey's harness during lunch but quickly slipped it back on. As she patted his head she noticed that his hackles were drawn as if he too sensed that trouble was on its way.

'Oh my God, it's Mrs Milton,' Kathy said.

Elsa looked up through bleary eyes and could only make out tiny speckles of sunlight as it trickled through the canopy of swaying branches creaking under the weight of lilacs. She willed the tears not to fall; she had done enough crying to last a life-time. When Freddie had died, she had locked herself away in her room and howled until she was hoarse. She'd barely slept and when she did, she prayed she would never wake up again. There was nothing left for her. She had lost the only man she could ever love and very soon she would lose her baby too.

Anne and her perfect husband had circled like vultures in the last weeks of her pregnancy, waiting patiently to pick the remaining piece of life from her bones. They had claimed concern but the tears in Anne's eyes as she watched Elsa stricken down by grief were surely tears of joy. There was nothing to stop her now, the baby was hers for the taking or so she thought.

What Anne didn't know was that in the depths of her despair, Elsa had reached out for the tiniest shred of hope that would give her a reason to carry on living. That reason had kicked some sense into her with its tiny feet. She had a duty to her unborn child and, as her baby grew stronger, so did her maternal instincts. Anne wasn't the only one who craved motherhood.

Elsa had vowed to stay strong and as the next contraction tore through her body, she pressed her hand to her mouth to stifle her cries. The baby was early and she wasn't yet ready. She had tried to persuade Celia to help, either by taking her in or speaking to their parents, but Celia had refused, saying it would be the ruination of her. Everyone kept telling her she was too immature but she would show them. She had been saving what little wages she received from Mrs Jackson. It wouldn't go far but it was enough to get her and the baby on a bus and out of Sedgefield. She had thought there would be more time to come up with a proper plan but when her first contractions had woken her in the early hours of the morning and she realised there was no more time, her first impulse was to run and she hadn't resisted.

Only now did she regret her haste. She should have stayed in her room; she should have called for Mrs Jackson when the dull but regular pains tightened around her stomach but instead she had crept downstairs and out of the house. She had barely made it onto the driveway when the pulling sensation that accompanied the pain had made it impossible to walk. The baby was coming.

In a fit of panic she had staggered back towards the yawning entrance of the house. She stopped with her hand on the door but couldn't bring herself to go inside. The house felt wrong, everything felt wrong and she was paralysed by fear. She thought she glimpsed movement through the stained glass windows and her heart froze. As another contraction began to build she stumbled towards the cover of the lilac trees but the pain was becoming too much to bear. She needed help and as her contractions intensified so did her fear that both she and her baby might die. Elsa released a primal scream that would have woken up half of Sedgefield.

As Kathy and Judith continued to stare out of the window in disbelief, Maggie and Harvey were already heading out of the room and down the hall. Nerves and unfamiliarity would not get the better of her and she fumbled only briefly with the lock before pulling open the front door. The scent of lilac was still there but now it had an all too familiar synthetic undertone. It was then that she heard the scream.

'Find Mrs Milton, Harvey,' Maggie pleaded. It wasn't a recognised command but somehow the Labrador knew where they were needed. Kathy's front garden was vast, at least twice as wide as the double-fronted house. A curved driveway came from the left towards the centre of the house but Harvey took Maggie to the right. She didn't slow as she stepped off solid tarmac onto the soft, spongy lawn or when her shoulders thumped against creeping branches that tugged at her dress. There was no time to wait, and even as Kathy and Judith emerged from the house, Maggie was immersing herself in the shade of the lilac trees.

The ground sloped gently and Harvey led Maggie with ease and urgency. When he stopped, Elsie's perfume had been overpowered by the more natural scent of lilacs but Maggie knew she was there. Above the sound of whispering leaves she could hear heavy, shuddering breaths. It wasn't the image of an old lady that came to mind, but that of a young woman cowering in fear.

'Elsa?' Maggie asked. 'What are you doing here?'

'The baby's coming,' she answered in gasping sobs. 'I'm scared. I don't want to lose her.'

Crouching down as best she could and using Harvey to balance herself, Maggie reached out a hand but found empty space. Twigs snapped as Elsa scrambled backwards. 'It's Maggie. You're safe. I won't let anything happen to you.'

Cold, trembling fingers wrapped themselves around Maggie's hand but when the grip tightened, it was like iron. 'Help me, please.'

'That's why I'm here. You're safe now,' Maggie said. She could hear Kathy and Judith approaching from behind her. 'Please come into the house with me. You can't stay here.'

Maggie wanted to believe it was Elsa she was helping to her feet but it was the frail and broken body of Mrs Milton she led back towards the house with Kathy's help. It was a task made doubly hard because Maggie needed both arms to support the old lady. Harvey remained a few steps behind with Judith who was giving whispered directions to Maggie so she could find her way safely.

'I'll go to my room now,' the old lady said with a youthful lilt as they stepped over the threshold.

Kathy made no objection to opening up her home to this relative stranger and Maggie helped Mrs Milton up the stairs. The old lady appeared to be far more familiar with the layout than Maggie and turned immediately left and through a door. The smell of stale air and musty drapery suggested the room had been shut up for a long time.

Springs creaked as Mrs Milton sank onto the bed while Maggie made her way around to the other side, feeling her way as she went. The bed was a double with a wooden frame and a bedspread folded at the bottom, which Maggie lifted up and over Mrs Milton before slipping off her shoes and lying down next to her. The pillows were musty but the cotton cases cool and crisp.

'Everything's going to be fine, Elsa,' Maggie whispered but the lie brought tears to her eyes.

'Where's Mrs Jackson?'

'We'll let her know.' Kathy was standing at the bedroom door with Judith. Harvey was close by panting with anxiety rather than exertion. 'We'll go downstairs and phone for help,' she added meaningfully.

'Thanks, Kath.'

Mrs Milton tensed her body and cried out in pain. 'It's nearly here. Oh, my God I don't want this to happen. Please, please, I don't want to lose her,' Elsa continued, sobbing now. 'I won't let them take her. I'd rather die. I want to die. She's all that I have. There's no point in carrying on without her.'

'Yes, there is,' Maggie insisted. 'You have a future where you're going to be happy again, Elsa. You're going to find someone who will love you and never leave you.'

Elsa moaned as she twisted and turned beneath the bedcover. 'No, no, I don't want anyone else. I want my Freddie. No one else, not ever!'

Maggie wondered if Ted had been forced to witness this too. She couldn't imagine the pain he would feel listening to his wife cry out for a lost love and at the same time dismiss nearly sixty years of marriage.

Instinctively, Maggie began to rock her friend and slowly but surely the sobs began to ebb and her body relaxed. It seemed to take forever but it was probably only minutes before Elsa fell silent. Her breathing was nasal but less laboured, and with a sense of relief Maggie realised she had fallen asleep.

'Is there anything I can do?' Judith whispered.

Maggie raised herself onto her elbow. 'Actually, could you bring Harvey over here,' she said, keeping her voice as low as she could. 'He might help keep her calm when she wakes.'

The dog padded over to Elsie's side of the bed and put his head on the mattress. She heard what she thought was Harvey licking his chops then realised too late that he was licking Elsie's face.

'What?' Elsie groaned as she tried to cover her face. Her grasping found Harvey instead but rather than push the dog away she began to stroke him. 'Hello, fella, what are you doing here? Ted, what's going on?'

As Elsie twisted around she actually jumped with fright when she discovered it was Maggie lying

269

next to her. 'It's all right, Elsie.' Maggie gave her a confident smile but she suspected Elsie, unlike Elsa, would be less willing to accept her futile assurances. 'You're in Kathy's house. We found you in the garden. You were upset.'

Elsie eased herself up into a sitting position. As she rubbed away her dried tears, the weathered skin on her hands made the sound of sandpaper across her cheeks. 'Oh, what a silly old bat I am,' she said with a note of self-admonishment and more importantly, without a hint of the vulnerable young woman who had cried herself to sleep. She took a deep breath. 'At least I get to see you and this chap again. I've missed you both.'

Harvey groaned as she rubbed behind his ear.

'We've missed you too,' Maggie said as she slipped off the bed and retraced her steps to sit on the edge of the bed next to Elsie.

Judith was still standing at the door. 'I'll let Kathy know Mrs Milton's feeling better,' she said diplomatically.

'Thanks, Judith.'

'Oh dear, not again,' Elsie whispered. 'Isn't that your mother-in-law? Goodness knows what she thinks of me.'

'She has a good heart,' Maggie offered. 'Deeply hidden but I think I've been convinced that it's in there somewhere.'

'I can see we have a lot of catching up to do. Ted meant well but it looks like you can't get rid of me that easily. I'm getting worse, Maggie, so no more keeping away. If that's all right with you?' Her last question sounded less confident with echoes of Elsa's voice.

'That's more than fine by me.'

'Good. You can begin by helping me up if you can manage? These joints of mine seize up as soon as they come within two feet of a bed or a comfy chair,' she joked.

There were plenty of grunts and groans as Maggie did as she was bidden and she followed Elsie not to the door but towards the light that streamed through the window and danced across her limited vision. Maggie could feel the sun warming her face as she waited for Elsie to collect her thoughts.

'I've been here before,' Elsie said with mild curiosity rather than shock.

The statement didn't come as a surprise to Maggie either. 'We found you in the garden. Is this the house that belonged to the lady who made her own lilac-scented soap?'

'Yes.'

'Mrs Jackson?'

'Yes.'

'And this room?'

'It's where I stayed,' she said, turning away from the window to focus on her surroundings. 'I tried to run away but I was already in labour at that point. I was a silly girl back then and it was Aunt Flo who got me back in here. This is where Tess was born.'

'Is it the first time you've been back since then?'

'It's the first time I've been back in this room, yes.'

'But you came back to visit Mrs Jackson afterwards, didn't you?'

'I couldn't talk to anyone about what happened here. I still can't, but with Mrs Jackson, I didn't need to. She understood how I felt without me having to explain. She became an honorary member of my family: in fact, my girls called her Aunt Flo too. It was a shame she didn't get the same kind of attention from her own family. The way her niece behaved was just awful. The only time Anne came back here was to bury her and collect her inheritance. I think she was terrified of the past catching up with her. She didn't even have the courage to tell me Flo had died. We turned up here one day and a bunch of nurses were renting the place, that's how we found out.'

'Alice said she remembers playing with your girls.'

'Yes and it's nice being able to share some good memories. You may not believe it but there were plenty of good times in my life.'

'Just not here.'

Elsie sighed. 'I never, ever wanted to return to this room.'

'But you wanted to return to the park,' Maggie said. 'Why?'

'Sometimes even the bad memories can be precious. I was a mother when I sat on that park bench. I couldn't see my baby or hold her but she was growing inside me and I kept her safe,' she said, her voice reduced to a whisper as she reached towards Maggie and touched the swell of her stomach. 'Until the day she was born.'

'I want to help you find her again,' Maggie said.

Elsie was shaking her head. 'It's too late.'

Maggie wasn't ready to take no for an answer; something told her that Elsa's spirit wouldn't rest until Tess was found but she didn't argue with the old lady who had been through enough for one day. They both turned to the door as they heard footsteps hurrying up the stairs and a moment later Kathy appeared, slightly out of breath. 'Ted's on his way, Elsie. He should be here soon.'

'You're good girls,' Elsie said. 'I'd be lost without you.'

'Yes, that garden is a bit overgrown. You could have been in there for days,' Kathy said. They all did their best to laugh and chase the ghosts back into the corners of the room.

When Elsie returned downstairs she was very quiet. The whole episode had left her exhausted but it was her embarrassment that kept her spirits low. Kathy and Judith were in the living room and, to their credit, chatted away as if Elsie was a long-lost friend while Maggie waited at the front door. She had made the excuse that Harvey needed a toilet break but she was waiting for Ted.

'It looks like I'm a bad penny that keeps turning up,' she said as he ambled towards her.

'I would have thought you could say the same thing of my wife.' He groaned as he negotiated the small step to reach Maggie. 'Thank you for being here.'

'More luck than management,' she said before lowering her voice. 'This was a bad one.'

'These days they all are, love. What happened?'

'She thought she was in labour. Once upon a time she gave birth in this house,' Maggie explained, 'but of course you already know that, don't you?'

'Yes, this is Aunt Flo's old place although I haven't been here for, oh, forty years, maybe? Flo died in the late sixties.'

As they talked, Maggie had one ear to the sounds coming from deeper within the house. There was still a lot of animated chatter. 'This was where she gave up her baby,' she said. It was an opening statement for her to launch into the arguments she had held back from Mrs Milton. 'Ted, we have to start the search for Tess. Elsie won't find peace until she knows what happened to her, that's why she came back here to Sedgefield.'

Ted reached over to give Maggie's arm a gentle squeeze. 'She already knows what happened to the baby, Maggie. I've done my own research and I've seen her medical records. The baby was stillborn.'

274

CHAPTER 17

Maggie pressed the palms of her hands down firmly onto the wooden slats. The bench was warm and the sun strong enough to soften the rough edges of the chipped paint, blurring the distinction between one layer and the next. She smiled as she listened to the sound of approaching footsteps. The greeting was on her lips long before the breeze lifted the scent of lilacs towards her.

Three weeks had passed since Kathy's birthday and July had slipped into August. Maggie had made up for lost time by visiting Elsie often. She couldn't match some of the practical support they were receiving from the health and social workers but she was still a friendly face and one that Elsie trusted if only after a little prompting. But today was a red-letter day. Ted had agreed to a little excursion to the park. If this was the only place where Elsie and her baby could be reunited, then this was where she needed to be.

'Here she is, Maggie,' he said. 'Now I'm expecting you to take good care of her.'

The sense of anticipation vanished into the ether

as Elsie remained silent and Maggie realised she wasn't with him, not in mind at least. 'How is she?' she asked.

'Quiet.'

Ted helped ease Elsie onto the bench with a few gentle instructions.

'Hello, Elsie. It's Maggie.'

When Elsie didn't reply, Ted tried again. 'You remember Maggie, don't you, love?' Again, nothing. 'Do you want me to stay?' he asked Maggie.

Maggie and Ted were still getting to know each other but at least now they both knew they were on the same side. 'We'll be fine,' she said with forced cheeriness.

'Then I'll leave you to it. I'll nip over to the shops and come back in about half an hour.'

There was more than a hint of exhaustion in Ted's voice that Maggie couldn't ignore. 'You sound tired; are you sleeping enough?'

'She was up in the night calling for her mum. I always thought she gave me a hard time, but you should have heard the language out of her when she thought I was one of her brothers.'

'Why don't you go home and take it easy? We can find our own way back.'

'Oh, don't you worry about me. I don't need that much sleep these days anyway.'

Maggie tried again but couldn't convince Ted to take any time off; in fact, it took some persuasion to get him to leave at all. After he'd gone, the two women sat in silence, both deep in thought but only one keenly aware of the other's presence. The sun was beating down on them and Harvey had crawled beneath the bench to find some shade. Maggie still held on tightly to his leash in case he was needed in an emergency.

'Phew, it's hot,' Elsie said suddenly. She was wafting her hand in front of her face.

'Elsie?' Maggie asked, more surprised that it was Mrs Milton resurfacing from her fugue state than by the exclamation itself.

'Oh, hello. I know you, don't I?'

'Yes, it's Maggie.'

'What on earth am I doing in Victoria Park?'

'You moved to Sedgefield with Ted,' Maggie said. 'Do you remember?'

'It's a lovely spot. No wonder I wanted to come back.'

Maggie felt as if she was talking to a stranger, not Elsie; not even someone who knew her particularly well. 'I think you liked to sit here and watch the swans once upon a time.'

'Is that what I told you?' There followed a mournful sigh then a poor attempt at a laugh. 'Don't go paying any attention to me, love. My mind's befuddled at the best of times. There weren't any swans in Victoria Park, not back in my time anyway. There were plenty in Sefton Park in Liverpool and that's probably what I was thinking of. That was where my beau used to take me. He told me how swans mate for life – it was his way of telling me how he felt about me.'

'Would that be Freddie?' Maggie asked. At last she could sense the sharpness of Elsie's mind slicing through the fog of her dementia.

'I told you about Freddie?'

'Yes, Elsie, you told me all about what happened here.'

'Everything?'

'You told me about Freddie and the baby,' Maggie confirmed, choosing her words carefully.

'I called her Tess.'

'I know and I'm so sorry, Elsie.'

Maggie imagined the forced smile being painted on Elsie's face. 'Oh, it's fine, don't let my woes wear you down. You've got your own life to look forward to. When's it due?'

Feeling Elsie's gaze upon her, Maggie rubbed her protruding belly. 'I've still got a few more months yet.'

'Yes, you don't look like you're at the waddling-duck stage just yet. There were times when I waddled down here on my lunch break and thought I'd never get up off this bench again. I was always late going back to the greengrocer's and Mrs Jackson would give me hell, but I could always get around her. She spoilt me rotten.'

'She was quite a lady.'

'Yes, she was the superwoman of her day. She ran the shop and a guesthouse all on her own and even tried her hand at midwifery now and again.'

'She delivered your baby?'

'Her mum was a midwife and Flo learnt enough to get by when she needed to.'

But not enough to save your baby, Maggie thought, but didn't say. The last pieces of Elsa's story were taking shape, although now Maggie wished they wouldn't. Elsa had tried to run away and had left it too late to call for medical help. Whatever problems there had been with the birth, it had been beyond Flo's limited experience.

'I wasn't the only one who was wracked with guilt,' Elsie continued as if she had read Maggie's thoughts. 'I suppose that was part of the reason Aunt Flo was determined to keep in touch after I went back home to Liverpool. She needed to know I was getting on with my life.'

'And you did,' Maggie said.

'Yes, but I can't help but wonder . . .'

The conversation stalled and Maggie felt Elsie's grip on the present slipping. Although Mrs Milton had been willing to relive the pain of the past, now was not the time, not when the memories of losing the baby were so prominent in her mind. Maggie tried to keep her focused on the here and now.

'I'm going to get a trial run at being a mum this weekend,' she said. 'Jenny and her husband are going away on a little boat trip so I'm babysitting Lily from Friday morning until Sunday night. She's almost ten months old now, crawling everywhere and getting into everything. I'm going to have my hands full but I can't wait. You remember Jenny, don't you?'

'Hmm,' Elsie said but she wasn't listening.

Maggie heard the sound of Elsie's wedding ring scrape along the bench as she explored its surface. When she did eventually speak, her voice had that unmistakeable youthfulness.

Elsa was looking out across the lake: the reflection of the sun so bright that it stung her eyes. 'What I wouldn't give to hold her one more time,' she said.

'I know and I'm so, so sorry,' said the woman sitting on her right.

Rather than turn towards her, Elsa's gaze drifted across the empty seat on her left. Her fingers were splayed out across the surface of the bench and she dug her fingernails into the wood as if she could imbibe the memories trapped beneath the layers of paint. Memories were all she had left. Her suitcase was packed and it was time to go home . . .

'Elsa?'

She snapped up her head. The sunshine was blinding and the tears welling in her eyes obscured her vision but she knew immediately that it was Aunt Flo who had appeared in front of her. No more than an amorphous silhouette, the old lady sat down in the vacant seat.

'I feel so empty,' Elsa said.

'It will pass.'

'Will it? Will these arms ever feel anything but emptiness?' she asked. She lifted up her arms as if to cradle her baby then dropped them down on her lap. 'Will I ever stop seeing that perfect little face with those beautiful eyes and cupid's bow mouth? Will I ever forget the feeling of those tiny little fingers and toes?'

'It will pass.'

Elsa shook her head. 'I won't forget.'

Flo tried to soothe her with promises of a bright and happy future but to no avail; it didn't matter how many babies she went on to have, they wouldn't replace Tess. 'I made a mistake and now I'm going to pay for it for the rest of my life.'

Guilty tears trickled down Flo's face. She had played her part.

'Don't blame yourself,' Elsa said. 'You did everything you could, I know that.'

But Aunt Flo's conscience wouldn't be appeased, not then, not ever. Her silhouette shimmered before it was whipped away by a soft summer breeze. When she had completely disappeared and was little more than a memory, Elsa began to sob. She clamped a hand over her mouth and for one blessed moment there was silence but then the unmistakeable sound of her newborn baby's cries began to echo across her mind. It was a sound that would haunt her for the rest of her life.

The scene being played out next to her on the bench was devastating. Maggie could only hear Elsa's responses to an imaginary visitor but it had made her skin crawl and her heart ache at the same time. It had been a mistake bringing Elsie

281

to the park. Her condition was deteriorating and it had been foolhardy to think that their beloved bench would help resurrect precious memories that would bring her comfort. Elsie's fractured mind was intent on making her suffer and had returned her to what must have been the bleakest point in her life, when she had lost everything she held dear.

When Elsa fell silent again, Maggie allowed her to drift mercifully towards a void between the present and the past. She waited patiently for Ted to return, but it was his wife who reappeared first.

'I was just thinking about Tess,' Elsie said. 'Did you know I didn't get to spend one single minute with her on my own?'

'I can't begin to imagine what it must have been like for you,' Maggie said with a shudder, hoping and praying that her own baby would be born safely.

'She cried and cried but I couldn't soothe her.'

Maggie was temporarily thrown by the remark but it wouldn't be the first time that Elsie's memory had misfired. Like the layers of paint on the bench, Mrs Milton's memories had been laid one on top of the other. Time had chipped away at those layers and occasionally one memory could peek through the cracks of another. It was true of her recollection of the swans and, despite its significance, it was true of the memories of the births of her three children.

'You were a good mum. Nancy and Yvonne are testament to that,' she offered.

'Gosh, the girls!' Elsie said, scrambling to her feet. 'I need to pick them up from school.'

'Harvey!' Maggie called so quickly that she made the dog jump in alarm. He was still lying beneath the bench and banged his head.

'Not so fast,' Ted called. He was some distance away but was rushing down the slope towards them with a laden shopping bag banging against his leg. He was out of breath by the time he reached them.

'Do I know you?' Elsie asked curtly.

'I hope so. We sleep together every night.'

'The nerve of him,' she said to Maggie. 'Postmen are so cheeky these days.'

It wasn't the first time Maggie had witnessed Elsie dismissing her husband and Ted saw the look of dismay on her face. 'Don't worry,' he whispered. 'I was a postie. That's how we met.'

Maggie had been focusing on one chapter of Elsie's life and a painful one at that. It was refreshing to hear how the next had begun. 'You'll have to tell me all about it.'

Ted didn't need much encouragement and as they ambled out of the park, he told her more of their earlier life together. He had first met Elsa when delivering post to her parents' house shortly after her return home from Sedgefield. Ted was proud of his fifty-eight-year marriage if not a little amazed that his wife had put up with him for so long. As he reminisced, he turned occasionally to Elsie for agreement but her responses were non-committal and eventually she disconnected herself from her surroundings. Maggie could only hope that wherever Elsie's mind was taking her, it held the kind of joy that Ted was recalling and not the horrors that Maggie couldn't help but imagine.

Elsa walked quietly out of the park. She was heading home to Liverpool but she would come back to Sedgefield one day. She was ready to face life again and all because Aunt Flo had given her something to live for. Mrs Jackson had promised her that she could see her baby one more time. Only once, mind, to say goodbye properly and to satisfy herself that Anne was giving Tess the love and care she deserved. Once would be enough, Elsa was sure of it.

CHAPTER 18

Lily slept soundly as the adults clucked around her like mother hens.

'Every packet has a label,' Jenny was explaining. She had known Maggie for nearly twenty years and not all of that time had been wasted on idle gossip and secret fantasies. As a teenager she had been curious about Braille and Maggie had been eager to share her knowledge. They had used it to send secret messages to each other at school but now it had more practical applications. Jenny had borrowed Maggie's Braille label maker a few days earlier but had been a little overzealous.

'You've even put a label on the nappies!' laughed Maggie. 'I think I could have worked that one out for myself.' She was trying to sound calm but she had woken up with butterflies in her stomach and they were now gathering up a storm and making her queasy.

'Better safe than sorry.' Jenny sounded petulant but there was a smile there too.

'She's even put labels on the things we didn't bring,' Mark added. 'Jenny, it's eight forty-five already. We said we'd be at the boat for nine.'

'You'll have a great time,' James said to Mark as they hustled out into the hallway, leaving the two women standing in the middle of the living room amidst the paraphernalia that had accompanied Lily's arrival.

'Don't worry, she'll be fine,' Maggie said when she noticed her friend hadn't made a move to follow Mark. 'I might be using Lily as a guinea pig to try out my new pram but I promise you Harvey and I are fully trained up and by the time you get back she'll be expecting you to pull her buggy along backwards too.' Guide Dogs for the Blind had provided the training and the pram was one specifically approved by them. The purchase of the pram marked the first tangible steps Maggie had taken in preparing for her baby's arrival and the sense of anticipation she felt as she looked forward to the day when she would be using it for her own baby was something she wasn't used to, but she embraced it.

'Don't blame me if Lily drools all over it.'

'Oh, don't worry. I'll make sure Baby Carter returns the favour when they're fighting over toys.'

Jenny still hadn't moved.

'I won't let you down,' Maggie promised. 'And James will be here too.'

'Maggie, I trust you with my life and more importantly, with my baby. You'll be the one taking charge whether James is here or not.'

'So leave.'

Jenny gave Maggie a hug goodbye and then

crouched down in front of the baby carrier. 'It's just that, for all my complaining about sleepless nights, I'm really going to miss her.'

'Well, while you're missing her, don't forget to enjoy yourself. You've got a very important job interview coming up and you need time to de-stress.'

'I don't know why. I'm going to have to get used to stress if I do end up getting the promotion,' Jenny answered miserably.

'It's a new challenge and you'll enjoy it.'

'Jenny, can we go now?' Mark called.

There was a loud smacking sound as Jenny planted a kiss on her sleeping daughter's cheek. 'You be a good girl for your Auntie Mags,' she whispered.

'Erm, Maggie?' It was James back in the living room. 'Would you mind if I went with them to help out? Just until they're ready to set off.'

'And how exactly will you be helping?' Maggie was smiling but her stomach twisted, crushing the butterflies and leaving nothing to hold back the wave of nausea. This was it. She was going to be left alone in charge of Lily and all of a sudden the self-doubt that had plagued her early pregnancy came back with a vengeance. She willed James to have second thoughts but she refused to ask him to stay.

'Jack's going to give Mark a crash course but if he has to rush off, I can stay around until he gets the hang of it.'

'You went on one boating holiday when you were a teenager. That hardly qualifies you as an expert.'

'It won't take me long to get my sea legs back,' he insisted.

'OK, but try to remember it's not *your* holiday. You'd better come back, James,' Maggie replied, only just holding her nerve.

She remained standing in the middle of the living room as the front door closed. Peace came in the form of the soft sighs of a sleeping baby. Stepping around the newly constructed assault course, Maggie worked quickly and methodically, finding homes for all of Lily's things, aware that she could wake up at any moment. Rather than follow her from room to room, Harvey stayed where he was. His baby training was paying off and he hadn't once tried to lick Lily's face or gnaw her toys but chose instead to sit and watch over her. The trust that Jenny had placed in Maggie extended to her faithful companion and deservedly so.

'How's she doing, boy?' Maggie whispered once she had everything in order. Lily's next drink of juice was ready and waiting in the fridge along with her lunch. A baby-sized spoon and bowl had been set out on the kitchen counter. Maggie had even prepared a changing area on the dining room floor with clean nappies at hand and a fresh set of clothes in case a quick change of outfit was required. There was nothing left to do except wait for Lily to wake.

Harvey licked Maggie's hand but when she went to pet him, he had already turned his head back to Lily. Maggie followed suit and sat down on the sofa to be lulled by the sound of the baby's steady breaths. Her nerves had all but disappeared. She was ready for anything, she told herself.

When the phone rang it cut through the silence and gave Maggie a start. She used one hand as leverage to heave herself up as quickly as she could while the other covered the rise of her stomach. Her baby objected to being disturbed and kicked her. Lily joined in and began to wriggle as she struggled into wakefulness.

Maggie scrambled out of the living room, pulling the door half closed before picking up the phone in the hallway. 'Hello?' she whispered.

'Hi, Maggie – it's Mel. I'm not disturbing you, am I?'

A frown furrowed Maggie's brow and her anxiety returned with renewed force. 'What's wrong?'

'Before I tell you, I need you to understand that it's nothing to worry about,' Mel explained carefully.

Maggie wasn't reassured. 'Is there something wrong with the baby?'

'No, Maggie, nothing like that. Is James with you?'

'No.' Her voice was quivering now. 'Mel, please, you're scaring me.'

Her midwife began to explain, taking her time to go through what had happened. Maggie had the presence of mind to ask some pertinent questions but once she knew all there was to tell, she stopped listening to Mel's continued assurances and focused instead on her growing anger and the voice inside her head repeatedly telling her that this wasn't happening; it *couldn't* be happening. Maggie's ears pricked to Lily waking up in the next room, reminding her of the simple joys of motherhood that seemed more out of reach than ever. No longer able to deny what she was being told, Maggie was filled with such a feeling of cold dread that by the time she ended the call with Mel, Lily wasn't the only one crying.

Lily was sitting in her baby recliner, kicking her legs as she drank her juice. She was old enough to hold her bottle by herself but kept dropping it onto the floor deliberately to make her new babysitter gasp. It might have entertained Lily but Maggie's smile was forced, the curve of her mouth catching the tears slipping silently down her face.

Moving towards the window, she checked her watch. It was almost ten o'clock and her ears strained for the sound of a car pulling up. It was only when she heard the knock on the door she realised Kathy had chosen to walk the short distance between the salon and the house.

'Sorry, Maggie, I tried to get away as soon as I could.'

The call she had received half an hour earlier had been fraught. Maggie had barely been able to speak but it hadn't been the sobbing that had frightened Kathy most, it had been the anger in her voice.

'So what exactly happened?' Kathy asked once they were sitting in the living room where Lily had been waiting noisily for someone to pick up her bottle.

Maggie swallowed hard but the lump wedged in her throat wouldn't budge. 'Mel's been talking to someone from social services,' she began but had to stop to take a breath. She felt woozy and willed herself to calm down but the fury only burned brighter as she explained to Kathy exactly what her midwife had told her: a social worker from the Child Protection Unit had been in touch. Mel had assured her that Maggie was receiving all the support she needed and there were absolutely no concerns, and the social worker had been satisfied with the response. Mel had hoped that would be the end of the matter and Maggie need never know but she had just received a copy letter from the social worker confirming the case was closed. The original was winging its way to Maggie.

If that had been all that Mel had told her then Maggie might have been able to keep things in perspective, but she knew that for Child Protection to be involved, someone had to think her baby was at risk and eventually Maggie had forced it out of her.

The inquiry had been triggered by a call made from a well-meaning member of the public who had been eager to share her concerns, one of which had been that the baby might be born with disabilities or might suffer learning difficulties as a result of being brought up by a disabled parent. The questions were familiar ones and Maggie had no doubt that the person asking them would be just as familiar to her.

'I can't believe how easily I've been fooled,' Maggie said, her voice trembling. 'I thought we'd turned a corner. Judith actually phoned me up this morning to wish me luck! Why has she done this, Kathy? How could she be so cruel?'

'Maybe it wasn't her,' Kathy suggested.

'There you go! I can tell straight away that *you're* lying. Why couldn't I see through her lies as easily?' Her jaw was clenched but she couldn't hold back the sob.

'Have you phoned James yet?'

Maggie shook her head. 'He'll still be playing on the boat and I don't want Jenny to find out and worry. Oh my God, what if she gets into trouble for leaving Lily with me?'

Kathy took hold of Maggie's trembling hand. 'Maggie, think about it,' she said firmly. 'No one with any sense doubts your abilities and especially not social services. They've had enough dealings with you over the years, haven't they? To support you, not condemn you. If they've had an inquiry then they have to follow it up but the case is already closed. You've been looking forward to having Lily over to stay so please don't let this spoil anything. There's no reason to change your plans. Enjoy your weekend, let Jenny enjoy hers and everything else can wait.'

Lily dropped her bottle on the floor again. It was empty and, without even thinking, Maggie picked it up and put it on a nearby table. From the same table, she picked up the baby's comforter doll and dangled it in front of the recliner. Lily grasped it in her chubby fingers and pulled it to her with a contented chuckle. 'I can't look after her,' Maggie whispered.

'You're a natural, Maggie. All you have to do is believe in yourself.'

Maggie gulped back another sob but the tears were already falling. 'I can't do it any more, Kathy. I'm sick of it. What's the point in building myself up to do something when there are people queuing up to knock me down?' In the distance, Maggie thought she heard the creak of the park gate. Where once she would immediately think of the park bench, now she thought only of the murky waters of the lake.

Kathy read her mind. 'You're scaring me, Maggie.'

'I won't do anything silly,' she promised. 'It's just that . . . I just thought Judith had finally accepted me. I wish it didn't matter but it does. Oh, God, Kathy, what's James going to say?'

'To his mum? Quite a lot I should think – I know I certainly will. Would you like me to hang around until he's home?'

'No, I'd rather speak to him on my own,' Maggie said, taking a juddering breath as she tried to staunch her tears. 'All I need you to do is take care of Lily.'

'No.'

Maggie couldn't hide the shock. 'Please, Kathy, I need you to take her. This morning I was anxious about looking after her but now I'm downright terrified,' Maggie said, her voice quaking. 'What if something happens while she's in my care? I can't take that chance. I don't want to end up on the "At Risk Register" or whatever it's called before I've even given birth.'

'That won't happen.'

'Please, Kathy,' Maggie said and now her whole body was shaking. 'Do you want me to beg? Because I will.' Terrified that her friend might refuse again, she quickly added, 'In fact I *am* begging you.'

There was a loud sigh. 'I can't believe Judith has reduced you to this. While I'm so glad I brought you and James together, I can't help feeling I need to apologise for inflicting his mother on you.' She paused a moment and then said, 'I suppose the salon could do without me for the rest of the day. That gives you time to explain everything to James and decide what you want to do. But I'm afraid I have far too much to do this weekend already so looking after Lily for three days is simply out of the question. If you're not prepared to stand and fight then you're going to have to call off what will probably be Jenny and Mark's last chance to have a break for a very long time. And who knows what kind of stress that will put on their marriage?'

Relieved that the immediate problem of Lily's care had been taken care of and in spite of her tears, Maggie felt the sides of her mouth twitch in response to Kathy's brazen manipulation. 'That was a bit harsh. What is it that's keeping you so busy anyway? I know you're not working in the salon over the weekend.'

'Oh, the simple matter of buying one house and clearing out another two.'

'Your mum's agreed to the move?'

'She's still dragging her heels but after taking her around to see the granny flat she's started to show a bit more interest. I have to go over tomorrow to sort through the mountains of paper-work she and Dad have accumulated over the years. Most of it is to do with the property busi-ness so that means I'll probably end up bringing it all home. So much for me downsizing.'

'But you could still look after Lily until then,' Maggie said desperately.

'I'll take her for the rest of the day but no more. Speak to James and let me know when you're ready to pick her up. Tonight,' Kathy added firmly.

'But . . .'

'I'm just telling you how it is,' Kathy said with a dismissive sniff. 'Oh dear, I think someone needs changing! You can do this one and show me how it's done.'

'You really don't take any prisoners, do you?' Maggie remarked.

'Sorry.'

Maggie groaned as she stood up to see to Lily. 'It's not for you to apologise, Kath, but we both know who should.'

Maggie didn't know which way to turn, so she stood staring at the front door long after Kathy had left. The house felt empty but it wasn't Lily's departure that had opened up a gaping hole in her life; that had already been created by a human version of a wrecking ball.

All her preparations from earlier that morning had been swept away. What Kathy hadn't taken with her had been piled into a store cupboard ready to be collected by whoever was going to take over Lily's care. Kathy was still holding out hope that Maggie would change her mind but in stark contrast, Maggie held out no hope at all, in anything.

Maggie couldn't bring herself to return to the living room, or the kitchen, or the dining room where even the faintest hint of Lily's chamomile and calendula baby lotion would set off her emotions again. With nowhere else to turn, she fled to her bedroom and almost made it to her refuge before stubbing her toe on the corner of the bed. The howl of pain quickly escalated into a scream, first through gritted teeth and then at full force. When the last ounce of air had been ripped from her lungs, she collapsed onto the bed and wrapped the bedspread around her. Harvey jumped up next to her and his wet nose sought out her face, which was buried in a pillow. When she didn't respond, he lay down quietly by her side.

Maggie was barely aware of the dog, wasn't even aware of the throbbing pain in her toe. She was, however, conscious of the bedspread that cocooned her. She and her mum had made the quilt together in preparation for moving into her new home with James. It had been made from a series of six-inch squares in a variety of materials with different designs to create depth and texture but, more importantly, it was made from love. Exhausted by the barrage of thoughts and emotions that had assaulted her, the quilt gave her an escape route into the relative safety of the past and eventually lulled her into a fitful sleep.

In her dream, Maggie was riding her friend's bike through the park. She could hear the wheels whirring and the sound of her mum running behind. Joan was calling out instructions, mostly to Maggie but occasionally to pedestrians who dared to get in her daughter's way. 'You're doing it on your own!' she shouted. Maggie's heart soared but then she veered off course onto grass and the crunch of gravel was replaced by ominous silence. The bike began to judder as it hit potholes and Maggie reached behind her in panic. She touched her mum's arm – which had been holding the bike upright all along. The shock made Maggie cry out and as she felt herself fall she heard a door slam and woke with a start. James was home.

Without saying a word, James took off his boots in the hallway and then shuffled off into the kitchen. Maggie huddled deeper under the quilt. He would have noticed that the pram was missing and assumed that impatience had got the better of his wife and she had gone out with Lily. Harvey was the one to take charge and the thud as he dropped down off the bed was loud enough to be heard downstairs.

'Maggie? Is that you?'

She felt sick to her stomach. It might only have been an illusion but life had been good in the last few weeks, she had belonged to a family again. She really didn't want to do this and a fresh wave of despair washed over her as she felt more alone than ever. She tried to draw herself tighter into a ball but her bump made bringing her knees any closer to her chest impossible.

James crept into the bedroom then stumbled to a stop. 'Where's Lily?'

Maggie rubbed her face and the salty flakes of dried tears stung her eyes. She took a deep breath and held it as long as she could but the time for prevarication was over. 'Kathy's taken her for the day.'

'Jesus, Maggie, what's wrong? Is it the baby?' James asked as he rushed to her side.

As James wrapped her in his arms, Maggie could feel the tension in his body. 'The baby's fine, I'm fine,' she said. 'I've had a call from Mel and before I tell you, I need you to promise me that you'll stay calm.'

'What's happened?' James asked, his voice confirming he was already far from calm.

She tried to massage the back of his neck but his flesh was as hard as iron. 'There's been some interest from social services into my case.' Maggie paused long enough to let the idea that she had become a case sink in for both of them. 'Someone has expressed concern and it was referred to Child Protection.'

'Someone?'

'A concerned citizen. I don't know who, I doubt we would ever be told but,' Maggie added, 'Mel assured me that it was only an informal inquiry and she isn't expecting it to go any further.'

'A concerned citizen,' James repeated under his breath.

Maggie didn't reply. She wanted James to reach his own conclusions. It was more than Judith deserved but if this was going to destroy James's trust in his mother, it would be because of Judith's actions and not her own.

'And what was this citizen so concerned about?'

'She was worried that I wouldn't be able to take care of the baby properly.'

'She?'

'Or he,' Maggie added lamely.

'Yes, of course. And what exactly were her concerns?'

Maggie shrugged. 'I can't remember.'

The blatant lie only served to confirm the truth and James didn't need to push her further on the subject. 'But I still don't understand. Why has Kathy taken Lily?'

'Mel may have convinced the social worker that I'm capable of caring for a child but what if something happened to Lily this weekend?' Maggie said, the panic rising in her voice. 'I'd never be trusted with a baby again and I won't take that kind of risk. I know it's stupid but I can't shake this vision of a social worker being there at the birth, ready to snatch my baby from me.'

'*You're* not stupid, Maggie. I'm the one who's been an idiot all these years,' James said. As he pulled away from her, she knew the anger tensing his body was begging to be released and a different kind of fear bloomed inside her.

'Please, James. Let's sit down and talk this through.'

He kissed the top of her head, the gentleness of his lips a stark contrast to the steel in his voice. 'We will, but first I need to make a quick call.'

James stormed out of the room and when he ran downstairs it sounded like a rumble of thunder. Maggie abandoned her quilt and ran after him with Harvey in hot pursuit.

'Wait,' she said as she caught up with him. She grabbed his arm as he was reaching for the phone in the living room.

'I'll never forgive her for this.'

'There'll be an explanation, there has to be,' Maggie said. She was trying to sound stronger than she felt, but without warning she burst into tears. She had detected Lily's sweet baby smells still hanging in the air.

'I have to do this. Please, Maggie,' James said, each word breaking his heart a little more. His hands were shaking as he led her very gently into the hallway before returning to the living room. Maggie rested her head on the door he had closed behind him and listened as he picked up the phone.

'What the hell have you done?' he asked.

There was a short pause but probably not long enough for Judith to give any kind of answer.

'I know you've been in touch with social services. What in God's name did you think you were doing?'

Maggie willed Judith to deny it. She didn't want to believe that the last few weeks had been a lie. She didn't want to consider that Judith had stepped closer into her world only to be better positioned to raze it to the ground. But with James's next response all remaining doubt was removed.

'I don't give a damn what your intentions were! You may not have meant to cause harm but you

301

have. No, Mum, it doesn't matter. I don't want to hear it. I've spent thirty-five years letting you inter- fere in my life but it stops here and now. I don't want you anywhere near my family. Stay away from me and stay away from Maggie. Stay *away*, Mum.'

There was only a soft beep as James ended the call but he didn't replace the phone in its cradle immediately. Maggie imagined him standing only feet away, lost and bereft. She wished she could go to him but the confirmation of Judith's betrayal had felt like a punch to the stomach. If James didn't hear Maggie drop to her knees he certainly heard Harvey bark an alert and the next thing she knew they were both at her side. Rather than try to lift her up, James sank to the floor next to her and she clung to him.

'I want my mum,' she whispered, managing somehow to smile at her vulnerability.

'I know.'

'For a while there I thought maybe your mum could . . .'

'I know, Maggie, but she's no one's mum, not any more.'

'You're really prepared to do this?'

She heard him put a hand over his face, his words muffled as he spoke. 'I won't deny it's killing me. My mum has been an indomitable force in my life for so long, always made me feel protected and safe.'

'That's what mums do.'

James straightened his back and he sounded

resolute when he said, 'Not now. Do you want to spend the rest of your life worrying about what other schemes she might be thinking up to come between us?'

'No, I don't but . . .' Maggie began, not sure where her thoughts were leading her. What she wanted was impossible. She wished the call from Mel had never happened or, for that matter, the call Judith had made to social services; she wanted that feeling of hope for the future again, a future where Judith would be there to lend a motherly hand if called upon. 'I can't do this on my own.'

'You're not on your own.'

'OK, I don't want *us* to do this on our own. I'm scared, James. I'm scared you're rushing into this decision and one day you'll regret it and, worse still, resent me.'

'I'm scared too but if I regret anything it's that I didn't see this sooner. I said I'd look after you and that's what I'm going to do.' James placed a hand on her wet cheek and lifted her head towards him. 'The tears end here,' he said.

While Maggie put her faith in her husband and dried her tears, James worked out a plan. 'And the first thing we're going to do is prove to ourselves as much as anyone else that we can do this. We're going to pick up Lily.'

'But . . .'

James silenced her with a gentle kiss. When she tried to object a second time, he kissed her again.

He pulled away, his lips still hovering over hers. 'No buts. You were perfectly capable of looking after her this morning and nothing, absolutely nothing, has happened to change that. I'm going to keep on kissing you, Maggie, until I get what I want.'

Maggie felt a rush of love that didn't quite wash away the pain but it eased her fears enough to agree. 'But not right this minute,' she said. 'I need you to hold me a little longer.' When he leaned in to kiss her again, Maggie hungrily met his lips. As they held on to each other, she was aware of their unborn child nestled safely between them. She knew it was time to stop looking for a replacement mother figure in her life. There was no pretence at independence now; this was it. With James as her foundation, she was the only mother her baby needed and that would have to be enough for her too.

CHAPTER 19

When Maggie entered the salon, the scent of flowers cut through the warm air, vanquishing the less appealing smells of hairspray and singed hair. From the rustle of cellophane Maggie guessed there was someone standing at reception with a bouquet.

Her first thought was that Judith was standing there, but when Harvey shivered in excitement and wagged his tail ferociously, Maggie relaxed her guard. 'They smell nice,' she said.

'They're for you,' Jenny replied.

An unscathed Lily had been handed over to her parents the previous evening, but even after a lie-in that morning, Maggie was still exhausted. Lily had missed her parents and her chosen form of protest had been to cry – and she had cried a lot, mostly during the night. She refused to be soothed by either Maggie or James, so they had been forced to call in the cavalry. It would seem that Harvey had the same winning charm with Lily as he'd had with Liam and Sam and even Maggie was forced to admit that, between the three of them, they had made the perfect team.

'Thank you but you really didn't have to. It was a pleasure having Lily and she wasn't a bit of bother.' Maggie took the bouquet and buried her nose in soft petals. She picked up the soft pink of rose, the citrus orange of geranium, a sprinkling of lavender blue and deep green grass. The flowers had been carefully chosen by someone who knew how to colour her world.

'However, I do have a bone to pick with you,' Jenny added. 'Why didn't you tell me about the call from Mel?'

The rainbow began to fade as Maggie lifted her head. 'I didn't want to worry you.'

'Should I be worried?'

Maggie shrugged. 'The letter from social services arrived this morning and no, there's nothing to worry about. As always, there's plenty of support on offer but thankfully no suspicions. The only lasting damage is James's relationship with his mum.'

'How's he taking it?' Kathy asked, returning to the reception desk from the main salon just in time to catch the gist of the conversation.

'Badly,' Maggie answered candidly. James's initial anger had been the precursor for a whole raft of emotions, the latest being guilt. He was ashamed of himself for allowing his mum's rejection of Maggie to go unchecked for so long. He had left other people to deal with her in the past but he was determined to prove to his wife that he had changed. 'He's refusing to answer any of

Judith's calls and I really can't see him forgiving her any time soon.'

'Good for him, I hope he cuts her out of your lives completely,' Jenny said. She didn't even try to hide her contempt. 'I can't believe she lulled you into a false sense of security only to stab you in the back. What has that woman got against you? Did she really think you'd let any harm come to Lily? Did she—'

'I've spoken to Judith,' Kathy interjected.

There was something in Kathy's tone that brought Jenny's blustering to a stop but it was Maggie who asked the question. 'And?'

'I started by giving her a piece of my mind but, to use Judith's own words, she doesn't need me telling her what a nasty piece of work she is.'

'I'd agree with that,' muttered Jenny.

'She was misguided and she knows it. But . . .' Her pause was a deliberate warning; there was another bombshell on its way. 'She did tell me that she made that call to social services months ago, shortly after you told her you were pregnant and before she went with you to your antenatal appointment. Long before my birthday party.'

In the silence that followed, Maggie felt something akin to relief. While the latest news didn't completely absolve Judith of blame, it gave Maggie some hope that the woman who had finally opened up her arms to her still existed. 'But even if I could forgive her, I'm not sure James will.'

'Where you go, James will follow,' Kathy persisted.

'Don't be so sure. It won't matter to him *when* she made the call, it's the fact she made it at all. I just can't see him getting over that kind of betrayal. I'm not saying he won't come around eventually but I don't think it's something he can be rushed into. We're going away in a couple of weeks, which gives everyone some breathing space, and I'll try to talk it through with him when we get back, I promise.'

'You're really going to consider letting her off the hook?' Jenny asked in disbelief.

'It's not going to be my decision.'

'Like you wouldn't interfere!' Kathy accused.

'No, I won't. I've never seen him so determined to protect me, Kathy. He won't let her near me, I'm sure of it.'

'OK, I'll try to persuade her to give you the space you need,' Kathy said, aware she had pushed the matter as much as she dared. 'But speaking of mothers, I have some other news. We've put in an offer for the house we wanted and it's been accepted!'

There was a smattering of applause which helped lift the sombre atmosphere that had settled around them.

'We could be moving into our new home in six weeks,' Kathy continued but she didn't sound so confident any more, 'although I don't know what I'm letting myself in for. Not only have I acquired more paperwork after the clear-out at Mum's house, but more work too, and I'm snowed under already.'

The corners of Maggie's mouth twitched. There was something about Kathy's complaint that sounded engineered.

'Is this the property management stuff?' Jenny asked innocently.

'Yes,' Kathy said with a long sigh. 'I'm sure I'll get to grips with it eventually.'

'But you already have so much on your plate. You'll burn yourself out if you're not careful and then your mum will be the one looking after you,' Jenny said.

In Maggie's current mood, the way the two women were skirting around the issue was nothing short of irritating. 'Oh, for goodness' sake! Kathy needs help and, as of next month, Mark needs a job. Kathy needs someone who knows the property business and Mark is an estate agent. Do I need to spell it out?'

'But Mark was so keen on retraining as a joiner and I couldn't offer him full-time work,' Kathy said.

'Can't he do both?' Maggie asked.

'I don't see why not,' Jenny agreed. 'To be honest, Kath, I think he would bite your hand off even if it was only part-time.'

'Sorted then,' Maggie said. 'Now, if you'll excuse me, I've got my own work to do and you'll be late back at the bank if you don't hurry.'

When Maggie withdrew into her treatment room with Harvey and an armful of flowers, she tried not to let the rose thorns prick her conscience. Still haunted by the image of Elsa sitting at the side of the lake mourning her baby, Maggie thought of the anguish her mother-in-law would be going through. Judith's arms were empty too – but they didn't need to be, there was still hope.

Maggie could feel her resolve weakening but she was determined that James and his mother should make their own peace in their own time. They needed to establish new boundaries that would make a better future for them all and they should do that without interference. Maggie was starting to think that their holiday couldn't come soon enough so she could remove herself from temptation.

Aware that she was wishing her life away, Maggie reminded herself that time was sometimes the enemy. Her thoughts turned to Mrs Milton who was deteriorating so quickly that even her devoted husband couldn't stop her from disappearing into the ether.

CHAPTER 20

Elsie was sitting quietly with a cup in her hand. Intent on stirring her tea, she hadn't spoken a word. It was a task that so far had taken fifteen minutes.

'I think that's enough stirring,' Ted said. He leaned over to still her hand. 'How about taking a sip before it gets cold?'

'Is there any sugar in it?' Elsie asked.

'Yes, love.'

As Elsie slurped her tea dutifully, Maggie said to Ted, 'Are you sure you don't want to go out for a little while, if only for some fresh air? It's going to be at least two weeks before I can come back.'

James was already en route to pick up Sam and Liam for their holiday and they would spend Friday night in Sedgefield before setting off for France first thing in the morning. But as much as Maggie was looking forward to the break, it was going to be a wrench leaving the Miltons. It was her third visit that week and so far Elsie hadn't recognised her at all. The strain on Ted was telling and it was agonising to hear the pain etched in his voice.

'I don't like leaving her when she's like this,' Ted said. 'But don't worry, the district nurse said she'd call in over the weekend and Yvonne's coming down next week to check up on me. I won't be on my own.'

'And there's always Alice,' Maggie added by way of consolation, as much for her benefit as for Ted.

'Yes, of course.' He didn't sound so sure.

'I bumped into her last week. She knows I'm going away and promised to call around more often.'

'Elsie, you're nodding off, love,' Ted said turning his attention back to his wife a little too swiftly. 'You'll spill that tea if you're not careful. Here, it's gone cold anyway.' He took the cup and placed it on the coffee table. 'Why don't we get you to bed?'

Elsie gasped. 'If my dad hears you saying that he'll punch your lights out.'

Maggie only witnessed a fraction of Ted's daily battles but this small exchange was enough to imagine how tortuous it must be to watch a loved one's soul being stripped away, layer by layer.

'Would you like me to take you?' she offered.

Elsie didn't answer but as Maggie stood up and reached out an arm, the old lady grasped it and unsteadily pulled herself to her feet. With a little encouragement, they made it out of the living room and down the hall towards her bedroom. Ted followed but remained at a safe distance.

'Are you warm enough?' Maggie asked as she pulled the bedspread over Elsie's shoulders. The ever-present scent of lilac wasn't enough to disguise the smell of stale linen which held no trace of the essential oils she had given Elsie to ease her symptoms.

'Don't leave me,' Elsie whispered and Maggie sensed her looking towards the door.

Ted shuffled away, his progress laboured as he went down the hallway to deadbolt the front door. He was taking no chances that his wife might slip out of her bedroom unnoticed.

'Go to sleep,' Maggie urged but when she made a move to leave, Elsie took hold of her arm.

'Maggie?'

'Yes, it's me,' she whispered. 'You were about to have a little nap.'

'Oh, OK.'

Maggie was tempted to stay and make the most of the tenuous connection she had made with her old friend but Elsie sounded tired. She tried again to leave but Elsie's grip on her arm tightened.

'Where's Ted?'

'He's close by.'

Elsie fell silent and Maggie presumed she was nodding off. When she spoke again, she sounded more wistful than tired. 'He's a good man. Did I tell you how we met?' she asked then paused as she tried to keep the memory within her grasp. 'He was a postman. A bit of a chancer, but he made me laugh when I thought I'd never laugh again. He was the one who started calling me Elsie and it was a new beginning for me. I took one look into those twinkling eyes and I just knew.'

'Knew what?' Maggie asked, imagining the moment when Elsa found her happy ending or as near to it as she would ever get.

'Oh, you know,' she said, suddenly bashful.

'He loves you very much.'

'Too much. It's not fair on him, is it?' she said as the present caught up with her. 'I know what I'm putting him through, Maggie. I can sometimes hear myself screaming at him, or worse. One minute I think he's going to attack me, and the next I see my Ted in front of me, telling me it's going to be all right. But it's *not* all right. It would be better for both of us if I walked in front of a bus.'

'Or threw yourself in a lake?' Maggie added. 'But you won't do that because that would break his heart. You know that, don't you?'

'It's still not fair,' she insisted. 'He shouldn't have to look after me as if I'm a baby. I should go into one of those homes.'

'He wants to look after you,' Maggie insisted.

'That's the problem . . .'

Returning to the living room, Elsie's words haunted Maggie. She hadn't been ready to hear her friend resigning herself to her fate, not yet, probably not ever. All too soon, Elsie would be beyond her reach and her comfort and, in some ways, so would

314

Elsa. Her ghost would forever remain sitting on the bench by the side of the lake, trapped by her grief. Maggie felt powerless to help. The signs were all around that the Miltons' life was disintegrating. Ted was struggling to cope and it wasn't only the house falling into disrepair.

'Did I hear you limping before?' Maggie asked. She had noticed him shuffling more than usual when she had arrived but it was his sharp gasps of pain when he had reached up to deadbolt the front door, when he thought he was out of earshot, that made her suspect he was concealing an injury.

'Oh, it's nothing. I slipped in the bathroom but I'll be right as rain in a day or two.'

'So that's why you didn't want to go out for a walk. Do you need to see a doctor?'

'I'm fine, Maggie.'

She could hear the strain in his voice so didn't press him further, on his own health at least. 'I never imagined she could get so bad so quickly,' she said. 'The drugs don't seem to be helping.'

'I'm not even sure she takes them. I caught her spitting some out the other day when she thought I wasn't looking. She thinks I'm trying to poison her.'

'All the more reason to accept any help you can. Did Alice say when she'll be calling in next?' Maggie hadn't forgotten Ted's earlier evasion.

Ted rubbed a hand over his face. The stubble on his chin made a chafing sound against his calloused hands. 'I didn't want to mention it while

Elsie was here, but Alice has had some bad news. She called around yesterday to tell me.' He sighed heavily as if the memory was too much to bear. 'An x-ray picked up a shadow on her lungs and she was rushed in for more tests. She has an appointment next week with an oncologist.'

Maggie's mouth went dry as she struggled with the news. 'I kept *telling* her to go to the doctor.'

'I know, she's told me to thank you. She wanted to tell you herself but she couldn't face going into the salon. She says there's no point in getting her hair done if she's facing the prospect of losing it to chemo.'

'Where there's life there's hope,' Maggie said, knowing it was lame but she couldn't think of anything else to say.

'Is there?' Ted's voice sounded much further away than it should. 'What about my Elsie? Her body is working pretty well for her age but what good does it do her? Where's *her* cure?'

Maggie wanted to go over and give Ted a hug but knew he wouldn't appreciate being pitied. Harvey had no such reservations and was quickly at his side. He groaned when Ted began to rub his back fiercely.

'It's wrong, I know that,' she said. 'I just wish I wasn't going away now and leaving you.'

Ted cleared his throat. 'Thanks, Maggie, but I really don't deserve your kindness.'

'Of course you do and I promise I'll come straight over as soon as I get back.'

'No, you don't understand.' There was a stran-
gled breath as he tried to rein in his emotions.
'Do you want to know what I was thinking when
Alice came over? When she was trying to make
light of her illness in case she upset me?' His next
words were full of self-loathing and his voice trembled with anger. 'I was thinking of myself, that's
what, worrying too much about who was going to
help me stand up to Yvonne when she arrives next
week to think about anyone else. It's unforgiveable, Maggie, especially when I'm now taking
advantage of a pregnant woman and resenting the
fact that she's going on holiday. I can't begin to
tell you how ashamed I am of myself. I'm a selfish,
self-centred, cantankerous old misery!'

'Now you listen to me, Ted. You're anything
but selfish. You're not thinking of yourself, you're
thinking of Elsie. We need to keep you well so
you can look after your wife.'

'But I'm not looking after her, am I? She doesn't
even know who I am most of the time. It's not
her husband she sees, but a deadly assassin who's
broken into her home.' His voice had started to
waver.

'Oh Ted, she still loves you. She's just been
telling me so,' Maggie said, choosing not to
mention what else Elsie had said. Would Ted want
to know that in that brief moment of clarity his
wife had wanted him to relinquish his duties and
leave her to someone else's care? Had Elsie already
said the same to him?

317

He was shaking his head. 'It's Freddie who's been immortalised. I hadn't quite realised how important he was to her.'

'Ted, Freddie's love was never tested. We'll never know if he would have given her the kind of love and devotion that you give her.'

He sighed. 'I suppose it's not only me she's forgotten; sometimes she forgets who she is, too. She told me she had a hot date with David Niven the other night,' Ted said with a forced laugh that Maggie couldn't share.

While Maggie struggled to find words of comfort, it was Ted who filled the silence. 'And sometimes she thinks the baby survived.'

The statement came out of nowhere and it stabbed at Maggie's heart. 'Tess? But you said you'd seen her medical records.'

'Yes, it's there, written in black and white that the baby was stillborn. Like I said, you can't rely too much on what she says.'

Maggie wasn't convinced. Ted had become adept at keeping Elsie's secrets, so the confession was out of character. He was telling Maggie for a reason. 'What if Elsie did come back to Sedgefield for Tess after all?' she murmured.

'Next you'll be going on about tracing her again.'

'Isn't that why you told me?' Maggie challenged. '*You* think Tess survived, don't you?'

'Oh, Maggie! She mentions her all the time, not only the baby, but the woman she might have become. All those questions she must have been asking herself for the last sixty years, she's now asking me as if I know the answers.'

'So why don't we try to find those answers?'

Wending her way back through Elsie's life, all the way back to Elsa, would be anything but an easy path, but if there was a glimmer of hope that the baby hadn't been lost forever then Maggie was prepared to grasp it. And Ted didn't answer her question, which she took as an indication that he was ready too.

'Did you ever sit down with Elsie and talk about her time at Sedgefield? Ever?' she asked him.

'I knew Mrs Jackson wasn't her real aunt but she was always vague about how they were connected. And of course I knew a little about Freddie, but as for the rest, she wanted to keep her secrets and I had to respect that.'

'But?'

She waited patiently for Ted to answer but he appeared more intent on massaging Harvey's back. There was the sound of an escaping sob being cut short. 'I watch her sitting in her chair sobbing her heart out, cradling a cushion and refusing to let it go. She can hear the baby crying and it's not only breaking her heart, it's breaking mine too.'

Harvey's groans intensified as Ted dug his fingers deeper into his fur. Maggie sensed the pleasure was turning to pain although her faithful dog wasn't going to let Ted down in his hour of need. Wanting to comfort them both, Maggie joined Ted on the sofa. She put her hand gently on top of Ted's and brought Harvey's distress to an end.

'I'm worried about you, Ted, and so is Elsie. I hate to say it, but maybe you should look at some respite care if only to give yourself a chance to recharge your batteries.'

'You're beginning to sound like Yvonne. I won't hear of it! Once Elsie's in a home, Yvonne will make it difficult for me to bring her back here. I know my daughter.'

'Difficult but not impossible, not if you can get yourself back to fighting strength. Ted, you can't carry on like this,' Maggie said. 'Even you would be hard-pressed to take care of her from the grave.'

Ted's laughter was hollow. He had taken hold of her hand and clasped it in both of his. 'You don't mince your words, do you?'

'And if you need someone to back you up when Yvonne gets here, then I will. I'm only a phone call away even if it is long distance,' Maggie offered. 'And what about Nancy? Would she take your side? Is she coming home?'

The pressure Ted was applying to her hand briefly intensified. 'Nancy? No, I don't think she'll be over until there's a funeral to attend. She doesn't even phone that much any more, not now that Elsie isn't well enough to chat. I think she speaks to Yvonne or maybe writes one of those email things but that's about it.'

'Sounds like Elsie was lucky to get flowers on

her birthday.' As she spoke, she realised. 'Nancy didn't send them, did she?'

'No,' Ted said. 'I bought them.'

Maggie thought of Elsa and her desperate fight to keep her first-born. 'I can't imagine anyone not feeling blessed to have Elsie as their mum.'

'Maybe I shouldn't have let her spoil them so much. Don't get me wrong, I'm proud of them both. We brought them up to believe they could achieve anything they set their minds to and not to worry about us. I wouldn't want to be a burden to them in my old age and Elsie felt the same but . . . but if it's the difference between keeping Elsie here or sending her away . . .' Ted's voice cracked and he wasn't even trying to disguise his sobs now.

Maggie pulled her hand free so she could wrap her arm around his shoulders. She had formed an impression of Ted in her mind from the limited physical contact they'd had so far. From the projection of his voice, she had always imagined him to be at least as tall as James and his hands were certainly wide and his fingers long and thin, but as she pulled him closer she was surprised at how insubstantial his frame seemed.

'I'll help as much as I can,' Maggie promised.

'I can't bear the thought of her going into one of those places, I just can't.'

'Then let's do everything we can to help her stay in the present. I know Alzheimer's is a cruel and wicked disease but what if we could give her a reason to fight it? Will you help me try to find Tess?'

'I'm getting desperate enough to try anything,' Ted admitted.

Maggie knew her logic was flawed. The appearance of a long-lost daughter wasn't going to provide a miracle cure but she wasn't ready to give up on Elsie and neither was Ted. She felt a flutter of nerves as she contemplated the idea of cancelling the holiday to France. Time was of the essence and Elsie needed and deserved her help now. The fluttering grew into a storm as Maggie realised how seriously she was considering the idea.

'Please tell me you're joking.' James was standing in the kitchen and had almost choked on his cup of coffee when Maggie had told him what she was thinking. Sam and Liam could be heard playing football in the garden with Harvey, blissfully unaware that their holiday plans had been called into doubt.

The grim look on Maggie's face should have been enough to tell him that there was no punch line, but for avoidance of doubt she shook her head and then held her breath.

James stuttered as he grappled with his response. His half-formed words came out as little clicks that would have made Maggie smile if the subject under discussion hadn't been so grave.

'No, Maggie,' he said quickly when his power of speech returned.

His reaction wasn't unexpected and she couldn't blame him but cancelling the holiday completely had been her starting position. She was holding out for a compromise.

'What if we put it off for a few days?'

'No!'

Undeterred, Maggie stood her ground. 'James, if you had seen how Ted was struggling physically as well as emotionally . . . He's already had a fall and if he can't look after Elsie then that's the end of their fifty-odd years together.'

'I know it's harsh, Maggie, but maybe that's for the best. I'm sure if Elsie was in her right mind she would be saying the same thing.'

Maggie wasn't quick enough and James glimpsed a shadow passing across her face.

'It *is* what Elsie wants, isn't it?' He sounded less exasperated now; he knew he was winning the argument.

'Only because she knows Ted needs more help and that's why I want to stay here.'

'But there's only so much you can do, Maggie. You'll have your hands full in a couple of months anyway.'

'Yes, in a couple of months,' she repeated as if he had missed the point. 'My hands look pretty empty now.' She waved her hands at him in frustration, only vaguely aware of how crazed she must look. 'Ted thinks the baby survived and we suspect her medical records were falsified. If Tess was adopted and we can find her then I'm hoping Elsie can find some peace – or at least stop focusing on the most painful period of her life.'

'She has Alzheimer's, Maggie,' James said as kindly as he could. 'You're never going to put her mind at rest.'

Maggie's lip began to tremble. 'It will help. It has to.'

James put down his coffee and didn't say anything until he had stepped close enough to hold her arms in case she started flailing again.

'I know how strongly you feel and how much you want to help, but seriously, Maggie, you're clutching at straws. You need to put yourself first – and if not you, then think of the baby. If Ted had a fall then isn't there a risk you could hurt yourself too?' James was getting better at reading Maggie and caught another look on her face. 'What happened to him exactly?'

She rested her forehead on his chest and listened to the steadiness of his heartbeat. He was far calmer than she. 'He wouldn't tell me at first but I finally got it out of him.'

'And?'

'Elsie had gone into the bathroom and left the taps running. When he heard the water spilling over he rushed in and frightened her. She launched herself at him and they both ended up on the floor.'

'That could have been you!'

'I know.' Her heart filled with dread as she anticipated what would come next.

'And I know you don't want to hear this but . . . maybe you need to become less involved.'

Maggie lifted her head and waited for the tears that were welling up in her eyes to trickle down her cheeks. James had promised her no more tears but he needed to know what this was doing to her. She knew it wasn't playing fair but she was desperate. 'I can't do that, so please don't ask me,' she said. 'I'm willing to accept that it was a bad idea to suggest cancelling the holiday but I won't desert them completely, not when they're both more alone than ever. They barely have each other.'

A pair of strong if slightly calloused hands cupped her face. Two thumbs wiped away her tears. 'As long as you're careful and you let other people do their bit too. I don't see why their daughter couldn't come down from Scotland a couple of days early if he's struggling that much. Or what about the other one in America? I know it's far, but it's getting desperate.'

'Don't get me started,' she said with a low growl. 'Nancy was happy enough to be spoilt by her parents but now she has a family of her own, she's turned her back on them. How she can live with herself, I'll never know.'

There was an awkward pause as they both became painfully aware of the parallels in James's life. The last time they had spoken about Judith was when Maggie had repeated her conversation with Kathy but James had refused to listen. Maggie had been prepared at that point to bide her time, time for James to miss his mum and for Judith to appreciate exactly how seriously he had been affected. But at that moment there was a void crying out to be filled.

'Your mum probably deserves better too.'

'No, Maggie.' His voice was resolute. 'Mum didn't spoil, she smothered, and it's only now that I'm beginning to appreciate how much she took over my life. I won't let her back in if there's even a remote chance she could threaten our life together.'

James hugged her close and she felt safe within the protective circle of his arms. His heart was beating a little faster now but she couldn't keep quiet. She couldn't bear the thought of another mother being denied access to her child for a moment longer.

'Her actions were indefensible but not unforgiveable,' Maggie whispered. 'When she phoned social services she barely knew me and hadn't been ready to accept me.'

'I know when she phoned, Maggie, and it doesn't make it any better.'

'But it does,' she said, raising her voice and her head towards him. 'Her actions were borne of ignorance not malice and she's learnt some harsh lessons since then. I'm not saying you have to make your peace with her right now but it's not good to harbour so much ill feeling. It's your decision, but couldn't you at least let her know that you're willing to start building some bridges when you get back off holiday?'

'You're right. It *is* my decision.' James had taken

a step back and put his hand on Maggie's protruding stomach. 'And my decision is not to let anything or anyone threaten this new life.' As if in response, a rogue hand or perhaps a foot pushed against the taut wall of flesh that kept her baby safe from harm.

'I know but wouldn't it be good if—'

Out in the garden, Liam and Sam's voices were getting louder. There was a dispute erupting over whether a goal had been scored and James pulled back from her. 'Wouldn't it be good if we didn't start the holiday with an argument? I need to go and sort the boys out.'

'James, please!' The boys weren't the only ones raising their voices now, but she was determined to stand her ground.

James had been moving towards the back door but he turned to face her again. 'It's not going to happen, Maggie. Not now, and not when I get back,' he growled. 'I can't forgive her. Don't you see what's happening? She's still driving that damned wedge between us. Do you want her to get what she wants?'

'She might have wanted to break us up once but—' Maggie didn't finish the sentence she wished she hadn't started. She had picked up the sound of Harvey panting and the scent of fresh earth and macerated grass too late.

'Dad?' It was Sam's trembling voice.

'Are you and Maggie going to get divorced?' Liam added.

James spun around but not quick enough to catch

his youngest son who rushed out of the kitchen as fast as he had arrived. Liam remained stock-still.

'No, son, of course not; there's absolutely nothing to worry about on that score. Grown-ups are allowed to have disagreements just like you and Sam. It doesn't mean I don't love Maggie, I do. With all my heart.' He had turned his head towards Maggie as he cast his last remark towards her. 'I'd better go after Sam.'

James's footsteps, closely followed by Harvey's, receded into the distance and silence fell in the space between Maggie and Liam. 'Everything's fine,' she assured him.

'Dad's not speaking to Nana Judith, is he?'

Maggie took a few tentative steps towards him. She listened acutely for any telltale signs that Liam was backing away. He wasn't. When she was close enough to feel the air from his harsh breaths, she reached out and found his shoulder. Tracing her hand upwards, she stroked the side of his face. 'Your dad's angry with her at the moment. She did something which even she would agree now was very silly. It's probably a good thing that they stay away from each other for a while. I should have known your dad was still very angry about it.'

'What did she do?'

Maggie hesitated. She didn't like keeping secrets, her own parents had been very open with her when she was growing up, but she didn't want to say something that might harm Liam and Sam's relationship with their grandmother. 'You know, Liam, I could tell you but I would think Nana Judith is upset enough as it is. It might make her feel worse if I told you.'

She had pulled away her hand and, in response, Liam rushed towards her and wrapped his arms around her waist. Where once he would have buried his head in her chest, now he rested it on her stomach. She leant down and kissed the top of his head.

'If you do get divorced, will the baby have to live with us?'

Maggie laughed despite herself and Liam raised his head.

'I promise you here and now that we are not getting divorced,' she said candidly, 'so the baby is staying here with me and your dad.'

'But how do you know that for sure?'

'Listen to me, Liam. Your dad is a wonderful man and he tries so hard to make everyone happy but that's not been fair on him.' As Maggie was talking, she could hear footsteps marking her husband's return but it didn't stop her from saying what needed to be said. 'It's a good thing that he's finally stopped putting other people's feelings before his own. I won't lie to you, it's going to be a bit of a learning curve for me but that's not a bad thing, not if it means he's finally going to be happy for himself.'

'It's going to be a bit of learning curve for me too,' James said. He groaned as he shifted position and it was then that Maggie realised he was carrying Sam on his shoulders. 'There's no reason why we can't consider each other's feelings and that way we'll both be happy. I'm sorry, Maggie.'

A glimmer of hope sparkled in the darkness but that was all it was. Maggie had to accept that there was nothing more she could do for now. She would have to pack away her anxieties along with her sun hat and sandals and hope that when she returned there was something left of the mess she was leaving behind to salvage.

CHAPTER 21

Elsa's eyes snapped open to find darkness staring back at her. She didn't know where she was and her pulse raced as she failed to make sense of the shadows forming in the gloom. Squeezing her eyes shut again, she let her other senses take over. Tentatively, she slid clammy hands across the cotton sheets until her fingers curled around the edges of a single bed. There had only been one time in her life when she had slept alone and the faint smell of lilac confirmed it. Elsa's lip trembled, she didn't want to be at Aunt Flo's house any more; she wanted to go home to her mum. She wanted to be back in the double bed she'd shared with her younger sister, even if she was a conniving little minx who had to be bribed every time Elsa wanted to sneak out in the middle of the night to meet Freddie. The memory felt like a stab to the heart.

'Oh, Freddie,' she murmured, wrapping her arms around herself in the knowledge that she would never feel his loving embrace ever again. It was then that she became aware of her sagging body, little more than an empty vessel now. She had never felt so utterly bereft.

'I'm sorry, I'm so, so, sorry, Tess,' she said as the first tear trickled down the side of her face. 'Why did I ever give you up? How will you ever forgive me?'

Her ears strained for answers that would never come. She was going to spend the rest of her life being tormented by memories of abandoning her first-born and as if to give substance to her fears, a long, pitiful howl cut through the silence of the night and turned Elsa's blood to ice. It had sounded as if it was coming from another room close by but Elsa imagined it was a ghost from the future – her ghost, her future. She couldn't bear the sound and clamped her hands over her ears but she could still hear the screams – which were now being wrenched from her own lungs. A moment later light flooded the room, silencing her with dread.

'Don't be frightened. You're safe here, Elsie,' a woman soothed.

With bright light stinging her eyes and tears blurring her vision, Elsa couldn't see the woman clearly but she could see enough. 'Who are you? Where's Aunt Flo?' she panted.

'Not far,' the woman said softly as she perched herself on the edge of the bed. 'We don't like to see you so upset, though. Do you think you could take your medicine now? It'll help you sleep.'

Elsa tried to hide beneath the covers. 'No, go away!' she cried. 'Leave me alone to my misery!'

Maggie's reintroduction to the blustery British weather at Manchester airport was a refreshing change from the cloying heat of southern France, but the weather wasn't the reason she was glad to be back on home soil. Her self-restraint had lasted but only just. She and James had avoided mentioning either the Miltons or his parents while they were at the farmhouse, although it was fair to say that his sons had shown significantly less self-control. Liam, in particular, was taking a guilty pleasure in mentioning Nana Judith at every given opportunity. Fortunately his mischievousness entertained rather than annoyed his father and they had all enjoyed what had been a relaxing and yet exhausting holiday.

After disembarking, Maggie had been temporarily separated from James and the boys. A member of the cabin crew had kindly offered to escort her or, to be more precise, Harvey, through the throng of arrivals towards a security door and the great outdoors so the dog could relieve himself. Travelling by plane wasn't something he was either used to or enjoyed but he had been impeccably well-behaved and made the most of all the fuss and attention showered on him by the cabin crew and passengers alike.

As soon as they found a patch of clear ground Maggie issued the command so he would do his business and he dutifully obliged. Maggie insisted on cleaning up after him but gave in when the over-eager stewardess asked to take Harvey for a quick walk to stretch his legs. If nothing else, it gave Maggie time to do the one thing she had put off for as long as she could. For two whole weeks there had been no calls home. She had made it known to her friends that she didn't want to hear any bad news while she was too far away to help, and although she had told Ted to phone if he needed her, he hadn't. She could only hope that his silence was a good sign.

Frustratingly, Jenny's phone rang out and with a sinking heart Maggie cut the call. Undeterred, she tried Kathy. Saturday afternoon was always busy at the salon so she was relieved when her friend answered the call so quickly.

'Hi, Maggie, home already?' In the background, the incessant, high-pitched buzz of hairdryers was somehow soothing.

'Still at the airport but we'll be back soon.'

'How was the holiday?'

'Lovely, thanks. The weather was glorious, a bit too hot for me sometimes but James and the boys loved it. They went on long walks roaming the countryside while I stayed at home with my feet up.'

'That's exactly as it should be – enjoy it while you can. I take it there were no problems with the farmhouse, then?'

'It was perfect – and you might get a pleasant surprise when you go there next. I put James to good use and even Sam and Liam helped out.'

'Now you know I wasn't expecting you to earn your keep,' Kathy said before quickly adding, 'So what did he do?'

'Don't get too excited, it was nothing major. Just

the odd fence mended and he's re-plastered the wall in front bedroom.'

'Nothing major? Maggie, it would have taken Joe years before he got around to repairing that wall.'

'It was the least we could do or should I say, the least James could do. I barely moved. I think I've doubled in size since I left – and before you say anything, it's not because I've been gorging myself.' Maggie was smiling as she gave Kathy the obligatory update about her holiday but at the back of her mind she was rushing towards the real reason she had phoned. 'Now, enough about me; what have I been missing? Do you know how Mrs Milton's doing?'

'She's fine.'

Goose bumps confirmed what Maggie had been expecting to hear. 'Something's happened, hasn't it?'

'I'm sorry, Maggie, she's been moved into a care home but it's a pretty good one by all accounts.'

Kathy had tried to sound upbeat but Maggie's heart sank. 'So Yvonne got her way, then?' she said.

'It's for the best, everyone agrees, even Elsie.'

'I bet Ted doesn't.'

'Oh, he'll come around to the idea. Look, we can talk more when you're back in Sedgefield,' Kathy said above the tinkling of a bell in the background that announced the arrival of a customer. 'Maggie, I'm really sorry but I have to go. Call me later.'

'I have to go too,' Maggie added solemnly. She

had heard the sound of claws scraping against tarmac. 'But I'll phone you the minute I get back.'

Maggie was guided through the arrivals gate and reunited with James who was too busy keeping Sam from wandering off to notice that the curve of her smile had a distinct quiver at its edges.

'Mark said he'd text me when he got here but so far nothing,' he told her.

'Hello, son.' Ken's voice came from behind them and, as he approached, he reached out and gave Maggie a quick squeeze. 'Wow, *you've* grown.'

Maggie felt a glow rise in her cheeks, but it wasn't the comment about her size that made her blush, Liam and Sam had said far worse. She was wondering where Judith was and by the tone of James's response, so was he. 'What are you doing here, Dad?'

'I told Mark I didn't mind picking you up.'

A host of questions flooded Maggie's mind, including how Ken had managed to coordinate arrangements with Mark when they barely knew each other. Maggie clearly wasn't the only one growing impatient to mend bridges.

'Don't worry, I'm on my own,' Ken said to fill the awkward silence and answer one of the unspoken questions. 'I am allowed to see you, aren't I?'

'Of course you are, Dad,' James said. He sounded sad and Maggie was glad of it.

There was a chorus of hellos from the boys and then everyone was talking at once. Liam and Sam were eager to tell their granddad all about their holiday and how Maggie had been teaching them the way to train their puppy. As Maggie listened, she couldn't ignore the persistent pull of home. 'Do you mind if we catch up properly when we're in the car? The flight has tired me out.'

Her pretence at exhaustion gave Maggie a good excuse to withdraw from the chatter on the journey home and there were no arguments when she suggested going straight to bed for a little nap. But sleep was the last thing on her mind and by the time she heard James saying goodbye to his dad and closing the front door, Maggie had finished the call to Kathy. She remained where she was, lying on top of the quilt with Harvey by her side. She didn't know what else to do.

James crept upstairs as quietly as he could which, for a man with giant-sized feet, wasn't quiet at all. He struggled as he tried to find room next to her on the other side of the bed from Harvey who wasn't about to surrender space for anyone, not even his master. James balanced precariously on the edge of the bed and, despite herself, Maggie smiled.

'Sorry, I thought you were asleep,' he whispered.

'Even if I was, I wouldn't be now,' she countered as she tried to nudge Harvey over to give James more room.

James let a finger trace the side of Maggie's face. He had found the damp trail of tears that lined her cheeks from the corner of her eyes to the back of her ears. 'What's happened?'

'Elsie's been moved into a care home. She left

a message for me not to worry.' Maggie was trying to sound strong but her voice cracked at the last.

James rested his head on the pillow next to her, his nose brushing the side of her face, his breath evaporating her tears as he spoke. 'So don't worry, Maggie, she wants what's best for Ted and you knew there was a possibility this would happen.'

His words were meant to reassure Maggie but had the opposite effect. 'Of course I knew! That was why I didn't want to go to France,' she barked.

James didn't reply and regretting her sharpness she forced her voice to soften. 'I know that if I'd been thinking objectively then I would have been the first to admit that Ted couldn't manage on his own any more. I had been hoping that maybe Yvonne would move in with them for a while and let Elsie stay at home that little bit longer, long enough for us to find out more about Tess.'

'Yvonne lives in Scotland, doesn't she?' The question was also an answer.

Maggie sighed and tried to let go of her anger. 'According to Kathy, she's not the ogre I thought she was. Ted had been telling her everything was fine, so it came as a massive shock for her to see how much Elsie had deteriorated. And apparently her daughter is expecting a baby soon, so now Yvonne's torn between the two. The last thing she'll need is someone like me judging her. Apparently she's already wracked with guilt – but then so is Ted for letting her take over.'

'He'd still feel like a failure no matter who took

the decision.' James buried his head into the curve of her neck. Big as he was, he felt impossibly vulnerable. 'It's his responsibility to look after his wife. Always was, always will be.' When he kissed her bare neck it sent a shiver down her spine.

There were shouts from downstairs as the boys demanded attention. Harvey jumped up and, as he bounded off the bed, the aftershock almost knocked James off too. Maggie grabbed hold of him.

'I'd better go,' he said, kissing her neck one last time. 'Try not to worry. At least Mrs Milton's not going to stumble around the park any more.'

When Maggie was alone again, she wrapped her mother's quilt around her and let her thoughts lead her to the old park bench. Another empty space had opened up in her life. She had lost a dear friend and could only imagine how keenly Ted would be grieving the loss of his wife who had left him in more ways than one. Tears trickled down the side of her face with renewed force.

CHAPTER 22

Elsa's body heaved as yet another heart-rending sob tore from her lungs and burned the back of her throat. She couldn't live with the pain and resisted the urge to breathe in again. She was going to drown in her own tears.

Her arms were aching as she wrapped them tightly around the pillow in a futile attempt to fill the crushing void. For purchase, her fingers were digging into her flesh but she welcomed the pain. She deserved no less. With a reflexive gasp of unwelcomed air she breathed in the scent of fresh laundry. Her nose was blocked so it was more a sense of taste than smell, clinical and sterile. Every shred of her baby's existence had been erased.

A memory flashed before her eyes and she lost herself to it. Instinctively she loosened her grip and began to cradle the pillow. She was in her bedroom at Flo Jackson's house. The towels that had been laid on the bed as she gave birth lay crumpled in a corner of the room and the smell of her exertions lingered in the air. She had been lucky to get back in time: the urge to push had overpowered her as soon as she had raised the alarm and Tess had been born within minutes.

With the baby's arrival had come less welcome guests. Anne and the doctor had been called as soon as Aunt Flo had noticed Elsa was missing and they had appeared like spectres at the side of her bed even as her body was recovering from the throes of childbirth. When Aunt Flo cut the cord, Elsa had held out her arms to comfort her baby girl but Anne was reaching out for her too.

'She deserves to hold her child! Don't you dare deny her that,' Flo had growled to her niece.

'You know you have to give her up, don't you?' Anne had said. 'You know it's for the best.'

Elsa ignored her. She couldn't take her eyes from the baby as Flo quickly bathed her with warm water and a damp cloth before swaddling her in a cotton sheet. She watched unblinking as Tess was placed in her arms, her tiny hands pulling free of her swaddling, her long, pink fingers grasping for purchase as she cried.

Gently rocking her baby, Elsa could feel her breasts tingle as they began to produce milk, her body's response a contradiction to everything she had been told of her ability to be a mother. But when she asked to feed her, Flo had simply shaken her head, letting loose a single tear that slipped down her cheek. Elsa began to stroke her daughter's face to soothe her cries and the baby sought out her finger and suckled hungrily. It was Elsa's turn to cry and her vision blurred as she looked

341

into her daughter's bright blue eyes and silently begged her forgiveness.

At Anne's insistence, her husband wrote up the medical notes that would describe another version of events, while Elsa held on to the living proof that Freddie had loved her once. She hadn't needed Anne reminding her what must be done, she already knew. She wanted to hate the woman who would take her place in Tess's life but Elsa knew, deep down, it was the right thing to do and she had no one to blame but herself. Anne wasn't a bad person and she would be the better mother but when the time came, she couldn't let go and her tears fell on the baby's face as she grappled with Flo in a desperate tug-of-war.

'Please, Flo, I can't do this. I'll do anything you ask, just don't take her from me,' Elsa begged. 'Please, please, I can't do it, don't make me.'

'You love your daughter, I know that,' Aunt Flo answered softly as she forced her hands between Elsa's arms and the baby to prise her free. 'Love her enough to let her go.'

'I can't . . . I can't . . . I can't . . .' Elsa repeated between desolate sobs. But she did love Tess enough, and with more strength than she imagined she could ever possess, she leant forward and rested her lips on her daughter's forehead. The baby's downy soft skin was wet and Elsa tasted the saltiness of her own tears. Her nose was completely blocked but she could still smell that unique mix of scents that was and always would

342

be Tess. 'I will never forget you,' she whispered, 'not ever.' Her grip on her daughter had loosened just enough for Flo to take the baby from her and there had been a physical wrench in her chest as she felt her heart break.

The memory sent a shudder down Elsa's spine. Even now she could hear herself and the baby wailing in perfect synchronicity. She buried her head deeper into the pillow and inhaled slowly, searching out even the subtlest scent of her baby's wet skin or the lilac-scented water Flo Jackson had used to bathe her.

'Will you describe every single detail to me? I want to know what the home looks like and if it looks well maintained. I want to know how many staff there are and what they're wearing and how clean the place is. And tell me about the residents, do they look cared for, do they look happy?' Maggie instructed.

'I'll describe everything,' confirmed Jenny.

'And be honest.'

'Maggie, please . . .' Jenny said. She had fifteen years' experience of being Maggie's eyes and she was losing patience. 'I've never been able to pull the wool over your eyes before and I'm not about to start now.'

'Sorry.' Maggie leant back against the headrest. She was grateful that Jenny had sacrificed a precious Sunday afternoon to take her to the care home. James had offered but he had to take the boys home and she wasn't prepared to wait another day.

'How was the holiday?'

'Fine, everything was fine. How's Mark getting on?'

'The holiday was *that* good?' Jenny remarked with more than a hint of sarcasm.

'Sorry, Jen, I promise I'll tell you all about France when my mind's settled. Now, back to you and Mark.'

Jenny didn't argue, there was still plenty of other news to catch up on. 'I got the job.'

'No!' Maggie said. 'Really?'

Jenny had the good grace to laugh at her friend's disbelief. 'Yes, that seems to be the general reaction I'm getting from people. I'm not sure I can believe it myself. I don't start until October, which gives Mark plenty of time to get settled with his own career, or should I say careers.'

'Is he working for Kathy yet?'

'Yes, he was over at the salon all last week. You do know they're using the treatment room as his office, don't you?'

Maggie nodded. Before her holiday she had packed everything away so Kathy could make a start on transforming the room into temporary office space. 'At least she hasn't rented it out on a long-term lease which leaves my options open for the future, for a while longer at least.'

'Should I ask if you've heard anything from Judith?'

'James has arranged to meet his dad for a game of golf but that's about as far as he's prepared to go at the moment. Anyway, weren't we talking about Mark? Has he sorted through all the paperwork Kathy took from her mum's yet?'

Jenny was starting to suspect that Maggie's persistent questioning had little to do with Mark's welfare. 'What are you after?' she asked.

Maggie took a deep breath before explaining how she was about to embark on a hopeless and most likely thankless task. 'I want to trace the history of Kathy's house. I know Flo Jackson lived there until the late sixties and Kathy's dad bought it about ten years later. If Mrs Jackson's niece inherited her estate then there must be a paper trail that leads back to her.'

'And why would you need to track down the niece?'

'I want to find Elsa's baby,' Maggie said as if it was that simple.

'I thought the baby was stillborn?'

'That's what her records say but both Ted and I think she survived.'

'I don't know what it was like in the fifties, Maggie, but I'm pretty sure it would be illegal for a doctor to falsify medical records.'

'Illegal – but not implausible, Jen. It was the doctor's wife, Flo's niece, who was so desperate for the baby. Maybe he was too.'

'He'd have to be to risk doing that.'

The car was slowing down now and there was

a sharp right turn. Wheels left tarmac and began to crunch gravel.

'Can you tell Mark to expect a visit from me?'

Jenny pulled the car into a parking space and switched off the engine. 'I'll tell him – but even if you're right, it's not going to be easy uncovering an illegal adoption. And why go to all that trouble anyway? Elsie may never be in a fit state to under-stand what you're trying to do.'

'I know, Jen, but please don't start talking me out of it. I have to at least try.'

'Then I'll help as much as I can.' Jenny reached over and squeezed Maggie's hand. 'Now, let me describe what I can see.'

Sunny Days lived up to its name and the bright lemon sun in a cloudless blue sky shone brightly across the imposing Victorian house, which had been extended over the years. The glimmering whitewashed walls flickered occasionally with the shadows of tall beeches and sycamores that were scattered throughout the large, rambling gardens and bordered lush, green lawns. A long, curved drive led towards the entrance and was punctuated by an ornate water fountain that sprinkled rain-bows into the cooling September air.

'Does it look well maintained?' Maggie asked. She sniffed the air and detected a hint of sweet, freshly cut grass.

'A few rust spots here and there but nothing to suggest disrepair.' Jenny sounded cautious in her verdict, which made Maggie relax a little. Neither of them would rush their opinion.

As they crossed the drive and neared the entrance, the soft tinkling of water from the fountain was the perfect accompaniment to the languorous birdsong that rolled in waves from the shade of the whispering trees. Again, Maggie sniffed. The water was just a little stagnant.

The deep gravel path made their progress difficult and Maggie held on tightly to Jenny's arm. She was glad she had decided against bringing Harvey who would have struggled too.

'I can't imagine this stuff is great for the residents to walk on,' Jenny said.

'Maybe it's so they can't escape . . .'

With perfect but unnerving timing, they heard an almighty scream from somewhere deep within the house. It was too distant to distinguish whether it was a man or a woman but the mournful cry set every one of Maggie's nerves on edge. They rang the bell and by the time the door was answered, the screams had been stifled.

'Hi, I phoned earlier. My name's Maggie Carter and we're here to see Elsie Milton,' Maggie said.

'Yes, of course. I'm Carol, the manager,' the woman said before inviting them into a small vestibule. 'Would you mind signing in for me?'

While Jenny completed the visitors' book, Maggie tried to process as much information as she could about the home. She'd had some preconceptions but the smell wasn't nearly as bad as she had expected, although not exactly pleasant either. Industrial strength air fresheners burned the back of her sinuses but it was impossible to tell if they were disguising bad odours or were an overenthusiastic attempt to make a strong first impression.

'So you didn't bring your dog, then?' Carol asked. Maggie had forewarned the home that she would be bringing her guide dog but then had second thoughts that morning. Carol sounded disappointed.

'He's had a busy couple of weeks so I thought he needed to catch up on some me time,' Maggie explained.

'That's a shame.'

Maggie tilted her head as she concentrated on the woman's voice. 'Is something wrong?'

Carol pursed her lips before she spoke. 'I'm afraid Mrs Milton isn't too well. It's nothing to be concerned about, but she's a little agitated this morning. It happens now and again, and of course it can take a while for our residents to settle into their new surroundings. She's insisting on going into the garden so Rachel's upstairs trying to get her ready. Maybe you could go into the visitors' room and wait or perhaps you could come back later when she's a little calmer.'

'No, take me up to her; I might be able to help,' Maggie said, immediately regretting leaving Harvey at home.

Before Carol could reply there was another scream, much clearer this time. The voice belonged

348

to Elsie but the tone belonged to a young woman whose life was being ripped in two.

Maggie took hold of Jenny's arm. 'Take me to her now,' she said, more forcefully this time.

'I'm sorry but I don't think that would be possible . . . health and safety . . .' Carol began.

'Oh, I wouldn't argue with her,' Jenny warned, although her tone remained disarmingly light. 'Once she's set her mind on something you can't stop her.'

The howling grew louder as they hurried upstairs. Maggie was so intent on reaching Mrs Milton that she didn't even register the pain when her ankle knocked against the chair lift at the top of the stairs.

Rachel was doing her best to stop the old lady from running out of the room half-dressed when they arrived. 'We're nearly there, Elsie,' she panted. 'Now please let go of the pillow so I can put your dress on.'

Even though the room was probably a fair size, it felt claustrophobic as everyone squeezed in. Elsie's terror was palpable and wouldn't be helped by a room full of strangers. 'Maybe I could try?' Maggie asked with restrained diplomacy. 'Do you think you could all give her some space?'

Rachel didn't argue and slipped past Maggie. Rather than the towering bully of Maggie's worst imaginings, she was probably only a little taller than her. 'She thinks someone has stolen her baby,' she whispered as she passed. 'I've never seen anyone so devastated – it's heartbreaking.'

From the concern etched in Rachel's voice, Maggie took some solace that Elsie was well cared for but there was no time to relax. Elsa had retreated to the furthest corner of the room, sobbing.

'We could always give her a sedative if you could persuade her to take it,' Carol suggested.

'Let me speak to her first.'

Maggie took a moment to get a better sense of where she was. There was an open window, which brought fresh air and sunlight into the room and flickering warmth across her face. The faint smell of cut grass added some colour to the sterile scent of disinfectant, but it couldn't sweep away the pungent aroma of sweat created by collective exertion.

Maggie stepped carefully across unchartered territory towards Elsa's sobs. Despite her best endeavours, she received another bump worthy of a bruise, this time to her shin. She felt her way past the bed on one side and a wardrobe on the other, continuing until she reached the wall opposite the door. Eventually her fingers touched a curtain that billowed in the gentle breeze. The birdsong from outside was only just audible over the wracked sobs.

From the projection of the sobbing Maggie gauged that the old lady was sitting on the floor and put a hand on the dressing table to balance herself as she bent down. Her pregnancy made the position cumbersome but she would stay there as long as necessary. With her other hand she reached out and made contact with a trembling knee. Elsa flinched.

'Elsa, it's Maggie. Tell me what's wrong.'

'I want my baby!' she mewled. 'They've taken her but I want her back. Oh God, how I want her back!'

Elsa's tears didn't abate and now Maggie was threatening to join her.

'I know you do, Elsa. You're a good mum and you would have looked after her.'

'Then help me! Please! I can't go on like this.'

'I swear I'll do everything I can to find her for you,' Maggie said with such conviction it frightened her.

There was a mumbled response, wet sniffs and hiccups which at least gave Maggie hope that Elsa was trying to stifle her tears.

'I have to get to the park,' Elsa explained. 'I have to meet Aunt Flo or I'll never see Tess again.'

'There's a little rose garden outside,' whispered Carol who had remained on the threshold. 'She likes to sit on the bench out there sometimes, so that's where we were going to take her.'

There was a soft mewl as the tears began to build once again. 'I need to go to the park!'

'Then let's get you dressed,' Maggie said, choosing a tone that was firm rather than cajoling.

There was a pause and Maggie felt herself being scrutinised.

'You have a dog. You're Molly, aren't you?'

'Maggie. We've sat together in Victoria Park a few times but I'm afraid I haven't brought Harvey with me today.'

'You know how to get to the park? Will you take me there?'

With a little awkward manoeuvring, Maggie helped Elsa to her feet, a task made doubly hard because Elsa was still holding on to the offending pillow. 'Can I take that for you?'

Elsa grasped the pillow tighter still. She lifted it to her face and breathed in deeply but then released a painful sob. 'I know it's not her,' she said, needing to explain herself. 'But I can't even smell her any more. She had a damp, baby smell but there was a hint of lilac too, from the water Mrs Jackson bathed her with. It's not there. I've lost everything.'

Two thoughts occurred to Maggie in quick succession. The first was the connection that could now be made between Elsie's choice of fragrance and her long-lost daughter, but it was the second thought that caused alarm. Elsie wasn't wearing her perfume. She didn't have the one thing that had helped ease her pain for over half a century.

'I can remember holding her, all wet and wrinkly. It was like being in the eye of a storm. The labour pains had vanished and she was still mine. There was just that one moment, only a few precious minutes, but I won't forget it and I won't forget that smell either. I let go of Tess, but I'll never let go of the memory.'

Maggie didn't try to take the pillow again but Elsa offered it up anyway. 'It's not her,' she repeated.

With a little help from Jenny, Maggie began to dress Mrs Milton who huffed and puffed as she obediently sat down on the bed to allow Jenny to put on her shoes. The final touch was a spray of lilac scent and then Elsie fell into an unnerving silence.

'You must always remember the perfume,' Maggie told Carol. 'Make sure all the staff know that.'

'Are we still taking her outside?' Jenny asked.

There was a gasp of shock. 'The park, I have to get to the park.'

This time there was no need for restraint and it was Jenny who helped Mrs Milton out of the room and towards fresh air with Maggie and Carol following close behind.

The rose garden was alive with colour; a mixture of light and shade that blended warm air with cool and delicate perfumes with earthy mulch. It was a distinct improvement on air fresheners and helped Maggie remain calm as she sat down next to Mrs Milton on the small bench. Placing her hands on the warm wood, her fingers resisted the flattened surface, yearning for the curve of wooden slats painted with layers of the past.

Elsie noticed the absence of a connection too. 'We're in the wrong place,' she said. She sounded worn out and her voice had a painful rasp, her throat still raw from grief.

'It's not Victoria Park,' Maggie agreed.

'And that lawn isn't a lake.'

'Are you OK, Elsie?'

Elsie laughed softly. 'No. I'm in the wrong place. Why do I keep saying that?'

'You've been staying in a care home.'

Elsie took one of Maggie's hands, which had been searching in vain for the familiarity of wooded knots and chipped paint. 'I know – and it's the right place for me to be. What I meant was, why do I feel like I should be somewhere else? I wanted to get to the park, didn't I?'

'You said you had to meet Flo there or you'd never see Tess again.'

Keeping hold of Maggie's hand, Elsie sat back on a bench that squarely resisted the curve of her spine. 'Yes, of course,' she said and then turned her mind to the memories she had so recently been reliving. 'I gave up my daughter within minutes of her birth and in the days that followed I became completely numb. It was the only way to survive the pain but I think it frightened Aunt Flo. On the day I left I didn't even say goodbye to her; I simply packed my bags and walked out the door. I stopped off at the park one last time and that was where Aunt Flo tracked me down. After trying so hard to convince me that a clean break was for the best, she was the one who begged me to come back to visit her. She finally swayed me by promising to bring Tess to me behind Anne's back so I could say goodbye properly.'

'The baby wasn't stillborn, was she?' Maggie still needed that all-important confirmation.

'No.'

For a moment Maggie was without words. The skeleton of Elsa's story had been given flesh and bone and her picture of Elsa's time in Sedgefield was almost complete. 'And did you get to see her again?' she asked when she could.

'It was all arranged. Aunt Flo would sneak out with the baby while Anne was visiting and I would wait in the park. Oh, how I waited and waited,' Elsie told her. 'I'm waiting still . . .'

'More heartbreak?'

Elsie went quiet for a moment. 'Dark times,' she said but would say no more.

'And it was Anne who adopted Tess?'

'Yes, she whisked away my beautiful baby while her husband wrote his lies. I suppose we all thought the good doctor could rewrite history too but I was never going to forget, not even with a mind as befuddled as mine.'

'What was Anne's surname, Elsie?'

Elsie squeezed Maggie's hand as if it would force the name from her memory. 'Anne and Dr . . .' There was a sigh of defeat but it caught in her throat. 'Hammond! That was it, Dr Hammond. Why do you ask?'

'I want to find Tess for you, or at least find out what happened to her. Would you want that?'

Elsie thought for a while then said, 'I've spent my whole life wondering if she was happy and, more than anything, if she was loved. I would never have handed her over if I thought Anne wouldn't take good care of her but you never can tell, can you? So yes. Yes, I would like to know.' Then Elsie sighed unhappily. 'But I'm not me very often these days, am I? I won't remember this conversation by teatime, so how could anything you find out help?'

Jenny had said the same thing. Elsa had lived her life and suffered her losses and there was nothing Maggie could do in the present to lessen that pain, least of all as Elsie relived it.

'But even though I go away,' Elsie continued, 'I'd like to think I'd find my way back for the right reason. If you can tell me that my baby went on to lead a happy life and that I made the right decision then I'd find my way back, for Tess. Of course, you'd probably have to tell me again an hour later but I'd never get tired of hearing it. I would like to know.'

'If I can find out, I promise you Elsie, I'll never get tired of telling you either.'

CHAPTER 23

It was as noisy and lively as ever in the salon, the incessant chatter competing with the screech of hairdryers, but for once Maggie didn't feel part of it. She was only a visitor today and one without an appointment.

'So is it you or Harvey on autopilot?' Kathy asked when she noticed the dog steering his mistress towards the treatment room.

Maggie brought Harvey to a reluctant stop and absent-mindedly rubbed her stomach. 'I've managed four whole days at home twiddling my thumbs but it's driving me crazy already.'

'Don't try pretending you've been stuck at home all of this time. I bumped into Ted and I know you've been visiting Elsie almost as much as he has.'

'I haven't,' Maggie answered a little too quickly. 'He's there at least twice a day.'

'It wasn't an accusation, Maggie.'

'Sorry, for a moment there I thought I was talking to James. He's the one who thinks I should be housebound. I've only been there twice, no, three times but someone has to. Yvonne didn't exactly hang around, did she?'

Kathy sighed. 'It wasn't easy for her. When she brought Elsie into the salon for a bit of pampering the day before she went into Sunny Days, Yvonne was in bits. It was as if she was already grieving for her mum. It made me think about James and how one day he might regret cutting his mum out of his life.'

Maggie's only response was to smile at the tenuous connection that steered the conversation towards another family in crisis.

'I know she doesn't deserve your sympathy,' Kathy continued, 'but the last few weeks have been torture for Judith. She's terrified of leaving the house in case she misses that all-important call from James.'

'It may surprise you to know that she does have my sympathy; unfortunately, James doesn't share that view. He's being uncharacteristically stubborn but I'll wear him down, I promise.'

'Thank you.'

'If you want to thank me then perhaps you could help me on another matter close to my heart.'

'OK. I give in – that room over there is yours whenever you're ready to come back. I'll even go so far as to let you have it rent-free if it helps the figures add up.'

Maggie laughed, surprised. 'Where did that come from? Kathy, I couldn't!'

'I run this salon because I enjoy being here, not because I rely on the income,' Kathy explained. 'I'm only thinking of myself – and I miss you. You and James are like family to me and I want to help. Besides, I'm expecting a lot from James in return.'

Kathy had been talking to him about putting together a property maintenance contract for her newly acquired responsibilities, and if he came up with the right deal it would put his own business on a more secure footing. 'Even so, that's too generous.'

'It's there whenever you're ready,' Kathy repeated.

There was iron in her voice and Maggie knew better than to argue. 'Thank you,' she said, stunned and immensely grateful, but the future would have to wait. It was the present and the past that would continue to preoccupy her, at least until the baby arrived. 'Would it be pushing it if I asked another favour?'

'Mark is sifting his way through a mountain of paperwork as we speak,' Kathy said. 'I've already heard about your fool's errand to find Elsie's long-lost daughter.'

'You think I'm mad, don't you?'

'Have you really thought through what will happen if you do find her?'

'I know I can't go back to 1953 but Elsa is still a lost soul and a wretched one at that. She had her heart broken when Freddie died and then ripped out of her chest when Tess was taken away. Even if she can't find complete peace, if there's one fleeting moment, just one, when she knows what became of her baby, then it'll be worth it.'

'It was Tess I was thinking about. Have you thought how this might affect her?'

'If I'm honest, I'm trying not to. There's no way of knowing if she's been looking for her birth mother or if she even knows she's adopted – after all, it wouldn't have been recorded officially. So how do I drop that kind of bombshell and then explain that Elsie has Alzheimer's and would struggle to recognise her husband, let alone the child she gave up sixty years ago?'

'It doesn't bear thinking about,' Kathy said. 'We can only hope that she would want to know the truth; and I suppose even a glimpse of the person Elsie was is better than nothing.'

'Exactly! And if it was me, I'd want to know,' Maggie agreed. 'But first we need to find her.'

There was a flutter of cotton sleeves as Kathy held her hands up in surrender. 'OK, you've convinced me. I'll even help Mark go through the paperwork. Come on.'

'And how may I help you today, madam?' Mark asked when Maggie knocked politely and then stepped into what had been her treatment room. 'Let me guess . . . You're having trouble sleeping because you're too busy delving into the past and uncovering dastardly plots. Mmm. I'm sure I have a bottle of smelly stuff around here somewhere that will cure you of your ills.'

'Those bottles of smelly stuff are my bread and butter,' growled Maggie, referring to the stack of removal boxes that were the last remnants of her beloved business.

'Ah, so it's an insatiable appetite you're struggling with. No wonder you've doubled in size since I saw you last.'

Maggie took another step. 'Would you like to come here and say that?'

'Certainly,' he said. Mark stood up from behind the desk that had taken the place of Maggie's treatment table and came over to give her a hug.

'We're here to help you track down the elusive Flo Jackson,' Kathy said. 'Maggie's getting impatient and time is of the essence.'

Mark pulled up two chairs for them before returning to his desk. 'You couldn't have come at a better time,' he said. Papers rustled in his hand. 'I've only just found these. One is a copy letter from your dad's solicitor, Kath. It's dated 1978 and terminates a ten-year lease on your house.'

'That was the year we moved in,' Kathy explained. 'It had been a nurses' home before that, but I didn't realise Dad already owned it.'

'A ten-year lease?' Maggie repeated. The squeak from the chair as she sat forward was achingly familiar. 'That means he bought it in the late sixties, which was around the time Flo Jackson died, so chances are her niece was the one who sold it. Mark, we're looking for anything that refers to either Anne or her husband, Dr Hammond.'

There was the sound of a box sliding across the table as Kathy started to rummage through musty paperwork while they talked.

'So what else did you find?' Maggie asked Mark.

'Nothing about the Hammonds, I'm afraid,' he said, starting with the bad news, 'but this is an almost identical letter serving notice to the proprietor of a shoe shop "formerly known as Flo's Fruit and Veg".'

'Kathy's dad owned Mrs Jackson's shop too?' Maggie asked before Kathy had the chance. The shuffling next to her had stopped.

'Yes.'

Mark was giving nothing away but suddenly he didn't need to. Maggie had already made the connection. 'Alice told me the salon was once a shoe shop . . .'

'And before that it was a greengrocer's,' Mark concluded.

'I don't care how we do it, but we have to track down the sale documents!'

'Have you found something, Kathy?' Mark asked, directing his attention to the one person who hadn't been swept up by the revelations.

'Hmm? No. No, nothing,' she said a little too quickly for Maggie's liking.

'Kathy, what is it?'

Her friend's chair squeaked as she moved away from the box. 'Oh, ignore me,' she said at last. 'It's probably just seeing all this stuff my dad accumulated. He's been gone eight years but 1 look at his handwriting and it's as if it were only yesterday.'

'He must have been an amazing dad, setting you up with all this property,' Mark said.

362

Kathy took a while to answer and Maggie sensed her staring at the papers strewn onto the desk. 'If you don't mind, I'll call it a day,' she said, and before anyone could object she was up and leaving. 'It'll be chaos out there.' Her voice sounded stronger the further she removed herself from her dad's archives. 'My girls are already in a tizzy as it is, with Mark on the scene.'

Mark cleared his throat. 'No need to mention that to Jenny,' he said when Kathy had left them. 'To be perfectly honest, they terrify me.'

'Your secret's safe with me. Now, back to work.'

An hour later and the door Maggie thought she was opening onto the past had begun to close again. Mark had found nothing more.

'What if Kathy's mum still has more boxes, Mark?' she said. 'It's worth a try, surely.'

'Sorry, I've been cataloguing everything and we have all there is.'

Maggie could feel four walls closing in on her. The room she thought she knew so well had been stripped of its identity in more ways than one. She didn't need to see to know that all her rows of bottles and jars with their explosion of colours at the twist of a cap had disappeared, replaced by countless brown boxes of musty, decaying paper. But it wasn't the latest reincarnation of the room that played on her mind but an earlier version, one that would have been known intimately by the young woman who was always one step ahead of her; in fact, so far ahead that she risked disappearing completely from view.

Maggie's eyes were closed and she made no acknowledgement of James's return to the bedroom. He placed a cup of tea on the bedside table and then leaned over to kiss her.

'You're not fooling anyone. I know you're awake,' he said, 'but at least try to get some rest. You don't need to get up yet, Harvey's been fed and watered.'

'I'll try.'

'What I wouldn't give for an opportunity to stay in bed.' He groaned as he pulled himself upright and away from temptation. 'All your tossing and turning kept me awake too. I don't suppose I need to ask what's playing on your mind, but isn't it time you accepted that tracking down Tess might be an impossible task?'

'And that's precisely what's keeping me awake,' Maggie said as she pulled herself up on one elbow. Her bump stayed where it was. 'Jenny's scouring through lists of Manchester GPs on the internet but it feels like clutching at straws. It would have been so much easier if the adoption had been legal. At least then there would be proper channels to go through.'

'It's probably a blessing in disguise that you can't trace her, for Tess at least. How's she going to feel if a complete stranger tells her how her so-called parents illegally adopted her?'

Maggie felt the ever-present knot in her stomach twist and tighten. 'Thanks, I needed that encouragement.'

'I'm not encouraging you, Maggie. I'm worried about you – and for the record, so is Kathy.'

'Kathy knows how important this is and she agrees with me; we need to find Tess and at least give her the chance of meeting her mum.'

'She also agrees with me. You've taken it as far as you can but it's time to let go. You can't though, can you? You're obsessed with that family. Isn't it enough that you're visiting Elsie every other day? Do you have to spend every waking hour thinking about her too?'

Maggie's jaw tensed as she spoke. 'You should be glad I've got Elsie to divert my attention or I might start making plans to reunite another mother with her child.'

There was a sigh of exasperation but James heeded the threat. 'Is it a crime to be worried about you?' he said before stepping away. 'I have to go to work.'

'You can't prevaricate forever,' she called before he had escaped completely. When he turned, he would see the self-righteous look his wife was casting in his direction.

'Are you actually looking for more ways to stress us both out?'

'The stress is there anyway. If this morning is anything to go by, then you're not the usual patient and supporting James I know and love.'

'I *am* being patient, that's the point. I've told you what I think about your search for Tess; I haven't told you what to do even though I'm sorely tempted. And for the record, I'm not prevaricating about Mum; I'm playing the long game.'

It was the first indication that his resolve was weakening, helped no doubt by the browbeating he would be receiving from Kathy while they worked on their business deal. Maggie was tempted to add her own argument for Judith's defence, but if she was honest, life was simpler dealing with one crisis at a time. 'I know, and I won't tell you what to do either. Now go, you're keeping me from my beauty sleep.' But even with all the lotions and potions at her disposal, Maggie couldn't find sleep. Her stomach churned as it followed the same twists and turns as her thoughts. She pushed her head into a pillow and breathed in the lavender and chamomile scent she had added to her linen, it was a trick her mum had once used. The wave of nostalgia brought with it an inescapable sense of loneliness and there was only one person left to turn to.

'Is it too early?' Maggie asked when the call was answered.

'It's never too early to hear from you, love. Is everything OK with the baby?'

'Yes, everything's fine, Dad,' Maggie said, rubbing her stomach in curved caresses as she spoke. 'I just had a few spare minutes and thought I'd find out how you are.'

'Oh, we're all fine and dandy. We get up, have breakfast, Jim goes out for a round of golf, I help Dot with the chores, we have lunch, we have a siesta, we have dinner and then Dot makes us watch the English soaps. We might have a game of cards and then it's a nightcap and bed: nonstop excitement.'

Stan made the routine sound tortuous, but Maggie knew he was enjoying his new life, or at least as much as he would allow himself without the wife who had been the other half of his whole for the majority of his life. He would never acknowledge that life was good again, so Maggie had to read between the lines and find her own assurances. 'Poor you,' she said.

'How's the weather over there? It's showing no signs of cooling down here yet.'

'Oh, it's teeming down as usual.'

'Bloody British weather,' he muttered and then yawned.

'Don't, you'll make me start,' Maggie said but she was already stifling a yawn.

'Actually, you do sound tired. Are you sure everything's all right?' he asked.

Maggie leant back and tried to stretch some of the knots out of her spine. On the other end of the phone she could hear her dad shifting position and imagined him out on the veranda with his straw hat and a cup of tea. She had heard the telltale rattle of a cup and saucer, the whispered instructions from Dot not to let it go cold and then the occasional, satisfied slurp. The picture made Maggie feel strangely homesick, not for a villa in Spain but the Sedgefield terraced house she had grown up in.

'I'm not sleeping too well,' she said although she wasn't about to tell him why. His reaction to her hopeless search would be the same as everyone else's and she didn't want another dose of realism. 'It's hard to find a comfortable position anywhere these days. I'm as big as a house.'

'Whereas I could sleep standing up. Ah, you've just reminded me, I had a dream last night.' He took another sip of tea and then said, 'Your mum was in it.'

'Do you dream of her often?'

Stan cleared his throat. 'No, that's the thing. This was the first one. I was watching the two of you laughing together.'

Maggie smiled as a hundred memories came flooding back from her childhood. 'What were we doing?'

'You were in the park, down by the lake.'

Maggie strained her ears as if she might be able to hear the sound of their laughter. What she did hear was a distant quack. 'Feeding the ducks?'

'No, you were too old to be feeding ducks, you were sitting on the bench talking.'

Maggie dug a hand into her pocket, slipped her fingers into a plastic bag and pulled out a crust. With perfect precision, she launched the bread into the air and it fell to the water with a plop.

'I'll never be too old to feed the ducks,' she said with a smile.

'You're not there now, are you?' An approaching family of ducks had given her away. 'I thought you said it was teeming down?'

Maggie raised her head to the muted warmth of the mid-September sun. 'Ever heard of an umbrella?' she asked not wanting to give up the lie she had used to ease her dad's home-sickness.

Stan laughed. 'Not for a while. But I don't suppose there's any point talking sense into you. You're as stubborn as your mum.'

Maggie's free hand had been resting on her stomach but only now did she feel brave enough to make contact with the past. As her fingers traced the surface of the bench she could read its history as if it was written in Braille. There were one or two deep cuts where someone had crudely carved out initials, and patches of chipped paint revealing hidden layers beneath, each one a differing shade. The latest layer was chocolate brown, she'd been told, but Maggie could remember when the bench had been painted a verdant green to match the moss that grew around the tree trunks, back when she could see with colours and not scent. She pushed her finger-nails deep into the cuts and sliced into her own past.

'Do you remember that time Mum padlocked your shed?'

'I don't know what she thought she'd achieve.

369

I could hardly finish the decorating with all my tools locked away in there.'

'And yet somehow she managed to get you to paint and decorate the kitchen in record time.'

'Yes, she always got her way in the end,' Stan said softly.

'I hope I have half her determination,' Maggie confessed. 'I'm going to need it.'

'You're going to do just fine,' Stan said, assuming innocently that his daughter would be concentrating solely on impending motherhood and not inveigling herself in other people's problems. 'Dot's making all the arrangements and we'll be over there as soon as you've had the baby.'

'I can't wait to see you all,' Maggie said.

When the call ended, Maggie stayed where she was. Closing down each of her senses she detached herself from the present and waited. There was enough room on the bench for someone to sit on each side of her and it didn't take long for the bench to summon up the ghosts of the past and give them substance. On her left, Elsa sat in silence, waiting desperately for that one last chance to see her baby. On her left sat her mum. She gave Maggie's arm a quick squeeze. 'Now is not the time to feel sorry for yourself, Maggie,' she told her. 'Don't waste time grieving for the things you can't do, get on and do the things you can.'

CHAPTER 24

Sapped dry by autumn winds, the leaves above Maggie's head rattled as she made her way through Victoria Park. She paused momentarily at the top of the slope that would take her down towards the lake but she didn't give in to its pull.

'Not today, Harvey,' she said with only a faint hint of regret.

Maggie tucked her chin into her chest and fought against the biting wind as she carried on towards the main entrance gates and the High Street where they paused again. To the right, the road wended its way to the salon. Maggie turned left.

Harvey knew the route to Ted and Elsie's house well enough, although they hadn't visited for over a month; before her holiday; and before Elsie had gone on her own travels. She wondered how much had changed at the bungalow since then and she wasn't looking forward to finding out. Ted was spending all his time at the care home, too intent on looking after his wife to consider his own needs, so there was little hope that he had kept up with the housework.

She had promised to be there by two, giving Ted enough time to return home after visiting Elsie. She arrived with two minutes to spare and dropped a heavy shopping bag onto the step to knock at the door. She had brought a hearty lunch for the two of them along with a selection of other dishes that would give Ted at least one substantial meal a day for the rest of the week. She had considered bringing some cleaning supplies too but there had only been so much she could carry.

'Hello, you two,' Ted said brightly when he opened the door. 'Come on in out of the cold.'

No sooner had Maggie stepped into the house than Harvey bounded down the hallway, his claws scraping along the wooden floor before being silenced by the soft carpeting in the living room.

As she unbuttoned her coat and swapped pleasantries with Ted, Maggie was already trying to detect the telltale signs of the squalor she had expected but instead picked up the unmistakeable scent of lilacs. The image of Ted spraying his wife's perfume to ward off his loneliness was too much to bear.

'I'll pop this in the kitchen,' Ted said. He groaned theatrically as he tested the weight of her shopping bag. 'You can find your way to the living room, can't you?'

'Of course I can.' Maggie's smile was tentative; she wasn't about to be fooled by his false bravado. It was only when she walked into the living room and heard Harvey wagging his tail energetically that she realised it hadn't been an act.

'Hello,' came a familiar voice.

Words completely failed Maggie as she quickly navigated her way across the room. When she reached the old lady, Elsie was standing up and ready to grasp her outstretched hand. They hugged each other desperately.

'So do you like my surprise?' Ted asked from the doorway.

'Is this an official visit or is there a search party on your heels as we speak?' Maggie asked, not daring to hope that this was anything more than a temporary reprieve.

'It is official, but it's not a visit. I picked Elsie up this morning and despite a lengthy debate with Carol, my wife isn't going back to Sunny Days. Not if I can help it. Isn't that right, love?'

'There's no arguing with him,' Elsie confirmed.

It was the ache in Maggie's cheeks that made her realise how broad her smile was. Elsie was back, in more ways than one.

'Make yourself at home and I'll put the kettle on,' Ted said.

Maggie raised a hand in objection. 'Oh, no, you're not going anywhere until you tell me exactly what's happened.'

Ted didn't argue. He took the seat opposite while Maggie sat next to Elsie on the sofa, holding her hand and squeezing it as if to confirm that she really was there.

'I only agreed to Elsie going into that place for respite but, as I expected, Yvonne was already making long-term arrangements. It's taken me a while to get fighting fit but I'm back in charge now and I won't hear another word said on the matter. She stays with me.'

'I'm sure Yvonne was only doing what she thought was best, for both of you.'

'I don't need other people dictating what's best for me,' countered Ted.

Maggie could sympathise: she had been the victim of well-meaning interference often enough, but it wasn't only Ted's opinion that counted. 'Elsie thought it was for the best too.'

'Yes, she did,' Elsie agreed, reminding Maggie that she was still in the room.

Ted sighed. 'I know, love, and I think I'd say the same thing if I was in your position. No one wants to be a burden – but it's not your choice and you're not getting your own way this time.'

Elsie tutted but didn't argue.

'She didn't belong in there,' he said turning back to Maggie. 'Don't get me wrong, they looked after her well enough but . . . I don't know, it was as if it was OK for Elsie to forget herself. No one cared whether she came back or stayed lost forever.'

Maggie ignored her first instinct to remind Ted that Elsie's illness was progressive and eventually she wouldn't come back, but of course he knew that. 'So you brought her back here to you.'

'Yes.'

'I know you want to stay together for as long as you can but . . .'

'No "buts", Maggie,' Ted said firmly. 'I'm her husband and I have a duty to take care of her. It's going to be tough but that's what marriage is all about, the good times and the bad. I won't abandon her to the care of strangers, even if she thinks I'm a stranger too. *I* know who she is, she's my wife and her illness can't take away my memories.'

As Ted gave his speech, Maggie gave Elsie's hand a quick squeeze but rather than acknowledge the outpouring of love and loyalty, the old lady's hand slackened. 'And how about you, Elsie?' she asked. 'Are you glad to be home?'

'Oh good, are we going home soon?' she said.

Maggie turned back towards Ted and raised an eyebrow but he wouldn't be challenged. 'She's better off here,' he said.

'I think I will have that cuppa now,' Maggie said. The beaming smile had faded and she was making an effort not to frown.

The two women sat in silence for a while as Ted busied himself in the kitchen. Maggie was reluctant to speak because she didn't want the confirmation that Elsie's presence had been fleeting. Nor did she want to acknowledge the secret hope that Elsa might emerge like a ghost from the past to guide her along the trail that would lead to Tess, a trail that had gone distinctly cold. 'Harvey's missed you,' she said at last.

The dog had been sitting in front of them, waiting quietly until his patience was rewarded with a rub behind the ear from Elsie. Harvey sighed before laying his head on her lap. 'He should go back to Mr Woodhouse, he'll be missing him.'

'He looks quite happy where he is for now,' Maggie assured her.

'Tea's up,' Ted said as he returned to the room.

'I was just saying that Mr Woodhouse will want his guide dog back. Do you think he'll be all right without him, Ted?'

'He doesn't need him at the moment,' Ted said as he put a tray down on the coffee table.

'You will be able to cope, won't you?' Maggie asked in a low voice when Ted handed her a cup of tea. 'Have you organised for the home help to come back again?'

'I will,' he said. 'Once we're all settled.'

'How about the district nurse?'

'Like I said,' he replied patiently, 'all in good time.'

Maggie wasn't convinced and considered making the call to social services herself, stopping only when she recognised the parallels with her own life.

'We knew a lady who was blind too,' Elsie continued. 'What was her name, Ted?'

'That would be Maggie.'

'Oh yes, Maggie, that's it. She was lovely. I don't think there was anything she couldn't do; in fact, half the time you'd forget she was blind. She was having a baby last time I saw her. Did we ever find out what she had?'

'She hasn't had the baby yet. A few more weeks,' Ted told her.

'Ooh, that's so exciting. Who's her doctor? Tell her not to go to Dr what's-his-name, Dr Hammond.'

'Dr Hammond retired years ago,' Ted told her gently.

The clatter of china was so loud it was lucky Maggie didn't break her cup on the saucer. 'You knew Dr Hammond?'

'He was our GP for years,' Ted replied. 'In Liverpool.'

'But he was Anne's husband, the doctor we've been looking for so we can trace the baby,' Maggie said, trying to sound calm despite her heart thumping against her chest.

'Sorry, Maggie, but he couldn't have been.'

'But that was the name Elsie gave me. I've been searching for the Hammonds.' Maggie was refusing to listen to what common sense was telling her until Ted spelt it out for her.

'It's possible there were two doctors with the same name but it's more likely that she simply confused the two.'

Maggie turned towards Elsie and felt a pang of guilt as she silently urged her to hold on to the memories she had spent a lifetime trying to bury. 'Elsie, do you remember Anne?'

'No,' she said in a tone that suggested she did.

'Not today, Maggie,' Ted warned.

'But I promised her I'd find Tess! How can I do that if I can't rely on anything she's told me?

What if she got the year wrong too, what if . . .'
Maggie began but dared not consider how much
of Elsa's story might be flawed.

'Maggie, I know for a fact she was here in 1953.
I'm not likely to forget the year she returned to
Liverpool – it was the same year I fell in love with
her.'

'But I can't find Tess without a name,' Maggie
told him desperately.

'Then maybe it's time to stop looking.'

Maggie was stunned by the full force of the brick
wall her amateur investigations had just hit. As
Ted consoled her as best he could and promised
to ask Elsie if ever she was of a mind to remember,
Maggie realised with a sinking heart that it was
time to accept what everyone else had been telling
her. It was time to give up on Elsa.

CHAPTER 25

'Is there anything worrying you at the moment?' Mel asked above the hiss of air being released from the blood pressure cuff.

Maggie shook her head nonchalantly. 'No, everything's fine.'

'Not according to your blood pressure, it's not. You've already stopped working so I presume you've had plenty of time to put your feet up?'

'Yes,' Maggie said, slipping her arm from the cuff that could detect her lies.

'And you're not still worried about the letter from social services, are you?'

'No, of course not.'

'Hmm,' Mel said as she scribbled some notes. 'I've been speaking to the health visitor who'll take over your care once my job is done. We thought it would be a good idea to start working together to make the handover as smooth as possible, so I'd like to sort out a home visit soon. That won't be a problem, will it, now that you're at home all the time with your feet up?'

Maggie gave Mel a winning smile. 'No, no problem at all.'

Seemingly satisfied with Maggie's answers, the midwife helped her on to the examination bed but as she began to explore the mountainous rise of Maggie's stomach, the questioning resumed.

'So are you ready to become a mum?'

Maggie refused to let the smile she had painted on her face falter. 'I will be,' she said, honestly this time. Playing mother to Lily and then the boys, along with the practice sessions Mel had arranged for her, had all played their part in boosting her confidence.

'You had better be, because this baby is preparing to enter the world. Baby's head is engaged.'

The surge of fear and excitement made Maggie's pulse race. 'Really? Does that mean it could be soon?' Panic was added to the mix as she realised how quickly time was running out and how much there was still to do. Her preparations for the baby were on track but nothing else in her life was even close to being resolved. Her search for Tess had reached a dead end and she hadn't been able to make any progress with James either. Meeting his dad for a game of golf had been the nearest he had come to a reunion with his parents so far.

Mel was laughing. 'Everything is still on track for your due date which is . . .'

'Three weeks on Wednesday,' Maggie offered.

'OK, three weeks, but I am a little bit concerned about your blood pressure. I'd like you to come back in on Thursday and we'll check it again.'

'Should I be worried?'

'No, Maggie, that's the point. You shouldn't be worrying about *anything*,' Mel said. 'Spend the next few days at home, with bed rest if you can manage it, and avoid stress.'

Maggie decided not to point out that this was a contradiction in terms. Staying at home doing nothing would only make her stress levels soar and so it was no surprise that rather than head straight there, Maggie found herself sitting on her favourite bench as she tried to decide what to do next.

Every time she convinced herself she was ready to slow down, a counter-argument formed. There was still time to make a difference – but she couldn't work out how, and the longer she sat there deliberating, the more agitated she became. Mel wouldn't be impressed.

She imagined two other mothers sitting on each side of her, reminding her that her first priority was her unborn child. They would have moved heaven and earth for their children. All Maggie was being asked to do was stay at home to keep her baby safe. How difficult could that be?

A week later Maggie's blood pressure was showing no sign of improvement and although it wasn't dangerously high, it could easily go that way. Mel was disappointed but not as much as Maggie who had made some effort to stay at home and had even cut back on her visits to Ted and Elsie. Clearly, it wasn't enough and Mel had told her in no uncertain terms that if she couldn't be trusted to take it easy then they would enforce bed rest in hospital and the last weeks of her confinement would be exactly that.

Maggie redoubled her efforts, but while she could slow down her body, her mind wouldn't be stilled. She was desperate for any kind of distraction and it came in the form of Jenny, who had phoned to say she was taking an early lunch and would call round. Judging by the agitation in her voice, it sounded like her promotion was getting to her even though she had only been in the job a matter of days. Maggie happily called a halt to the mind-numbing task of itemising her remaining stock, which had been relocated to James's workshop, and was at the door waiting when Jenny arrived.

'I can't stay long,' Jenny apologised, 'but I had to come and tell you. I could have waited, but you know what I'm like. Anyway, the thing is, I need you to promise me that you won't go rushing off and doing something you might regret before we've had the chance to come up with a plan of action. It'll have to be tomorrow, though, because Mark's at night school later. He's really enjoying his joinery course – I don't think he realised how much he regretted not finishing his apprenticeship – but don't worry, I'm not going to hound you any more about James taking him on. The college is going to arrange a placement for him.'

Jenny had gone off at a tangent and when she

took a breath, Maggie jumped in. 'Good. That's great news, Jen, but I'm guessing that's not what's got you all excitable. Now, do you want to stand on the doorstep all day or would you like to come inside?'

Jenny whisked past her and at the very last moment grabbed hold of Maggie's arm and pulled her along with her. Maggie barely had a chance to close the front door. 'This had better be good,' she laughed.

In the living room, Jenny waited for Maggie to sit down before sliding a footstool over so she could face her when she spoke. 'You have to promise to stay calm if I tell you I've found Flo Jackson's niece.'

The shock of the news left Maggie's entire body quaking. 'Too late! Tell me everything.'

Jenny cleared her throat, a sure sign she had a tale to tell. 'I know we wasted time looking for a Dr Hammond but that wasn't my only line of enquiry,' she began. 'I surmised there would be other records available in relation to the said properties formerly owned by one Florence Jackson. My investigations led me to Her Majesty's Probate Office where I submitted a request for said records in relation to Mrs Jackson's estate.'

Maggie put a hand gently on Jenny's knee. 'If you don't stop playing policeman and tell me what you know,' she said carefully, 'I won't be responsible for my actions.'

'I've had a response from the probate office.'

Maggie's heart quickened. 'You have a copy of Flo's will?'

'Yes,' Jenny said, suddenly sounding as meek as a mouse.

'And she mentions Anne?'

'Yes.'

'So who is she? *Where* is she?'

'I'm not sure I should tell you.'

Maggie's jaw dropped. 'Don't make me hit you, Jenny!' If her friend had wanted to send her blood pressure soaring then she couldn't have planned it better.

'The will mentions Elsa too.'

'She left her something?'

'Not exactly. Flo left everything to Anne Walters but there were a few caveats and a reference to Elsa and her daughter.'

'Anne *Walters*?' Maggie repeated. It was then, as the words formed on her tongue and spilled over her lips that she recognised the name. Her hand immediately went to her mouth but it was too late, the secret that had remained hidden for sixty years was out and, pressure rising or not, her blood ran cold.

No sooner had Jenny left than Maggie made two phone calls, one to her husband to tell him she was taking Harvey for a quick walk in the park and the other to Ted, to explain her real intentions. Both took some convincing but Maggie wasn't going to take no for an answer.

As she walked through Victoria Park, Maggie tried to concentrate on her breathing in a vain attempt to calm herself. The sun broke through the thick cloud above her and she raised her face to greet it. The air around her began to warm, invigorating the damp scent that was more rotting mulch than fragrant blooms. Autumn was making its presence known.

Maggie released Harvey's harness but kept hold of his leash as they settled in their usual spot by the lake. Her hands immediately began to trace the contours of the bench. The knots in the wood were hidden beneath layers of paint but they could still be found.

'Hello there, Maggie.'

The woman's voice was little more than a breathless rasp and Maggie struggled to identify it. Even as she approached, the woman's scent was tantalisingly familiar but still not enough to place the voice. It was only when she cupped her hand under Maggie's chin and gave it a squeeze that Maggie realised that it wasn't only the unfamiliarity of the voice but the absence of cigarette smoke that had thrown her.

'How are you, Alice? I've been thinking about you.'

'Bless your heart, Maggie, I'm doing fine,' she said. She sounded chirpy, but the gasps for breath were a reminder that she was anything but. 'I'm in and out of that hospital so much I keep telling them I should have my own parking space.'

'Are you still having chemo?' Maggie hadn't seen

Alice since her cancer had been diagnosed but between Jenny and Ted, she had been keeping track of her progress. Despite everything she was going through, Alice still managed to call in occasionally to see the Miltons.

'I'm having a bit of a rest at the moment.'

'I hope that means you're putting your feet up.'

There was a raspy chuckle. 'I'll have plenty of time for that when I'm in my grave. By the look of you, I'd say *you're* the one who should be putting your feet up.'

Maggie stretched her back in response and groaned. 'Actually, I'm under house arrest, but I'm still allowed to come out for fresh air once in a while, if only for Harvey's sake.'

'So is it Harvey who drags you over to see Elsie and Ted all the time?'

'I've only been there once in the last week. Even I can accept that I need to take a step back and, as it happens, I've arranged to meet them here for a change. They should be along soon.'

'Sooner than you think,' rasped Alice but Maggie had already recognised the sound of Elsie's heels scraping along the path.

'How is she today?' Alice asked Ted.

'Quiet.'

'And you?'

'Getting plenty of help so you two can stop fretting,' Ted said. 'Your friend Kathy came around to organise the home help. She refused to leave until all the paperwork was sorted.'

'That's Kathy for you,' Alice said.

Maggie smiled with relief. 'I'm glad.'

There was a lull in the conversation and they all turned their attention to the one person who had yet to speak.

'Hello, Elsie, love,' Alice said, her voice rising to a harsh whisper. 'I have to go to the shops now but I'll be around to see you tomorrow. Why don't you rest your legs and take a seat next to Maggie?'

As Elsie sat down, Maggie pushed her hand harder against the surface of the bench, willing it to trigger the connections that would allow Elsie's mind to remember the long-lost daughter she said she would never forget.

'No hair under that scarf,' Elsie remarked.

'Saves me a fortune in shampoo, I can tell you,' Alice said.

There were gentle smiles rather than laughter and then Alice was saying her goodbyes. Maggie made a move to stand up but was told in no uncertain terms to stay where she was. She didn't argue. Unlike a hug goodbye, a squeeze on the shoulder wouldn't give her the slightest hint of the rigours of Alice's cancer treatment. There were occasional benefits to being blind.

'There's something I need to tell you, Elsie,' Maggie said when Alice had gone.

'Do you want me to go?' Ted asked.

'No, please stay. I need someone to hear what I have to say, even if it's only Elsie who can give me the answers I'm looking for. If she can't do that, Ted, then I don't know what I'm going to do.'

There was a clamour at the water's edge where half a dozen ducks demanded their attention. Some splashed their wings against the water while others slapped webbed feet on the slipway, waiting noisily to be fed. It wasn't the ducks but the lake itself that caught Maggie's imagination. The secrets of the past were rising to the surface and Maggie's body tensed as she prepared to grasp Elsa's hand and free her from its murky depths.

'Where have the swans gone?'

Maggie tipped her head as she analysed Mrs Milton's voice, which had neither the gravity of the older woman nor the youthful lilt that heralded Elsa's return.

'Maybe they've made their nests somewhere else,' Maggie suggested. 'It does happen.'

'Is that what happened to me?'

'Yes, I think it was.'

'But I came back.'

'You came back for a reason, Elsie.'

'To feed the ducks?'

Maggie felt sick with nerves and could barely get the words out. 'No, Elsie, you came back for Tess.'

Sensing where Maggie was leading the conversation, Ted took a seat on the other side of his wife. Elsie's body stiffened and she shuffled closer to Maggie but didn't say a word.

Like Jenny, the burden of knowledge was

impossible for Maggie to contain but she would have to lead Elsie gently towards the revelation and then hope against hope that she would keep up with her. 'When you were twenty-two, you fell in love,' Maggie began, aware her voice was shaking. 'You gave your heart to Freddie and when you lost him, you wanted to hold on to the one thing you had left, the baby you were carrying. But you gave your baby up because you thought she would have a better life with Anne Walters and her husband. Do you remember that, Elsie?'

There was no indication that Elsie was listening, but Maggie carried on as if she was.

'You went on to marry a wonderful man and had two more daughters, Nancy and Yvonne. You had a happy, fulfilling life but you never forgot Tess and maybe, as the years went by, you began to doubt whether or not you made the right decision.'

Whenever Maggie wanted to reach out to Elsie, she would offer her hand and more often than not, Elsie would grasp it. But today Maggie's hands were firmly planted on the bench, still searching for that elusive connection. Shadows danced across her face as the sun dipped in and out of the clouds and the breeze that swirled around her sapped the moisture from her lips. Her mouth felt dry and her throat strained as she tried to contain the desperation in her voice. 'You told me not so long ago that if I could tell you what happened to Tess then you would find your way back,' she said. 'Elsie, I think I've found your daughter.'

She had arranged to meet Aunt Flo at noon in the park. It was a glorious summer's day and Elsa had warmed herself beneath the sun's rays as she waited; and waited; and waited. After only half an hour, her excitement had begun to wane as doubt crept in. An hour later and the knot of fear growing inside her felt heavier than the baby she had once carried. Two hours later and the first tear slipped down her face. When four hours had crawled by and Aunt Flo still hadn't arrived, Elsa had stopped scanning the top of the embankment for her first glimpse of her baby. She was looking out over the lake now, ignoring the polite hellos from passers-by. When she began to sob uncontrollably, Elsa thought she would never stop but at some point she lost herself to her grief and fell into an uneasy trance.

All she wanted was to hold her baby just one more time so she could tell Tess that she would always be loved and to beg her forgiveness. She would never feel complete, she knew that, but she might be able to find an uneasy peace that would allow her to get on with the rest of her life. She might even consider returning the attention of the persistent postman who was determined to make her smile. Maybe one day she could be happy again. But if she couldn't find some kind of absolution, then what was the point in carrying on? The lake glinted in the sunshine.

Five hours passed but time had lost all meaning because Elsa had no intention of leaving the park. Without warning she stood up and began to walk, her pace brisk as if late for an appointment. She didn't stop at the slipway or when the shock of the cold water took her breath away. She forced her way forward even though her feet slipped on the slime at the bottom of the lake and when she fell forwards, she refused the final breath as she plunged beneath its surface. She waited calmly for her burning lungs to stop fighting for air and only began thrashing when arms grabbed at her to pull her from the water. She put up a good fight but was eventually manhandled back to the bench by a passer-by. Aunt Flo had been called and arrived soon after, empty-handed and full of apologies. Elsa could hear voices around her now, more promises that would be broken but she wasn't listening. Her mind had taken her to a place where no one could reach her.

Maggie's pulse was racing as she listened for even the smallest indication that Elsie understood what she had said. Still nothing.

'Elsie, I really need you to say something,' Maggie said, aware she was begging. 'Right now I'm keeping your secret safe but I don't know where to go from here. I need you to tell me what to do next.'

At first the silence that followed was broken only by the disgruntled ducks but then a voice filled the void.

'You found her?'

Maggie turned towards the sound of Ted's voice and the first tear slipped down her cheek. 'Why won't she answer? She promised me she would find a way back.'

'She still has her good days,' he told her. 'This just isn't one of them.'

She was about to reply when Elsie stood up. Maggie grabbed frantically for the old lady's arm but Mrs Milton moved faster than her stiffened joints should have allowed. She strode towards the lake but Ted was there to save her, as he always would be.

'It's all right, Elsie, love. I've got you,' he reassured her.

Elsie's mournful wails as she fought off her husband were painful to hear and there was nothing Maggie could do to help. Her dream of reuniting mother and daughter was turning into the nightmare everyone had warned her it would be.

Slowly but surely Ted soothed his wife who was still refusing to utter a single word. 'I'd better take her home,' he said.

Maggie summoned up the courage to ask the question she didn't want answering. 'I've found Tess too late, haven't I?'

'Where there's life . . .'

Maggie put her hand over her mouth to hold back her emotions until she was calm enough to speak. 'I don't know what to do. Tess isn't a faceless stranger any more and I came here hoping for Elsie's permission to approach her. I can't take the decision on my own.'

'Then ask her other mother. Ask Anne.'

It was only when James slipped onto the bed next to her that Maggie realised she had fallen asleep. He kissed the back of her neck, his lips warm against her cold skin. The patchwork quilt hadn't been quite thick enough to protect her from the afternoon chill.

'What time is it?' she asked.

James was lying on top of the quilt, his body gently spooning Maggie's. He wrapped an arm around her waist and traced his fingers across her stomach. 'Gone six.'

Maggie groaned as she pushed back against him, a reaction not to her stiffened joints but to the roiling wave of emotions that coursed through her body as she remembered what she had done. 'I should get up.'

'No,' James told her, tightening his grip oh so slightly. 'It's nice to see you taking Mel's advice for once. I hope you didn't exert yourself too much in the park with Harvey?'

'We weren't out long.'

'So there weren't any detours to see the Miltons?'

On that one matter at least, Maggie's conscience was clear. 'I didn't need to; I bumped into them by the lake.'

'How was she?'

Maggie played with the soft satin edging of the

quilt, having resisted the urge to pull it over her head. 'Not the Elsie I know and love.'

Without warning, a dull pain pulled Maggie's abdomen taut. James felt her body tense. 'Are you OK?'

It took a moment for Maggie to catch her breath. 'Yes, it's only a Braxton Hicks contraction, those practice ones Mel told us about that prepare my body for the real thing.'

'You're sure?' James asked, pushing up on to his elbow and leaning over her. She could feel his heart hammering against his chest wall.

'Yes, I had one earlier today.'

James lay back down and together they remained still for a while, both waiting for the next contraction. When it didn't happen, they began to relax a little.

'I *will* start taking things easier,' Maggie said.

'Would that be a confession that you haven't been?' When Maggie didn't answer, James added, 'I think I should cut back on work and start staying home more.'

'It's too soon; maybe next week,' Maggie suggested. She didn't want James finding out what she was up to, not yet. With her blood pressure still high, he was hardly going to approve of plans that made Maggie's stress levels soar just thinking about them.

The warm draught from James's throaty laugh prickled the back of her neck. 'I should have known it was impossible to clip your wings. I suppose I have your mum to thank for that.'

Maggie hugged the quilt closer still. 'I miss her so much,' she said, a tremor in her voice.

'She was an amazing woman.'

'Yes, she was. It must have been so hard for her to find that balance between protecting me and letting me find my own way. I suppose it's difficult for any mum to let go.'

'Would you be including my mum in that observation?'

Maggie had actually been thinking of Elsa. 'Possibly.'

'The difference is that while your mum gave you wings, mine gave me a route map.'

'Your mum interferes because she wants what's best for you. She sees a single path for you to follow, one that she thinks will keep you safe and happy.'

'I know.'

'And I think the message has got through to her that your happiness includes me.'

James pressed his head against hers as if her optimism could be transferred by osmosis. 'That doesn't automatically mean she's going to make you happy too. I can put up with her interference – I've had a lifetime getting used to it – but it's you I'm worried about. I'm not sure you could cope with her, despite all your good intentions.'

'It would be a shame not to try.'

'Would it help if I said I'll think about it after the baby's born?' he asked cautiously. 'But only once we've settled into our new routines and we know what we're doing.'

Maggie bit her lip. She ought to be delighted and relieved by the breakthrough but Judith was about to make a reappearance in their lives much sooner than James could possibly imagine.

CHAPTER 26

When Maggie opened the front door, fresh air curled around her, leaving a scented trail of damp grass and decaying leaves. She fought an impulse to rush past her visitor and flee to the park.

'Come in,' she said.

'Thanks, Maggie. Thank you so much.' Judith still sounded as nervous as she had the day before when Maggie had phoned. The conviction she had once held about what was best for her family had been shattered and the formidable matriarch had shrunk back to more human proportions. Of course Maggie was only making this assumption from a single phone call and a greeting on her doorstep. It would take time to tell if her mother-in-law was ready to let her son lead his own life.

'You look so well,' Judith said. 'It's good to see you.'

'I'm just sorry your son isn't here to greet you too.'

'Still, it's good to see you,' Judith repeated.

Maggie led the way into the kitchen and, as she

set about brewing the tea, Judith made a fuss of Harvey, something that surprised the dog as much as it did his mistress. The conversation between the two women was stilted at first. They opted for safe topics such as their husbands' renewed interest in golf which was far easier than confronting the past – or the immediate future for that matter. Maggie had yet to explain to Judith her reasons for asking her to accompany her on a visit to see Anne Walters.

Neither was in a frame of mind to sit and relax so they stayed in the kitchen but it wasn't long before Maggie abandoned her mug of tea on the counter top. She was too sick with nerves to stomach it and wondered, not for the first time that day, if she was doing the right thing. The midwife had told her to avoid stress and yet she was about to charge straight into the eye of a storm. But there was no choice – she had to act now. A little more of Elsie's life was being erased with each passing day but there was another reason time wasn't on her side.

'What is it?' Judith asked when she saw Maggie grimace.

'Only a twinge,' she said, dismissing yet another practice contraction. She'd had a couple during the night too. 'Would you like to see the nursery?'

Judith had last seen the room when it had been stripped bare and she gasped at the transformation. With barely two weeks to go, the nursery was more than ready to receive the new addition to the Carter family, but rather than the smell of fresh paint and clean linen, it was jasmine with just a hint of lavender and rose that greeted Judith. The colour scheme complemented the aromas perfectly. The butter-cream walls provided a soothing backdrop to the swirling meadows of pink and blue flowers on the soft furnishings, blooms bright enough to tempt the bumble bees hanging from a mobile above the baby's bed.

'James made the cot,' Maggie explained and couldn't resist sweeping her fingers across the carving on the headboard where she followed a trail of leaping rabbits. It had been a labour of love.

'It's beautiful. And this baby quilt too, where did you get it, Maggie?'

'I made it,' she answered proudly. 'It's not quite as good as the ones my mum used to make, and I did get some help from Jenny, but I think Mum would approve.'

'Your little one is lucky to have such talented parents.'

Maggie wondered where this woman had been hiding for the last two years. Perhaps there was something in Maggie's smile that gave Judith the courage to speak more openly. 'I know when we spoke yesterday you said that what was done was done and we should put it all behind us, but I really do need to explain myself.'

'Honestly, Judith, you don't have to. I know you made that call to social services before we had both said our piece at Kathy's house. It really doesn't matter what happened before then.'

'It matters to James, and I wouldn't blame him if he never forgave me,' Judith said quietly as if she were afraid to say it out loud. She swallowed hard before adding, 'I betrayed my own son, Maggie. I betrayed both of you and I'm so, so sorry for what I did.'

In a room brimming with hope for the future, the desolation in Judith's voice tore at Maggie's heart. 'If you need my forgiveness, then you have it.'

'And James?' Judith asked, her voice quaking.

'You're his mum. He loves you and he will forgive you . . . eventually.'

'But he was so angry that day when he phoned me. He's never been like that before. It scared me, Maggie.'

'I think it scared him too.'

'It's because he loves you so much. You're his priority and I understand that now more than ever. Would it offend you if I told you that I've been the one who's been blind?'

'No, it wouldn't but I'd add that we've both had our eyes opened in the last few months. James isn't going to be the pushover he once was.'

Judith's voice was growing stronger as she dared to hope. 'Do you really think he'll let me back in?'

'Yes, I do.'

Judith released a breath that might have been a laugh if she hadn't been so tense. 'I promise that if we can get through this then I won't interfere. In fact, you have my permission to give me a not-so-gentle nudge if I ever step out of line.'

'It'll be my pleasure,' Maggie said with a wicked smile.

The hug from Judith was unexpected and brought with it a sense of relief that lasted only until her mother-in-law pulled away. It was time to go.

'You haven't told Mrs Walters I'm coming with you, have you?'

'No, not a word,' Judith said. 'But I still don't understand why it's me you've asked to take you. Not that I'm complaining,' she added quickly.

'You mean why didn't I ask Kathy to take me to see her mum?'

'I suppose she'll be up to her eyes with the move right now,' Judith said in answer to her own question.

'And she doesn't know either?'

'No, I've done exactly as you've asked,' Judith insisted. 'Now, are you going to tell me what this is all about?'

Maggie inhaled deeply to steel herself. 'Let's set off first,' she said, wanting to give Judith as little time as possible to talk her out of it.

'I don't know what to think,' Judith said.

So far Maggie had done most of the talking as Judith drove, explaining not only the basic facts she had uncovered about Elsa's life, but why a story told by an elderly woman with a tenuous grip on reality had been so persuasive. What Maggie failed to mention was what might have happened after the baby was born. That, she told Judith, was why she needed to speak to Anne Walters.

'I have to be honest with you, Maggie,' she added. 'I do feel a bit awkward about not fore-warning Anne. You think she has something to hide, don't you?'

Maggie shrugged in response as she tried to reconcile the two images of Mrs Walters in her mind. One was a scheming and heartless woman who had falsified records and torn a newborn baby from its mother's arms while the other was the wily octogenarian Maggie had admired from afar.

'Anne might be getting on in years but she isn't frail by any means,' Judith warned. 'She's not someone you would want to cross.'

The comment only served to compound Maggie's fears and her legs felt wobbly as she hauled herself out of the car with a little assistance.

'Are you sure you want to do this?' Judith asked.

'I've come this far.'

Once they had closed the wrought iron gate behind them, the walk up the driveway to Anne Walters's bungalow was surprisingly long. By comparison, the front door of Ted and Elsie's home was only a couple of steps from the pavement. Maggie brushed against a tall hedge on her right and a little probing with her cane revealed a neat stone border beneath it. Under other circumstances she would have asked Judith to describe the house and its grounds but this was not a social call. Instead, she allowed herself the luxury of forming her own impressions as her imagination saw fit. This was an imposing house, spacious and well maintained. Anne Walters certainly knew how to look after herself: she had invested the profits from other people's misery very well indeed.

Judith rang the bell but there was an interminable delay before the door opened.

'You're right on time, sweetheart. I've already put the kettle on. Oh, who's this, Judith?'

'This is my daughter-in-law, Maggie.'

Maggie could feel a wary pair of eyes scrutinising her. 'Oh, hello,' Anne said. 'You're my Kathy's friend, aren't you?'

'Yes, that's right.'

'How lovely to meet you at last.'

Maggie was taken aback by the insincerity in Anne's voice but then remembered who she was dealing with. Kathy must have mentioned Elsie in passing to her mum and Anne was sharp enough to quickly surmise the motives behind Maggie's unexpected visit. Her guilt was showing and Maggie half expected the greengrocer's niece to close the door in her face. She didn't, but neither did she open it wide.

'Can we come in?' Judith ventured when no one else had made a move.

'Yes, how rude of me – please do.'

The hallway was airy and the echo of their footsteps on the hardwood floor only served to reinforce Maggie's assumptions that the bungalow was spacious. Beneath the welcoming aroma of home baking she detected the smell of fresh paint. Kathy had been preparing the place for renting out but Maggie would rather believe that Anne commanded pristine living conditions.

'I thought you'd be overrun with removal crates by now,' Judith said.

'Oh, I'm not moving just yet. Kathy needs to settle into the new house first and apparently there's dry rot in the granny flat that needs some attention.'

This was news to Maggie and a frown was creasing her brow when Anne turned to her and said, 'I can't believe we've never met before. I've heard a lot about you though.' Her voice was soft and light with only a touch of graininess that gave away her age. From her light, slow footsteps as she led them into the living room, Maggie gauged that Anne was of slight build and the dipped projection of her voice suggested that she walked with a stoop. Maggie's senses were forming the image of a harmless old lady – but her heart held on stubbornly to a more monstrous figure.

'Yes, it is surprising, but then I don't think you like coming over to Sedgefield, do you?' It was the first shot across the bow.

Anne's answer was succinct and to the point. 'No, I don't.'

'Why don't you two sit down and I'll make the tea,' Judith offered. 'I know where everything is.'

Maggie took a seat on the edge of a wide

armchair. Her hands gripped the plush Jacquard upholstery as a twinge pulled across her stomach. She ignored it, concentrating instead on where to start her interrogation. Nerves got the better of her though and she found herself saying, 'This is a lovely house. I imagine it's going to be a big upheaval when you do move.'

'But a nice change too,' corrected Anne. 'I've been on my own for too long now and it will be good having family around. They are so very important to me, now more than ever.'

The deep breath Maggie took forced the next words from her mouth. 'You know why I'm here, don't you?'

'I think I'd prefer you to tell me.'

Maggie cleared her throat. 'I know I have no right to invade your privacy and demand answers, but I've recently become very close to someone who knew you in the fifties. Elsie, or Elsa as you would have known her, moved back to Sedgefield earlier this year. I think she wanted some kind of resolution after everything that had happened to her all those years ago when she stayed with your aunt, Flo Jackson.'

'Wanted, not wants?' Anne asked, pouncing immediately upon the weak point in Maggie's prepared argument.

'She has Alzheimer's and we lose a little more of her every day, but there are still times when she remembers and times, too, when she thinks she's back in 1953.'

The tinkle of china announced Judith's return to the room. 'Tea's up,' she said. 'I can leave it here if you would rather talk to Maggie alone?'

'No, please stay. You're practically family anyway. So, where were we?' Anne continued as Judith busied herself pouring the tea. 'Ah, yes, Elsa was quite a character; what we would have called flighty in my day.'

'She was a young woman who made one mistake,' Maggie protested.

Upholstery creaked as Anne struggled to get comfortable in her chair. 'I didn't mean to sound so harsh,' she offered, 'but it was very different back in our day. Respectable girls didn't go to dances at Burtonwood airbase and they certainly didn't become unmarried mothers. Elsa would have been in her early twenties when we met but she was still very much a teenager. Although, when all's said and done, it was hard not to like her.'

Maggie recognised something akin to genuine affection in Anne's voice and she found herself smiling. 'She complained a lot about working at the greengrocer's.'

Anne allowed herself a smile too. 'Yes, she tried to use her pregnancy to get out of work but my aunt was no fool.'

'Now I know where you get it from,' mumbled Judith as she passed Anne her cup.

'Why did you help her?' Maggie asked.

'My husband was her sister's GP and I was his receptionist so I knew Celia quite well. I was there

406

when she dragged Elsa along to the surgery to confirm her suspicions.'

'Gordon was a doctor?' gasped Judith. 'I never knew.'

'Yes, that came as a surprise to me too,' added Maggie. She was about to ask what had caused the dramatic change in career but Anne was eager to continue with her story.

'The two sisters had a very strict Catholic upbringing and, unlike Elsa, Celia conformed to tradition. She married young and already had a brood. I think she would have taken Elsa's baby as her own if she hadn't been pregnant at the time. I felt sorry for them and mentioned my aunt's guesthouse. Aunt Flo agreed to take her in until she had the baby on the condition that Elsa earned her keep.'

'That took care of Elsa, but you also had plans for the baby, didn't you?'

'Here's your tea, Maggie,' Judith said.

Maggie's hand wrapped around the warmth of the cup then gripped it a little tighter as a twinge tried to take away her breath. It was her third that morning or was it the fourth? She refused to be distracted.

Anne sniffed dismissively. 'Elsa couldn't have looked after a baby! She barely knew how to take care of herself.'

'She did a good enough job only a few years later,' remarked Maggie.

'By all accounts she married and went on to lead

407

a happy life and I'm glad – but when she was in Sedgefield, Elsa was completely on her own.'

Maggie was about to reply but Anne stole her thunder. 'I suppose she told you all about Freddie,' she said barely disguising the barbs in her voice. 'The handsome Yank who was going to whisk her off on his white charger so they could live happily ever after?'

Maggie shrugged. 'Maybe it did sound too much like a flight of fancy but there's no denying it turned into her worst nightmare. Elsa lost Freddie; she didn't deserve to lose Tess too.'

'Tess? Oh, yes, that was the name she gave the baby. It was so desperately sad.'

'What happened to her?' Judith asked.

Maggie's pulse raced as she waited for Anne to decide whether to set free the truth or continue with a sixty-year lie.

'She was stillborn, I'm afraid.'

'That's not how Elsie recalls it,' countered Maggie.

'And how reliable is her memory again? If you would care to check her medical records, they will tell you all you need to know.'

'And it was your husband who recorded those details.'

'I don't know what you're inferring but you would be well advised not to smear my late husband's name.' The sweetness had disappeared from Anne's voice. She was losing patience but then so was Maggie.

'By suggesting he had falsified birth records, you

mean?' Maggie asked bluntly. 'What happened to make him leave the medical profession?'

Anne's breathing had become shallow and she swallowed before saying, 'I don't want to appear rude but I really don't think there's anything more I have to say on the matter.'

Maggie cursed herself for antagonising Anne. Although she could prove she was lying, Maggie had wanted Anne Walters to give the information freely. There seemed little chance of that now.

'It must have been so awful for you.'

'I'm sorry?' Anne asked, as stunned by Judith's comment as Maggie.

'I was only thinking that you would have been pregnant with Kathy around the same time that Elsa lost the baby. This all happened in 1953, you said?'

Maggie couldn't read Judith's face but she could read her voice. It hadn't been an innocent comment at all.

'Yes, although I have to say, I always thought Kathy was born later. Up until recently that is . . .' Maggie added but stopped herself from mentioning how she had come across Kathy's date of birth. Flo Jackson's will was the final piece of the puzzle and revealing it would come soon enough; Anne was leaving her no choice. 'I'd assumed that because you went to school together you were the same age but you're not, are you? I can't believe she let us celebrate her sixtieth in the summer with paninis and a glass of wine.'

Judith laughed. 'It wasn't exactly a milestone Kathy wanted to celebrate and she would love people to think she was the younger one but she was a couple of years ahead of me at school.'

'Elsie never mentioned that you were pregnant,' Maggie said, turning her attention back to Anne. 'In fact, she was under the impression that you couldn't have children.'

'It was a long time ago and even I'm struggling to remember things clearly,' Anne said, feigning vulnerability. 'I'm sorry, but all of these questions have worn me out. I can't give you the answers you want, Maggie. History can't be rewritten.'

'No, I'm afraid it can't and I would be doing Elsa a disservice by not finishing the job I came here to do.' She let Judith take her half-empty cup and then fumbled around in her handbag. Her hands were shaking but she found the piece of paper that Jenny had typed out on her Braillewriter. 'This is only an excerpt of your aunt's will but I think it says it all. Shall I read it out?'

When Anne spoke, her tongue clicked against the roof of her dry mouth. 'Can I stop you?'

As Maggie was about to begin, she felt a now-familiar pain pull across her abdomen. This time she checked her watch. She was going to have to stop calling them twinges and start timing her contractions. Her baby seemed determined to be as much a part of Elsa's story as Tess and that somehow felt right. She took a moment and when she could speak, she said, 'There's one section

410

that lists the estate but I think this is the important part. It says, "The property stated above shall remain in the possession of my niece Anne Walters and shall not be sold during her lifetime but passed in its entirety to her daughter, Katherine Margaret Walters. To Elsa Milton, nee O'Brien, I leave only my heartfelt apology. Wrongs have been done to you and for my sins I played my part. I can only hope that you eventually discover the door I have left open to the past and my dying wish is that one day you will be reunited with your daughter."'

The moment she had finished, Maggie shivered as she imagined that door being flung open. 'I'd say Flo's final words speak volumes, wouldn't you agree? She wanted Kathy to have the house so that one day her birth mother would come and find her. And it looks as if she has,' Maggie said in a short summation of the truth that could finally be spoken aloud.

'Have you told Kathy?' Anne's voice sounded further away than it should.

Maggie's elation was swept away by guilt. 'No. The only connection she's aware of is that Elsa knew the woman who once owned her house and the salon. She presumes her dad bought them from Flo Jackson's estate.'

'No, she doesn't,' Anne said, her voice choking on the last remnants of emotional restraint. 'She found the deeds of transfer and wanted me to explain why we had inherited the properties. My daughter waited for me to explain the family connection but I couldn't do it. I desperately wanted the secret to stay buried.'

'So if Kathy has worked out that you're Flo Jackson's niece then she knows the truth,' Judith said.

In the pause that followed, Maggie imagined Anne nodding grimly.

'She knows, but she's still waiting for you to tell her, isn't she?' Maggie demanded.

'I should have told her a long time ago,' Anne said, her voice quaking. Her defences had been destroyed and had left her broken. 'But I didn't want to hurt her. I only ever wanted to protect my daughter, more than you could possibly know.'

'No one could ever doubt that you love Kathy,' Judith said, her voice a gentle balm in response to Anne's roiling emotions. 'You've been a good mum to her.'

'I'm not the evil baby snatcher you think I am,' Anne said, casting her remark towards the silent Maggie. 'Although I will admit, I was jealous when Elsa and her sister asked for my help. It was so unfair that some girls could fall pregnant without even trying. I had struggled for years and yes, Judith, it is awful to witness a baby being stillborn; in fact, it's harrowing. But you have to believe me – it was only after Elsa mentioned having the baby adopted that I realised what an amazing opportunity had presented itself. By the time Elsa began to have doubts, I had already started to think of the

412

baby as my own and I was prepared to go to any lengths to keep her safe from those who would only do her harm.'

Maggie was tensing herself for the next contraction but it didn't stop her hearing another secret being swept over. 'You actually thought Elsa would harm her own child?'

'Not Elsa.'

'Then who?'

'Think ill of me if you must, but please, there are some things that Elsa would be better off never knowing; ghosts that should remain buried in the past.' There was no strength left in Anne's words. She wasn't going to fight if Maggie insisted.

A gasp escaped her as the next contraction took hold and the only way Maggie could disguise it was to talk through it without pausing to think. 'Let me be the judge of that.'

Anne went quiet but Maggie and Judith were prepared to wait. When Anne's confession came the flare of anger in it took them both by surprise. 'Did you ever stop to wonder how convenient it was that Freddie died when he did? No, of course not, and why would you? You fell for his charm just like Elsa did but Freddie didn't die! He killed himself off and played the hero to the end.'

Maggie felt her jaw drop. 'How could you know that?'

'When Elsa wrote to Freddie and explained that she was pregnant, she also told him about me and how desperate I was to adopt the baby. I wasn't only the answer to his problems; I was a potential source of income. While he was wooing Elsa with promises, he was busily extorting money out of me, through Celia. He threatened to return to England and take Elsa and the baby away to their ultimate ruination or we could save her by buying his eternal silence.'

'So you put a pregnant woman through the torment of believing her fiancé had been killed?' Maggie asked in utter disbelief.

When Anne spoke, her words were muffled. She had covered her face with one hand as she accounted for her misdeeds. 'I know what I put Elsa through. I'm reminded of it every time I look at my daughter and see the same spark of life I once saw in her mother's eyes before we snuffed it out. She had her heart broken twice over but we did what we considered to be the lesser of two evils. Remaining the hero was more than Freddie deserved but Celia knew her sister and I had to agree; she would see no wrong in him and had to be shocked into her senses.'

'So Freddie was the real villain in all of this . . .' Judith added.

Maggie shook her head as if to rid herself of the memories of Elsa sitting on the bench grieving for her perfect hero. She had never experienced such a sense of loathing for another human being.

'And he's been a spectre in my life ever since,' Anne continued. 'We had intended seeking a court order to formally adopt the baby, but I was terrified Freddie might turn up again with more threats before it was finalised. I was the one who persuaded Gordon to misreport the birth, but of course, that left us even more vulnerable to black-mail. And there you have it, Maggie, the reason my husband gave up his medical career. We had no choice but to start afresh.'

'And that was why you cut off all ties with Flo Jackson,' Maggie guessed.

'I didn't want to do it; I was all the family she had but she left me no choice when I caught her trying to sneak off with the baby to see Elsa.'

'You stopped Flo from meeting up with Elsa?' Maggie asked, the emotional pain of that revela-tion almost as intense as the next contraction.

'I'd been visiting my aunt when she offered to take the baby to the park so I could do a bit of shopping. I was about to leave her on the High Street when someone stopped to say hello and mentioned that they'd seen Elsa sitting down by the lake. Even Aunt Flo couldn't talk her way out of that one,' Anne explained. 'Kathy was only a month old at the time and, however remote the possibility, I couldn't risk losing her.'

'That particular pleasure was left to Elsa.'

Despite the harsh assessment, there was no malice. Maggie had heard only painful truth from Anne and, despite her best efforts, she no longer thought of her as a monster. She was a frail old woman who had been driven by circumstance and longings for a child to call her own. Maggie had seen Jenny go through a similar kind of misery so it was impossible to condemn Anne.

'I know it looks like I was the one who got what I wanted,' Anne said, 'but I think, on balance, Elsa got what she needed at the time, however cruel it may seem now. I still have the letters Freddie sent to Celia, setting out his stall, along with the forged note supposedly from his commanding officer informing Elsa of the accident. I keep them to remind me that we did the right thing, for Kathy most of all. She couldn't have been more loved.'

Maggie couldn't reply, her jaw was set in a grimace and she dug her fingers deeper into the armchair.

'So what will you do now?' Judith asked Anne.

It was Anne's turn to catch her breath as emotions overwhelmed her. 'I need to speak to my daughter. I just hope she can forgive me.'

'Kathy was willing to accept your silence on the matter: if that isn't testament to how much she loves and admires you then I don't know what is,' Maggie said.

'And will you tell Elsa?' Anne whispered.

'I had hopes of reuniting her with her daughter but I have to consider other people's feelings. It pains me to say it but it might have to be enough to simply tell Elsie that her daughter is happy and loved.'

There was nothing left to say and no one argued when Maggie suggested it was time to go. Anne had laid bare her soul but it was a measure of her character that she retained her dignity to the last. She was courteous enough to give her persecutor a kiss on the cheek as they stood at the door, leaving a trail of damp tears on Maggie's face.

There was still one secret to be revealed but this one had nothing to do with the past and everything to do with the future. Maggie's contractions had been getting more regular and increasingly stronger so when she reached the car and the next one took hold, she let the gasp of pain escape unchecked for the first time.

'My God, what is it? Is it the baby?' Judith was by her side in moments and began to rub Maggie's back.

'If I told you my contractions were five minutes apart would you panic?'

'I'll phone for an ambulance.' Judith's voice was surprisingly calm and reassuring.

'No, I'll be fine. Do you think you could find your way to the hospital?'

'It's where Sam and Liam were born so yes, of course I know the way but . . .'

'Less chat, more driving I think.'

As Judith set off, Maggie searched for her phone. It wasn't in her bag. She'd forgotten – she'd deliberately left it at home so that she had an excuse, however feeble, for not telling James where she was and what she was doing. 'Do you have your mobile with you?'

'It's in my handbag,' Judith said with a grunt as

she reached an arm behind her seat, scrambling around while she continued to drive. 'Here, it's in the side pocket.'

Maggie tried not to panic when she realised that Judith's mobile wasn't one she was familiar with. Even though her fingers found the number pad, without her voice commands and contact list, it was worse than useless. 'I can't remember James's number. My brain has turned to mush.'

Judith laughed. 'Get used to it. My brain was mush for years after James was born. Maybe it still is, because I can't remember the number either. Hand it over,' she said calmly. The car swerved to the side of the road and Judith pulled on the handbrake. 'I don't care what the emergency; I'm not using the phone and driving at the same time.'

'It's good to know you're a careful driver,' Maggie said and was about to suggest she might be called upon to drive around with her new grandchild soon but her words were cut short by another contraction.

'It's ringing,' Judith said. She handed the phone back to Maggie and the car indicators briefly clicked in sync with the ringing tone. They were on the move again.

The phone rang out until it switched to voice-mail. Maggie cut off the call. 'No answer,' she said with a shuddering gasp as the contraction subsided.

'Ah, he's probably seen who the caller is. Try again. The button on the bottom left is the redial.'

Maggie redialled only to have the call diverted yet again. She hung up and hit the redial button. This time the call switched to divert almost immediately. 'He's deliberately ignoring the call!' Maggie screamed through gritted teeth. 'The stubborn, useless idiot!'

The car swerved to another stop. 'We'll try someone else and they can get through to the stubborn, useless idiot.'

'How about Ken?'

'He's out on site this morning and I'm afraid he's a bit of a technophobe. He doesn't have a mobile. How about Kathy?' Judith still sounded calm but it was taking a little more effort.

'No.' It didn't matter how desperate Maggie was, she had caused enough chaos in Kathy's life for one day.

'This is an emergency,' Judith insisted. She made the call herself. 'It's engaged. How about Jenny?'

Another contraction pulled Maggie's abdomen tight and the pain could no longer be described as a twinge by any stretch of the imagination. 'I can't remember her number either. Do you have it?' she panted.

'Sorry.'

'Ted! I know the Miltons' home phone number by heart and I'm sure they'll be there.'

Maggie repeated the number and Judith, whose hands were shaking only marginally less than Maggie's, pressed the buttons. With the phone ringing in her ear, Maggie was pushed back in her seat as Judith set off again, accelerating much faster than before.

'Hi, Ted, it's Maggie. Yes, I'm fine,' she began. 'Well, actually I'm not. I'm in labour and I'm on my way to the hospital but I can't get in touch with James. He's doing a job at Sedgefield Primary School.' The school was close enough for Ted to walk there but she now realised that she couldn't ask him to leave Elsie by herself. 'Do you think you could phone the school or is there someone you could ask to go over there?'

For once, fortune was on their side. Elsie's home help was with them and Ted had been on his way out anyway. He told her not to worry; he would march over there and bang James's head against the wall he was building before sending him off to find her. He was going to be her hero.

CHAPTER 27

'Don't leave me!'

Maggie had grabbed Judith's arm when she suggested slipping out to help track down her wayward son. The midwife with them in the delivery suite wasn't someone Maggie knew and she wasn't particularly keen on her matronly style. There had always been a good chance Mel wouldn't be on duty when the time came but it was still another bitter blow. Her original birth plan, which had never in her wildest dreams included Judith as a potential birth partner, lay in tatters.

'I won't be long.'

'No, please, Judith, don't go. I'm so scared.' Maggie had been given a tour of the delivery suite as part of her antenatal preparations but without Mel's comforting and confident presence, the once-safe environment felt intimidating and frightening but there were other fears too. 'It's too early for the baby to come.'

'You're in safe hands. Don't worry.'

Maggie couldn't answer as another contraction took hold and was the strongest yet. She was lying prone on a hospital bed and the Pethidine she had been given was having little to no effect. She breathed in the gas and air, biting down on the mouthpiece to stifle a cry of pain. A heavy wave of wooziness washed over her, although it wasn't enough to completely block out the pain. Eventually the contraction began to subside and a couple of deep, cleansing breaths lifted the drunken haze.

'Don't leave me,' she repeated.

'OK, I'll stay.'

'You've still got a while to go yet, Maggie, so if you don't mind, I'll leave you with your mum-in-law,' the midwife said, then slipped something into Maggie's hand. 'This is the alarm button. Press it if there are any problems or if you're worried at all.'

As soon as the midwife had left, Maggie said, 'Why don't you try phoning in here? There's no one to stop us now.'

Judith pulled her mobile out of her pocket. 'No messages and no missed calls.'

'Try James again.' The tremor in her voice was an aftershock from the contraction that had exacerbated her sense of abandonment.

'It's ringing.'

'Yes, I know,' Maggie said with a quivering smile. Tears sprang to her eyes as she heard the distinctive ringtone from James's phone echoing along the corridor outside. She strained her ears and thought she heard him apologise to someone for using the mobile, presumably their busybody midwife.

The door was flung open. 'I'm sorry,' James said. He sounded out of breath as he rushed to her side. 'How the hell did this happen?'

Maggie reached towards him, seeking out the warmth and firmness of his forearm. The sense of relief was palpable as she ran her hand up towards his shoulder, her fingers tracing the thickness of his neck and the square of his jaw before she cupped his face in her hand. Her breathing was shallow and she could feel the next contraction beginning to build and the fear of its arrival made her stomach churn. She still hadn't spoken, choosing instead to let her fingers do the talking. She took her hand from his face, slowly pulling away, sensing the distance between her fingertips and the warmth of his skin. Four inches, six, ten. She could feel the sterile hospital air filling the space between them and then, without warning, she brought her hand deftly back towards his face with almost as much force as the contraction that wrapped itself around her.

'Ow! What was that for?'

The reply was more of a groan, muffled by the gas-and-air mouthpiece she was biting down on. In her throes of agony, Maggie had forgotten how to suck in the air from the tube and then out through her mouth. 'I keep blowing when I should be sucking,' she cried.

James had the temerity to laugh and even Judith let a chuckle escape. Maggie's free arm flailed out to hit her husband again but James sidestepped the blow and Maggie only managed to grab hold of his T-shirt.

'I'm getting the feeling you don't want me here,' he said, still laughing.

Maggie drew one last, long breath of gas and air as the pain eased. Still on her drug-induced high, she drew James closer as she slowly regained her speech if not her composure. 'You idiot! I needed you and all you could do was ignore my calls. I can't believe I was forced to send Ted on a fool's errand because the fool in question was too stubborn and hard-headed to give in and speak to his mother. Judith did something stupid and she realises that now. But she's been amazing today. She's believed in me and stood by me through a pretty harrowing morning and if that's a taste of how supportive she can be then I want her in my life! Now, do you have a problem with that?'

'I wouldn't dare,' James said. 'I'm sorry.'

'Don't apologise to me, apologise to your mother!' Maggie screamed between gritted teeth.

The door opened again. 'I don't know about your blood pressure but mine's shot through the roof!'

Mel had arrived but there was no time to relax and Maggie steeled herself for the next contraction. 'I think I want to push,' she groaned.

'So do what your body is telling you.'

'But it's too soon!' It was two weeks too soon to be precise and a part of her was willing to endure any pain to keep her baby safe.

'The baby's vital signs are looking strong and your blood pressure is actually lower now than it's been for weeks. The doctor has already told you you're both doing fine, hasn't she?'

Maggie could only nod as she gave into the urge to bear down.

'Then it's time.'

Maggie breathed in deeply and slowly. The air carried a damp, metallic taste and the odours that filled her senses were both alien and familiar, as if the newborn placed on her chest was still a part of her. Her body continued to tremble from her exertions but the pain had vanished into the ether to be replaced by pure elation at the sound of her baby's first cries. She wrapped him in her arms and gently let her fingers search out the precious contours of his skin, all damp wrinkles and wriggling fingers and toes. 'He's beautiful,' she said.

James sniffed. 'Yes.'

Maggie turned her face towards her husband and he kissed her gently on the lips and then the top of his son's head.

'Another boy! I am going to be outnumbered, aren't I?'

'We can try for a girl next time.'

Maggie laughed softly. 'Let me catch my breath first.'

She held on to Aiden for as long as she could, which wasn't long at all, but she didn't object when Mel took him from her. She knew she would be getting him back.

Maggie had been running on pure adrenalin for the last couple of days and the relief that washed over her brought with it a heavy wave of fatigue but she wouldn't give in, not until she knew her baby was safe and well.

'Five pounds ten ounces and a pair of lungs that will keep you awake for the next two years at least. The doctor's on her way to check him over but if you want my assessment then I think you have one sturdy little man here,' Mel announced.

'Takes after his dad,' Maggie said with a woozy smile.

It was only as she was nodding off that she remembered Judith. She had remained in the room the whole time and Maggie wanted to encourage her out of the shadows but she was too tired to fight the pull of sleep. Her concern for Judith chased her through her dreams and half an hour later, when Maggie raised herself back into consciousness, she was relieved to hear Judith's voice amongst the hushed whispers.

'I panicked,' Judith was saying. 'I thought you were throwing your life away and it was my fault because I'd convinced you not to go to Portsmouth.'

'I wasn't throwing my life away. If anything, Maggie gave me something to live for. She has given me a sense of completeness that I've never experienced before, not even with Carolyn, not even close.'

'You're lucky to have her, I can see that now.'

'So can I, Mum,' James said. It was a warning. 'I didn't realise until recently exactly how much at risk our marriage was and the blame was all mine. I kept my feelings to myself. I thought that in time you would realise how much I loved her: that my actions spoke louder than words, but you weren't listening. We were both responsible for Maggie being left isolated. I ignored the problem, and I ignored her pain. I'm supposed to be the strong one, strong enough to protect my wife and family, but I didn't even have the courage to stand up and tell you, of all people, how I felt.'

'And now?'

'There's nothing I wouldn't sacrifice for my wife or my kids.'

'Including me?' Judith asked in the barest whisper, afraid to speak but even more afraid of the answer.

'I'm sorry, Mum, but I can't let you back into our lives if there's even the slightest chance that it would put a strain on my marriage. You and Maggie are too alike. You both expect to get your own way and you each have your own ways of making that happen.'

'Manipulative, you mean?' Maggie joined the conversation. She sat up in bed and rubbed the sleep from her eyes. Her ears strained for the sounds of life in the room. To her immediate left, she could hear Aiden's soft breaths and when she stretched

427

out an arm, she found the hard plastic surface of a hospital crib. 'Is he OK?'

There was the scrape of a chair on the far side of the room as James hurried over to her. 'They were going to put him in an incubator but he's doing so well they've said he can stay with us. How are you feeling?'

Maggie smiled as she counted her blessings. 'Surprisingly well. Now, what's this about me being manipulative?'

'I think that was your word, not mine,' James said. 'Are you going to hit me again?'

The offending hand rushed to Maggie's mouth rather than James's cheek. 'I'd forgotten about that. I'm sorry, James.'

'I'll forgive you if you can forgive me for not answering your phone calls.'

'You're forgiven – but the jury's still out on whether you're an idiot or not.'

James didn't take the bait. 'Mel said they need to move you to the ward soon. Even though Aiden's arrived earlier than we expected, everything is going to plan and she's said you should be able to go home in the next day or two as long as he's feeding OK and you're feeling confident enough.'

'I'm not sure I ever will be,' Maggie said. Her voice quivered. 'The theory was daunting enough but this is such a huge responsibility. I don't think I can do this on my own. I'm going to need all the support I can get.' She bit her lip nervously.

'I'm not daft,' James warned. 'And I'm not falling for the weak and feeble act.'

'I don't know what you mean,' she answered curtly.

James sighed. 'I give in,' he said. 'But I'm warning the two of you now: I expect you both to behave impeccably or you'll have me to answer to.'

'Thank you, James,' Maggie said. Her face actually felt warm as she basked in a self-made glow of smugness. She had brought one problem to a satisfactory conclusion.

Another chair scraped across the floor and tentative steps drew closer. 'I promise you that I'll be making up for lost time and you'll have nothing to worry about, James. We're already quite a team, aren't we, Maggie?'

It was then that a shadow passed across Maggie's thoughts. 'Have you been in touch with everyone yet?'

'I've spoken to your dad and Dot's trying to change their flights. I've texted everyone else,' James said.

'Any replies?'

'Tons of them. Jenny is going to come in to see you later.'

'Did you tell Ted?'

'Of course I did. He and Elsie send their love.'

'Has he forgiven me for sending him out looking for you?'

'He said he hasn't had that much excitement for years.'

'Have you told Harvey yet?' she asked with a trembling smile that threatened to send the tears spilling down her cheeks.

'I thought we might do that together.'

There was still one crucial name that had yet to be mentioned. 'Have you heard from Kathy?' she asked, directing her question to Judith.

'James sent her a text and I tried phoning but no answer.'

Maggie turned back to James. 'No reply to the text?'

'Not yet.'

Back to Judith. 'Have you told him?'

'No, I thought you might want to do the explaining.'

'Yes, I suppose it is all down to me.' Maggie was biting her lip again, although there was no acting involved this time and it did little to steady her nerves. 'I've done something that's going to turn Kathy's world upside down and I don't know who she'll think has betrayed her most, me or her mum.'

CHAPTER 28

Maggie left hospital two days after the birth and her return home had been an emotional one. Her first task had been to introduce her son to the second most important member of their household. Harvey, excited at the return of his mistress, had calmed immediately when the baby carrier was placed in front of him. His tail swished across the floor as he leant forward and gently touched Aiden's cheek with the tip of his nose and breathed him in. He was the only one to keep his composure: even James had struggled to hold back the tears, and he didn't have raging hormones as an excuse.

Maggie's moods went from one extreme to the other. With her baby cradled in her arms, sleeping or feeding, she was blissfully happy; without him, she was desolate and if he cried, then the pain she felt was unbearable. His cries carried echoes of another baby and another time and she couldn't help but imagine what it would be like to have him wrenched from her arms and not be allowed to comfort him. It was little consolation when she reminded herself that the baby whose cries

431

tormented her, the little girl born to Elsa, now had a voice of her own.

It was Saturday morning and five days had passed since she had opened Pandora's Box. Although there had been plenty of visitors to see the new arrival, Kathy hadn't been one of them and Maggie's guilty conscience had so far stopped her from making the first move. Judith had no such reservations but even her direct approach had proved inconclusive.

'Has Anne told her? I mean, has she told her everything?'

Judith sighed down the phone line. 'I'm sorry, Maggie, it was like getting blood out of a stone. As soon as I mentioned going to see her mum with you she couldn't wait to cut the conversation short. Apparently she's still in the middle of the house move and there was an emergency she had to attend to there and then.'

Maggie was in the kitchen. Her mouth was parched but she couldn't stomach the orange juice she had just poured for herself. She felt drained as she rested her head on the refrigerator door. 'It's the not knowing that's driving me mad.'

'Maggie, the fact that Kathy is refusing to talk to either of us speaks volumes. She *knows*.'

A wet nose prodded her leg and Maggie rubbed Harvey's head in response. 'She must be absolutely furious with me.'

She could almost hear Judith's mind turning as she tried to think of something reassuring to say.

'Yes, probably,' she said, 'but she's mad at me too and she can't ignore both of us forever. Don't worry; it'll sort itself out eventually. Now tell me, how is my little love?'

'He's as beautiful as ever. James is in the living room with him now, and I think he's just got him to sleep. I've only just fed him and I have to say this breastfeeding lark is thirsty business.'

'So make yourself a drink while you've got the chance.'

'I'm already on the case,' Maggie said. She felt mothered and allowed herself a brief smile before sipping her drink. Next she launched into a lengthy description of every amazing little thing Judith's new grandson had done in the sixteen hours since her last update. Without warning, Harvey chuffed lightly and scampered out of the kitchen.

'I think I might have a visitor,' she said and a second later there was a knock at the door. 'I'd better go before whoever it is wakes up Aiden.'

Maggie tried not to build up her hopes as she pulled open the front door – they had been dashed too many times already, and her unwitting guests didn't deserve her disappointment. It wasn't their fault that they weren't Kathy.

The rush of cold air was filled with the unmistakeable scent of lilacs. The smile on her face was only half formed as doubt crept in. These were fresh flowers.

'Don't think that just because I'm bringing you flowers that it's some kind of peace offering.'

Maggie swept up the bouquet and breathed in the delicious floral scents. 'Lilacs, how lovely.'

'Yes, they are. But wipe that smile off your face, Maggie Carter. I'm still very angry.'

There was something in Kathy's voice that confirmed it was no idle warning. 'If you're going to shout at me then let's not do it on the doorstep. Come in.'

'Babies first,' Kathy said as she accepted Maggie's invitation. 'Where is that gorgeous boy of yours?'

'I'm here,' James said. He was standing at the living room door, his voice hushed and a softly snoring baby in his arms.

'Oh, you're absolutely gorgeous! Not like your daddy at all,' Kathy added. 'Here, can I have a go?'

Aiden was bundled into Kathy's waiting arms and she disappeared into the living room to make herself comfortable. James, who had heard the exchange at the door, gave Maggie an encouraging kiss on the forehead. 'I'll make myself scarce,' he said, taking the flowers.

'Tea, two sugars,' Kathy called after him.

Aiden whimpered in his sleep as Maggie was about to take a seat on the sofa opposite Kathy. 'Is he all right?' she asked.

'Sit down, he's absolutely fine. Aren't you, sweetheart?' Kathy had dropped her voice to a whisper.

She spent a good minute gently coaxing the baby back to sleep and another minute or two letting the silence stretch out. Maggie was feeling distinctly uncomfortable in Kathy's company and that made her feel even worse. Kathy was more than a friend, she was a major influence in her life and Maggie had betrayed her trust. 'So, are you ready to shout at me now?' she managed.

'You had no right to go behind my back.'

'I know.'

'It wasn't only my family you rode roughshod over, Maggie, it was my entire life. You took my identity and ripped it in two. I'm not who I thought I was – and even worse than that, my parents aren't who I thought they were either.' Kathy kept her voice low and it was almost a growl.

'I know, and if Aiden wasn't already keeping me awake then my conscience would be. But I couldn't exactly ask you if you wanted to know or not. The only option I had was to ask your mum.'

'Which one?'

'Both,' Maggie confessed. 'Although Elsie couldn't really give me the answers I needed.'

'So you wrenched a confession out of Mum,' Kathy said before adding a confession of her own. 'But I already knew, Maggie.'

'I know that now.'

'I found copies of the deeds for the house and shop while you were sitting next to me talking to Mark. I was about to say something when I spotted a letter from the executor of Flo Jackson's estate. It didn't explain everything but it was enough to turn my world upside down.'

'Sorry.'

'I know you are; and for what it's worth, I'm sorry too,' Kathy offered. 'I should have trusted you, Maggie, but I was scared. Part of me wanted to know the truth and I even made a half-hearted attempt to ask Mum . . . But I've lived in this skin for sixty years and I wasn't looking for a new identity. I wanted the past to stay exactly where it was and I even dropped a hint or two to James so he would convince you to stop your damned search for Tess – for me.' Kathy paused to draw breath. 'And of course your timing was awful. Not only was I in the middle of a house move but I had also been planning on setting up home with mum.'

Maggie's conscience prepared to take another blow. 'You made up problems with the granny flat to stop your mum moving in, didn't you?' she asked, remembering how Anne had mentioned the dry rot. 'Please don't say it's not going to happen.'

'How can it?'

'Oh, Kathy, I'm so, so sorry.'

Kathy shifted uncomfortably and her head was bowed when she spoke. 'I'm not saying it won't happen eventually. She's still the woman who brought me up, still my mum, but right now I'm even more angry with her than I am with you.' There was a heavy sigh that sounded wet with tears but, like her adoptive mother, Kathy fought against them. 'Shush there,' she said to the sleeping baby who needed the words of comfort far less than she did.

'Are you okay?' Maggie asked quietly.

'I went to see Ted and Elsie after I found out,' Kathy said, as if that answered the question.

'Ted mentioned you'd arranged the home help for them.'

There was another sigh as if Kathy's lungs were slowly being crushed by the weight of her new-found knowledge. 'Elsie wasn't there, but Elsa was. She was clinging on to a cushion and pleading with us not to take her baby. What they did to her? Maggie, it broke her heart and now it's breaking mine . . .'

'Has your mum explained to you why they did what they did?'

'Yes, and I might need your newly found detective skills to trace my so-called father. I swear, if I could track him down I wouldn't be responsible for my actions.'

'I'm so sorry, Kathy.'

'So you keep saying. But don't worry, I *will* forgive you. I have to.'

For the first time since Kathy had arrived, Maggie relaxed a little. 'And why would that be?'

'Because my head is all over the place and I need my friends now more than ever. What's done is done. It's how we move on from here that's causing me some sleepless nights of my own. So you say you tried to tell Elsie? Does that mean Ted knows?'

'Not everything. He only knows that I've found Tess, nothing more. I didn't want to make things any worse than I already had,' Maggie said. 'But . . .'

'Let me guess, you think I should.'

There was an apologetic look to accompany the nod.

'We both know how ill Elsie has become. It's not going to be the fairy-tale reunion you've had in mind for the last six months.'

'I know, but she still has her moments. I'll help as much as I can, but if you're going to do it then do it soon.'

Kathy cleared her throat, the threat of tears over for the moment. 'No pressure then,' she said, and Maggie was grateful that at least it wasn't an outright refusal.

'And don't forget that it's not only about you and Elsie. You have two sisters you never knew you had,' Maggie added, aware she had to tread carefully but unable to stop herself from pushing the positives.

'That's the only thing I'm looking forward to – or, I should say, the thing I'm dreading least. I've already met Yvonne and we got on really well so I'm hoping that in time we could all get used to the idea.'

'I'm sure they'll learn to love their older sister.'

'Less of the old.'

'Sorry.'

'Stop being so meek, it doesn't suit you. I wouldn't have been surprised if you'd sat there telling me I should count myself lucky for having two mothers.'

'I wouldn't say such a thing,' Maggie said, although she had thought it. Her first outing with Aiden had been to the cemetery to introduce her mum to the baby. She had gone with her dad who had managed to get back to England within days of the birth and he had been there to hold onto while she sobbed uncontrollably at her mum's grave.

There was a tentative knock at the door. 'Is it safe to come in yet?' James asked.

'Yes, I've had enough of the serious talk and I'm ready for that cuppa now,' Kathy told him. 'There's only one mother I want to talk about now and that's the new one. I hope you're looking after her.'

'As if I need to,' James said.

Maggie allowed the smile to spread across her face as she listened to James extol her virtues. She felt warmth flooding her body and it was the perfect remedy to the stress she had put herself through in the last week. She had felt sick with dread after Jenny produced the will and then, after the confrontation with Anne, the mixture of guilt and fear had been overwhelming. It had sullied the birth of her son and the days that followed.

She hadn't allowed herself to enjoy the moment but she did now. Tears of joy slipped down her cheeks while James and Kathy were too involved in their conversation to notice. Harvey, who had been standing guard over the baby, whimpered. Maggie heard him take a couple of steps towards her but then he stopped as Aiden let out a tiny whimper of his own.

'Can I hold him?' Maggie asked, interrupting James mid-sentence.

'Who am I to come between a mother and her child?' Kathy said as she placed the sleeping baby gently into Maggie's arms.

Kathy put her hand on Maggie's face and wiped away a tear. 'Don't make me cry too.'

'You don't know how much I would hate to do that,' Maggie said as her mind stretched back sixty years. She could still hear the baby's cries but they no longer haunted her.

CHAPTER 29

'Hand lotion?'

'It'll help,' Maggie promised.

Kathy gave a deep heavy sigh that emptied every ounce of air from her lungs. 'I suppose it's packed full of essential oils to help me relax.'

As Maggie waited for her friend to open the bottle, she listened to the scrape of leaves being blown across the ground towards a watery grave. 'Try it.'

Kathy unscrewed the top and Maggie imagined a frown creasing her brow.

'Lilacs? I should have known.'

'I'm trying to recapture the fragrance that Elsie associates with Tess. This is a better match than her perfume and might be enough to make the link to you.'

'Sounds more like a leap of faith to me.'

'Isn't everything these days? All I know is Elsie relies on her perfume to keep you close. She's never let go of you,' Maggie said as she reached over unconsciously for her own baby. Aiden's pram was tucked away to the side of the bench to protect him from the blustery November weather.

'But she barely knows who she is these days. What hope is there that she'll be able to recognise me as the baby taken from her all of those years ago?'

Maggie wasn't ready to admit defeat. 'I spoke to Ted before we left. He said she's not too bad today and being here will help.'

'Your bench is going to have to have some pretty impressive powers to make this work.'

As she spoke, Kathy had poured out a generous amount of lotion into the palm of her hand. She inhaled the lilac-scented air and held her breath. So did Maggie.

'Anything?'

'Hmm, I'd like to say yes, in fact I almost *could* say yes but . . . no. It's wishful thinking.' Kathy began to rub her hands together then added, 'I can't believe how much my hands are shaking.'

Maggie reached over to her. 'Here, let me do that.'

A gust of wind picked up the fragrance and coiled it around them. With Maggie's steadying hand, Kathy began to calm as they continued to wait. Harvey was the first to notice Elsie and Ted approaching. He had been sitting next to the pram but slipped closer to Maggie as his excitement began to build.

'Look who this is,' Ted said. 'You remember Maggie and Kathy, don't you?'

'Yes of course, how lovely to see you and who's this then?' Elsie said to the dog licking her hand voraciously.

'This is Harvey,' Maggie said. 'You and he are old friends.'

'Yes,' Elsie replied, more out of politeness than recollection.

Maggie gently nudged Kathy so a space opened up between them. 'Why don't you sit here and we'll keep you nice and snug.'

'You know, I think I will. My feet are killing me.'

As Elsie sat down, Maggie said a silent prayer. This had to work.

'I'm going to stretch my legs for a bit,' Ted said. 'Just shout if you need anything. I won't go far.'

Maggie strained her ears as she waited for Kathy to speak but other than Ted's receding footsteps all she heard was the whisper of trembling leaves. She cleared her throat deliberately but Kathy didn't take the hint. She had been struck dumb.

'You came here when you were younger,' Maggie said to Elsie when her patience was exhausted. 'But that was a long time ago, wasn't it?' Her question was guarded. More often than not these days, Mrs Milton was neither in the past nor the present. She had fallen between the cracks and, as Maggie tried to ease her back towards the present, she knew she was just as likely to push her into the past. 'You told me about your stay with Mrs Jackson.'

443

Elsie fidgeted. 'Judging by these hands I'd say that was a long time ago. Thirty years maybe?' she guessed. 'I think my feet were killing me back then too.' There was a soft chuckle.

'Yes, you worked at a greengrocer's and it was hard work. You were pregnant at the time.'

'I told you that?' she asked with a gasp of disbelief. 'I didn't think I'd ever tell anyone.'

'You told me about Freddie and the baby, Elsie. You told me about Tess.'

Elsie nodded solemnly. 'I lost them both.'

Maggie reached out for Elsie's hand. 'I know,' she said but her pity was tinged with bitterness. Freddie didn't deserve Elsie's grief and while Maggie fought the urge to say something the old lady's body stiffened. She took hold of Maggie's hand and raised it to her face.

'I know that smell.'

Maggie wanted to pull away but Elsie's grip was uncompromising. 'It's not the same as your perfume, is it? This scent is from *real* lilacs. I think Tess was bathed in something similar when she was born. Do you remember?'

'How could I forget? I know I'll have to face the prospect of forgetting most things but not that, please God, not that.'

'What if I were to tell you that you don't have to remember? What if Tess was here to remind you?' Elsie's fingers had been curled tightly around Maggie's but her grip slackened and Maggie could feel her slipping away. 'Elsie,' she said, her heartbeat providing her very own drum roll, 'I've found your daughter.'

'Yes, she's in Scotland,' she said. 'Or is it America? No of course not, that's the other one, Yvonne, no Nancy. Yvonne went to Scotland, that's it.' There was a sigh as she let go of Maggie's hand completely. 'I really must get going or I'll be late for work.'

In the pram next to her, Maggie could hear Aiden stirring. It was an opportune moment for her to withdraw from the conversation. She leaned forward. 'Kathy?'

'It's Sunday, Elsie. No work today so we've got plenty of time to sit and chat,' Kathy said with an urgency that belied her reassurances. Time was very much against them but still Kathy paused, grappling with the words she had been rehearsing in her head for days. 'Anne Walters and her husband Gordon took your baby as their own.'

'Anne Walters? I haven't heard that name in years. She disappeared off the face of the earth.'

'Yes, I know. She didn't want anyone to know what they'd done. But whatever you think of her for taking your baby, you need to know that she was a good mother. She kept Tess safe and happy.' Kathy's breath caught in her throat before she added, 'Your baby couldn't have been more loved.'

'No!' Elsie cried out and recoiled from Kathy as if she meant to harm her. 'No one would have loved her more than me. She was *mine*. I would have kept her safe if I'd been given the chance.'

Elsie was pushing her weight against Maggie, her body shaking, but she wasn't the only one who had become agitated. Aiden was four weeks old and Maggie could already distinguish between his different cries. He wasn't hungry but he was uncomfortable and either needed changing or winding. She couldn't and wouldn't ignore him. When she stood up, Elsie squeezed into the space she had vacated but at least she had stayed seated.

Maggie picked up Aiden and cradled him in an upright position. He was trying to lift his head from her shoulder as she patted his back. There were a couple of polite belches in quick succession. 'There you go. That's better, isn't it?'

With Aiden comforted, Maggie began rocking him in her arms, all the while aware of the two women sitting on the bench. They sat in stony silence and it was enough to try her patience. 'Elsie, are you ready to meet your daughter?'

There was a gasp of excitement and Maggie realised her mistake too late.

The cold had seeped into her bones and Elsa couldn't stop shivering. Her fingers brushed across her woollen coat, expecting it to be dripping wet but it was bone dry. She had no idea how much time had passed since she had been pulled from the lake, long enough for her clothes to dry out but not for her heart to heal. She could remember

Aunt Flo appearing at one point but she had been on her own and Elsa's arms had remained achingly empty. But she was going to carry on waiting, forever if necessary, holding out for a miracle. And then it happened.

Elsa couldn't believe her eyes when the woman appeared in front of her cradling Tess in her arms. Her baby was wrapped in a white blanket and she could see her tiny hands reaching up towards the woman's face, little fingers grasping the air.

'Can I hold her?' Elsa asked. Her voice was tremulous but she was giddy with excitement.

The woman froze and for one heart-stopping moment Elsa thought she was going to turn away.

'Please,' she begged.

When the tiny bundle of wriggling arms and legs was offered into her outstretched arms, the joy Elsa felt was almost too much to bear but she willed herself to remain calm. She wanted this moment to be perfect and did her best to ignore the other woman sidling up closer, hemming her in.

'It's all right,' she said and helped tuck the blanket around the baby. 'I'm only making sure you're both comfortable.'

Elsa turned to look at the woman. There was something about her face that reminded her of Celia. She had the same eyes and Elsa returned a tentative smile.

With some relief, the lady standing in front of her took a step back. Her escape was clear but Elsa stayed where she was. Her arms were full and her heart fit to burst. She tried not to cry so she could absorb every detail of her daughter's features but the tears were already blurring her vision. Her finger trembled as she traced the side of her baby's face. 'You have no idea how long I've dreamt of this moment,' she said in a hoarse whisper.

Elsa recalled the last time she had held her baby and the full force of that memory took her breath away in a shuddering gasp. She couldn't survive having her wrenched from her arms again.

'Don't worry,' the woman next to her said. 'You're both safe.'

Elsa inhaled the sweet scent of lilacs, still not quite believing this was really happening. 'Is she mine to keep?' she asked, her lip quivering at the possibility.

The woman shook her head and a rogue tear trickled down her cheek. She looked as if she was going to say something else but her words faltered and Elsa turned back to the baby. She didn't think she could speak either, but she knew she must. She already knew what she had to say, she had rehearsed it often enough.

'Oh, my sweet, sweet baby girl. I should never have let you go. I'm sorry. I'm so, so sorry.'

She had to stop to catch her breath and rein in her emotions. This was her one and only chance and she had to get it right. Leaning forward, she kissed Tess gently on the forehead. She breathed her in then tried again.

'I've never stopped loving you or thinking about you, not for one second. Not a day goes by that I don't regret giving you up – I should have found a way to keep you; I should have fought harder. You have a right to hate me because I hate myself. I was all on my own, you see. Once I'd lost Freddie there was no one else. Celia couldn't help and my mum and dad would have disowned me. But still . . .' The baby stretched her hand towards her as if to offer comfort but Elsa wouldn't be consoled. 'I was a silly girl, I know that – your dad was my downfall, Tess, but I was his willing victim. We made all kinds of plans to see the world together on the back of his motorbike but then he left for Germany and I thought he'd forget all about me. I couldn't believe it when he said he was going to come back and marry me.'

'But he didn't come back for you, did he?'

Elsa tore her eyes away briefly from the baby to glare at the woman next to her. 'You make it sound like it was his choice.'

Tess wriggled in her arms as if she knew her father would never hold her and Elsa began to rock her, coaxing her back to sleep with gentle words that belied the pain rending her heart in two.

'I joked once that your dad was more interested in his bike than he was in me and it was the bike that won in the end. After he died, though, I couldn't bear the thought of losing you. But I left it too late, Tess. I was in labour when I tried to run away and goodness knows what I thought I was doing. Like I said, I was a silly girl and I panicked. I would have kept you inside me forever if I could, but you came into the world kicking and screaming. I think you knew what I was about to do and it was your way of shouting at me to grow a backbone. I should have listened to you instead of Anne and Aunt Flo. I'm sorry, Tess. I let you down.'

The baby had drifted off to sleep but Elsa still had one last thing to say and it was going to be the hardest.

'I want you to be happy and more than anything I want you to be loved. Anne has a good heart and she'll bring you up as her own,' Elsa said as the tears rolled down her cheeks, unchecked now. 'But I'll never know for sure. I'll never know if I'm doing the right thing.'

The woman put an arm around Elsa's shoulder and the other around the baby. 'You did the right thing, Elsa. Tess was happy and she was loved. Very much.'

Elsa wailed as she tried to wriggle free. 'Get away from me! Get away! I'm not ready to let her go! I'm not ready!'

Horrified, the woman shrank back and for a moment the shadows that had been hovering around Elsa and her baby were pushed away. She looked at the baby's face, her closed eyes flickering across a dreamscape. Did she dream of those precious minutes she had spent in her mother's arms on the day she was born? Elsa dreamt of them: over and over again.

The shadows returned as the second woman stepped closer. All Elsa had ever wanted was to have one single moment alone with Tess, just the two of them. Was that too much to ask?

'I can't . . . I can't . . . I can't,' she began to repeat as her grip tightened on the baby. 'I can't do this again. Please, I'm begging you.'

The woman in front of her leant down and rested her hands on each side of the bench, penning her in. Any moment now her daughter would be wrenched from her arms and she would never hold her again. Elsa let out a painful mewl that sounded like a trapped animal. She craned her neck to look past the woman, searching desperately for a means of escape. At first it was the wide expanse of water that drew her in but then a flash of white caught her attention and her heart skipped a beat. The swans had returned! If they could find their way back then maybe Freddie would too. What if he hadn't died? What if it had all been a terrible mistake? But the flicker of white disappeared and all she could see was the lonely figure of an old man at the side of the lake. He turned towards her and Elsa saw the flicker of white again. It was a cotton handkerchief and it flapped in the breeze: there were no swans, she knew now, no hope. As she felt her mind pulling her towards the watery abyss her eyes remained focused on the fluttering white sail.

Elsa watched as the man wiped his eyes. He looked towards her and caught her in his gaze. The decades that had passed since the birth of her first child paraded across her mind and the memories came flooding back.

When Maggie had crouched down in front of Elsie her first priority had been to protect Aiden. It was only when she was satisfied that Elsie wasn't going to make a bid for freedom that she turned her attention back to the problem at hand. How on earth was she was going to salvage anything from this?

'Elsa?'

'Where am I?'

Maggie was now an expert at reading Elsie's voice and sensed that her mind was releasing her from the past, but her relief was short-lived.

'I don't think I can bear this any longer,' Kathy said. 'Ted's on his way over to help. I'm sorry, Maggie, I can't stay.'

The raw pain in her voice tore at Maggie's heart. She had made such a mess of everything. She had drawn Kathy into an emotional maelstrom where she didn't know who she was any more, and in a bitter twist of fate, neither did her birth mother. The meeting had become more painful than anyone could have imagined and one that Kathy would be unwilling to repeat. This was Elsa's one and only chance to be reunited with her baby.

'Please, Kathy, stay. I think we're nearly there,' Maggie begged.

Kathy didn't answer but Maggie heard her settle back in her seat, signalling that she was willing to stay a little longer at least. Maggie dug her fingernails deep into the painted surface of the bench. 'Elsie, you're in Victoria Park in Sedgefield.'

'The swans have gone,' Elsie said, sniffing away her tears absent-mindedly.

'They were never here. Your mind has been playing tricks on you.'

'You can say that again,' Elsie said with a gentle chuckle. 'Where did this baby come from?'

'This is my son, Aiden.'

'Oh, yes. You're the blind girl who's pregnant, aren't you?'

'Yes, I'm Maggie and I'm still blind but I'm not pregnant any more,' she said with a smile.

'He's a beauty.'

'Yes, he is, isn't he? But if you don't mind, I'd like us to have some time on our own. Do you mind if Ted takes him for a little walk?' She had heard Ted approach. 'Kathy, could you put Aiden in his pram and show Ted how it works?'

Kathy stood up and put a hand on Maggie's shoulder. 'Don't panic, I'll come back,' she said with grim resolve.

Elsie didn't complain as she relinquished the baby, hesitating only long enough to hold his hand one last time. 'Sweet dreams, precious one,' she whispered.

While Ted and Kathy fussed around the baby, Maggie remained crouching in front of Elsie. She wanted to be the anchor that would keep her fixed in the present, for the next few minutes at least.

'He's a beauty,' Elsie repeated.

'You and I are good friends, aren't we?'

'Yes, I think so,' she said, a little less sure of herself.

'Well, I know we are, and you've told me all about your time here in Sedgefield.' She was repeating herself, but this time she was more determined than ever to fight through the fog that inveigled Elsie's thoughts. She paused to give Elsie a chance to digest what she was being told. 'You told me your secrets.'

Elsie cleared her throat. 'Yes.'

Maggie wasn't convinced. 'Elsie, you're not well. You forget things and you get confused but sometimes you're aware of how ill you are.'

Elsie obliged with another confirmation but again without conviction.

'You promised me something, Elsie. You said you would find your way back if I found Tess for you but so far you're letting me down,' she said, emphasising each word with growing passion. 'Do you remember telling me that? Were you lying when you said you would fight your way back for Tess? Have you stopped caring about her?' Her voice broke at the last and her fingernails screamed out in pain as she dug them deeper into the wood in an effort to connect with Elsie.

'Yes.'

'Yes, you've stopped caring or yes, you remember?'

Maggie felt as if her chest was about to explode as she waited for Elsie's answer. She could hear the pram being pushed away and the click of Harvey's claws. Her own baby was in safe hands whilst Elsa's child was now standing behind her, holding her breath.

'Of course I haven't stopped caring. I'll never stop missing Tess, not until I draw my last breath.'

'Or we find her,' added Maggie.

Elsie's body stiffened but her voice was timorous as if she expected to shatter into a thousand pieces. 'You've found Tess?'

The goose bumps exploded across every inch of Maggie's skin and the shiver tingling down her neck and spine was electrifying. 'Yes, Elsie, I've found her.' The words gushed out as a sob and it was only when Elsie cupped her trembling hands around Maggie's face that the power of speech returned. 'It's 2013 and you're eighty-two years old. Your baby is all grown up now.'

'She's practically an old lady, then,' Elsie said with a laugh that was shared a moment later with her daughter.

Maggie's body had tensed so much that standing up was a painful process but once on her feet she held out her hand to Elsie. 'Would you like to join me?'

'I might need some help getting up too,' Elsie warned.

Maggie kept Elsie's hand firmly in hers and when all three women were standing together she took hold of Kathy's too.

'Anne Walters has taken care of your baby for sixty years and she did an amazing job. You don't have to feel guilty any longer because your daughter did very well for herself and she has led a very happy life surrounded by people who love her. You can be very proud of your daughter.'

'Can we get in touch with her? All I want is one last chance to tell her that I never stopped loving her, just one. Would that be too much to ask?' There was desperation in Elsie's voice, as if she was already preparing to be told it was as impossible now as it always had been.

'I think she already knows.'

Only rarely did Maggie miss her sight but there had been two such occasions in the last month. The first had been at the birth of her son and the second was now. She couldn't see the looks on Elsie and Kathy's faces so had to make do with the sensation of bringing two trembling hands together.

'This is Tess, Elsie.'

'No, you can't be my baby,' Elsie gasped, snapping her hand away as if she had received an electric shock.

Maggie didn't panic. She could read Elsie's voice perfectly and the old lady wasn't rejecting her daughter, she was simply awestruck. Kathy meanwhile thought the worst and let out a sob.

'Oh, my beautiful girl,' Elsie whispered, reaching her hand towards Kathy again. 'Don't cry.'

Maggie wanted to savour the moment but she knew she was intruding. 'I'll leave you alone with your daughter, Elsie.'

Stepping away, Maggie was riding on such a high that she almost walked straight into the lake. She sensed the vast expanse of water in front of her but the gnawing fear of its murky depths had vanished. She and Elsa were safe now. With nothing to fear, Maggie used the sound of sobbing on one side of her and the benign lap of water on the other to find her bearings. Without the benefit of a cane or her guide dog, she relied on her intimate knowledge of the park to remove herself from the scene and grant Elsie her longed-for wish of having Tess all to herself.

There was the sound of approaching wheels accompanied by the regular click of claws and Maggie waited for her own reunion. 'How's it going?' Ted asked.

'Better than I thought it would at one point. Elsie knows who Kathy is now and that she's found Tess. She really knows it, Ted.' The curve of her smile was collecting the tears that were falling freely but other than the ache in her cheeks, she barely noticed.

'You do realise that she'll have forgotten it all by the time we've stepped out of the park, don't you?'

'I know,' Maggie replied, refusing to let her smile falter. 'But even if her illness takes that memory from her, Kathy will remember for the two of them.'

'Your friend's a formidable lady, isn't she?'

Maggie laughed. 'It should have been obvious that she and Elsie were related. But it's going to be hard for her to come to terms with everything that's happened in the last few weeks.'

'It's such a shame she never got to know Elsie when she was . . . Elsie.'

'I think that's where you come in. You can help fill in the gaps.'

'I'll do as much as I can and the rest of the family can help too, once they know.'

Elsie's other daughters had yet to be told that they had another sister and only time would tell how they would take the news. She hoped that if Kathy were to be denied ever truly knowing her mother she would at least have a chance to know her sisters.

'Did I do the right thing?' she asked.

It was too much to hope that Elsie's mind would free her from the pain and guilt she had carried around for sixty years – her life had become too entrenched in the past to release her completely – so Maggie would have to look to others for confirmation that it had all been worth it in the end.

'*Elsa* would think so,' Ted said.

'Yes, she would.' There was still a half smile on Maggie's face as she wondered if there would be times to come when she could sit with the woman who called herself Elsa and tell her what the future held. But then the smile faded. 'Would she want to know everything, do you think?'

'Everything?'

Maggie had been reaching out to take hold of the pram but she found Ted's arm and held on to it. 'Freddie wasn't the hero we all thought he was, Ted.'

He patted her hand. 'I think I could have told you that, love. But my Elsie wouldn't be able to accept it, not then and not now.'

'What if I told you that he wasn't killed in a motorbike accident? That he had no intention of marrying Elsa? That he was only using her to blackmail Anne by proving how easily he could ruin her?' As Maggie proceeded to tell Ted everything, the old man's grip on her hand tightened. 'Don't you think we should at least try to tell her what kind of a man he really was?' she asked.

He squeezed her hand one last time and then let go. 'No. He's still her hero.'

Anger bloomed. 'No, Ted, you're her hero! You're the one who gave your life and your heart to that woman. You gave her hope for the future and then a life she could be proud of. You're the one who fights for her and cares for her. You're the hero who rescued her from the care home, for goodness' sake!' Maggie's fury burned up the oxygen in her lungs. When she paused for breath, Ted was ready with his reply.

'And I'm the one who will let her keep her dreams.'

The only response Maggie could offer was a stifled sob.

'Now, don't you go feeling sorry for me,' he warned. 'It's not always Freddie she's thinking about, even if she thinks she is.'

Maggie swallowed back her anger as best she could. 'How do you mean?'

'Elsie's hero used to take her to the park,' he explained. 'Not this one, but Sefton Park in Liverpool. She was very withdrawn after returning from Sedgefield and wouldn't speak to anyone. On the positive side, she couldn't say no when her hero insisted on taking her out. He would sit beside her on the park bench and tell her that she wasn't on her own. He would tell her all about the swans and how, once they found their mate, they never left each other's side. He told her over and over again until one day she realised that she was his swan and when he asked her to marry him, she said yes.'

'And that was you.'

Maggie couldn't help herself; she gave Ted a hug. Perhaps it was just her imagination but he had somehow grown in stature since she had last held him.

By the time they were all ready to leave the park, the autumn wind had lost its breath and a peaceful lull descended. Harvey led the way with Maggie, followed closely by Ted who was still pushing the pram while Kathy and Elsie trailed behind. Kathy was giving her birth mother a guided tour of her life from early childhood to the latest news that she was soon to be a grandmother again. At first Elsie listened in awe, occasionally asking questions but then, slowly and inevitably, she fell into silence. As they stepped through the iron gates that separated the park from the High Street, Ted's prediction was proven painfully true. Elsie said goodbye as if Kathy and Maggie were strangers but Kathy wasn't deterred.

'We're going to meet again, you and I,' she promised, 'and I'm going to remind you why today is worth remembering.'

EPILOGUE

Aiden was sitting up in his pushchair, squealing with delight as he spied the ducks approaching from the other side of the lake. It was hard to imagine that he had once been so tiny and defenceless. Hard, but not impossible, because Maggie had been acutely aware of how precious those first memories were. She never allowed herself to become complacent, and yet life had insisted on moving at an alarming pace.

To quell her nerves, Maggie took a deep breath before launching a handful of bread into the air. Amidst the cacophony of quacks, she detected the occasional cheep. The first brood of ducklings had arrived.

Deep in her own thoughts, she jumped when her phone rang. It was James. Harvey took a step nearer the pram. He would keep a watchful eye on Aiden while Maggie was temporarily distracted.

'Haven't you got work to do?' she asked.

'It's nearly lunchtime. I'm allowed a break once in a while.'

Maggie was only too aware of what time of day it was and James's reminder only served to

462

intensify her anxiety. 'How's it going?' she asked, eager for a diversion.

'It was going fine until Kathy turned up this morning. She's changed her mind on a couple of things. Again.'

'It won't put the completion date back, will it?'

'I won't let it, not while everyone's so impatient to move in.'

'Everyone except possibly Anne.'

The last six months had been difficult for Kathy, her two mums and their respective families, and Maggie still felt guilty. She had created the mess, albeit with good intentions, but it was Kathy who had been left to pick up the pieces. How she proposed to do that had surprised even Maggie.

'Actually, she was there this morning too. I wouldn't go so far as to say Anne was excited, but she seemed willing to make it work. She had her own ideas and there was a bit of friction between the two of them but Kathy knows how to handle her.'

'I'm just relieved they're still moving in together.' If Maggie regretted anything, it was the damage that had been done to Kathy's relationship with Anne. Whatever the rights and wrongs of Kathy's adoption and the secrecy surrounding it, there had never been any doubt that the bond between the two was worth fighting for. Thankfully, Kathy had never lost sight of that.

'Rather Kathy than me, though,' James said with

a laugh. 'To have one mother move in with you is bad enough, but two?'

James wasn't the only one wondering how it would work. Kathy hadn't been able to settle in the new house once she knew how much history she had left behind. The old Georgian villa in Sedgefield was, and always would be, her home and she wanted to move back. She still wanted her mum to move in with her and now she also wanted to help Elsie. Flo Jackson's guesthouse was big enough for all of them, and with a few alterations and a fair amount of renovation, no one could think of a reason why they couldn't all move in together, even Anne, who no longer had to fear returning to Sedgefield. It would give Kathy a chance to spend some time with her birth mother and everyone had to agree that it had a certain poetic justice.

'I wish Flo Jackson could have known what would happen. She wanted the house to remain in the family so that it might reunite a mother with her daughter – but even she couldn't have imagined they would all end up living there together, Anne included.'

'At least Kathy isn't going to be able to complain about rattling around in an empty house any more.'

Kathy's plan hadn't been that difficult to pull off in the end. Anne insisted on selling her house to pay for the redevelopment and James was commissioned to do the work. Ted was more than happy with the idea, not least because Yvonne had been making noises about her parents moving up to Scotland again. Joe wasn't too keen on having to deal with two mothers-in-law but he had found an ally in Ted and wasn't going to be completely outnumbered.

'I'd better go. Mark's waving frantically at me,' James said.

Mark had picked up his long-forgotten joinery skills with surprising ease and James hadn't needed much convincing to take him on, not with all the extra work Kathy was sending his way. Mark was now dividing his time between managing Kathy's property business and working for James and the arrangements were working so well that there was even a suggestion that the three might set up a joint company. But that was for the future.

'Oh, no, Kathy's back again,' James said. 'She said she was bringing Ted and Elsie for a quick guided tour this afternoon.'

'Then off you go,' Maggie ordered. 'You're not the only one with work to do.' Her stomach lurched without warning.

'It's going to be fine.'

'I know.' She didn't sound convinced.

'Have I told you lately that . . .'

'That you love me? Yes, I believe you told me that very thing this morning.' The smile creeping across her face eased her nerves.

'Ah, but did I tell you . . .'

'That I'm the best mother our son could possibly hope for? Yes, I think you mentioned that too.'

'Did I tell you that you're the most remarkable woman I've ever met and that I'm going to enjoy spending the rest of my life with you?'

The smile on her face broke free. 'Now that one I don't think I've heard today.'

'You're going to be fine and, more importantly, so is our little man. Now I really do have to go because all of this sweet talk is putting the lads off their lunch.'

When Maggie ended the call, she turned her back on the ducks. The bench was less than ten feet away but she hadn't been able to take her usual seat today and her plans for a picnic were in tatters. She was gripped by indecision. There was still an hour to kill and she briefly considered going back home. She could always carry on with the house-warming present she was making for Kathy. She had acquired another piece of wood from the house and James had carved it to match the one Maggie had already given her. Rather than 'Home' this one said 'Heart' and she was adding four names to it. Flo, Anne, Elsa and Tess.

When Harvey began nuzzling her hand in gentle encouragement, Maggie still didn't move, and following Harvey's example, Aiden began to grumble. They were both getting hungry but she couldn't face the thought of returning home. Not yet.

'The ducks are behind you.'

Maggie couldn't be sure if Lorna was joking or

not and she was in no mood to care. 'What colour have they painted it?' she asked.

'The bench? It's a sort of burgundy.' There was a question in her answer: Lorna was clearly confused by Maggie's interest in colours.

Maggie could smell wet paint but her imagination bloomed with scents of bergamot and cranberries.

'Can I have some bread? I want some bread!' Josh was already pulling at the plastic bag in Maggie's hand.

'Say please,' Lorna told her son.

'Please,' Josh recited.

'Of course you can.'

The child grabbed the bag and the first handful of bread sent the ducks into a frenzy. Harvey began to whine.

'Don't go too near the water's edge, Josh,' Maggie warned. 'Remember what happened last time.'

'Oh he's fallen in loads of times since then. I swear that child has no sense of danger.' Lorna took a few steps away from the lake to avoid the splashes and, grabbing Maggie's arm, pulled her away too.

Maggie almost stumbled. 'It's fine, Lorna, I can find my own way.' She deliberately stepped back and wrapped her hands around the handles of the pushchair. She could hear the water spray hitting the pram and while Aiden was more than happy to get soaked to the skin, she moved him away from the splash zone.

'I've been telling my husband how you pull that pram along the road. I've never seen anything like it. Are you sure it's safe?'

Maggie didn't trust herself to respond but simply nodded her head. She was starting to think that going home wasn't such a bad idea.

'So today's the big day then?' continued Lorna, unabashed.

'Yes, I'm looking forward to it,' Maggie said, hearing the lie even if Lorna didn't.

The truth was that she wasn't looking forward to returning to work at all. Jenny kept telling her that it wouldn't feel so bad once she was in a routine, but her response had been to remind her friend about the time she had walked out of the salon bawling. Maggie was allowed a wobble too, although she would be damned if she would let Lorna know that.

'At least you've got your mother-in-law to help.'

Suddenly Maggie's false bravado felt a little less forced. 'Yes, I'm so lucky. I can't believe Judith offered – so much for easing herself into retirement.'

'And you'll be able to find out all the gossip once you're back in the salon,' Lorna said, her voice lowered, although unfortunately Maggie could still hear it above Josh's shouts and Aiden's squeals. 'Is it really true that Kathy was adopted?'

'I believe that's what she told you,' Maggie answered carefully. Kathy had decided that she wanted everyone to know the basic facts of her adoption, if not the detail. She had Anne's permission and although Elsie was now rarely in a state of mind to form a view of her own, Ted had given *his* blessing.

'It's so sad that she should find her mum now,' Lorna said. 'She has Alzheimer's, by all accounts.'

'Yes, but at least they found each other.'

'And Kathy has two new sisters to boot. I bet they weren't happy hearing about all the secrets their mum had been keeping from them.'

'Actually they're absolutely delighted,' countered Maggie. Kathy had seen Yvonne at Christmas and they were getting on like a house on fire. She had even been in touch with the elusive Nancy and there were plans to all meet up once Kathy was back in the old house. Not that Maggie was prepared to share any of this information with Lorna, so she deliberately changed the subject. 'Will you be calling in at the salon soon?'

'Oh yes, I'm well overdue a massage.'

Maggie's ears pricked as she detected the sound of feet splashing in the water. Harvey whined. 'I think Josh is about to go in the lake again,' she warned and then the strangest thing happened. To accompany a fluttering shadow, she could feel the air in front of her face being wafted one way and then the other. There was a faint smell of soap. 'Did you just wave your hand in front of my face?' Her question was followed by a shocked laugh.

'Sorry, Maggie! It's just that I can't believe

you're really blind sometimes.' Lorna shuffled her feet in embarrassment.

Maggie opened her mouth to respond but Lorna was already on the move to rescue her son. Screeches of excitement had transformed to those of horror as Josh found himself floundering once more. There was a hurried goodbye as Lorna dragged a howling child away and in the calm that followed, Maggie turned her attention to her own family. She took hold of the pram but didn't immediately take hold of Harvey's harness. She knew her way to the bench.

The smell of wet paint was overpowering as she reached over and let her hand hover inches above the freshly painted wood. There would always be doubters in her life but as her mum had taught her, a person's true strength was hidden beneath the surface. With a glint in her eye, Maggie pressed a finger down into the sticky paint and smiled. The bench had been leaving impressions on people's lives for decades. She was simply returning the favour.

As Elsa stepped over the threshold, she kept her eyes cast down. The black-and-white tiled floor was covered in muddy footprints and there were drifts of sawdust gathering in the corners of the vestibule. She was afraid to lift her head only to have her suspicions confirmed. The house felt empty and if she looked up and didn't see Aunt Flo there to welcome her with open arms she knew she would cry. She missed the old lady who knew better than anyone how Elsa had lost everything including herself.

'It might look a bit of a mess now, but it's going to be amazing when it's finished.'

When Elsa did find the courage to look up, she tried to return the smile of the woman who had spoken. There was something familiar about her face but what that might be she couldn't quite recall. Panic bubbled. She knew she must fight to remember but still the memories slipped from her grasp like squirming eels. Panic was replaced by fear and she turned in a bid to escape but there was a man blocking her way. She wouldn't look at him as she wrestled from his grip.

'Elsie, it's going to be all right. I'm here, love.'

Lifting her eyes, Elsie was captured by the gaze of the man who had saved her all of those years ago. One singular thought sliced through the fog of her dementia like a swan gliding across the water. Aware how quickly that thought would slip away she held on to it as if her life depended on it. She didn't quite understand why, but for the first time in sixty years she felt whole again.